Cindi Myers is the autho[r of] novels. When she's not plotting new roma[nce story,] she enjoys skiing, gardening, cooking, crafting and daydreaming. A lover of small-town life, she lives with her husband and two spoiled dogs in the Colorado mountains.

Nicole Helm grew up with her nose in a book and the dream of one day becoming a writer. Luckily, after a few failed career choices, she gets to follow that dream—writing down-to-earth contemporary romance and romantic suspense. From farmers to cowboys, Midwest to *the* West, Nicole writes stories about people finding themselves and finding love in the process. She lives in Missouri with her husband and two sons, and dreams of someday owning a barn.

Also by Cindi Myers

Eagle Mountain: Unsolved Mysteries
Canyon Killer

Eagle Mountain: Criminal History
Twin Jeopardy
Mountain Captive

Eagle Mountain Search and Rescue
Eagle Mountain Cliffhanger
Canyon Kidnapping
Mountain Terror
Close Call in Colorado

Also by Nicole Helm

Bent County Protectors
Vanishing Point

Hudson Sibling Solutions
Cold Case Scandal
Cold Case Protection
Cold Case Discovery
Cold Case Murder Mystery

Covert Cowboy Soldiers
Casing the Copycat
Clandestine Baby

Discover more at millsandboon.co.uk

WILDERNESS SEARCH

CINDI MYERS

KILLER ON THE HOMESTEAD

NICOLE HELM

MILLS & BOON

All rights reserved including the right of reproduction in whole or in part in any form. This edition is published by arrangement with Harlequin Enterprises ULC.

This is a work of fiction. Names, characters, places, locations and incidents are purely fictional and bear no relationship to any real life individuals, living or dead, or to any actual places, business establishments, locations, events or incidents. Any resemblance is entirely coincidental.

Without limiting the author's and publisher's exclusive rights, any unauthorised use of this publication to train generative artificial intelligence (AI) technologies is expressly prohibited. HarperCollins also exercise their rights under Article 4(3) of the Digital Single Market Directive 2019/790 and expressly reserve this publication from the text and data mining exception.

® and ™ are trademarks owned and used by the trademark owner and/or its licensee. Trademarks marked with ® are registered with the United Kingdom Patent Office and/or the Office for Harmonisation in the Internal Market and in other countries.

First Published in Great Britain 2025
by Mills & Boon, an imprint of HarperCollins*Publishers* Ltd
1 London Bridge Street, London, SE1 9GF

www.harpercollins.co.uk

HarperCollins*Publishers*
Macken House, 39/40 Mayor Street Upper,
Dublin 1, D01 C9W8, Ireland

Wilderness Search © 2025 Cynthia Myers
Killer on the Homestead © 2025 Nicole Helm

ISBN: 978-0-263-39722-2

0825

This book contains FSC™ certified paper and other controlled sources to ensure responsible forest management.

For more information visit: www.harpercollins.co.uk/green

Printed and Bound in the UK using 100% Renewable Electricity at CPI Group (UK) Ltd, Croydon, CR0 4YY

WILDERNESS SEARCH

CINDI MYERS

For Lucy

Chapter One

Deputy Aaron Ames stood on the edge of the Colorado state highway and stared into the canyon below, his chest tight with dread. A small white sedan was wedged, nose first, between boulders at the bottom of the canyon. A passing motorist had spotted the glint of sun off the taillights and called to report the accident. Aaron squinted, trying to detect any movement in the car. Surely no one could survive a plunge like that. The canyon had to be at least two hundred feet deep at this point.

"Search and rescue are on the way." Jake Gwynn joined Aaron. The young deputy was close to Aaron's age—thirty—with dark curly hair and the deep tan of an outdoorsman. "The highway department is sending a team to block off this lane. We'll help with traffic control."

Aaron turned his back to the canyon and studied the roadway. This time of morning on a Sunday, there wasn't much traffic. Two lanes of pavement wound between rocky spires, sun glinting off the red granite peaks. This stretch of the highway was fairly straight, without the hairpin curves in other sections. "We haven't had any rain lately," he said. "I wonder what sent the driver off the side?"

"No skid marks," Jake pointed out. "I don't see any signs of another driver or an animal or anything." He glanced back into the canyon. "Unfortunately, some people choose to end things this way."

Aaron grimaced, but any reply he might have made was cut off by a siren. Seconds later, a large orange Jeep pulled in ahead of his sheriff's department SUV. The siren's wail still echoed off the canyon walls as half a dozen volunteers piled out of the vehicle and began unloading equipment. His sister, Bethany, waved. His two brothers, twins Carter and Dalton, were also search and rescue volunteers, but they must have been working when this call came in. Sundays were a busy time for the family's Jeep tour business.

SAR Captain Danny Irwin, a tall, lanky man in tactical pants and a blue Eagle Mountain Search and Rescue windbreaker, strode toward them. "Hey, Aaron, Jake."

The men shook hands, then looked down into the canyon. "I haven't seen any movement down there," Aaron said.

"Any idea when this happened?" Danny asked.

"No telling," Jake said. "No one's reported anyone missing. It's pure luck a passing motorist saw the wreck."

Danny looked down at the pavement. "No skid marks."

"Yeah," Jake said. "So maybe we've got a suicide."

"We'll get down there and see what we can find." Danny turned back toward the other volunteers.

"Get a plate number for us and we'll call it in," Jake said.

The highway department crew arrived to set up cones to close the lane to traffic, and Aaron went to help. By the time he returned to the accident site, the SAR volunteers had staged on the narrow shoulder. A man and a woman in climbing harnesses and helmets were beginning their descent into the canyon while other volunteers lined the roadside, watching. An aluminum-framed litter waited at the ready.

Aaron started to join the volunteers, then stopped as his

gaze fixed on one young woman, petite and slender, hair in a long blond braid down her back. Recognition jolted him—a knowing deep in his gut, more instinct than conscious knowledge.

"Kat?"

He hadn't realized he had spoken out loud until she turned. The same cool blond beauty—pale skin, blue eyes, delicate features that still haunted him. But the look on her face—surprise, followed by such raw hurt—hit him like a kick in the gut. It had always been like that with Kat—the very first time he had seen her he had felt the connection to his core. He had fallen so hard, and the impact when they had parted still hurt.

She quickly masked her own pain with a cold disdain he remembered from their last encounters. But instead of turning her back to him, she moved away from her friends, coming to stand beside him. "Don't call me Kat. My name is Willa Reynolds now." She spoke softly, so that he had to lean toward her to hear, and caught the soft scent of her hair, a sensory memory imprinted on his DNA.

But her words confused him. "You changed your name? Why?"

"I had to." She spoke in a clipped, angry tone. "Gareth changed his, too. He's just Gary now. Gary Reynolds. It makes it harder for the media and other people who want to harass us to find us."

Her words pained him. He knew things had been tough for her, but not that desperate. "I'm sorry you felt you had to do that," he said.

"Are you?" She glared at him and moved away once more.

He wanted to pull her back, to tell her how much he missed her. How sorry he was for the way things had ended between them. But what could he say? He had done the only thing he could under the circumstances, what he still believed was the right thing. Why couldn't she respect that?

He had so many questions he would probably never know the answers to. What was she doing here in Eagle Mountain, Colorado, anyway? Surely she hadn't known he was here. But it was so unexpected, that they had each moved so far from their hometown and ended up in the same small town.

She returned, not to where she had been standing, but farther away, where another volunteer was doing something with ropes and the litter. She moved in to help him, her back to Aaron. She bent over, and he had a view of her shapely backside. He forced himself to look away, not wanting to be caught ogling her.

Jake soon joined him. "I saw you talking to Willa," Jake said, and nodded toward where Kat and a young man were moving the litter closer to the edge of the canyon.

Aaron would have to get used to thinking of her with her new name. "How long has she been with search and rescue?" he asked.

Bethany or one of his brothers hadn't mentioned that Kat Delaney was with the group. Surely one of them would have recognized her, whatever name she went by now. Maybe not Bethany—she had moved to Eagle Mountain before things got really serious between Kat and Aaron. But surely the twins would have remembered a woman who was so striking.

"She's brand-new," Jake said. "When Hannah went on maternity leave she recruited Willa to fill in for her. I'm pretty sure today is her first call."

Aaron nodded. Jake's wife, Hannah, a paramedic, was expecting their first child.

"The group is always short medical personnel," Jake continued. "Willa is an RN, a new hire at the local clinic."

Aaron and Kat—Willa—had met when he had delivered a prisoner for treatment at the emergency room where she worked in Waterbury, Vermont. Two thousand miles and a lifetime from here.

"I hear she's single."

Aaron turned to see Jake grinning at him.

Aaron shook his head and turned away. Willa was never going to forgive him for arresting her brother for murder. Never mind that all the evidence had pointed to Gareth. In the end, the district attorney hadn't felt they had enough evidence to convict. The case had never gone to trial, and Gareth Delaney and his sister, Kat, had moved away, leaving behind a lot of suspicions and unanswered questions.

Now they were here in Eagle Mountain. Kat was a chapter in Aaron's life he considered closed. But in a town this small, where it was impossible to avoid running into people, they would have to find a way to at least maintain a facade of distant politeness. The prospect left a sour taste, but was it that different from the compromises people made every day for the sake of keeping peace? He had learned to hold back anger at people who broke the law, and to keep his opinions about some things to himself, out of respect for others. He could pretend he didn't care about Kat anymore. What was one more lie in the grand scheme of things?

WILLA TRIED TO concentrate on the knot she needed to tie, but every nerve vibrated with awareness of the man standing behind her. Aaron Ames. Tall, dark and handsome Double A, as his partner on the Waterbury police force had referred to him. The first time he had looked into her eyes and flashed his confident smile she had been lost. What were the odds of seeing him here, two thousand miles away from Vermont, in a town most people had never even heard of? Had he somehow followed her here? Or worse, did he think she had followed him? The idea shook her so badly she dropped one end of the rope.

"Take your time." Caleb Garrison picked up the dropped rope and returned it to her. A boyish-looking man with a mop of unruly blond hair, Caleb was helping train search and rescue rookies like Willa. He had the kind of patience that probably came in handy at his day job, teaching history to college students. "You don't need to rush," he said.

She nodded, and this time tied the knot correctly.

Danny Irwin joined them. "Sheri and Ryan say they're ready for the litter," he said. "Send a body bag down, too."

Willa swallowed a lump in her throat and nodded. As soon as she had seen the crumpled car, so far down below, she had told herself no one could have survived that plunge. Still, they always hoped for survivors.

"Just the one person in the vehicle?" Caleb asked.

"Seems so," Danny said.

Willa stepped back and watched as Caleb and volunteer Carrie Andrews lowered the litter. She was here to give medical assistance, but the driver of the car was beyond that. Suicide—if this was suicide—was always hard, on the families, but on everyone else, too.

In the weeks after nine-year-old Rachel Sherman's death, Willa had been afraid for Gary. He had been so upset not only by the girl's murder, but also by the fact that everyone suspected he had killed her. Willa had never seen him so despairing; she had worried he might take his own life. She had been furious on his behalf, and more afraid than she had allowed herself to admit. And Aaron, the one person she had counted on to help them through this ordeal, had turned out to be involved in Gary's arrest.

At first, she had told herself it was Aaron's job to follow

orders given by his superiors. He had been one of the arresting officers, but that didn't mean he wasn't on her side. She had even told herself it was good that Gary had a friend on the inside. But when Aaron had expressed his own doubts about Gary's innocence, Willa had been devastated. Her brother wasn't a murderer. Why couldn't Aaron see that? The memory of that betrayal still tore at her.

There were a lot of employees at the youth camp where Rachel Sherman had been murdered, but the police zeroed in on Gary right away. They said he was known to be friendly with the girls—as if this was something sinister. They had two witnesses who had seen him talking to Rachel shortly before she was last seen. Just talking, but that was enough to make him their only suspect. It wasn't evidence, and the district attorney had seen that, but not before Gary had been held and questioned for several days.

She and Gary had naively thought when the DA declined to press charges that he would be absolved from guilt, but the harassment only intensified—snide letters to the editor and stories in the paper. Emails and phone calls from strangers making accusations. An outcry from Rachel's family to prosecute him.

"Willa?" She turned to see a young woman with dark braids and a tentative smile approaching. "I'm Bethany Ames. We didn't get a chance to meet at the training meeting the other night. Welcome to the group."

Bethany Ames. Aaron's sister. Willa had taken pains to avoid her, and Aaron's two brothers, Carter and Dalton, at the search and rescue training session. She knew she would eventually have to explain herself, but she wasn't ready to deal with that yet.

Bethany had already been living in Colorado when Aaron and Kat were together, but surely she had seen pictures of her brother's girlfriend. But Willa detected no sign of recognition in the younger woman's eyes. Bethany had probably been too wrapped up in her own life to pay attention to Willa – she had suffered a broken engagement before she left town. "It's nice to meet you, Bethany," Willa said. "And thanks. It's good to be part of the group."

"Not a great first call." Bethany looked over Willa's shoulder at the scene in the canyon below. "So sad."

"Yes."

"Anyway, I just wanted to introduce myself. How are you doing?"

"I'm okay," Willa said.

"Good. It can be overwhelming at first." Bethany swept her hand to indicate the array of equipment and personnel. "All this. But you'll catch on really quick and every one of us is here to help you." She tilted her head, considering. "Have we met before? You look so familiar."

Willa shook her head. "No, I don't think so."

Bethany shrugged. "I guess you just have one of those faces." Someone called her name and she took a step back. "I have to go, but let me know if you need anything, or have any questions."

"Thanks," Willa said, but Bethany was already moving away.

The litter had reached the lip of the canyon, and Willa stepped back to allow those managing it to haul it to the top.

"Did you find any identification?" Aaron's voice shook her once more, but he wasn't speaking to her. He moved forward to meet Sheri and Ryan, who were climbing out of the canyon.

Ryan handed over a worn leather wallet. Aaron opened it, then passed the driver's license to Jake.

"Trevor Lawson," Jake said. He looked at the volunteers who had gathered. "Do any of you know him?"

"I know the name." Grace Wilcox stepped forward. "I'm pretty sure he works at Mount Wilson Lodge."

The lines around Jake's eyes tightened. "That's Dwight's place."

"Dwight Prentice?" Aaron asked. "The former deputy?"

"Right. He inherited the lodge from his uncle and he and his wife, Brenda, decided to continue operating it." Jake tucked the wallet in his pocket. "Any sign of other passengers?"

"No," Ryan said. "We took a good look around, but I'm pretty sure he was alone."

Sheri stepped out of her climbing harness. "He was wearing his seat belt and the air bags deployed, but the car is destroyed."

"Does he have family in town?" Aaron asked.

No one knew. "We'll talk to Dwight," Jake said. "Did you find anything else we should know about?"

"We smelled alcohol," Sheri said. "Like he'd been drinking a lot. That could be a factor in the accident."

"We'll ask the coroner to run a tox screen." Jake looked down into the canyon. "We'll have to arrange to get the car out later, line up a wrecker and schedule with the highway department to close the road while we haul up the vehicle."

He and Aaron walked back to the sheriff's department SUV and stood, heads together, talking.

Willa didn't want to look, but she couldn't help it. Aaron's and Jake's khaki uniforms and duty belts stood out in the sea of tactical black and navy worn by the SAR volunteers. Her eyes met Aaron's and she felt again that buzzing acknowledgment of a connection, humming through her body like a low-voltage current.

She looked away, but his expression stuck with her—not hurt or angry, just *intense*. She had appreciated his serious approach to life when they first met but now, after all she had been through with Gary, she needed more light in her life. She had hoped to find that here in Eagle Mountain. She wanted a refuge and a fresh start, not reminders of the past.

Chapter Two

Aaron and Jake stayed to process the accident scene—at least the portion of it on the highway—then made the drive to Mount Wilson Lodge to meet with Dwight Prentice. Aaron had yet to meet the popular former deputy, though he had heard a few stories. And he was aware that the reason he had a job was that Dwight had left an opening on the small force when he decided to leave and run his late uncle's hunting and fishing lodge.

The lodge itself was a soaring A-frame made of massive logs with large windows looking out onto a turquoise lake—the kind of place people pictured when they heard about a retreat in the Colorado mountains. Smaller cabins were scattered like dice around the lodge, and a sign at the entrance advertised the availability of fishing, hunting and boating access.

Dwight Prentice waited on the front porch as Jake parked the SUV. "Civilian life seems to suit you," Jake said as he and Dwight shook hands. "This is Aaron Ames."

"My replacement." Dwight shook Aaron's hand. A tall man with a thick shock of dark hair, dressed in faded jeans and a denim shirt with the sleeves rolled up, he fixed Aaron with the assessing gaze of a law enforcement officer. "Good to meet you. What brings you two here?"

"Can we go inside and talk?" Jake asked.

"Sure." Dwight led the way through a lobby area with soaring ceilings, to a cramped office.

A freckled blonde, her hair caught up in a clip on top of her head, fine lines at the corners of her eyes, looked up from behind the desk. "Hello, Jake." Her gaze darted to Aaron. "Is something wrong?"

"This is my wife, Brenda," Dwight introduced her to Aaron. He leaned against the end of the desk and crossed his arms. "What is this about?"

"Do you know a Trevor Lawson?" Jake asked.

"He's one of my employees," Dwight said. "Is he in some kind of trouble?"

"I'm sorry to tell you he's dead. His car went off Dixon Pass, along that big straightaway on the descent toward town."

"He went off the road?" Dwight uncrossed his arms and leaned forward.

"Into the canyon?" Brenda asked.

Jake glanced at her. "Yes. Maybe last night or early this morning. A passing motorist noticed the wreck and called it in. When was the last time you saw him?"

"Yesterday," Dwight said. "He's off work today. I knew he wasn't at his cabin, but I thought he might be off somewhere with his brother."

"Who's his brother?"

"Wade Lawson. He's a counselor at the youth camp down the road—Mountain Kingdom. What happened to Trevor, exactly? How did he go off the road in that straightaway?"

"There's some indication it might be deliberate," Jake said. "There weren't any skid marks or other indications that he tried to stop. We don't have a toxicology report, but the first responders who brought him up said the car smelled strongly of alcohol."

"That doesn't sound like Trevor," Brenda said.

Dwight nodded. "I never knew him to be much of a drinker."

"How long have you known him?" Aaron asked.

"Not long. He worked for Uncle Dave and I kept him on after Brenda and I took over the place. He's been a good worker."

"Did he seem upset about anything lately?" Jake asked.

"Not at all," Brenda said.

"He seemed fine to me," Dwight agreed. "You might ask Wade. The two of them seemed close."

"We'll talk to his brother," Jake said.

"Tell him to call me anytime," Dwight said. "I'm sure he'll want Trevor's things."

They said goodbye to Brenda, and Dwight walked with them to the parking lot. "Let me know if you find out anything," he said.

"Is there anyone else we should talk to about Trevor?" Jake asked. "A girlfriend? Other family or close friends?"

"I don't know much about his personal life. Maybe Wade will know more. You could ask the camp owner, Scott Sprague. Trevor did odd jobs for him sometimes."

"Thanks."

MOUNTAIN KINGDOM KIDS CAMP was only two miles from Mount Wilson Lodge. As soon as Jake turned into the long, wooded drive leading up to camp headquarters, Aaron felt thrust back in time. The countryside around his hometown in Vermont had been dotted with similar summer camps, with their open-air pavilions filled with picnic tables, clusters of batten-and-board-sided cabins, scattered canoes along the shores of a small lake, archery targets set in fields and trees festooned with yarn-and-stick creations or braided-leather ornaments crafted by generations of campers who returned summer after summer.

He spotted several groups of children in matching T-shirts near the lake and a few milling around the cabins as he and Jake parked in front of a square wooden building labeled Office.

A harried-looking woman with shoulder-length gray hair looked up as they entered. "Can I help you?" she asked.

"We're looking for Wade Lawson," Jake said.

A deep furrow formed between her sparse eyebrows. "Has Wade done something wrong?"

"No. Can you tell us where to find him?"

"You should talk to Mr. Sprague." She picked up a radio and keyed the button on the side. "Mr. Sprague, there are two sheriff's deputies here. They're looking for Wade."

"Tell them I'll be right up," said a deep voice.

The woman's gaze met theirs. "If you could wait just a minute."

While they waited, Aaron studied the posters tacked to the wall by the door—instructions on how to thoroughly douse a campfire, first aid diagrams and handwritten lost-and-found notices. Found: Red Flashlight on Lanyard. Lost: One Silver Earring with a Green Stone. He paused before a large poster with a long list of Rules for Campers. At the bottom, in bold letters: "Campers in violation of rules will be punished with loss of privileges. Multiple violations will result in a call to your parents." Words to strike fear in the heart of most children, he thought.

The door opened and a stocky man with a graying crew cut stepped in. "I'm Scott Sprague," he said. "I'm the owner of Mountain Kingdom. What seems to be the problem?"

"No problem," Jake said. "Mr. Sprague, we need to talk to Wade Lawson."

"Call me Scott. What's this about?"

"Do you know his brother, Trevor?"

"Sure, I know Trevor. Is he in some kind of trouble?"

"He was killed in an accident on Dixon Pass," Jake said.

Scott blinked. "I'm sorry to hear that."

"Can you tell us where we can find Wade?" Jake asked.

"Sure. I'll take you to him." Scott turned to the woman. "Track down Veronica and ask her to come over to the boat launch and take over from Wade," he said.

Then he opened the door and exited the cabin.

Jake and Aaron hurried to keep up with Scott, who, despite his stocky stature and graying hair, set a brisk pace. He cut through the trees, headed directly for the shoreline and a dock where a group of girls in green T-shirts paddled about in yellow-and-red canoes.

"Wade!" Scott called.

A slight blond man with gold wire-rimmed glasses—Aaron had mistaken him originally for one of the campers—turned to frown at them.

"Come here," Scott called, and motioned with his hand.

Wade glanced toward the girls, then lifted the whistle that hung from a cord around his neck and blew it. "Everybody out of the water," he called.

The girls had noticed the two uniformed deputies, and stared, motionless, some in mid-paddle. Wade blew the whistle a second time. "Out of the water!"

"You heard the man," Scott shouted.

The girls all headed for the dock at once, resulting in a traffic jam it took several minutes to sort out. But at last all the canoes were beached and the girls gathered in a knot on the shore. A young woman with long dark hair loped toward them. "Mrs. Mason said you needed me," she panted as she approached Scott.

"Take over the canoeing instruction from Wade," Scott said.

Wade had joined them, and was giving the two deputies nervous looks. "What's going on?" he asked.

"These two want to talk to you about Trevor," Scott said.

What little color was in the pale young man's face drained away. "Do you know where he is?" he asked. "Is he in some kind of trouble?"

"When was the last time you saw your brother?" Jake asked, his voice gentle.

"Last night. About seven thirty." He glanced at Scott. Aaron thought he looked nervous.

"Thanks for your help, Scott," Jake said. "We'll let you get back to work now."

"I don't have anything pressing," Scott said.

"We'd like to speak with Mr. Lawson alone," Jake said.

Scott's mouth tightened. Aaron wondered if he was going to argue, but after a tense moment, he nodded. "Let me know if you need anything else," he said, and turned away.

No one said anything until the older man was out of sight, then Wade said, "What is this about? Is Trevor okay? I've been trying all day to get hold of him, but he's not answering his phone."

"Let's go over here and sit down." Jake led the way to a picnic table about fifty feet away and sat. Wade sat across from him, hands clasped between his knees.

"I'm afraid your brother was killed in an accident on Dixon Pass," Jake said. "His car went over the side into the canyon."

Wade made a choking sound and looked away. He swallowed, his Adam's apple bobbing up and down. After a long moment, he faced them again. "Are you sure? You're positive it's Trevor?"

"The photo on the driver's license in his wallet confirmed his identity," Jake said.

Wade blinked rapidly, eyes reddening. He swallowed again, struggling for control. "When did this happen?" he asked, his voice a harsh whisper.

"We're not sure. A passing motorist saw the sun glinting off a taillight and called it in this morning."

"He went off the road? What happened?"

"We don't know," Jake said. "When you spoke to your brother last night, was he upset about something?"

"No. I mean, I don't think so." He looked down at his hands. "I didn't actually talk to him before he left. I mean, he didn't say goodbye. He was just here, and then he wasn't."

"Was that unusual? Him not saying goodbye?" Aaron asked.

"Well, yeah. I mean, he never went off like that before. I didn't know what to think."

"When you saw your brother last night, had he been drinking?" Jake asked.

Wade's eyes widened. "No! Alcohol isn't allowed here. Mr. Sprague would have thrown us out on our ears if he caught us with any beer or liquor." He leaned forward. "Are you saying Trevor was drunk? That's why he went off the road?"

"We're waiting on a report from the coroner. Was your brother much of a drinker?"

"No. I mean, he might have a beer or two from time to time, but he didn't make it a habit. And when I did see him last night, he was stone cold sober."

"Tell us about last night," Jake said. "What time did Trevor get here and what did you do?"

Wade sat up straighter. "He got here around six. He finished for the day at Mount Wilson Lodge, where he works full-time, then came up here. We have a bonfire on Saturday nights, by the lake. Trevor helped me get the fire ready.

We moved a bunch of picnic tables down by the water and helped Veronica and Tatum—they're other counselors—carry the food down from the mess hall. We do hot dogs and chips and stuff on bonfire night, roast marshmallows, sing songs and stuff."

"Did Trevor often help out on bonfire nights?" Aaron asked.

"Oh yeah. All the time. Mr. Sprague pays him for that and other odd jobs—cleaning cabins, maintenance and stuff. Trevor was saving to buy a new dirt bike, so he picked up as much extra work as he could." His lips trembled and he looked away.

Aaron and Jake waited, letting him compose himself. After a long moment, Jake asked, "Did Trevor seem normal to you—not upset about anything?"

"Nothing. He was joking with a couple of the maintenance staff who were helping with the picnic tables."

"When was the last time you saw him?" Jake asked again. "What was he doing?"

Wade thought a minute. "We had all finished eating and Veronica was playing the guitar and leading the campers in a sing-along. Trevor tossed his paper plate in the trash, then said he was headed to the outhouse. He walked off and that's the last time I saw him."

"What time was that?" Jake asked.

"About seven thirty."

"Where was the outhouse?"

He pointed behind them. "It's past that first group of cabins. There are a couple of composting pit toilets."

"Were you worried when he didn't come back?" Aaron asked.

"One of the girls burned her hand on a flaming marshmallow and I had to take her up to the first aid room. Mrs.

Mason checked her out and decided she didn't need to go to the hospital. We bandaged her up and I walked her back down here to her cabin mates. I looked for Trevor, but when I didn't see him, I figured he had got tired of waiting for me and gone home." He frowned. "But usually he stays to help put out the fire and move the picnic tables and stuff. I tried calling him to ask what was up, but he didn't answer his phone. I was annoyed, to tell you the truth." He rubbed the back of his neck. "It doesn't make sense that he would leave here and get drunk. That wasn't like him at all."

"Was Trevor in a relationship with anyone?" Jake asked. "Could he have gotten bad news from a romantic partner, maybe had an upsetting phone call?"

"He wasn't dating anyone."

"What about other family, or close friends?"

"Our parents are in California and last I heard, they're fine. And Trevor didn't really have any close friends. Just me." His voice broke and he looked away again.

"I need to ask you a question that's going to be hard to hear," Jake said. "But do you think your brother would have taken his own life? Had he ever talked about suicide?"

"No!" Wade jumped up. "No way! Are you saying that's what happened? Because it didn't."

"There weren't any skid marks or any indication that the car swerved to avoid anything," Jake said. "And the first responders who retrieved your brother's body said there was a strong smell of alcohol."

"No." Wade shook his head. "Trevor wouldn't do that. I know he wouldn't."

"Is everything all right here?" They turned to see Scott stalking toward them. He had a short stride, but covered ground quickly, arms swinging.

"Mr. Sprague, they're saying Trevor killed himself," Wade said. "You know him. He wouldn't have done that."

Scott put his hand on Wade's shoulder. "Trevor was a good man, no doubt about it," he said. "But we can never really know what another person is thinking, can we?"

"Scott, did you see Trevor when he was here yesterday evening?" Jake asked.

"I saw him working with the others to get the bonfire ready," Scott said. "I may have said hello, but I didn't speak to him."

"Did you get an impression as to his mood?" Aaron asked. "Was there anything unusual about his demeanor?"

"No. But I was busy making sure the bonfire was organized. It takes a lot of preparation to make sure the campers have a good time, but are also safe."

"Can I see my brother?" Wade asked.

"Someone will call you," Jake said. "And Dwight Prentice says to get in touch with him about collecting your brother's belongings."

"I'll help with any arrangements," Scott said. He was still gripping Wade's shoulder. "Why don't you take a couple of days to pull yourself together and do whatever you need to do? And remember, we're all here to help."

Wade nodded. He stared at the ground, looking miserable.

Jake handed Wade a business card. "Call me if you think of anything we should know, or if you have any questions. I'm very sorry for your loss."

Scott led Wade away and Aaron and Jake headed back to the parking lot. "I know people never like to think their loved one committed suicide, but Wade seemed really shocked by the idea his brother might have taken his own life," Aaron said. "And driving into a canyon doesn't seem like the easiest way to go."

"Still, it happens," Jake said. "Maybe the autopsy will tell us something, or they'll find some malfunction on the car when they haul it up."

"Maybe so."

"Not the best way to begin the week." Jake nudged him. "Still, you met Willa. You should ask her out, though I hear she's turned down everyone else who's approached her."

Hearing this didn't make Aaron feel any better. Had he hurt her so badly she couldn't bear to get involved with anyone else? Not that he had jumped back into the dating scene, either. He told himself it was because he'd been busy—with the move, and a new job.

But really, the thought of starting over, with someone who wasn't Kat, made his chest hurt. Now that he knew she was here, the pain had started up again. No sense going out of his way to make it any worse.

Chapter Three

When Willa arrived home from running errands Sunday afternoon, Gary was just coming out of the shower. Neither of them could afford rent on their own, so sharing a place had made the most sense. Plus, it allowed Willa to keep an eye on her little brother. He would have protested that, at twenty-three, he didn't need her to look after him, but she needed to reassure herself that he was all right.

"How was your day?" she asked as she put away groceries.

"Okay." He rubbed his shoulder. "I had to dig, like, a mile of ditch for a water line."

"By yourself? That sounds horrible."

"I was supposed to have help, but the guy didn't show up. And it had to be done today. Supposedly there's a big storm coming in tonight."

"Maybe you should look for another job."

He had a degree in physical education but all he had been able to find here was a job doing maintenance at a local ranch.

"Nah. I like this one. Working outside, nobody to hassle me. And it keeps me in shape." He moved to the refrigerator and took out a can of flavored seltzer. "You want anything?"

"No, thanks." She closed the cabinet, then stood by the counter, unable to think what to do next.

"Is something wrong?" Gary asked.

"What makes you ask that?"

"You look upset." He took a drink of seltzer, gaze fixed on her. "Did something happen at the clinic yesterday?"

"We had a bad search and rescue call this morning. A guy drove his car off Dixon Pass. They think he did it deliberately."

"Wow. That's rough. Was he really messed up?"

"No. I mean, I don't know. I didn't see him."

"Maybe you shouldn't do this search and rescue stuff if it's going to upset you so much."

"It's not the call that upset me."

He frowned. Before he could ask any more questions, she added, "I saw Aaron today. He was at the scene. He's a sheriff's deputy. Here, in Eagle Mountain." There. She had told him. She hated to upset him, but he needed to know. Better to hear the news from her than to run into Aaron somewhere in town.

But Gary didn't look upset. "Yeah, I know."

"You knew?" Her vision grayed at the edges for a moment, she was so shocked. "And you didn't tell me?"

He shrugged. "Because I knew it would upset you. And see, it has." He gestured to her with the seltzer can.

"When did you see him? Did he say anything to you?"

"I was at the hardware store, and I saw him outside, talking to someone. He didn't see me. Then I saw him one other time, at Mo's Pub. We never spoke. It was no big deal. Did he say anything to you?"

"He said he was sorry."

"Maybe he really is."

She hugged her arms across her stomach. "I don't care

if he's sorry or not. I can't forgive him for believing you would ever do something so horrible."

"What did you expect? He's a cop. That's how they're trained to think." He drained the rest of the can of seltzer and tossed it into the recycling bin.

"But there wasn't any evidence against you."

"There wasn't any evidence against anyone else, either. And two people saw me talking to Rachel that night."

"How can you be so calm about something so horrible?"

He had spent time in jail because of police insistence on focusing on him as their only suspect in Rachel Sherman's murder. The two of them had had to leave everything behind and start over because of that terrible mistake.

Gary shrugged. "I don't see any sense in brooding over something that happened in the past that was completely out of my control. I'd rather get on with my life."

It was a sensible attitude. A healthy one. But one she couldn't adopt. "Aaron should have given you the benefit of the doubt," she said.

"I don't think that's how these things ever work. And it's not like he was the only cop pointing the finger at me. He wasn't even a detective or an investigator. The important thing is that the DA didn't file charges and I'm a free man now." He opened the refrigerator again. "Spaghetti sound good for dinner? I'll make it."

"Sure. Thanks."

But he didn't start dinner right away. He continued to study her. "Don't let Aaron get to you," he said. "He made a mistake and he paid for it. He lost you. Someone else will step up to the plate and realize how great you are. In case you haven't noticed, this place is crawling with single men. Seriously, I can't believe you don't have guys standing in line to ask you out."

She laughed, more from frustration than mirth. "I'm not interested in going out with anyone right now." She had turned down half a dozen men who had shown up at the clinic, asking to see "the new nurse" with their mystery ailments. They had all been polite, ranging from slick and charming to bashful and sweet.

"That's cool, too." He pulled a package of ground beef from the refrigerator and shut the door. "But the next time you see Aaron, look right past him. Let him know you don't care what he thinks."

"I'll do that." She didn't need Aaron. She didn't need any man.

But she did need for Gary to be all right. He said he was free now, but was he, really? The two of them had given up so much to escape the cloud that hung over him because of those charges. They had told themselves taking new names and moving was a chance to reinvent themselves. They could do whatever they wanted, and be whoever they wanted to be.

But seeing Aaron had made her feel the past would always be hanging on to their heels, pulling them backward whether she wanted it or not.

THEIR SHIFTS HAD ended by the time Jake and Aaron left Mountain Kingdom Kids Camp, but they still needed to return to the station and file reports. Aaron was used to the long hours. It wasn't as if he had anything else to devote himself to, though he knew Jake was anxious to get home to his wife.

"I wonder why Trevor left the bonfire without speaking to his brother?" Jake asked as he and Aaron drove away from the camp. "And how he ended up smelling of alcohol if he wasn't a drinker?"

"Maybe he wasn't drinking at all. Maybe a bottle broke in the car or something."

"Yeah. We need to wait until we hear from the coroner." He slowed as a quartet of turkeys crossed the road in front of them, sun angling through the trees glinting off their bronzed feathers. "Did you ever go to summer camp as a kid? Someplace like Mountain Kingdom?"

"I spent a couple of weeks at Boy Scout camp one summer," Aaron said. "But not places like this, where kids stay for a month at a time, or the whole summer. There were a lot of those in Vermont, where I'm from. When I was on the force in Waterbury, we would occasionally get calls."

"What kind of calls?"

"Usually petty things—theft or vandalism. But we had a murder case once. A little girl was killed." Rachel Sherman.

"Did they find the killer?"

"We never did."

"That's rough."

"Yeah." Aaron and another officer had interviewed the girls in Rachel's cabin. They had said they had seen Rachel talking to Gareth Delaney. Aaron remembered the shock of hearing Kat's brother's name in connection with a crime. He hadn't known Gareth well, but he had seemed like such an ordinary, likable guy.

But the more Aaron and his fellow officers talked to Gareth, the more nervous and suspicious Gareth acted. At first he denied knowing Rachel. When confronted with her cabin mates' statements, he admitted talking to her, but said he hadn't even known her name. Another lie. And though everyone was supposed to be innocent until proven guilty, you didn't have to be a cop long to learn that guilty people often lied.

Aaron realized Jake had been talking to him. He shook his head. "Sorry. What did you say?"

"I asked how you're settling in. New town, new job, all that?"

"It's good. I like it here."

"Small towns aren't for everyone, but I guess it helps that you have family here."

"Yeah. It's great." Not that he couldn't have moved away from his parents and siblings, but when they had decided to follow his sister, Bethany, to Eagle Mountain, it seemed like a good opportunity for him to make a fresh start. Get away from bad memories.

Except this morning the biggest memory had confronted him on the side of the highway. As beautiful as he remembered.

And just as unforgiving.

WILLA SLEPT LITTLE that night, her mind too full of worries about Aaron and Gary. Would Aaron spill their secret to others in the community? Would the media—or some true-crime enthusiast online—track them down and make their lives miserable, as had happened back in Waterbury? The murder of Rachel Sherman remained unsolved and the internet was full of amateur sleuths who were sure they could find the real killer. A good number of those people started with the assumption that Gary was guilty. All they had to do was find the right proof to convict him, or persuade him to confess.

She dozed off after 4:00 a.m. and woke at six to crashing thunder and pounding rain. She gave up trying to sleep and rose, showered and made coffee. By seven, she was sipping her second cup, scrolling through her phone, searching for any distraction, when it vibrated in her hand with an alert from the first responders' app. For a moment she thought she must have dreamed the last hour as she read the message:

Volunteers needed to search for missing girl, Mountain Kingdom Kids Camp. Muster at SAR Headquarters.

She was still staring at the message when Gary shuffled into the kitchen. He must have said something, but she didn't hear him. Her head buzzed with the dizzying sensation of having been here before.

"Sis? Is something wrong? You look like you're going to be sick."

She looked up and focused on her brother's face: He was blond like her, with a boyish face that had many people still mistaking him for a teenager. Despite everything that had happened to him, he maintained his open, optimistic attitude about life. People liked Gary. They trusted him.

Most people did. The cops hadn't. Aaron hadn't.

She wet her dry lips, and struggled to speak. "It's a search and rescue call," she said. "There's a girl missing from a kids camp."

Alarm flashed in his eyes. "What camp?"

"Some place called Mountain Kingdom Kids Camp."

He groped for a chair and sank into it, so pale even the blond hairs of his unshaven chin stood out against his pasty skin. "Who? Did they say who?"

"They don't say." She leaned forward and covered his hand with hers. "What's wrong? Why are you acting like this?"

He wiped his hand across his face, and wouldn't meet her gaze. "Mountain Kingdom is where I work."

He wasn't making any sense. "You work at a ranch."

"That's what I told you, but I actually work at the camp." He grimaced. "I didn't tell you because I knew you'd lose it."

Her stomach clenched. "Gary, how could you do that? How could you risk that?"

"It was the only job I could find, okay? And it's a good one. I didn't have anything to do with Rachel's death, so what does it matter if I work at this camp instead of that one? I didn't do anything wrong."

"Of course you didn't. But what if someone finds out about what happened in Vermont—what you were accused of? They could jump to the wrong conclusion."

They could think he had sought out another job working with kids on purpose. That he was some kind of predator.

"Whatever they think, it's not true. We have to live in the present, sis. Not stay stuck in the past."

She wanted to argue with him that their present was shaped by the past, but her phone buzzed again, reminding her she didn't have time for this. "I have to go," she said, and stood.

"I should go, too," he said. "Maybe I can help."

"No. I don't want you anywhere near the camp or this girl. Not until she's safe. I won't risk anyone thinking you had anything to do with her going missing."

"I didn't."

"I know. But it will be better if you stay away."

He didn't say anything, just stared at her, jaw set in a stubborn line. She turned away, her heart pounding and a voice in her head chanting over and over, *This can't be happening again.*

Chapter Four

As the volunteers assembled to begin the search for thirteen-year-old Olivia Pryor, Willa reminded herself that a missing child didn't mean she was a victim of foul play. Children wandered off and got lost all the time. They sometimes ran away. Most of them were found safe. Surely that would happen this time, too.

"As a reminder for those of you who are new, we're going to search in teams." Captain Danny Irwin addressed the assembled volunteers at Eagle Mountain Search and Rescue headquarters. Almost two dozen volunteers had responded to the early-morning summons, despite the rain that pounded so loudly on the metal roof of the headquarters building that Danny had to raise his voice in order to be heard.

"Each team of four to five people will search an assigned area, as indicated on this map." Danny held up a piece of copy paper. "Anna Trent and her search dog, Jacqui, are already headed for the camp to see if Jacqui can pick up Olivia's scent. With a lot of luck, by the time we get there, they'll have located the girl and we can all go home. But the rain is going to make things more difficult, so we need to be prepared to conduct a ground search."

He consulted the piece of paper in his hand once more.

"Olivia is five feet, one inches tall and weighs approximately one hundred pounds. She has sandy brown hair, olive skin and brown eyes. There's a photo of her on the map each of you will be given. She was reported missing this morning when a bunk mate told her counselor that Oliva wasn't in her bunk. Another cabin mate said she thought Olivia had sneaked out of the cabin a little after midnight."

"She's probably hiding somewhere, trying to stay out of this rain," someone in the back of the room said.

"Keep that in mind as you're searching," Danny said. "Also remember that she may believe she's in trouble for sneaking out of the cabin, so she might not respond to your calls, even if she hears you. It's not unusual for children to hide from searchers. There's also the possibility she's hurt and unable to respond, so don't rely solely on your sense of hearing. Search for flashes of color or anything out of the ordinary in your surroundings such as piles of brush or dislodged rocks or broken branches."

"We might find footprints in the mud," someone else said.

"Or the rain might wash them away," someone else countered.

"Do we know what she was wearing when she left?" Bethany Ames, standing a short distance from Willa, asked.

"We don't," Danny said. "Though the usual camp uniform is shorts or jeans and T-shirts."

"Let's hope she thought to put on a raincoat," someone said.

"Any more questions?" Danny asked.

No one had any, so they headed out to the parking lot for the drive to the camp. Willa found herself in an SUV with Bethany, Grace Wilcox, Tony Meisner and Harper Stanick. There was little conversation on the drive to the camp, the steady thump of windshield wipers and the drum of raindrops providing background noise for their thoughts. Willa texted Gary with Olivia's name and information, asking if he knew the girl, but he made no reply.

Mountain Kingdom Kids Camp looked like a typical summer retreat, with clusters of wooden cabins, a main lodge and recreation areas set amid tall pine trees. This morning the grounds teemed with people in uniform—both camp staff and law enforcement. A deputy checked them in at the front gate and directed them to a staging area in front of the main lodge, an impressive log-and-glass structure where at least twenty people—all adults, from what Willa could see—milled about in plastic ponchos or more substantial rain gear.

Willa pulled the hood of her rain jacket over her hair as she exited the SUV and looked around. She didn't realize she was searching for Aaron until she spotted him standing with two other deputies at one corner of the lodge. He wore a black raincoat, but the bottoms of his khaki uniform pants were soaked.

She turned away, hoping he wouldn't see her, but as she shifted her gaze another familiar figure made her gasp. Gary was there, talking to another young man. They were both wearing green jackets with an emblem on the chest she assumed was the camp's logo. As if he had heard her he looked up, his expression defiant.

"Thank you all for coming." An older man had mounted the steps leading to the lodge entrance and was addressing the gathered crowd with a hailer. He, too, wore a green rain jacket and green rain pants. He had pushed back the hood of the jacket to reveal a gray crew cut. He had a beefy build but he wasn't fat. Willa guessed he was in his late forties. "My name is Scott Sprague and my family has owned and managed Mountain Kingdom Kids Camp for forty years," he said. "This is the first time we've had to deal with something like this, and I want to thank you all for coming to help. Olivia is a bright, smart child, and I'm confident she'll be found safely. But she could be hurt, or scared, or just confused. So I want to ask you to be gentle with her when you find her. Don't worry about finding out what happened. We don't care about that. We just want her safely returned to us." He lowered the hailer and looked out at them, the picture of a man in distress.

Willa was paired with Grace, Tony and Bethany to search an area near the camp's kitchen and mess hall. A group of camp employees were combing through the interior of the buildings. Willa's group was supposed to cover the exterior between the buildings and the lake, to a group of campers' cabins on the east and a dirt road on the west. They kept close together, looking behind and up in trees, behind boulders and along the foundations of the buildings. They investigated two pit toilets, a massive rock barbecue grill, and turned over half a dozen canoes beached along the lakeshore, in case Olivia had taken shelter there. All the while the rain beat down. Within ten minutes Willa was shivering and clammy, despite her rain gear.

Her phone buzzed and she answered the call. It was Danny. "Willa, can you return to the headquarters building? We've got one of the campers who slipped and hurt her leg. She might need some medical attention. I'm tied up in another part of the camp."

"Of course. I'll be right there." She ended the call, then told the others what had happened and left them. She spotted other SAR volunteers, law enforcement officers and camp employees searching for Olivia as she hurried toward the lodge. The sound of the girl's name rang out from all directions. Though the rain had slackened a little, water still dripped from trees and the sun remained behind heavy cloud cover, lending the whole scene a twilight feeling.

The girl in question—two thin brown braids framing a round face, with a streak of mud on one cheek—sat on a sofa in the lobby, one foot on a pile of cushions. She looked as if she had been crying. "I was just trying to find my friend," she said before Willa could even ask her name. "I know I wasn't supposed to be out of the cabin, but I couldn't sit in there and do nothing. Am I going to be in trouble?"

A young woman with swimmer's shoulders and short blond hair sat next to the injured girl on the sofa. "I'm Tatum," she said. "And this is Stella. She was climbing on some rocks behind her cabin and slipped and fell."

"Stella, I'm Willa. I'm a nurse. What hurts?"

"My ankle." Stella leaned forward and gingerly touched her left ankle. "It hurts a lot." Tears welled, and clung to her thick lashes.

"I got her shoe off right away," Tatum said. "But I left the sock so maybe her foot wouldn't be so cold."

The foot was ice-cold, to be expected with this damp. "Maybe you could find a couple of blankets," Willa said as she gently examined the swollen foot.

Stella cried out when Willa tried to move the foot, and Willa took her hands away. "No more of that," she said. "But I think you've sprained it. To be sure, you'll need to have an X-ray."

"My parents are going to be so mad," she wailed.

"They'll be relieved you're okay," Willa said.

"You don't know my parents."

"No. But think about it. One girl is missing. They'll hear about that. Then they'll learn that you're hurt, but safe. In comparison, an injured ankle isn't going to seem like a big deal."

"I can't believe all these people are looking and they haven't found Olivia," Stella said.

"I hope they'll find her soon." Willa opened her pack and took out a roll of elastic bandage. "I'm going to wrap your ankle," she said. "That's going to make it feel a lot better. We'll also get an ice pack for you."

Stella sniffed and watched as Willa began to wind the tape around her foot and ankle. "Are you in the same cabin as Olivia?" Willa asked.

"Yeah. She and I are good friends."

"When was the last time you saw her?"

"About ten o'clock. That's lights out. We said good-night."

"I heard she sneaked out of the cabin later."

Stella sighed. "I guess so. She's done it before. I didn't see her this time, but Marissa did, and she wouldn't have any reason to lie."

"Why did Olivia sneak out?" Willa said.

Stella didn't say anything. Willa focused on wrapping the ankle, letting the silence tease an answer from the girl. "I think she was meeting someone," Stella said at last.

"Another girl?" Willa asked. "Or a boy?"

"Probably a boy." She looked up as Tatum returned.

"I found a couple of blankets," Tatum said, and laid them on the sofa next to Stella. "And I brought an ice pack." Her eyes met Willa's, then she turned to Stella. "I heard what you said about Olivia sneaking out." She shrugged, deliberately casual. "It happens. I mean, there are rules, but not everybody follows them. Do you know who she was meeting? One of the other campers?"

"I don't know," Stella said. "Honest, I don't. She wouldn't say." She looked miserable.

Willa gently patted the wrapped ankle. "Does that feel better?" she asked.

"A little."

Willa settled the ice pack in place. "She's going to need X-rays," she told Tatum.

"Mrs. Mason is going to take her to the clinic in town in a little bit," Tatum said. She turned back to Stella. "Did Olivia tell you anything else? Maybe about her boyfriend back home?"

"You know about that?" Stella's eyes widened.

"I heard her parents sent her to camp to get her away from an older boy she had been seeing," Tatum said. She glanced at Willa. "She wouldn't be the first camper to come here in an effort to get her away from someone the parents thought inappropriate."

"Olivia said her boyfriend was sixteen," Stella said. "But that they weren't doing anything wrong."

"It might help find Olivia if the sheriff knew about this," Willa said. "Someone could try to track down this person Olivia had been going to meet."

"Good idea." Tatum pulled a radio from her pocket. "I'll let someone know." She took a few steps away.

"I'm really going to be in trouble now, aren't I?" Stella said.

"You're helping your friend," Willa said. "No need for you to be in trouble for that."

"Will you stay with me until Mrs. Mason gets here?" Stella asked.

"Of course." She was finally beginning to feel warm again, and Stella was a sweet child. She liked Tatum, too, who was close enough to Stella's age—was she even eighteen?—to sympathize with the girl.

Willa regretted that decision when she heard footsteps approaching and turned to see an older woman walking toward her, accompanied by a sheriff's deputy. An expression Willa couldn't read passed across Aaron's handsome face when he recognized her, but he quickly masked it, and focused on the girl.

"Hello, Stella," he said. "I'm Deputy Ames. I understand you have some information that might help us find your friend Olivia."

Stella picked at the pink and purple woven bracelet around her left wrist. "I don't know if it will help or not. I mean, I didn't actually see Olivia leave the cabin."

Aaron sat on the sofa beside the girl, but not too close. "Tell me what you know," he said. "I promise, you're not in trouble. But the more information we have, the better we'll be able to narrow our search and find Olivia."

"All I know is that Olivia had sneaked out of the cabin before. She went to meet someone, but she wouldn't say who."

"Did she have any special friends among the other campers?" Aaron asked. "Boys or girls?"

"No one in particular." She bit her bottom lip, then looked up, as if just realizing something. "I can't think of a single time I ever saw her even talk to a boy. I mean, they're all the time trying to get our attention, or teasing us. But Olivia ignored them all. So it couldn't have been a boy she was meeting." Stella looked relieved.

"What about staff?" Aaron asked. "Was Olivia friendly with any of them?"

"Veronica is our counselor," Stella said. "We're all friendly with her. And Tatum. She does crafts with us and stuff."

"What about male staff?" Aaron asked. "Did you ever see Olivia talking to one of them?"

Willa stiffened. She thought she knew where this was going and she didn't like it.

Stella shifted, as if suddenly uncomfortable. "The other

male counselors—Wade and Crispin—tell us what to do, or they'll ask questions if they're teaching us something. And Mr. Sprague talks to all of us if he sees us. He's always asking how we're doing and stuff like that."

"Did you ever see Olivia alone with any of the staff members?" Aaron asked. "When they weren't instructing you?"

Stella shook her head. "No."

"Tatum said something about Olivia having a boyfriend back home," Aaron said. "Did she ever say anything about him coming to see her here?"

"No." Stella brightened. "Do you think that's what happened? Maybe they ran away together. I mean, if he's sixteen he can drive, right?"

"Did she ever mention running away with this boy?" Aaron asked.

"No."

"What did she tell you about him?" Aaron asked.

Stella slumped, her elation having vanished. "She said after her parents found out she was sneaking off to see him, they made him promise to never contact her again and he hadn't. She was kind of mad about that and said she never wanted to see him again."

"Was Olivia happy here at camp?" Aaron asked.

Stella considered the question. "She seemed to really like it here until a couple of weeks ago."

"What happened a couple of weeks ago?" Aaron asked.

"I don't know. She just…" She ducked her head, gnawing her bottom lip again.

"Just what?" Aaron prompted.

"She was crying one night, after lights out. I asked her what was wrong and she just said she wanted to go home."

"Do you have any idea what was wrong? Do you remember anything happening?"

"I thought she was just homesick. We all feel that way sometimes."

"After that, was she still homesick?"

"She was just…quieter. Like maybe she was sad. But she didn't want to talk about it."

"Anything else you think we should know? Anything that might help us find her?"

"I'm sorry. I can't think of anything."

"Thank you for your help." He stood. Mrs. Mason moved forward. "I've got my car at the front door," she said. "Tatum has a wheelchair."

Tatum wheeled the chair forward and Stella left with her and Mrs. Mason.

When they were alone, Aaron turned to Willa. "I saw your brother. I was surprised to find out he works here."

Willa didn't mention that she had been surprised, too. "He was home with me all night," she said. "Until after I got the search and rescue call that Olivia was missing."

"Are you sure?" Aaron asked. "He could have slipped away while you were asleep."

"And abducted a girl in the middle of the night? I can't believe you're suggesting something so ridiculous." She struggled to keep her voice down, but fury made her shake. She clenched her fists, fighting the urge to physically attack him.

"It's my job to ask hard questions," he said. "Of everyone." Everything about him was hard—his voice, his clenched jaw, the look in his eyes. Cop mode, she had thought of it, before she had to face the demeanor herself after Gary was arrested.

"I've given you my answers," she said. "Why can't you accept them?" She didn't wait for his reply, but turned and stalked across the lobby, aware of the stares of people milling about the space.

"Aaron!"

Another deputy—a muscular blond—entered the lobby. He hurried past Willa and he and Aaron met beneath a massive antler chandelier in the middle of the space. They conferred, heads together, then raced outside, feet pounding hard on the floor, faces taut with urgency.

Willa hurried after them. She found Danny with a group of other people just outside. "What's going on?" she asked, reading the same urgency on his face.

"They've found something," he said. "Something that might be related to Olivia."

Chapter Five

Aaron stood with Deputies Shane Ellis, Jake Gwynn, Jamie Douglas, Ryker Vernon and Sheriff Travis Walker in a tight circle in an L formed by the cabin where Scott Sprague lived and a maintenance shed. Search and rescue volunteer Anna Trent was also there, holding tightly to the leash of a black standard poodle who wore a blue Search Dog vest. They were all staring at a ripped and muddy green T-shirt, splotched with a rusty red Aaron thought looked like blood.

"The dog located it at the corner of the foundation," the sheriff said. "That kept the worst of the rain off of it."

"And we're sure it belongs to Olivia?" Jamie asked. Her long hair had partially come loose from its bun, and hung in sodden strands around her face.

"Jacqui alerted on this, based on the scent she got from the sock the counselor retrieved from Olivia's dirty laundry bag," Anna said.

"We'll know for certain once we get results from the lab," the sheriff said. He nodded to Jake. "You can bag it now."

Wearing gloves, Jake picked up one edge of the shirt between thumb and forefinger and lifted it. "That looks like it was slashed with a knife or a razor or something," Shane said.

No one else said anything as Jake placed the garment in an evidence bag. Aaron wondered if they, like him, were focused on the blood.

"What's that on the ground?" Jamie asked. She pointed to what looked to Aaron like colored string, pressed into the mud where the torn shirt had lain.

The sheriff used a pen to tease the item from the mud. "It looks like colored string, woven into a pattern," he said.

"It's a friendship bracelet," Jamie said. When they all looked at her, she shrugged. "My sister, Donna, is into making them. Girls trade them with each other."

"Olivia's friend Stella was wearing a bracelet like that," Aaron said.

The sheriff placed the bracelet into an evidence bag. "We'll find out if Olivia had a bracelet like this."

"Was there anything else?" Aaron asked. "Any footprints or sign of a struggle?"

"Nothing," Ryker said. "I was with Anna when Jacqui found it and the ground isn't really disturbed at all. It's almost like someone just dropped it there."

"We'll keep searching, keeping in mind that we may be looking for a wounded girl," Travis said, his expression grim. He was a hard man to read, but Aaron knew he had children of his own. Was he thinking of them? He looked at each of them in turn. "We need to talk to everyone who had contact with Olivia in the last twenty-four hours—campers, counselors, other staff at the camp. Anyone who might have seen her with someone or heard her say something that might be relevant." He turned to Aaron. "Did you learn anything from her cabin mate?"

"Olivia had a relationship with a sixteen-year-old boy at home. Her parents didn't approve. They forbade her to see him again and sent her here for the summer to get her away from him. The friend, Stella, says Olivia told her she was mad at the boy and didn't want to see him again, but she may have been lying to cover up a planned meeting. Stella said this wasn't the first time Olivia sneaked out of the cabin after lights out. She thinks Olivia was meeting someone, but doesn't know who, or even if it was a boy or a girl. She did say she had never seen Olivia interact with the boys at camp, or with male staff, outside of the incidental contact you would expect."

"I'll talk to the parents, get the name of this boy and follow up on his whereabouts," Travis said.

He turned and started walking away, but Aaron followed. "There's something else you should know," he said.

Travis stopped and waited. "There's a man on staff here, Gary Reynolds," Aaron said. "He's a maintenance man. A relatively new hire, from what I can gather. I know him. He's from Vermont."

Again, Travis said nothing, waiting for Aaron to elaborate. "I knew him as Gareth Delaney. He worked at a youth camp there, also. He was a counselor. A little girl disappeared there and she was later found in the woods nearby. She'd been strangled. At least two people said they saw her with Gareth shortly before she disappeared. He was arrested and questioned, but there was never any further evidence to link him to the crime. The murder is still unsolved."

"Do you know if he had any connection to Olivia?" Travis asked.

"No, sir. But I thought you should know."

Travis nodded. "Let's find this man and talk to him."

WORD HAD SPREAD that something of Olivia's had been found near one of the cabins, some bit of evidence that hinted at violence. There were whispers of blood, even talk that the search had morphed from one for a live girl to a hunt for a body. Over the course of the day, the search teams had shifted and re-formed, some people taking breaks to warm up inside and change into dry clothes, then heading out with different partners to look in different areas. Some areas had already been searched and were being gone over again, while other groups moved out farther away from camp to comb through the forest and rocky cliffs beyond the grounds of the camp.

Willa joined one of these groups, accompanying Carrie Andrews, Caleb Garrison and Harper Stanick on a hike through dense forest. They scrambled over fallen trees and around massive boulders, and stopped to shout Olivia's name and listen to their own voices echo back to them. They moved slowly, scanning the ground for disturbed leaf litter, shoe prints in the mud, broken branches or blood. None of them were trained trackers, but they tried to notice anything in the dripping landscape that might be out of place. Anything to show that a young girl, possibly frightened, possibly injured, had passed this way.

The rain had stopped an hour before, but everything still dripped moisture. They were quickly as soaked as if they had walked through a downpour, simply from brushing against foliage and walking under sodden branches.

Caleb stopped and prodded at a mound of dirt and leaves.

"Did you see something?" Willa asked.

"Bears hide their kills by partially burying them," he said. "I figure a human killer might do the same."

Willa shuddered, but nodded. Statistics weren't on their side here. If Olivia hadn't run away with a boy or other friend, and if she had been injured by something or someone, the more time that passed, the less likely they would find her alive. No one was saying that out loud—yet—but she was sure they were all thinking it.

She remembered when Rachel Sherman had been found. Willa hadn't been involved in looking for the girl, but everyone she knew was keeping track of the search efforts, constantly scrolling for updates on social media. Willa was at work when a paramedic came in and told them Rachel's body had been found. "I heard she was strangled and thrown in the creek," he said. "One of the cops said she probably died within hours of her disappearance." He made a fist. "They ought to find whoever did that to a kid and give him a taste of his own medicine."

Willa had nodded and agreed with the paramedic. That was before Gary had been arrested. Before she had had to listen to people call for the return of the death penalty for "people like him." So many people had assumed that because he had been arrested, Gary must have done those horrible things to an innocent child. No one seemed to believe her when she protested that her brother was innocent. Not even the man she loved.

Caleb's radio chirped with a message from Danny to return to the lodge. "We're calling the search for the night," he said. "It's too hazardous to keep going in the dark when everyone is exhausted. Go home. The sheriff will decide if he needs us tomorrow."

Willa was crossing the lobby when Bethany caught up with her. "Are you riding back with us?" she asked.

"No," Willa said. "My brother is here. I'm going to catch a ride with him."

"My brother is here, too," Bethany said. "But he's one of the sheriff's deputies, so I'll skip riding with him."

She waved and hurried off. Willa went in search of Gary. She approached several clusters of camp employees, but he wasn't among them. She tried texting him, but got no reply. She was standing in the light from a cluster of cabins when Scott Sprague approached. The events of the day had reduced the owner of the camp to a gray and wilted version of his burly self, his clothes disheveled, color drained by fatigue and the unflattering overhead light.

"Can I help you with something?" he asked.

"I'm looking for my brother," she said. "Gary Reynolds?"

His brows drew together. "You're Gary's sister?"

"Yes. Do you know where he is?"

"The sheriff took him away about half an hour ago."

She swayed—or felt as if she had, though perhaps the only thing that shifted was her perception. "They *arrested* him?"

"I believe they took him for questioning," he said. "Of course, I guess that amounts to the same thing, doesn't it?"

AARON STOOD AT the door to the interview room and studied the man at the table across the room. Gary Reynolds hadn't changed much since the last time Aaron had seen him. He had the same pale blond hair and boyish features. The papers in Vermont had played up the contrast of his cherubic appearance with the horrible crime he was accused of committing.

But Gary didn't look particularly cherubic at the moment. He was sweating and fidgeting in the hard chair across the table from Sheriff Walker. It was the kind of behavior Aaron had been taught indicated guilt. But could this also be the behavior of a man who had been wrongly accused once before, and was reliving his worst nightmare?

"What's your relationship with Olivia Pryor?" the sheriff asked.

"I don't have any relationship to Olivia," Gary said.

"You don't know her at all?"

"I'd never even heard her name before today." He had stopped fidgeting, and looked directly at the sheriff when he spoke.

"But you must have seen her around camp," the sheriff said.

"I work in the maintenance department. I don't have any contact with the campers. And I've only been there two weeks."

"Where did you work before you were employed by the camp?"

"I was unemployed."

"Before that, where did you live?"

"I lived in Vermont." His gaze slid to Aaron. "I'm sure Deputy Ames already told you that. I'm sure he told you the whole story."

Travis acted as if he hadn't heard this. "Is your real name Gary Reynolds?" he asked.

"It is now. I had it legally changed."

"Why did you change your name?"

"Because I was the chief suspect in the murder of a little girl in Vermont. I was released because there was no evidence against me, but my name was in the papers. It's in every story online about a famous unsolved crime. Me and my sister were harassed and threatened by people to the point where moving away and changing our names was the only way to have any peace."

"Why did you move to Eagle Mountain?"

"Because it was two thousand miles from Vermont, and a small town where nobody knew us from before. We hoped to make a fresh start here."

"Why did you go to work for Mountain Kingdom camp?"

"Because I needed a job and they agreed to hire me."

"Did you work yesterday?"

"Yes. I was at the camp from 8:00 a.m. to 6:00 p.m."

"What did you do yesterday?"

"I dug a ditch for a water line."

"All day?"

"Yes. It was a long ditch."

"And you left the camp at six?"

"A few minutes after six."

"Where did you go?"

"I went to the house I share with my sister, Willa." He rattled off the address. "I was there all night."

"She can verify that?"

"Yes." He looked at Aaron again. "You know Willa. She isn't a liar."

"I spoke with her," Aaron said. "She confirmed that Gary was at the house all evening."

"Then why are we even having this conversation?" Gary asked.

"When you saw the photo of Olivia Pryor, did you recognize her?" Travis asked.

"No."

"In two weeks working at the camp you didn't recognize her?"

"They're kids. Little girls. I don't pay attention to them. I'm not that kind of man."

"Is there anyone at the camp who does pay attention to the girls?" Travis asked. "The wrong kind of attention?"

"Not that I've noticed. I'm not there to keep tabs on other people. I'm there to do my job."

"Digging ditches."

"Or changing light bulbs or repairing the ice maker in the kitchen or anything else that needs doing."

"Did you know Trevor Lawson?"

Gary blinked. "Yeah, I knew him. He worked part-time at the camp. He was a good guy. I was sorry to hear he died."

"When was the last time you saw him?"

"The evening before last. We were setting up for the bonfire and he helped."

"How did he seem to you?"

"What do you mean?"

"Was he upset about anything? Did he seem agitated, or depressed?"

"No. He was his usual self. Easygoing. Joking around with his brother."

"Did you see him leave the camp?"

"No. I already told you, I left a little after six when my shift ended. Trevor was there, working." He leaned forward. "Why are you asking about Trevor? Do you think he has something to do with Olivia?"

"I just wondered if you knew him." Travis stood. "You can go now. We'll let you know if we have more questions."

"I need to call my sister to come get me."

"You can wait for her in the lobby."

Deputy Shane Ellis escorted Gary out of the room. When Travis and Aaron were alone, the sheriff said, "Tell me about Gary's sister."

Aaron crossed his arms over his chest, then uncrossed them. He had nothing to hide, yet he felt guilty. "Willa is a nurse at the clinic. She volunteers with search and rescue. Jake Gwynn's wife recruited her."

"You knew her in Vermont?"

The sheriff didn't miss anything, did he? "She and I were in a relationship."

The sheriff considered this. "How did she react when you questioned her about her brother's alibi for last night?"

"She was upset. She accused me of targeting him because of what happened in Vermont."

"Why was he a suspect in that girl's murder?"

"Two campers separately reported they saw him talking to her shortly before she was killed."

"Anything else?"

"We had a profile that pegged her killer as a white male in his late teens or early twenties who worked for the camp. Gary fit that description."

"Anything else? Any DNA?"

"No." At the time they had all been so sure he was Rachel's murderer. Only later did Aaron realize they had been guilty of tunnel vision.

"Do you believe his sister is telling the truth about him being at the house all evening?"

"Yes. Though there's always the possibility he sneaked out of the house after she went to bed. Olivia's cabin mate said Olivia was meeting someone. Maybe Gary arranged to meet up with her later."

"Talk to the neighbors. See if any of them remembers seeing him leaving."

"Yes, sir." He started to leave, then hesitated.

"Anything else?" Travis asked.

"Why were you asking about Trevor Lawson?"

"We got the autopsy report. His toxicology shows a blood alcohol level of twice the legal limit. He had also ingested secobarbital."

"Sleeping pills?"

"Yes. His brother says Trevor didn't take anything like that. Trevor also had a black eye and two broken fingers and a busted lip."

"Injuries suffered in the accident?" Aaron asked.

"The coroner doesn't think so. He estimates they happened a couple of hours before Trevor died."

Aaron frowned. "So, he was in a fight?"

"That's what I'd like to find out."

"I didn't notice any bruising on Gary Reynolds."

"Neither did I. Or Trevor's brother. It's probably unrelated to Olivia's disappearance, but they're both connected to the camp."

"Seems like an odd coincidence."

"It does." Travis moved toward the door. "Go home and get some rest. You can talk to the Reynolds' neighbors tomorrow."

Gary was gone by the time Aaron entered the front lobby. Willa must have arrived to pick him up. It was just as well Aaron hadn't been there to see her. Earlier today she had made it clear how much she hated him.

He got into his car but instead of heading home he drove to the street where Willa and Gary lived. It was too late to talk to the neighbors, but he wanted to see the house. It was a small, square, wooden building on a fieldstone foundation—a miner's cottage, dating from the turn of the twentieth century. The older part of town was full of these small homes, many of them converted to rentals. Willa's car was in the driveway—the same blue Toyota she had owned when they were dating.

He wished he could talk to her. He wanted to explain what it was like to work a serious case, like a murder. The pressure to find the killer. How easy it was to see things one way.

Things that had looked so obvious to him back then weren't so clear now.

This time was different. No one was going to charge Gary with anything. He wanted to reassure her of that, but she would never listen to him. Hate clouded her view of him.

As for him, he thought he could see her more clearly than ever. She was still beautiful, and passionate—about her job, her volunteer work and her family. But she would never feel that way about him again. He had made a mistake, and he would have to live with the consequences, wanting what they had once had, and could never have again.

Chapter Six

Willa was exhausted, but she had little hope of sleep. Gary had said very little after she picked him up at the sheriff's department, but they needed to talk. She put water on to boil for tea, and took two cups from the cabinet. "Do you want something to eat?" she asked.

Gary slumped at the kitchen table. He looked as bad as she felt. Worse, maybe, pale and heavy-eyed. "No. Though if you've got anything stronger to go into that tea, I'll take it."

She looked in the cabinet until she found a bottle of rum left over from some long-ago recipe, and set it on the table beside him. "Do we need to hire a lawyer?" she asked.

"I don't think so. We can't afford one anyway. Not a good one."

"I could borrow money." She hated the thought, but she would do it for him.

"You don't need to do that."

"How can you say that? You know what happened last time." Those three days when he had been in jail had been among the worst in her life.

"This wasn't like last time." He unscrewed the cap from the rum. "This was different."

The kettle whistled and she poured water over the tea bags in the two mugs. "What do you mean, different?"

"This sheriff is different. I mean, he didn't say much. He listened more than he talked."

She set a mug in front of him. "What did they ask you?"

"The usual. Did I know Olivia? Where was I last night?" He added rum to his mug. "Aaron was there."

Of course he was. "He's probably the one who told the sheriff to question you."

"Probably. He didn't have much to say, though he did tell the sheriff that you verified that I was here all last night."

"That was big of him."

"I always felt bad about busting you guys up. You seemed really happy with him."

"You didn't bust us up. And it's just as well. I got to see his true colors."

"I guess you wouldn't have made a good cop's wife."

But she could have been a good wife to Aaron. If he had been a good man.

"I'll never forgive him for putting you in this position a second time," she said. "When Scott Sprague told me they had arrested you—"

"They didn't arrest me. They questioned me. And not just about Olivia. They asked other stuff, too. They wanted to know if I had seen anyone else with Olivia. And they asked about Trevor." He picked up the mug and eyed her over the rim. "Why didn't you tell me he died? I found out when I showed up this morning that he drove his car into a canyon. They think it was suicide."

"The search and rescue call yesterday morning." She sat across from him and cradled her own mug. "That was a friend of yours?"

"Yeah." He sipped the tea.

"I'm sorry. I didn't know. Why were they asking about

him? They don't think you had anything to do with his death, do you?"

"No. At least I don't think so. They were asking when I saw him last, did he seem upset or depressed, stuff like that."

She sipped the tea, not even caring that it scalded her tongue. "I can't believe this is happening again," she said.

"It's going to be okay. No one can say I was with Olivia because I never even knew her."

"Did they say anything else about Olivia? Did they say what they found that had everyone so agitated? Was it something that belonged to her, or some other kind of evidence?"

"They didn't say anything about that. Someone at camp said it was a shirt or something. And that it had blood on it."

"What do the people at camp think happened to her?"

"No one knows. At first, people said she must have run away. Kids do that, sometimes, I guess. But if they found blood..." He shook his head. "There are some bad people out there."

She couldn't do anything to stop those people. All she could do was try to protect the people she loved. The only family she had left.

DANIEL AND SYLVIA PRYOR had the shattered look of people everywhere dealing with loss and uncertainty. They sat in two chairs in the sheriff's office Tuesday morning, untouched coffee cups in front of them.

"Olivia was happy at the camp," Sylvia said. "Every time we talked to her, she was excited about everything she was doing. All the fun she was having." She glanced at her husband. "We hadn't heard her that happy about anything in a long time."

"Her counselor told us she was sent to the camp to get her away from an older boy she was seeing," Travis said.

"Yes," Daniel Pryor said. "He was sixteen. Olivia was barely thirteen. We felt she was too young to be that serious about anyone. We caught her sneaking out to see him and felt we had to do something."

"Olivia was very upset with us at first," Sylvia said. "But she came around. After her first week at camp, I could tell she was really happy. It was like…like we had our little girl back." Her voice broke and she looked away.

"Who is this boy she was seeing?"

"Jared French," Daniel said. "As soon as the camp called to tell us Olivia was missing, I called Jared to find out if he knew anything. He swears he hasn't been in touch with Olivia. His parents believe he's telling the truth."

"And Jared is at his home now?" Travis asked.

"Actually, he and his family are in Michigan, visiting family," Daniel said. "So we know he and Olivia didn't run away together."

"Did she mention any special friends at camp? Other campers?" Travis asked.

"She talked about the girls in her cabin," Sylvia said. "But never any boys."

"She wouldn't have mentioned boys to us," Daniel said. "Not after what happened with Jared." At his wife's wounded look, he added, "She's a teenager. It's what teenagers do. They don't tell their parents everything."

"We questioned her cabin mates." Travis looked to Aaron. "They didn't mention any boys Olivia was particularly friends with."

"Her friend Stella said Olivia never paid attention to any of the boys," Aaron said. "They tried to tease and flirt with the other girls, but Olivia ignored them."

Sylvia nodded, but said nothing.

"Stella also said that starting about two weeks ago, Olivia

had been quieter," Aaron said. "As if she was upset about something. And about then is when she began sneaking out of the cabin at night."

"How can that happen?" Sylvia asked. "I thought a counselor slept in each cabin with the girls. Isn't she supposed to prevent that kind of thing?"

No one had an answer for this. Aaron remembered his own teenage years—how devious he and his friends had been in getting around restrictions and rules. They weren't bad kids, causing mischief and getting into trouble. But they had craved independence and tested their limits at every opportunity.

"I talked to Scott Sprague on the phone yesterday afternoon," Daniel said. "He said he keeps a close eye on the campers and he doesn't think Olivia was seeing anyone associated with the camp. He suggested someone from outside might have been coming onto the property."

"We've questioning everyone in and around the camp," Travis said. "We haven't identified any suspects at this point. We're sending out a couple of search dogs again today, and hope to get a drone up to do an aerial search now that the weather is better." He cleared his throat. "There's something else you should know. A search dog yesterday located a slashed T-shirt near the foundation of a storage building. There was blood on the shirt. It's the same blood type as your daughter's. We need a blood sample from one or both of you for DNA comparison."

"Blood?" Sylvia look as if she might faint.

Her husband gripped her hand. "You say the shirt was slashed?"

"With a knife or razor. But there was no blood on the ground in the area, and no blood trail leading away from the shirt. It's possible the rain washed away any trail. At this point, we don't know."

"But Olivia is hurt. She's out there alone somewhere. And hurt." Sylvia began to weep, head bowed, sobbing quietly.

Daniel rubbed her back. "I want to be a part of the search," he said. "If Olivia hears me, maybe she'll come."

"It's better if you and your wife stay together, so that we can notify you as soon as she's found," Travis said. He didn't say the last thing they wanted was for the girl's father to stumble upon her lifeless body, but Aaron knew that's what he was thinking. "Someone can take you to the lodge at camp. You can wait there, nearby. We'd also like you to go through Olivia's things at the camp. You might spot something unusual or out of place that we would miss." This task would give them something else to focus on, and a way to feel useful.

"Of course," Daniel said.

"Deputy Ames will drive you to the camp," Travis said.

"We have our own car," Daniel said.

"Then he'll follow you there," Travis said.

Aaron nodded. Neither he nor the sheriff believed the Pryors had anything to do with their daughter's disappearance, but it was good police procedure to keep an eye on them and gauge their initial reactions to the scene. And deputies were going to question everyone at the camp again, in the hope that this time someone would have something useful to say. Something that would lead them to Olivia.

A CASUAL VISITOR to the camp would have had no clue to the previous day's chaos. The sound of cheerful children's voices echoed among the pines and groups of campers gathered on the shore of the lake or around the cabins. Despite

Olivia's disappearance, everything appeared to be operating as usual at Mountain Kingdom.

Aaron escorted the Pryors to Olivia's cabin, and the bottom bunk where she had slept. At the end of the bed was a metal trunk that held her belongings. Her mother sat on the bed and sorted through the contents of the trunk, tears streaming down her face as she smoothed her hand over pajamas and swimsuits, and a stack of green Mountain Kingdom T-shirts, like the one the search dog had located.

"There's nothing unusual here," she said when the trunk was empty, its contents stacked on the bed beside her.

"Did she have a phone?" Aaron asked. Veronica had told him campers were not allowed to have cell phones, but he was curious if Olivia had sneaked one in.

"No, I have it with me." Sylvia dug in her purse and handed him the cell phone.

"Has it been on the whole time?" he asked.

She shook her head. "I switched it on after we found out she was missing. In case she tried to call." She bit her lip, holding back tears.

"Could you unlock it for me, please?"

She unlocked the screen and returned it to him. He scrolled through the history. No calls in almost a month, and before that calls to home and someone named Sara. "Who is Sara?"

"Her best friend at school."

He had to scroll back two more weeks to find a series of text messages to Jared—a furious discussion of her parents' anger and threats to tear the young lovers apart. Then a gap of a few days and an angry exchange in which Olivia said she was glad they broke up and she never wanted to see him again. That fit with the story Stella had told them.

He returned the phone. "Thank you for looking through these things. I'll take you to the lodge now."

"I can do that." Scott Sprague crossed the cabin to them. Freshly shaved and wearing pressed khakis and a green Mountain Kingdom polo, he looked less haggard than he had yesterday. "I'm sure you have questions for me," he told the Pryors. "I'll do my best to answer them."

"I have a question for you," Aaron said. "Are you intending to keep the camp open while Olivia is missing?"

Scott looked puzzled. "I don't think it's wise to disrupt the children's lives any further. While we don't know yet what happened to Olivia, I'm sure she's merely run away and will be found very soon. And I truly believe, despite this very unfortunate incident, that the children are safer here than almost anywhere. So far, the parents agree with me. Though any parent may remove their child at any time, none of them have elected to do so. I see it as a testament to their faith in me."

Aaron didn't want to point out the possible significance of the bloody shirt with Olivia's parents there, so he merely frowned and shook his head. He didn't think the sheriff could order a private business to shut down, though if he had been a parent in this situation, he would have been retrieving his child as soon as possible.

Aaron left the Pryors with Scott and was headed toward the parking lot when someone hailed him. He turned back to see Gary Reynolds jogging toward him. "I'm glad I caught you," Gary said and stopped beside Aaron, a little out of breath.

"What is it?" Aaron asked. He braced himself for anger. Maybe Gary wanted to berate him for telling the sheriff about Rachel's disappearance and Gary's role as a suspect.

But Willa's brother didn't appear angry. "I've found something," he said. "Something you need to see."

"What is it?"

"Come look."

He followed Gary across camp, around to the back of the mess hall to a small storage shed. "This is a shed where we keep extra canned goods, bottled water and stuff like that," he said. "I came out here this morning to get a case of spaghetti sauce for the cook and saw someone broke the lock." He stepped back so that Aaron could move in closer. The padlock which had fastened the door was intact, but the wood around it was splintered.

"I think they broke it with that crowbar." Gary pointed to an iron bar that lay on the ground nearby.

"Is anything missing?" Aaron asked.

"I don't know. I didn't want to touch anything until someone official got a look. But I know it wasn't like this yesterday."

Aaron nodded. Yesterday they had searched this area multiple times. Someone would have seen this damage. He took out his phone and snapped half a dozen photos of the door and the crowbar on the ground, then put on a pair of gloves. "Let's take a look inside."

He eased open the door and peered into the dark space. "There's a pull chain for a light overhead," Gary said.

Aaron tugged on the light. "Notice anything out of place?" he asked.

Gary shouldered his way into the small space. "That case of water wasn't open last time I was in here." He indicated a flat of water bottles, the plastic wrapping on one corner pulled back and three bottles missing. He moved farther into the space, toward the back. "There are bins back here where they store extra blankets and sleeping bags. The lid is off one of them and it looks like someone rifled through here. And there's some backpacking equipment that hangs on the wall. There's an empty spot where I think there might have been a pack. You'd have to ask the counselors what was in it."

Aaron joined him and took more photos, then they both backed out of the building. "What time did you get to work this morning?" Aaron asked.

"My shift starts at eight. I got here a few minutes before, parked and walked up to the mess hall for a cup of coffee. The cook asked me to fetch the spaghetti sauce, so I got the key from her and came back here and found the lock busted. I saw you walking across to the parking lot and thought I'd better have you take a look."

Aaron nodded. "Thanks."

Gary shifted from foot to foot, hands shoved in the pockets of his jeans. "Should I be worried?" he asked. "Willa says we should hire a lawyer. Should we?"

"I talked to your neighbors this morning," Aaron said. "The woman across the street says your truck was parked at the curb all night. Her kid was sick with a stomach virus and she was up and down all night and she could see it out of her front window. She's pretty sure Willa's car was there, too."

"So you're saying my alibi holds up."

"We had to question you. We wouldn't be doing our jobs if we didn't."

"You guys in Vermont wasted a lot of time with me. They never found who killed Rachel."

"No, they didn't."

Gary kicked a rock. "What is with these people, hurting little kids?"

"I don't know. We don't know Olivia is hurt. Maybe she took these things and ran away."

"I heard they found a shirt of hers. With blood on it."

"Where did you hear that?"

Gary shrugged. "People talk. And what about Trevor? Did he really kill himself? He didn't seem the type."

"What's the type?"

Gary sighed. "Yeah. I guess you never know. It just seems weird, him dying, then Olivia disappearing."

"Maybe she ran away because Trevor died. Maybe he was the person she was meeting when she sneaked out of the cabin."

"I don't know anything about that."

Aaron would talk to Trevor's brother again. Maybe there was something there. It didn't explain the ripped shirt or the blood, but it was something...

"How did Willa seem, when you talked to her?" Gary asked.

Aaron stared at Gary, surprised. "What do you mean?"

"Was she different from before?"

"She still hates my guts, if that's what you're asking," Aaron said.

Gary shook his head. "Did you notice she's thinner? And just, I don't know, sadder. I mean, I get that what happened, with Rachel and me being arrested, and then all the people who thought they could solve the case hassling us, was really awful. But when she decided we should change our names and move here, I thought it would be a good thing. A fresh start. She got a good job, then joined search and rescue. Guys ask her out all the time, but she won't say yes to any of them. She just seems, I don't know, stuck."

"She's been through a lot," Aaron said. Had he hurt her so badly she would never recover? "All this happening isn't helping any."

"Seeing you again upset her lot," Gary said. He shifted again. "But it got me thinking."

"About what?"

"You don't get upset about something you don't still care about."

"She cares about you," Aaron said.

"She does. But at one time she cared about you. A lot."

Aaron's throat tightened, making it difficult to speak. "Those days are gone." He forced out the words.

"I don't know about that," Gary said. "I mean, you have to wonder why we ended up here, in Eagle Mountain. Willa says she forgot that you had family here, but I wonder."

Aaron's radio crackled and Gary took a step back. "I have to get to work, but I'll be around if you need me."

Aaron keyed the mic and responded to a summons to meet the sheriff at the lodge. He needed to report the broken lock and the theft from the storage shed, but instead his mind raced with what Gary had told him. Did Willa still care about him? He certainly hadn't seen it in her eyes last time they had spoken. At one time he would have said he knew her better than almost anyone in the world. Now she was a stranger to him.

As for whether or not he still cared about her…it was a question he didn't have to think about very hard to know the answer. Willa would always be the one he measured every other relationship against. That didn't strike him as particularly healthy or well-adjusted, but it was the truth. She may have grown to hate him, but his heart had never let go of her.

Chapter Seven

Willa worked at the clinic all day Tuesday, checking her phone every hour for updates. Volunteers were still searching for Olivia, but the efforts were more targeted. Danny said the sheriff's department had launched a drone. They had brought in a second tracking dog, but they were having no luck picking up Olivia's scent, possibly because of the rain since she had disappeared.

At noon, she texted Gary to ask how he was doing. He replied OK, then refused to respond to further texts. He didn't like to be nagged, but she couldn't help it. Her mind kept replaying the nightmare of him being hauled away in handcuffs, outside their house in Vermont. Gary might have convinced himself that wasn't going to happen again, but she didn't have that kind of faith.

A little after four o'clock she was updating a patient chart when her phone buzzed with a search and rescue alert. Before she could respond, a call came in from Danny. "You're going to get an alert about a fallen climber," he said.

"It just came through," she said.

"I'm tied up here in Junction. And Dr. Rand Martin, our medical director, is in surgery. I know you're at the clinic today, but is there any way you can get free? It sounds like this climber is going to need medical attention and while there are plenty of people who can assess him and give the appropriate care to stabilize him until he can be transported, if he needs pain meds it's better if we have a licensed person on-site."

"Of course." She stood and began gathering her belongings. "We're not that busy, and there are people here who can cover for me."

"Thanks. Let me know how it goes."

She told her supervisor what was up and got permission to leave work early, texted Gary to let him know she might be home late and set out, grateful to have something new to focus on, even temporarily. Someone she didn't know was having what was probably one of the worst days of his life. She could help make that day a little bit better.

SCOTT SPRAGUE STUDIED the damage to the storage room door, unspeaking, then moved into the center of the small space. "I can't say for certain whether anything has been taken," he said. "When the counselors need things like water or a sleeping bag or pack, they're supposed to log what they take, but that doesn't always happen." He indicated a clipboard hanging by the door.

Aaron peered at the last listing on the board. "The last entry is dated two days ago. Someone took two bags of marshmallows for the bonfire."

"Employees wouldn't have broken the door to get in, would they?" Travis asked.

"They'd better not," Scott said. "You say Gary Reynolds reported this to you?"

"Yes."

"He should have told me first, and I would have notified you."

"I was nearby when he discovered the damage," Aaron said. "I think that's why he came to me first."

Scott said nothing. He exited the shed and Travis and Aaron followed. "Are you any closer to finding Olivia?" Scott asked.

"We're still searching," Travis said.

"But you're not finding. She's one little girl. How far could she have gotten in a rainstorm? You should have found some sign of her by now."

"Unfortunately, there are a lot of places to hide in this rugged country. A lot of places to get lost."

A lot of ways to get hurt, Aaron thought, but didn't say it out loud.

"You took Reynolds in for questioning," Scott said. "What did you find out from him?"

"Nothing," Travis said.

"He's my newest employee," Scott said. "I don't know much about him. Seems suspicious this girl disappears right after he shows up."

"Do you think he knew Olivia?" Travis asked.

"What do her friends say?"

"They don't remember ever seeing her alone with a staff member or even another camper," Travis said.

"Kids are good at hiding things. And they don't always tell the truth." Scott spread his hands wide. "Don't get me wrong. I love kids. It's why I run a kids camp. But they're not all little angels. You can't believe everything they say. Or don't say."

"Have you considered temporarily closing the camp and sending the children home?" Travis asked.

Scott's expression hardened. "I don't think you understand what a thin financial margin I operate on here, Sheriff," he said. "Closing the camp would be utter disaster for

Mountain Kingdom. We might never recover. Of course, if I believed the children were in any real danger, I wouldn't hesitate to send them away. But I really don't see how petty vandalism and one missing girl—who probably ran away—is a serious threat."

"Not everyone would agree with that assessment," Travis said.

"I've run this camp for decades," Scott said. "I know how to keep my campers safe."

The sheriff held his gaze for a long moment, but Scott didn't blink. "We'll let you know if we find anything," Travis said.

They left Scott contemplating the damaged door. "I want to talk to Wade Lawson," Travis said.

They found Wade with a group of boys and girls in an open-air pavilion, where they were working on some kind of leather craft. "Can we speak with you a minute?" Travis asked.

"Sure." He caught the eye of the woman across from him. "I'll just be a minute, Veronica."

He followed Travis and Aaron to a tree some distance away. "What's up?"

"We got the coroner's report back on your brother," Travis said.

Wade's expression tightened. "What did it show?"

"He had over twice the legal limit of alcohol in his system. And he had taken sleeping pills. A couple of them, at least. Seconal."

Wade shook his head. "Trevor didn't take sleeping pills. He wouldn't hardly even take an aspirin. He didn't like pills of any kind. And he never got drunk."

"Never?"

"I can think of maybe two or three times in his life I

ever saw him even tipsy. And he wouldn't drink and drive. Besides, when I saw him at the bonfire, he was perfectly sober and happy."

"He didn't argue with anyone that night?"

"No! What makes you think that?"

"He had a black eye, two broken fingers and a busted lip," Travis said. "The coroner thinks all those injuries happened several hours before he died."

Wade stared. "Somebody beat him up?"

"Have you seen anyone around here with bruised knuckles or any injuries like that?" Aaron asked.

"No." He took a deep breath, then looked Travis in the eye. "None of what you're describing is anything Trevor would do. Do you think someone could have kidnapped him, beat him up, filled him full of pills and alcohol, then forced him off the road? Because that's the only thing that makes sense to me."

"Who would do that?" Travis asked. "And why?"

"I can't figure it out. It sounds like a movie plot or something. But I can't believe he would kill himself. I know people probably say that all the time but Trevor really wasn't like that. He was a happy guy. And if something was bothering him, I would have heard about it. He wasn't the type to keep things to himself."

"Did Trevor know Olivia Pryor?" Aaron asked.

"Do you think this has anything to do with what happened to Olivia?" Wade asked.

"Did Trevor and Olivia know each other?" Travis asked.

"I don't think so. I mean, I never saw him talking to her or anything." He rubbed the back of his neck. "When he started working here part-time, I made a big deal about how he had to stay away from the kids, especially the girls. You don't ever want to be alone with them, or touch them, or do anything somebody might misconstrue. That's a sure way to get in big trouble. I harped on it a lot and Trevor took the warnings to heart. He was friendly, but not too friendly. Mostly, he just helped me out and focused on the job."

"We haven't found any connection between Olivia and your brother," Travis said.

"I hope they find her soon," Wade said. "She was a good kid. Polite. Smart. Her parents must be sick about this."

"We're not going to stop looking for her," Travis said. "Call me if you think of anything helpful."

"Yeah, sure. Thanks."

Wade returned to the crafts session, and Travis and Aaron headed for the main lodge. "We're sending the drone up again this afternoon," Travis said. "And tonight we've got a military helicopter flying over with heat-sensing technology. If she's out there, maybe they'll find her."

Aaron sensed the worry behind his words. The sheriff wasn't known for talking. Right now it was as if he was listing out loud everything they were doing to find Olivia, listening for anything he might have left out or overlooked.

"Tell me about the girl in Vermont," Travis said. "The one who was killed."

Aaron paused, gathering his thoughts. "Rachel Sherman was nine," he began. "She disappeared right after dinner. She was on her way back to her cabin with four friends and stopped to use the toilet. They went on without her. She never showed up at the cabin, so the counselor sent a couple of older girls to look for her. They couldn't find her, so she alerted the camp manager. A search was conducted by camp staff, then they called the police department. We searched and the next day found her body up under some brush on a creek about half a mile from the camp. She had been strangled. Sexually molested, but there was no DNA."

"And no idea who killed her?"

"None. There were rumors there had been a man camping in the area, but we never found him. It's always hard when you don't solve a case, but when it's a kid…"

Travis nodded. "I'm going to talk to the Pryors again. Maybe they can help me learn more about what kind of kid Olivia is. How she thinks. If she was attacked by someone and got free, where would she go?"

"Why wouldn't she run to someone in authority in the camp?" Aaron asked. "One of them could have called us right away."

"That's what I need to figure out."

INSTEAD OF DRIVING to search and rescue headquarters, Willa headed straight to Caspar Canyon, a popular rock climbing area where her patient was reportedly stranded on a rock face with a possible broken leg. Tony and Caleb were already there, and half a dozen other volunteers soon arrived. Climbers gathered around them.

"He was almost to the top when something went wrong and he slipped," an agitated man in a red climbing helmet said. "He was trying to hold on, but he slid about forty feet down the wall and landed on that narrow ledge." He pointed up to the sheer rock face above them.

There were several ledges that didn't look wide enough to hold anyone. Willa couldn't tell where the injured climber lay, but Tony said, "I see him."

"I was up top and looked down and could see his leg was bent at this awful angle," the other climber said. "And he was just screaming and screaming." He swallowed. "That stopped. I think he passed out or something. I thought about trying to get down to him, but I was afraid I might push him off the ledge trying to get to him."

"We need to come down from the top and lower him to here," Tony said. He started giving orders, using terms Willa couldn't understand.

"What can I do to help?" she asked.

"I'll radio you as soon as I get to him with a report on his condition," Tony said. "You can talk me through what I need to do."

She stood back and waited as others moved in to rig ropes and pulleys and assemble gear. Tony left and moments later appeared at the top of the cliff, descending toward the narrow ledge where Willa could just make out a slumped figure. No one spoke as Tony moved down the face of the rock. She found she was holding her breath as she watched him make the descent. Could she ever do something so risky to help someone she didn't even know? She had joined search and rescue primarily to lend her medical expertise, and her license that allowed her to prescribe and administer certain medications. But she had told Danny on her first day that she wanted to go through the regular training, like any rookie. She wanted to be a working member of the team, not merely someone on the sidelines.

When Tony reached the ledge, he hovered beside it for several moments before perching on the edge, leaning back against his ropes for balance.

Willa's radio crackled. "His leg's at a forty-degree angle in the wrong direction," Tony said. "I'm going to cut open his pants to get a better look." There was a ripping sound, then a loud moan. "Easy," Tony said. "I'm with search and rescue. We're going to take care of you." More moaning and the brush of fabric against rock. "Not a compound fracture," Tony said. "I need an air splint for this leg. I'll need to straighten it and that's not going to be any fun for either of us. His shoulder is injured, too. I can't tell how much.

It's going to take two of us to get him into a litter and lower him down. He could use some pain meds."

"I'll send up an injection for him." She got more information about his approximate weight, then retrieved the lockbox of drugs and drew up the appropriate dosage of painkiller. She placed this in a plastic case that snapped shut and handed it off to Ryan Welch, who was going to make the descent with the air cast and other first aid supplies.

A tense half hour followed. Ryan reached the other side of the ledge and handed off the painkiller. Tony gave the injection and they waited for it to take effect, talking with the semiconscious climber and doing their best to make him comfortable. Then they worked together to get the injured leg in the air splint and assess the shoulder. Willa listened in as they relayed details about the climber's medical condition, and she was able to suggest some things they could do to make transport easier. Then they began the awkward task of moving him from the ledge to a litter, first fitting him with a cervical collar and strapping the shoulder to immobilize it.

A Rayford County Sheriff's Department SUV escorted the ambulance into the canyon. Willa stiffened, then let out a sigh of relief when she saw the deputy was not Aaron, but a woman. She introduced herself as Deputy Jamie Douglas.

"How's it going?" Jamie asked, and nodded toward the suspended litter.

"They're getting ready to lower him down," Willa said.

One of the paramedics joined them. "What have we got?" he asked.

Willa explained the situation and what they had done to care for the man, including all medications administered.

"Sounds like all we need to do is get him to the hospital," the paramedic said.

It seemed to Willa to take forever for the man to arrive

safely on the ground, though by her watch only another twenty minutes passed. Ryan and Tony descended alongside the litter, keeping it steady and helping it over any outcroppings. By the time everyone was on the ground, Willa noticed the men were sweating from the exertion.

"You did a great job," she told them.

"He's going to be okay," Tony said as they watched the paramedics load the climber into the ambulance. "Thanks for your help."

"You did all the hard work," she said.

"Everyone's contribution matters," he said.

She stayed to help load equipment, then headed home, feeling calmer than she had all day. It had been good to focus on something else for a while. To remember that hers were not the most pressing concerns in the world.

She drove toward home, but on the edge of town found herself behind a familiar black pickup truck. Her gaze focused on the sticker on the left side of the bumper, advertising a popular Waterbury restaurant. She studied the driver's silhouette through the truck's rear window. She would know that erect, dark-haired figure anywhere. She let her foot off the gas and slowed. The last thing she wanted was for Aaron to think she was following him.

But when he put on his blinker and turned onto a side street, she found herself making the turn also. Two-thirds of the way down the street, he headed into the drive of a dark brown A-frame and parked. She sped past, catching a glimpse of him getting out of the truck as she did so. The house was small, like hers. A rental? Or had he purchased it? Did he live there alone, or with a roommate? A woman? The idea that he might be living with a woman made her stomach twist.

Not because she was jealous. But maybe because it hurt to think he had gotten over the pain of their parting so easily.

She gripped the steering wheel harder and made the block and headed home. What Aaron Ames did with his life was none of her business. All she cared about was taking care of Gary and herself.

She was surprised to see that Gary's truck wasn't in the driveway. He almost always got home before she did. Once inside, she texted him. Everything OK? But he didn't answer.

He's probably out with friends, she told herself. Except that Gary hadn't gone out with anyone during their short time in Eagle Mountain. He wasn't the type to party and almost always came straight home from work.

Half an hour later, she called his phone, but it went straight to voicemail. She was on the edge of panic. Had the sheriff picked him up again?

With trembling hands, she searched for the nonemergency number for the sheriff's department, but her call went to voicemail. She hung up, then tried to think what to do. She could go to the sheriff's department, but was anyone even there after hours? Or rather, was there anyone there who would let her in?

She stared at her phone again. She had deleted Aaron's number from her contacts a year ago, but she could still remember the digits. She dialed it, only to have an unfamiliar woman answer. That shook her. Did he had a girlfriend? A wife?

"Is Aaron there?" she asked.

"Aaron don't have this number anymore," the woman said, and hung up.

Willa tucked the phone away. She didn't know Aaron's new number, but she did know where he lived. And she was desperate to make sure Gary was safe.

Aaron's truck was still in the driveway of the A-frame. Willa parked her Toyota behind it, then forced herself to get out and walk up to the door. She knocked and waited for an answer.

She was about to turn around and retreat to her car once more when the door opened. Aaron, barefoot and shirtless, wearing only joggers and the St. Michael medallion his mother had given him when he became a police officer, opened the door. His dark hair was damp and he smelled of herbal shampoo and shaving soap. She had a horrifying vision of walking right into his arms and resting her head on his shoulder, surrendering to the comforting sensation of his strong arms around her.

"Willa? Is something wrong?"

She stared at him, embarrassment heating her face. What was she doing here? "I… I can't find Gary," she said. "I thought maybe…maybe you had arrested him again."

He stepped back, and the door opened wider. "We haven't arrested Gary," he said. "Come in and I'll help you find him."

She followed him into a small living area. He picked up a T-shirt from the end of the sofa and pulled it on. She stared, distracted by the ripple of his back muscles as he pulled the shirt over his head, but unable to look away. When he turned to find her watching him, her face heated again.

"Why did you think we had arrested Gary?" he asked.

"Because that's what happened before. You took him in for questioning and let him go, but the next day you arrested him."

"That was a different case," he said. "Sit down. Please."

He sat on the sofa and motioned for her to join him. Instead, she perched on the edge of a chair across from him. "You told the sheriff about what happened in Vermont," she said. "You told him to question Gary."

"We questioned a lot of people from the camp," he said.

"We're still questioning people. The more people we talk to, the more likely we'll learn something useful."

"Is Gary a suspect in Olivia's disappearance? He didn't even know her."

"He's not a suspect. A neighbor confirmed his alibi and we haven't found any connection between him and Olivia. Unless you know something he hasn't told us."

"No." She shook her head. "You double-checked his alibi? You didn't believe me?"

"It's not about what I believe or don't believe," he said. "All that matters is what a jury believes. Two witnesses are always better than one."

"Like the two girls who said they saw Gary talking to Rachel before she disappeared."

"Two witnesses would have been more convincing than one, yes."

"But not convincing enough for the DA to prosecute."

"We didn't have a strong case. All we had was an FBI profile and the statements of those two girls. It wasn't enough. I don't think the sheriff here would even have arrested your brother."

"Then why was he arrested in Vermont?"

He leaned forward, elbows on knees, his gaze locked to hers. She wanted to look away, but she couldn't. He spoke softly, but his words held an intensity that had her leaning toward him. "The police chief was under a lot of pressure to solve the case. All of us were. I'm not saying that to excuse what was done, only to try to help you see what was going on behind the scenes. We didn't have anything to go on. No suspects. Then we had Gary. He fit the profile. He had been seen with Rachel. The sheriff thought if we questioned him long enough, he would crack."

"You mean, he would confess."

"Yes. But he never did."

"Because he wasn't guilty!" She clenched her fists.

He reached out and put a hand over hers. "I see that now," he said. "I didn't see it then. I'm sorry."

She stared at his hand, the feeling of its weight and warmth so familiar. She told herself she should pull away, but she couldn't.

"I'm sorry this has hurt you so much," he said.

Was that *pity* in his voice? The idea repelled her. She pushed away. "We didn't leave Vermont because we were running away," she said. "We left because we didn't have a choice. Not if we wanted to have any kind of life. I tried so hard to find anyone else who might have killed Rachel. There were rumors of some guy living in the woods near the camp, but by the time the police looked for him, he was gone. I tried to find him. I even hired a private detective, but he couldn't find anything."

"We weren't even sure there was a guy in the woods," Aaron said. "It sounded like the kind of story that kids make up to scare themselves around the campfire."

"Did you even look for him?" She couldn't keep the bitterness from her voice.

"We did," he said. "I personally spent half a day out there, searching for some sign of a camp. But there wasn't anything."

"Until they find who really killed Rachel, Gary will always have that hanging over his head," she said. "Every true crime podcast that rehashes the case mentions him."

"Unfortunately, some cases are never solved," he said. "Especially when there's so little evidence, as in Rachel's case. I'm sorry."

Did she believe him? What difference did it make if she did?

"I'm afraid it will be the same thing all over again if Olivia isn't found safe," she said. "Did they really find her blood?"

He straightened, and pulled his hand away. "I can't say."

"I think that probably means yes."

"We're doing everything we can to find her," he said. "That's the most important thing right now. If she's alive, she can tell us herself what happened."

"And if she's not alive?"

"Then maybe she'll still tell us what happened, through the evidence at the scene."

She nodded, and bowed her head, suddenly so exhausted.

"Why Willa Reynolds?" he asked. "Your new name, I mean? Why did you choose that one?"

"Oh." She took a deep breath, trying to pull herself together. "Willa was my mom's name. Reynolds was my dad's middle name. It seemed a good way to still remember them, but it's the kind of thing it would be harder for a random person on the internet to figure out. At least, I hoped so." She sighed. "Gary didn't want to change his name at all, but I persuaded him to go by Gary instead of Gareth, and he agreed to Reynolds because at least it was still connected to our dad."

"And Eagle Mountain? How did you end up here?"

"I could get a job here," she said. "I answered an ad I found in a nursing publication. And it was a long way from Vermont, but it had mountains."

"Still, it seems like a big coincidence, both of us ending up here."

"The name of the town in the ad caught my attention," she said. "I didn't remember until later that Bethany had moved here and you raved about how beautiful it was. I guess the name stuck in my head. But I didn't know *you* were going to move here." She stood. "I should go."

He rose also, and moved toward her. She thought at first he was going to pull her to him, and she flinched. She didn't trust herself in his arms. She was too aware of him—the scent of him, the memory of his touch. He wasn't good for her, but her body wasn't paying any attention to that knowledge. Every part of her ached for him and she didn't know, right now, if she was strong enough to resist him. "I can help you look for Gary," he said.

She shook her head and pulled out her phone, and saw to her surprise that she had a new text message. She opened it. I'm home, Gary had texted.

"Gary's home," she said, shaky with relief.

"Good." Aaron still wasn't touching her, but he stood so close she could see the gold flecks in his brown eyes and the dot of shaving cream just beneath his left sideburn. Her gaze shifted to his mouth, and her own lips parted. Then their eyes met and she felt pulled to him.

He stepped back, and turned away. "Are you all right now?" he asked.

Would she ever be all right again? She felt wrung-out. Drained. "I'm fine," she said, and forced herself to move past him, toward the door.

She didn't remember walking out the door or to her car. She didn't even remember driving home, though she was soon there, parking behind Gary's truck. The conscious part of her was still back there with Aaron. Waiting for his kiss. Wanting it as much as her next breath.

Chapter Eight

Tuesday was Aaron's father's birthday, and nothing short of a genuine emergency could excuse Aaron and his siblings from their presence at the family table. "Everyone is pulling extra shifts right now, trying to find this missing girl," Aaron said when his mom called to remind him he was expected for the birthday celebration. When they weren't actively scrutinizing the countryside for any sign of the missing girl, they were combing through evidence for any clue as to her whereabouts.

"You still have to eat," his mother said. "If you can't join us, I'll bring a plate to you at the sheriff's department."

Aaron could only imagine the ribbing he would endure if his mother showed up with dinner for him. Though some of it would probably be jealousy—Diane Ames was a good cook. "I can stop by for a little while," he said. "But I have to eat and run."

Thus, he found himself in his usual seat at the family table, across from Bethany and her fiancé, Ian. Aaron hadn't been so sure about the professional mountain climber—and reputed billionaire—when they had first met. He had been afraid the guy would end up hurting Bethany, who had a tender heart and a history of poor judgment when it came to men. But he had been happy to admit he was wrong. Ian had proved to be a stand-up guy and he truly seemed to care about Bethany.

Twins Carter and Dalton sat on either side of Aaron—two years younger than him and showing no sign of settling down. They worked as drivers, tour guides and general handymen for the family business, Peak Jeep Tours and Rentals. Their parents—married thirty years and still doing everything together—were at either end of the table, which was loaded down with lasagna and a huge salad, a basket of bread sticks and a lemon birthday cake for dessert.

"A group of us are getting together to search those gullies and caves on the back side of Mount Wilson tomorrow afternoon," Carter said as he doused his salad in dressing.

"I'll help," Ian said. An internationally known climber, Ian Seabrook had settled in Eagle Mountain to open a via ferrata, a public climbing route.

"We should ask Willa to come with us," Bethany said. "I know she wants to help, and I'd like to get to know her better."

"Yeah, I want to meet her," Carter said. "Every search and rescue call she's been on, I haven't had a chance to speak to her. I hear she's really good-looking."

"I noticed her watching you, Aaron," Bethany said. "She was really checking you out."

Aaron forced himself not to react. "When was that?"

"When we responded to the call about the guy who drove off Dixon Pass. And again at the youth camp, that first day we searched for Olivia. Willa couldn't take her eyes off you. You should definitely ask her out."

He shook his head. "That's not going to happen."

"Why not?" his mother asked.

He debated lying but the truth was going to come out.

"Do you remember the woman I was seeing in Vermont?" he asked. "Kat Delaney?"

"I remember her," Carter said. "The two of you broke up after her brother was arrested for the murder of that little girl at the summer camp."

"What murder?" Bethany asked. "And the woman you were dating was named Kat?"

"Short for Katherine," Carter said. "And this little girl at a summer camp in Waterbury was murdered."

"You had already moved away when all that was going on," Dalton said.

"What about her?" Carter asked. He stabbed at his salad. "You can't ask Willa out because Kat broke your heart?"

"I can't ask Willa out because she *is* Kat." He shoveled a forkful of lasagna into his mouth and chewed, though he might as well have been eating packing peanuts.

"What?" Carter paused, fork halfway to his lips. "Willa and Kat are the same person?"

Aaron nodded and swallowed. "I guess she and her brother were harassed so much they moved and changed their names. They had no idea I was living here."

"If Willa is Kat, why didn't I recognize her?" Carter asked.

"She was out of context," Dalton said. "We didn't expect to run into Aaron's ex here. Plus, the name change threw us. And we never got that close to her."

"Still, makes me think I'm losing my touch." Carter returned his focus to his food. "I usually have a good memory for good-looking women."

"So do you think her brother did it?" Dalton asked. "Killed that girl? And does he have anything to do with Olivia's disappearance?"

"The charges were dismissed because we didn't have any

real evidence against him," Aaron said. "Just a couple of girls who had seen him talking to Rachel earlier in the day, and he fit the FBI profile. At the time, the sheriff thought he was acting guilty, but he was probably just scared."

"Yeah, but what does your cop instinct tell you?" Dalton asked.

Aaron shook his head. "I don't know if I believe in 'cop instinct.' At the time, I convinced myself he was guilty, because that's what everyone around me said they thought. Now—I don't think he was."

"What a terrible thing to happen," his mother said. "I can't imagine having to change my name and move all the way across the country to start over, just to get away from a scandal like that."

A scandal Aaron had helped to set in motion. Whatever Gary may or may not have done, Kat—Willa—was innocent. But she had suffered just as much as her brother had. She was still suffering.

This afternoon, when he had opened the door to find her there, it had taken all his will not to pull her close. She had looked so shaken and afraid. And when he had dared to touch her he had felt the connection like an electrical current. He had looked into her eyes and thought she felt it, too. The connection and the longing to be together again.

Then he had realized he was letting his emotions lead him in the wrong direction. Willa hadn't come to his home for help. She had come to accuse him of arresting her brother. That was still how she saw him—as the enemy. The person who had ruined her life.

So he had done the only thing he could see was right and let her walk away. She would never know how much that had cost him. He turned to Carter. "Do me a favor, and don't ask her out," he said. He doubted Willa would say yes—not when she realized who he was. But no sense taking chances. The only thing worse that not having Willa would be seeing her with his brother. "And don't say a word about her name change."

"I won't," Carter said. For once his brother wasn't making a joke out of the situation.

"Let me get this straight," Bethany said. "Kat—who is now Willa—broke up with you because her brother was suspected of murdering this little girl at the summer camp. Except now you don't think he did it, and in any case, he was never charged with the crime. And now your former girlfriend and her brother are living in Eagle Mountain, with new names."

"Yeah." Aaron looked down at the remains of his lasagna; his appetite vanished.

"Wow," Bethany said. "Of all the places for her to end up. Maybe it's because the two of you are meant to be together after all."

"That's not how life works, Bethany," Aaron said.

"You only say that because you're a cop," Bethany said. "But there are people who believe—"

"Bethany, did you look at those bridesmaids dresses in the link I sent you?" his mother interrupted.

Aaron guessed after so many years of raising four children his mom was an expert in heading off an argument. And he really didn't want to argue with his sister about fate and destiny and all that nonsense. He and Willa had been good together, but now she hated him and he had to learn to live with that.

"I did, Mom." Their mother couldn't see it, but Aaron didn't miss the conspiratorial look Bethany sent Ian. "We're thinking of something a little simpler."

"Some of those dresses were quite plain," his mother said.

"Yes, but we're looking or a more rustic wedding venue. We want to keep it very casual."

"I don't see why you can't have the wedding in a church and the reception in the canyon," his mother said.

It was an old argument. One his mother was not going to win. Bethany had defied her parents to see Ian and that had given her all the courage she needed to stand firm on her wedding plans. Good for her. But Aaron didn't want to get involved. He slid back his chair.

"I have to go now," he said. "Thanks for the dinner, Mom. It was great."

"But you haven't even had dessert. It's lemon Italian cream cake—your father's favorite."

"And we have to sing 'Happy Birthday' to Dad," Bethany said.

"Think I'll skip the cake tonight." He patted his flat stomach. "Have to stay in shape."

He lingered long enough for "Happy Birthday," then he left, back to the side of his life he felt better equipped to handle. He might not solve every crime, and they were no closer to finding Olivia after two days of intense searching, but he knew how to investigate and dig and the next steps he should take. Relationships—whether romantic or familial—were a lot more unpredictable.

WILLA'S FIRST PATIENT after lunch on Wednesday was a camper from Mountain Kingdom who had fallen on a hike and broken her arm. Juliet was twelve, with a cloud of curly red hair and a gangly frame. She had a tear in her shorts and tears running down her face, but Willa praised her for being brave and talked about what a great story she would have to tell her friends back home, and eventually coaxed a smile from her.

After X-rays and an examination by the nurse practitioner, Willa presented Juliet with a lollipop and set about casting the injured arm. While this was being done, the counselor was called into the business office to complete some paperwork.

Willa watched the woman leave, then asked, "Did you know Olivia, the girl everyone is looking for?"

"Uh-huh. But I don't know what happened to her." Juliet licked the lollipop. "The adults keep asking everyone over and over, but we don't know anything." The girl's voice rose, and Willa looked nervously toward the office. She could see the counselor's back from here. Could the woman hear how upset her charge was becoming? Willa was liable to be reprimanded for meddling in something that wasn't her concern.

"I'm sorry about your friend," she said, and applied the last of the wet plaster. "How does that feel?"

"Funny. Is it going to itch?"

"It shouldn't itch too much. Is it too tight?"

"I don't think so." She met Willa's gaze, her expression serious. "I don't know Olivia that well," she said. "But her best friend at camp, Stella, is really upset. I heard her crying in her bunk last night, and I think it was because of Olivia. Or maybe it's because she sprained her ankle. But I don't think that's it. The ankle is all wrapped up and Stella told me it hardly hurts at all anymore. And she gets to skip all the hikes and stuff. But she also has to miss out on swimming, so maybe she's just sad about that." Juliet shrugged. "Some kids cry all the time, especially the little ones who get homesick, but Stella isn't like that, so I figure she just misses Olivia."

"I imagine she does."

"How are we doing?" The counselor returned to the room.

She frowned at Willa. Had she overheard part of the conversation?

"Would you like pink, orange, purple or green for the final layer?" Willa asked, and showed the box of colored wraps.

"Purple," Juliet said.

Ten minutes later, the counselor and the girl left, the child showing off her purple cast.

The door opened and Aaron entered. Willa stiffened. "How can I help you, Deputy?"

"Would you be willing to go to lunch with me? Just to talk."

This wasn't the first time she had been asked out in front of a waiting room full of patients. She had even heard a rumor that there was a secret betting pool on how long it would be before the new nurse agreed to go out with someone. She was used to turning men down with a minimum of fuss, but Aaron's invitation caught her off guard. What made him think she would even consider going out with him?

But she remembered those moments of connection the other night at his house. She had wanted to believe those feelings were all one-sided. Apparently not, and he had gotten the wrong message. "I don't think that would be a good idea," she said, keeping her voice low.

He nodded, showing no disappointment or surprise at her rejection. "Could you answer a medical question for me?"

Almost everyone in the waiting room was watching the two of them, not even pretending interest in anything else.

"Come back here," she said, and led the way to an empty exam room. She closed the door behind them, then thought perhaps she shouldn't have. The room was small, and suddenly intimate, with the two of them so close together. "What kind of medical question? Are you sick?" The idea alarmed her. He looked healthy. Better than healthy—he looked perfect. But you couldn't always tell…

"I'm trying to figure out how you could give sleeping pills to someone against their will," he said.

Not what she expected. "Do you have someone in mind?"

"It's a hypothetical. It's related to a case I'm working on."

"All right. Well, there are lots of ways. You could crush them up and put them in food or a drink. How many pills are we talking about?"

"Two or three."

"Depending on what you put them in, the person you're giving them to might not even notice."

"This person didn't have any food in their stomach."

"Then I'm not sure how you would do it."

"Could you force the pills down their throat? The way you'd pill a dog or cat?"

"I suppose so. If they were restrained."

"Could you do that with alcohol, too? Pour booze down their throat?"

"Not without choking them." She knew better than to ask him for details. She had learned very early in their relationship that he took privacy concerns very seriously. As did she. She didn't talk about her patients, and he didn't talk about his cases. It hadn't mattered, because they had so much else to talk about—books, music, news and life itself. She had been a little smug at times. One thing she and Aaron did well was communicate, and that was supposed to be the key to a good relationship, wasn't it?

"I suppose you could make someone drink anything if you threatened them with a weapon," she said. "Or threatened someone they loved." The idea made her queasy. "Who is doing these horrible things?"

"I'm not sure anyone is doing anything. At this point, I'm just speculating."

"Does this have anything to do with Olivia?" she asked.

"No. This is something else. And don't tell anyone we had this conversation. It's so far-fetched they'd probably laugh me off the force if they knew. I was just curious." He moved a little closer, his tone confiding. "To tell the truth, it gave me an excuse to talk to you. I've missed that."

She had missed it, too. But that didn't mean it was a good idea to spend too much time talking with him. "I have to get back to work," she said.

"Me, too." But he lingered, his gaze like the brush of his fingers across her skin.

A knock on the door made them both jump. "Willa, is everything all right? You have a patient ready."

She glanced up at him, a desperate look, and he stepped aside and opened the door. She rushed past him and hurried toward the examining room, fleeing her own worst impulses.

JAKE RADIOED AS Aaron was leaving the clinic. "What's your twenty?" Jake asked.

"I'm headed back to the sheriff's department. I'm about a block away."

"Do you have time to run back out to Mount Wilson Lodge with me? Dwight has something he wants to show us."

"Sure. What's he got?"

"He didn't say. He wants us to take a look and arrive at our own conclusions."

They met at Jake's sheriff's department SUV. He looked as exhausted as they all did, worn out but determined to keep going, desperately hoping for some sign of that missing little girl. Every day that passed made it less likely they would find her alive. Gradually the case was moving from a rescue mission to a search for a body to give the family closure and, they hoped, provide more clues to what had happened.

Aaron might have dozed on the drive out to the fishing and hunting lodge. He snapped to as they turned in at the gate. Dwight met them in front of the lodge with two quadrunners. "This is the best way to get to where we need to go," he said.

Jake got behind the wheel of one vehicle, while Aaron rode with Dwight in the other. They headed down a trail, past a large lake where two men stood, fly-fishing.

"The wife of one of those guys went hiking this morning," Dwight said. "When she came back she asked me about this place. I couldn't really figure out what she was talking about, so after she went back to her cabin, I rode out here to take a look. That's when I decided to call this in."

"Call what in?" Aaron asked.

"It's hard to describe. You'll have to see and decide for yourself." Past the lake, he turned off on another trail that led up an incline to the east. "We're headed toward Mountain Kingdom Kids Camp now," Dwight said.

"How far is the camp from here?" Aaron asked.

"About a mile as the crow flies. A little farther on foot. It's pretty rough country—a lot of blow-down trees and big boulders scattered around. Some of the search and rescue people came through there the day Olivia was reported missing. They didn't find anything, but it would have been easy to miss someone in that kind of terrain."

They threaded their way through dense forest, then across a high meadow, until they reached a three-strand barbed wire fence. Dwight stopped and shut off the machine. Jake parked beside him.

"We have to walk from here," Dwight said. "We'll be on national forest property."

"How did your hiker end up out here?" Jake asked as he ducked between the strands of barbed wire.

"She said she was following a trail that just stopped," Dwight said. "I think she must have gotten off on a deer trail. Fortunately, she has a good sense of direction and was able to find her way back to the fence and the main trail from there." He pulled out his phone. "I marked the GPS coordinates after I found what she was talking about."

They walked for another hundred yards, Dwight frequently consulting the screen on his phone. They detoured around a thick stand of aspen, then came to a stop.

"What are we looking for?" Aaron asked.

"Over there." Dwight pointed to what at first looked like a clump of brush. But as Aaron moved closer he could see it was actually branches that had been bent over, the ends weighted down with rocks to form a tunnel.

He crouched down and looked inside. "Did you go in?" he asked.

"No. Look there, just inside. Do you see it?"

Jake moved in to peer over Aaron's shoulder. "It's a shoe print," he said. "A small shoe print."

Aaron studied the faint outline, as if from the sole of an athletic shoe. "About the size a thirteen-year-old girl might wear," he said.

"My guest didn't notice that," Dwight said. "She was asking me what kind of animal made the tunnel."

Jake and Aaron looked at each other. "One of us has to go in there," Jake said. "In case she's in there."

"I'll do it," Aaron said.

"Let's photograph that shoe impression first." Jake took out his phone. "And the structure, too, in case you tear it up."

Photographs taken, Aaron prepared to crawl on his hands and knees down the narrow tunnel. It was a tight fit, and branches scraped his back in several places, but after approximately four feet he emerged into a larger space. "It's like an igloo made of branches," he said. He could hear Dwight and Jake just outside. An igloo just big enough for one half-grown person to shelter.

"Is anyone in there?" Jake called.

"No. But the grass is all pressed down, like someone was sleeping here." He studied the ground closely and spotted a blue label. He placed this in an evidence envelope, then retraced his path down the tunnel.

He was grateful to stand upright once more, his back protesting as he straightened. He handed the evidence bag to Jake. "I found this. It's the same brand of water as the ones taken from the Mountain Kingdom storage shed."

Jake looked back at the tunnel. "Do you think Olivia was hiding out here? Why?"

"Maybe she wanted to prove she could?" he guessed.

"When I was a kid I read a series of books about a kid who lived alone in the wilderness after a plane wreck," Dwight said. "I used to daydream about doing something like that, but I never would have really tried it."

"I read those books, too," Aaron said. "Maybe Olivia did, too."

"That doesn't explain the bloody shirt," Jake said.

"No, it doesn't," Aaron said. "Unless that shirt is the reason she's hiding. She's afraid whoever did that to her is still after her." He looked around then. "You would have to be right up on this place to ever see it."

"Smart kid, to figure all this out," Jake said. He pulled a coin from his pocket. "You want heads or tails?"

"What for?" Aaron asked.

"The loser waits here while the other one goes back to Dwight's house and calls it in. We'll have to get forensics, see if we can find any definitive evidence that Olivia was here."

"She was here," Aaron said. "No adult made this. Everything about it is kid sized."

"Heads or tails?" Jake repeated.

"Heads."

The coin came up tails. Aaron settled in to wait while Jake and Dwight returned to the lodge. After a while he sat, his back against a tree, warm sun on his face. For the first time in days, he felt at peace. This wasn't a place where someone had been held captive. This was a hideout. A safe place. Olivia had been here recently; he was sure. And she was alive.

The only questions were why had she hidden out here, and where was she now?

Chapter Nine

"We're asking search and rescue to assist with an intense, targeted search in this section of national forest between Mountain Kingdom Kids Camp and Mount Wilson Lodge." Sheriff Travis Walker stood before the gathered search and rescue volunteers Wednesday afternoon inside the main building of the Mount Wilson Lodge. He indicated a section outlined in red on an enlarged map pinned to the wall. "We've found some indication that Olivia Pryor has been in this area recently."

A murmur rose among the volunteers. "What did you find?" Bethany asked, addressing the sheriff.

"We're passing around a smaller copy of the map," Travis continued. "On the back is a photograph of a brush shelter where we believe Olivia spent at least one night. The location of this shelter is marked on the map. Keep your eyes open for similar primitive shelters like this."

"How would a thirteen-year-old girl know how to build something like this?" Dr. Rand Martin, Eagle Mountain Search and Rescue's chief medical officer, asked.

"Mountain Kingdom has a three-day wilderness adventure course where they take the kids out and teach them survival techniques, including building shelters," Sergeant Gage Walker, the sheriff's brother, spoke up. "Olivia's parents also say she is a big fan of adventure novels and TV shows. Looks like she was paying close attention."

"Do we know why she ran away from camp?" Danny asked. "Can we expect her to try to hide from us?"

"We don't know why she left camp," Travis said. "And yes, she may try to hide. But she's been out there three days now and may be ready to return, if not to Mountain Kingdom, then to her family."

"May I say something, Sheriff?" Scott Sprague stepped forward. The camp owner had added a silver Stetson to his khaki-and-polo uniform, the hat mimicking those worn by some members of the sheriff's department. "Thank you all for volunteering to help with the search for Olivia," he said, his voice projecting clearly in the large room. "All we want is for her to be safe. Whatever reason she decided to run away, it wasn't because of anything that happened at the camp. We know she was happy there."

"Already working on covering his reputation," Carrie Andrews, on Willa's right, whispered.

Scott continued, talking about the illustrious history of his family's camp, and reminding everyone that this was the first time anything like this had happened. The gathered volunteers exchanged glances and shuffled their feet.

"Thank you, Mr. Sprague." Gage put a hand on the camp owner's arm, silencing him. "Let's get out there and start searching. We want to take advantage of every bit of daylight."

Willa turned away, but found herself face-to-face with Carter and Dalton Ames.

"Hi, Willa." Carter offered his hand. "I don't know if you remember us. We're Aaron's brothers. We saw each other a few times in Vermont, but I didn't recognize you until Aaron told us about your name change."

"Of course." She shook hands with each of them in turn. What was she supposed to say? "Um, this is a little awkward."

"Don't worry," Carter said. "We won't tell anyone your secret identity."

She winced. "Thanks."

"Aaron told us the whole story," Dalton said. "Sorry you were being harassed back in Waterbury. And it's great that you joined search and rescue."

"Yeah. If you need anything, let us know," Carter said. He glanced over his shoulder as someone called his name. "We just wanted to say, no hard feelings or anything."

"Yeah." Dalton clapped his brother on the shoulder. "We'd better go."

Willa stared after them. She had a memory of Aaron's brothers as friendly but involved in their own world. All her focus had been on Aaron. At least they didn't hold any grudges about the way she had ended her relationship with their brother.

Willa was assigned to search with Bethany and Carrie. "I saw you talking with Carter and Dalton," Bethany said as Willa approached. "I hope they didn't embarrass you or anything."

"No." She glanced at Carrie, who was studying her phone screen. "They just welcomed me to search and rescue."

"Aaron made them promise not to ask you out," Bethany said.

"No! They didn't ask me out." Aaron had told them that? Why? Of course, she would never have agreed to go out with them. Talk about awkward! "What else did Aaron say about me?" She couldn't help it—she had to know.

"Well…" Bethany looked over to see that Carrie had turned away and was talking with another volunteer. Then she leaned closer to Willa and lowered her voice. "He said he doesn't think your brother had anything to do with that little girl's murder back in Vermont, that he was only acting guilty because he was scared."

Willa stared. Why couldn't Aaron have seen this at the time of Gary's arrest? Why change his mind now, when it was too late to undo the damage?

Bethany shrugged, maybe reading the unanswered questions in Willa's eyes. "He's not one to admit he's wrong very often."

Carrie turned to them. "We'd better get started."

As they moved out of the building, a fourth person joined them. Aaron, dressed in jeans and a black T-shirt, held up a copy of the map. "I'll be with you three," he said. He looked at Willa, then away. He couldn't have overheard her conversation with his sister, but she still felt the impact of Bethany's words. Aaron had admitted he was wrong about Gary, but wasn't that too little, too late?

"You're out of uniform," Bethany said to her brother.

"We thought the uniforms might scare off Olivia." He slipped a daypack onto his back and glanced at Willa again. "You're the trained professionals. I'm here to follow your lead."

Carrie turned the map over and studied the photograph of the shelter. "They really think Olivia built this thing?" she asked.

"I saw it," Aaron said. "It was really clever."

"Why would a kid go to all that trouble?" Bethany asked. "The camp looks like it would be a blast. Was Olivia secretly bullied or something?"

"No one we talked to mentioned anything like that," Aaron said. "The other girls in her cabin seemed to really like her."

"I heard the same thing," Willa said. When they all turned to look to her, she added, "We had one of her cabin mates in the clinic yesterday. She said Olivia's best friend at camp really misses her."

"Her poor parents," Carrie said. "I hope we find her soon."

They set out for the section of the map they were assigned to search—a brush-choked half acre of forest bisected by a deep gully. It was easier to forget about Aaron's close proximity as they fought their way over and around the massive, rotting trunks of fallen trees, pausing to look under each one in case Olivia had hollowed out the space for shelter.

After forty-five minutes of this, they stopped to drink water and catch their breath.

"I don't see how a kid could get through all of that," Bethany said.

"She would probably have an easier time of it than us," Willa said. "She's smaller and probably more flexible."

"It would be a good place to hide," Aaron said. He looked around them. "We're making so much noise thrashing through here, she would hear us coming from a long way off. All she would have to do is double back to an area we had already searched and wait until we left."

"Come on out, Olivia!" Bethany shouted. "Your parents really want you to come home!"

Aaron was leaning against the same tree trunk as Willa, two feet of space between them. "Did the girl you saw at the clinic have anything else to say about Olivia?" he asked.

"She said she didn't know Olivia very well, but that her friend Stella cries at night now that Olivia is gone. She thinks it's because Stella misses her friend." She couldn't believe she was having a regular conversation with him. It didn't even feel that awkward. They were behaving like normal people, no messy past between them.

"We've still got a lot of ground to cover," Carrie said. "We'd better get going."

Another half hour of pulling aside thorny vines, slipping in mud and scrambling up rocks had Willa feeling bruised and battered. She stood atop a granite boulder and surveyed the surrounding wilderness. Then her breath caught.

"There's someone over there!" she said, and pointed straight ahead.

Aaron vaulted up beside her, and steadied himself by briefly holding her arm. He released his hold and followed her gaze. Someone was clearly moving around, ducking under branches and around rocks.

"There aren't supposed to be any other searchers assigned to this section," Carrie said.

Aaron cupped his hands around his mouth. "Hello!" he shouted.

The figure stopped. Aaron took a pair of binoculars from his pack and focused. "It's not Olivia," he said. He handed the binoculars to Willa.

She focused in on a burly older man in a green shirt and a silver Stetson. "It's Scott Sprague," she said.

Aaron waved. "Mr. Sprague!" he shouted.

Scott looked up, then began picking his way toward them. "What are you doing out here by yourself?" Aaron asked when Scott was almost to the boulder where they waited.

"I can't sit still and do nothing while Olivia is missing," he said. "I'm responsible for that little girl."

"It isn't safe to be in this rough country alone," Aaron said. "You need to go back to camp and leave the searching to us."

"It would be terrible if you were hurt while you were trying to help," Carrie said. "The camp needs you."

He slumped against the rock. "You're probably right. I

felt energized when that brush shelter was found. Now that we know that Olivia is alive and probably close by, it feels wrong not to be out here searching for her."

"I'm sure you're a big help to Olivia's parents," Bethany said. "You should go back to them."

He wiped a hand over his face. Up close, Willa could see slashes from vines across his cheek, and scraped knuckles on his hands. He didn't even have a pack or water. She pulled one of her own water bottles from her pack. "Drink this," she said.

"Bethany, could you go with Scott back to camp?" Aaron asked. At his sister's frown, he added, "Please?"

"I don't want to take one of you away from the search," Scott protested. "I'm sure I can find my way on my own." He looked around. "If you'll start me off in the right direction."

"I'd better go with you," Bethany said. "It's so easy to get turned around out here." She consulted the map. "It's going to be easier to retrace our steps to the lodge. Are you ready, Mr. Sprague?"

"Please, call me Scott." He returned the half-empty water bottle to Willa. "And I'm ready, thank you."

Bethany and Scott headed back the way they had come, and the other three pushed forward once more. Willa was more aware now of Aaron staying close to her. Once, when she lost her balance on a rolling log, he took her elbow to steady her. He released her as soon as she was secure, but she hadn't flinched from his touch.

"Thanks," she muttered, and moved on.

She slowed down after a moment, and let him get in front of her. She liked being able to watch him as he broke a trail through the thickest brush. The black T-shirt emphasized his muscular shoulders and arms. He wore a gun in a small holster on his hip, a badge clipped beside it. Even though he was out of uniform he was still on duty, she reminded herself.

"Do you remember the day we climbed Mount Hunger?" he asked.

She groaned. "That last mile was so hard. I was beginning to wonder if you were trying to get rid of me."

"But the view at the end was worth it."

"Yes." The end of the hike offered a spectacular view of the surrounding mountains. But it wasn't the view she remembered most—it was the kiss they had shared, and the euphoria of having conquered something difficult together. She had never felt closer to anyone in that moment and had been sure she could face anything with this man. But that feeling had been a mirage. They had climbed that mountain together, but when the most difficult thing she had ever endured in her life happened, Aaron wasn't beside her; he was opposing her. He was the one responsible for her problem.

THEY HAD COVERED every inch of their search area by 6:00 p.m., and returned to the lodge dirty, bruised and worn-out. The other searchers looked the same. No one had found any sign of Olivia.

"Maybe you were wrong about that shelter," Bethany said when she found Aaron eating dinner catered by the lodge. She slid onto the picnic table bench beside him and helped herself to a potato chip from his plate. "I was talking to Scott and he said that wilderness course they take the kids on didn't have anything about building brush shelters, just instructions on basic first aid and how to use a compass and the importance of staying put if you're lost."

"There was a shoe print just inside the shelter," Aaron

said. "The same size as Olivia's foot. And a label from the same brand of water bottles we found in camp."

"That's something, I guess." She ate another chip. "You were sticking pretty close to Willa today," she said. "Does that mean the two of you are going to get back together?"

"Not much chance of that." He crunched a chip. "I'll settle for her tolerating my presence."

"Oh, I think she more than tolerates you," Bethany said. "She was checking out your butt when you were hiking ahead of her."

He laughed, at the disgusted expression on his sister's face as much as at the idea that Willa had been ogling him. "Don't tell me you don't check out Ian's backside sometimes," he said.

"Well, yeah, but that's different. Ian isn't my brother."

"I'm not Willa's brother, either." And he wasn't exactly her friend. He hoped he wasn't her enemy. It wasn't all he wanted from her, but it was better than he had hoped for.

Jake approached the table, plate in hand. "Do you have room here?"

"Sure." Bethany scooted over to allow him to slip in beside her. "Where were you searching?"

"I was with a group searching the area where we found the shelter." Jake bit into a sandwich and chewed.

"I guess you didn't find anything," Bethany said.

He shook his head.

"I wish we knew why she ran away," Bethany said. "If we knew that, we might have a better feeling for where she would go. I mean, is she trying to get away from someone or to someone—or something?"

"Good question," Aaron said. Why hadn't he thought of that?

"If she was in that shelter, she didn't go that far from camp," Jake said.

"And that water and stuff was taken from the storage shed after she was reported missing," Aaron said. "So she was still close to camp, then."

"It's like she's sticking around to see what happens," Bethany said.

"If she's just playing a game, it's time to stop," Aaron said.

"There's still that shirt with the blood on it." Jake spoke quietly. He cut his eyes to Bethany. "And you didn't hear me say that."

"It's not a secret," she said. "But it's good to hear the rumor confirmed." She leaned toward them and spoke in a whisper. "Was the blood really Olivia's?"

Jake nodded.

"So, somebody hurt Olivia, she ran away and now she's hanging around," Bethany said. "Maybe she's waiting for the person who hurt her to get caught. When they are, she'll come out of hiding."

"Then it would help if she would leave a few more clues as to this person's identity," Aaron said. He pushed his plate away. "And that sounds awful. She's just a kid. Maybe hurt. Probably frightened. She's not supposed to have to do our job for us."

"There's no other DNA on that shirt," Jake said, still speaking quietly. "So we have no idea who might have attacked her."

"You would think one of the other campers would know something," Bethany said. "I mean, girls talk. Boys, too. They can't help it. They never stop. I remember going to a Girl Scout camp for two weeks when I was eleven. It was nonstop talking. By the end of the week I knew the darkest secrets of at least a dozen girls I would never see again. I knew whose parents were getting divorced and whose big brother had a drug habit and who had a creepy uncle they avoided being alone with at family gatherings. If Olivia had a secret, somebody must know it."

"No one's telling us anything," Aaron said. "We've questioned all the campers more than once."

"You two are cops. And you're men. And you're old. I mean, you're not old, but to a young teen anyone over twenty-five might as well be their parents."

"Do you think they'd tell you anything they wouldn't tell us?" Aaron asked.

"Maybe. Though by this point they've already either outright lied to you or just omitted to mention something important. And they've probably done it more than once. Which means they're even less likely to volunteer information to yet another stranger. Even a female who's not a cop." She paused, then turned to Aaron. "You could ask Willa to talk to them."

"Why Willa?" Jake asked.

"She's a nurse. Nurses are used to getting information out of people in a nonthreatening way. She's pretty. Girls like that. And she looks younger than she is. I think they would be more likely to trust her."

"It's not a bad idea," Jake said. "Though I'm not sure how we'd square it with Scott. He might not like the idea of bringing in another outsider when there's so much focus on a missing camper. I've heard some parents are questioning whether he's doing enough to protect the campers. They're questioning staff qualifications and security measures and things like that. A new person interacting with the kids might draw attention he doesn't need right now."

"It's something to think about." Bethany stood. "I have

to go. Some journalist is coming tomorrow to write up a feature about the via ferrata. I'm supposed to put together a press kit for her."

She left. "Do you think Willa would talk to the girls in Olivia's cabin?" Jake asked.

"I think she would do anything to help find Olivia," Aaron said. "But how would we ever make it happen?"

"Maybe she could volunteer to teach a first aid course at the camp."

"I'm sure they already have someone to do that."

"They probably don't have a nurse," Jake said. "And Bethany's right—Willa is pretty. Scott Sprague strikes me as a man who might be influenced by pretty."

"What makes you say that?"

Jake shrugged. "I was watching him that first day, when all the searchers were at camp. He wasn't exactly leering at some of the women, but he was definitely aware of them."

"Like most men," Aaron said.

"Talk to Willa. See what she thinks about the idea."

"Why should I be the one to talk to her?"

Jake gave him a pitying look. "You're not fooling anyone, Aaron. We've all seen the way you look at her. You might as well talk to her. Maybe you can even work the conversation around to asking her out. Though I'll warn you, she's turned down better men than you. Supposedly there's a pool at Mo's about how long it will take before she agrees to go out with the many men who've worked up the nerve to ask her."

Aaron could have told Jake he was certain he wouldn't be the one to win that lottery. Instead, he merely shook his head. "I'll ask Willa about proposing a first aid course for the campers, but don't blame me if she says no. Should we talk to the sheriff first?"

Jake considered this. "Probably not. He won't want to involve a civilian. If Willa does it and learns anything useful, she can pass it on as a concerned citizen and leave us out of it."

"Coward."

"Says the man who's afraid to talk to a beautiful woman."

Aaron scowled. He wasn't afraid of Willa—only fearful of ending the fragile peace between them.

Chapter Ten

The search and rescue volunteers were preparing to leave Mountain Kingdom when an alert came in from the 911 operator. "A woman called in, says her husband is injured, with a possible broken leg," the operator told Danny as the team listened in. "She says he's fallen into some kind of trap and can't get out."

"A trap? Like, a bear trap?" Danny frowned.

"She says it's a hole in the ground, with branches over it to hide it. He fell in and she thinks he broke his leg. I have GPS coordinates for you."

"All right. Go ahead." Danny nodded to Tony, who was standing next to him, and Tony took out his phone, prepared to enter the coordinates.

The dispatcher rattled off the numbers and Tony typed them in. "That's pretty close to here," Tony said. "Less than a mile away, down a different county road." He frowned at his phone screen. "It's not near any established trail."

"What were they doing out there?" Danny asked the dispatcher.

"The woman says they were looking for that missing little girl."

"Tell them we're on our way." He ended the call and turned his attention to the assembled volunteers. "Those of you who want or need to go home, do so," he said. "You've been out here all day. We only need about six people to handle this."

"I'll come," Willa said. Going home meant hours of sitting and worrying. Better to be active and help someone in need.

"I'll go, too," Ryan said. "I want to see this trap."

Tony, Vince Shepherd and Ryan's fiancée, Deni Traynor, made up the rest of the crew that set out toward the area where the couple was stranded.

"We'll have to hike in from here," Tony said, enlarging the area map on his phone.

Danny distributed first aid supplies, including a wheeled litter, splints, back, neck and leg braces, supplemental oxygen and fluids, as well as ropes and other gear for retrieving their patient from the pit he had fallen into. "Some of this is probably overkill," he said as he helped Willa stuff her pack with more bandages. "But we don't know the extent of his injuries and we have to be prepared for the worst."

They set out with Tony in the lead, breaking trail where there was none. The terrain looked like the country they had searched all day—pine and aspen forest pocked with boulders and gullies, choked with deadfall and impenetrable thickets of scrub oak. Tony had a machete to cut a path where absolutely necessary, but mostly they tried to detour around smaller obstacles, alert for hazards and for any sign of Olivia.

It took an hour to reach the couple. They heard them before they saw them, the woman calling out, "Over here!" and a man's very loud "Thank you!"

The group stopped at the edge of a small clearing and stared at the scene before them. The woman stood beside a boulder and looked from the group to a hole in the ground.

The hole was approximately six feet across, with green pine branches piled around it on two sides. Moving carefully, Danny led the way to the edge of the pit.

The man was approximately five feet down, on his back in the bowl-like depression on a bed of more green branches. The scent of pine perfumed the air. "We were walking along, taking our time, searching for any sign of the little girl," the woman, a forty-something blonde dressed in jeans, a pink T-shirt and a black day pack, said. "Luke was ahead of me. I heard a scream and looked toward him and he wasn't there."

"The ground gave way and I fell," Luke called up. He wore camo pants and a black T-shirt, a green ball cap over his short, sandy hair.

"Someone spread all these branches over this hole in the ground," the woman explained. "I pulled them away and piled them to the side. Who would do something like that? Were they trying to catch a deer or a bear or something?"

"What's your name, ma'am?" Danny asked.

"Melissa Wagner."

"I'm Danny Irwin. We're going to take care of your husband. It will take a few minutes for us to get down there to him. Meanwhile, you can answer some questions."

While the others helped Tony attach a rope to a sturdy tree nearby and assemble the needed equipment, Danny and Willa questioned Melissa about her husband's medical history and general health. "He said he heard the bone pop when he landed," she said.

"He's pretty sure it's broken, but there's no bone sticking out." She bit her lip, her eyes shiny. "I can't believe someone would do this."

"I've never seen anything like this, either," Danny said. "But right now, let's focus on Luke."

He used the rope to steady himself as he walked down

into the pit. Tony and Ryan followed, leaving Deni, Willa and Vince to stay with Melissa and lower supplies via another rope as needed.

"It's like something aboriginal hunters might use," Vince said. "I think I saw that in a book—they dug a pit, lined it with sharp sticks and drove game over it."

"Thank goodness this one didn't have any sharp sticks," Willa said.

"This pit wasn't really dug out," Deni said. "It looks like a tree died a long time ago and the stump rotted away and left this depression. All anyone had to do was scoop out the debris."

She walked a short distance away and stopped beside another downed tree. "The branches they used to cover the hole came from this tree. I can see where someone broke them off."

"They look like they're still green," Vince said.

"The tree has been down a little while," Deni said. "It takes a long time for pine to turn brown."

"Send that oxygen tank down, will you?" Danny radioed.

They returned their attention to caring for their patient, who turned out to have a probable fracture of the fibula and some cracked ribs. They stabilized his injuries, then secured him in the litter and carefully raised him from the pit using a combination of ropes and man power.

At ground level once more, they attached a large wheel to the center of the litter and stationed people at the four corners to steady its occupant and help the contraption over rough places in the ground.

While they were packing up the last of their gear, Ryan took several photographs of the pit and the surrounding area. "We should tell the sheriff about all of this," he said. "Someone will need to make sure there aren't more of these out here, waiting to trap some person or animal."

"This looks recent," Tony said. "Do you think someone did this to deliberately trap one of the people searching for Olivia?"

"Who would do that?" Deni asked.

"If someone kidnapped Olivia and is holding her around here somewhere, they might be trying to keep other people away," Ryan said.

"Or they could be someone who likes hurting other people for no good reason," Willa said.

Deni put a hand on Ryan's back. "It doesn't matter to us who did this, or why. We need to get Mr. Wagner to the hospital."

They took turns handling the litter. When Willa wasn't involved with that, she sought out Melissa and fell into step alongside her. "Did you see any sign of Olivia before your husband fell?" Willa asked.

"No. We were talking about turning back and going home when Luke fell."

"Why did you decide to search in this area?"

"We want to help, but when we showed up at the camp, they told us only trained search and rescue volunteers were needed there. So we decided to come here. It was close enough we could imagine the little girl might have wandered over." She sighed. "I guess there's a reason they only wanted trained searchers. We didn't realize how rough the country would be. I don't see how a little girl could be okay out here."

"It's hard to want to help and not be able to do anything," Willa said.

"Only now we've made more trouble for everyone."

"It's what we're here for," Willa said. They never wanted to discourage people from calling for help when they needed it. It was why they didn't charge for rescue missions.

An ambulance was waiting in the parking lot of Mountain

Kingdom Kids Camp and they loaded Luke Wagner into it, and Ryan and Deni drove Melissa to her car so that she could meet her husband at the hospital in Junction. Willa, adrenaline ebbing and exhaustion taking over, trudged to her own vehicle at the far edge of the parking lot.

She stiffened when she recognized the tall figure waiting for her. "What do you want?" she asked Aaron, the words coming out more brusquely than she had intended.

"I'm hoping you'll do something to help with our search for Olivia," he said.

She clicked the key fob to unlock her car, but didn't open the door. "What can I do?"

"You could teach a first aid class to the girls in Olivia's cabin. Talk to the kids and see if any of them know something about Olivia and her disappearance that they haven't told authorities."

"Why me?" she asked.

"You're a nurse, so you're qualified," he said. "We think the girls would like you and confide in you."

"Who is 'we'?"

"Me and Jake." He hurried on before she could ask why they had been discussing her in the first place. "The girl you saw in the clinic seemed willing to talk to you about Olivia."

"It seems a sneaky way to get information."

"We've already questioned every camper at least twice," he said. "They're suspicious of cops. They'll be more relaxed with you."

She could see the logic in that. Sort of. "What am I supposed to find out?"

"Why she ran away from camp," he said. "Was someone there bullying her? Was she afraid of anyone? Is she trying to get someone else in trouble? Having those answers might help us figure out how to find her."

She opened the car's rear door and shoved her pack inside. "All right. What do I have to do?"

"You have to persuade Scott Sprague to take you up on the offer."

She made a face. "So he doesn't even know you're planning this?"

"No one knows. Jake and I came up with the idea on our own. Well, with some help from Bethany. She's the one who pointed out that the campers wouldn't want to tell the truth to 'old' men like us."

She almost smiled in spite of herself. "What if Scott says no?"

"Don't take no for an answer." He grinned. "Besides, I don't think he'll turn you down."

"Oh? Why is that?"

"He's a single man. You're a beautiful woman."

She ignored the flutter in her stomach at his words. "You're suggesting I what—*seduce* him into saying yes?"

"No! Nothing like that. Just, you know, smile and make him think you want to do the class as a favor to him—and the campers."

She didn't want to agree to the idea, but she couldn't think of a better one, and she wanted to help find Olivia. "All right, I'll try," she said.

"At least you'll know you tried." He held the driver's door open for her. She gave him what she hoped was a look that told him she didn't need his help, and slid past him, into the seat.

"How did the call go?" he asked. "I heard it was a hiker with a broken leg."

"Fine. We had to pull him out of a hole in the ground he'd fallen into." She was about to start the car, but hesitated, wanting to tell someone about what had happened, and who better than a sheriff's deputy? "Someone had set a trap out there in the woods—a hole in the ground with a bunch of branches over it. This man—he and his wife were out searching for Olivia—stepped on the branches and fell into the hole."

"No pointed sticks at the bottom?" he asked.

She frowned. "No. Vince said something about that, too. I never heard of that."

"It's called a punji trap. They used them in the Vietnam War." At her questioning look, he added, "When I was a teenager I went through a phase where I was really interested in stuff like that. Anyway, someone dug a hole and set up a trap like that—without the sticks?"

"It didn't look like they dug the hole, exactly," she said. "A tree had died and most of it had rotted away. Whoever did this scraped out the rest of the dead tree, then pulled some branches off a pine that had fallen and scattered them around. There's a lot of branches and stuff on the ground around there anyway, so it was good camouflage."

"Was someone trying to trap Olivia?"

"I don't know. It was just…strange." She started the car. "I think Danny is going to contact the sheriff about it. Someone needs to make sure there aren't other traps out there. With so many searchers out in the woods, someone else could get hurt."

He stepped away from the car. "Thanks for agreeing to talk to the kids," he said.

She nodded, and put the car in gear. She didn't like how circumstances kept throwing her and Aaron together.

Most of all, she didn't like how seeing him made her feel—not like she was facing someone who had betrayed her. When she was with Aaron these days, she was reminded of how much she missed him.

Gage asked Aaron to come with him to check out the trap that had injured Luke Wagner. They said little as they hiked toward the location search and rescue had provided. Aaron was tired of tramping through the woods, or at least these woods, with their tangled deadfall and uneven terrain. He was constantly slipping on the thick carpet of pine needles or being slapped in the face by low-hanging branches.

"This isn't good," Gage said when they stopped briefly to rest and drink water. He pointed at something on the ground.

Aaron leaned over to look. "Bear scat," he said. There were plenty of black bears in Vermont, though most of his dealings with them had involved chasing them out of people's fruit trees or garbage cans. "Black or grizzly?"

"No grizzlies in Colorado," Gage said. "And the black bears around here usually shy away from people."

"Even if one ran away, it would probably terrify a little girl," Aaron said. The thought made his stomach ache. Forget his own troubles; they needed to find Olivia.

They reached the GPS coordinates they had been given and gathered around the hole in the ground.

"I see what Willa meant when she said this wasn't dug by hand." Aaron indicated the remains of a rotted tree nearby. "Someone used what was already here."

"It looks like they moved some rocks to sort of funnel traffic this way." Gage pointed at several piles of rocks on either side of a path that led toward the hole.

"They couldn't have known who would end up in it," Aaron said. "Even an animal might have been hurt."

Gage nodded and walked the perimeter of the hole, studying it. "It looks to me like something a kid would do," he said after a while. "My daughter and her friends are always coming up with schemes like this—you know, 'Let's dig a hole in the backyard, fill it with water and make our own swimming pool.' Or 'Let's build a fort by the back fence.' If they came across a big hole in the ground in the middle of the woods, they might remember a scene from a movie or book and decide to re-create it."

"The only kid we think is out here is Olivia," Ryan said. "Why would she do something like this?"

"Maybe she doesn't want to be found," Gage said.

Which again begged the question why. Olivia's parents seemed like decent people who were truly concerned about their daughter. No one had reported Olivia having a bad relationship with her parents. Everyone they had interviewed said she enjoyed camp, though there was Stella's report that Olivia had been sad about something for the past couple of weeks. What would have driven her away from the comforts of the camp to live alone in a rugged wilderness, through a rainstorm, cold nights and the possibility of encountering a bear? It didn't make sense to Aaron.

They took a lot of photos, then marked the spot with orange flags and moved rocks and branches to guide people away from the area.

"That should keep someone else, or any animals, from accidentally falling in," Gage said.

They searched for several hundred yards in all directions around the trap and didn't find anything else suspicious. "I think someone saw that hole and decided to turn it into a trap on the spur of the moment," Aaron said.

"More kid behavior," Gage said. "Olivia's parents said she was really into outdoor adventure and surviving in the wilderness stories. Maybe this is part of it. Maybe she isn't running away from anything or anyone—she's just out here having fun."

"She has to know people are looking for her. And her

parents are worried sick. That's a cruel game. Nothing I've heard about her makes her sound like a cruel kid."

"We won't stop searching for her," Gage said. "It's just something to keep in mind. Our first idea about a situation isn't always right."

Aaron knew that. His former department's first idea about Rachel's killing had been wrong, and look what a mess that had turned into.

Chapter Eleven

Scott Sprague did not turn Willa down when she called and asked to meet with him Thursday afternoon. She arrived for their appointment, not at the lodge, but at the cabin on the property where he lived. He was freshly shaved and smelled of expensive cologne and she immediately doubted her decision to wear a clingy sundress instead of her nurse's scrubs. She wanted this to work, but she didn't want Scott to think she was coming on to him.

He invited her to sit on the porch with him. "I would invite you to join me in the house, but I don't want to start any rumors," he said. "A man in my position has to guard his reputation carefully. Working with children is such a vulnerable responsibility. I can't even risk the appearance of scandal."

"It's a lovely day to sit outside," Willa said diplomatically. From this vantage point, she could see most of the camp—the cabins and mess hall, and the lakeshore beyond. Boys and girls in green T-shirts ran between the trees or clustered around counselors. Several canoes bobbed on the lake, and another group of kids swam in an area marked by yellow buoys.

"You said you wanted to discuss volunteering at the

camp?" Scott asked. "We're all trained in first aid, but having a nurse on-site would certainly be welcome."

"I was thinking I could teach a first aid class to the campers," she said. "A couple of hours for each cabin, with hands-on exercises. I find children really enjoy wrapping each other in bandages and trying on slings."

"Our counselors usually do some basic first aid instruction, but it might be good to have a medical professional teach a course." He rubbed his chin. "That would take our training to the next level. Parents would like it. When are you available?"

"We could start tomorrow," she said. Aaron hadn't specified, but it seemed reasonable to her to try to collect information about Olivia as soon as possible. "I have the day off. I could do the girls this Friday and teach the boys next week."

Scott rubbed his chin. "Friday afternoons we have our weekly canoe regatta, but the morning is open." He nodded. "We can sub in your class instead of the pottery workshop. The girls can do pottery next week. Could you be here at nine?"

"Yes."

He stood and extended his hand. "Thank you for offering. We'll see you tomorrow."

She texted Aaron on the walk back to her car.

Class is on for tomorrow. You have to help me figure out what to ask the girls.

He replied right away. When can you meet?

I get off at five.

We need somewhere we won't be overheard, he said.

She hesitated, then typed, Come to my place. Gary would be there, but that was a good thing. With her brother present, she wouldn't be tempted to let emotion get the better of sense. She didn't exactly hate Aaron anymore, but she would never be foolish enough to trust him.

This isn't a date, Aaron reminded himself as he shaved before meeting Willa Thursday evening. But unmet expectation charged every interaction with her. He was trying to get past that, to accept that the best he could hope for from her was casual friendship. His brain might agree, but his body wasn't listening.

He pulled on jeans and a button-down shirt. Blue—her favorite color. He had jotted some notes, and he carried those with him, adding to the illusion that he was viewing this as strictly business.

She answered the door promptly, still wearing pale blue scrubs from the clinic. "I was running late and just got home," she said. "Would you mind waiting while I change?"

"No problem." He followed her into the house.

"Make yourself comfortable," she said. "Gary should be home soon. I'm going to jump in the shower. I need to wash off any clinic germs."

She hurried away and moments later he heard water running. His mind immediately conjured memories of other showers, ones they had taken together. He groaned and closed his eyes. *Think about something else.* He sat on the sofa and picked up a magazine from the coffee table. *Modern Nursing.* He flipped through it, but could focus on nothing but the running water and the heat coursing through his body.

The back door opened and he stood and moved toward the kitchen. Gary took a step back when Aaron entered.

"Hey," Gary said. "What are you doing here?" He looked wary, but not hostile. Despite everything that had happened, Aaron had never sensed any particular animosity from Gary.

"I'm meeting with Willa." He held up his folder of notes. His prop to prove there was nothing to see here. No conclusions to leap to.

"Is this about the class she's holding at the camp?" Gary asked. He opened the refrigerator and leaned inside. "Do you want something to drink?"

"No, thanks. Yeah, it's about the first aid class."

"My sister, the police spy." Gary grinned. "Never saw that one coming." He leaned back against the yellow Formica counter.

The kitchen was small and dated—not that different from Aaron's own. But he could see the effort Willa had made to dress it up, with a stained glass piece in the window over the sink, and framed pen-and-ink drawings of fruit and flowers on the wall over the table.

"She's not really working for the sheriff's department," Aaron said.

"Right. It's a big secret." He popped the top on a Coke and sat at the kitchen table.

"Any changes at the camp since Olivia left?" Aaron asked.

"The counselors have to do bed checks every four hours," Gary said. "Whether they're actually doing that, who knows?"

"No more thefts from the storage shed?"

"Nope. It's locked up tight. I take it no one's gotten any closer to finding Olivia?"

"No."

"It's a long time for a girl to be on her own in the wilderness," Gary said. "There aren't many people out there, but there are bears and mountain lions. And what's she doing for food?"

"She may not be on her own. She might have arranged to meet up with someone, or someone might have taken her from the camp."

"Have you seen some sign of another person out there?" Gary asked.

"No, but we have to be open to all possibilities," Aaron said. "That's why I asked Willa to do this. I'm hoping one of Olivia's friends will mention something that will help—if she ever talked about leaving, where she might go, if someone had been bothering her."

"So maybe she didn't just run away?"

"We don't know," Aaron said. "That bloody shirt pointed to violence, but we haven't found any other sign of that. And someone crafted that shelter we found. It didn't look as if it had been there long. It's possible whoever took Olivia made it, but it's just as likely she built it herself. We simply don't know."

Willa came into the room. She had changed into pink shorts and a T-shirt, and had a blue towel wrapped around her head like a turban. "Hey, Gary. How was your day?"

"Okay." Gary stood. "I'm going to leave you two to it."

Willa looked alarmed. "You don't have to leave."

"It's okay. I'm going to check out that new pizza place in town. I heard it's really good." He nodded to Aaron, then left. Willa stared after him.

"Do you really think you need a chaperone?" Aaron asked.

Her cheeks flushed pink. "It's just...awkward."

"It doesn't have to be." He was amazed at how calm he

felt. Seeing her nervous made him feel steadier. She wasn't acting like someone who hated him.

"Why don't we sit here?" She indicated the kitchen table. "Do you want something to drink or eat first?" She pulled a can of Coke from the refrigerator and held it up. "Do you want one?"

"Sure."

He accepted the drink, then they sat across from each other and he laid his notes between them. "I should give Bethany credit for this idea," he said. "She thought if we could find out if Olivia was running from something or to something, we could figure out how to persuade her that it's safe to come home – or, if she was kidnapped, it might point to who took her. We're also still trying to determine if she's hurt, and who might have hurt her."

"Because of that bloody shirt?"

"Yes. She's doing a good job of avoiding all the searchers, so that makes me think she's in pretty good shape. We believe she stayed close to the camp for several days at least. We're hoping that's still the case."

"So she wanted to get away, but she stayed nearby. Why?"

"Bethany suggested it's because she's waiting for the person who hurt her to be caught. Then it will be safe for her to return."

"Why not go somewhere and tell someone in authority what happened?" Willa asked.

"I don't know. She seems like a bright kid, but maybe she doesn't feel like she can trust anyone with her secret."

"Or maybe the person who hurt her is someone in authority."

Aaron nodded. "We don't think it was another camper. So that leaves one of the counselors or other workers at the camp."

"Or a parent?" Willa wrinkled her nose.

"We've checked out her parents pretty thoroughly," he said. "There's nothing suspicious there. But you might see if you can find out how Olivia viewed their relationship."

She leaned back and grabbed a legal pad from the counter and began making notes. "Part of first aid is protecting our personal safety and our mental health, too," she said. "With kids, especially, there's an emphasis on not getting into dangerous situations in the first place. That includes identifying people who might be a danger or behave inappropriately. I can start a conversation with the kids from that direction. Maybe they'll mention a particular incident or person at camp."

"That's a good idea," Aaron said. "There's also the possibility that Olivia left on purpose. She wanted to play in the wilderness, see if she could live like people in stories she's read or heard about."

Willa frowned. "That sounds terribly cruel to her parents. Not to mention how she's endangered all the people who are searching for her."

"She probably didn't think about those things."

Willa made more notes. "There will probably be camp employees at my class," she said. "To assist and to keep tabs on me, too. I mean, if I was in charge of a bunch of kids, I wouldn't let any stranger interact with the children without oversight. That might limit how nosy I can be."

"I hadn't thought of that, but you're right. Do the best you can. And maybe you can get a feel for how the adults who are there react to all this talk of inappropriate behavior. You might pick up something we need to investigate further."

"I'm probably not going to find out anything useful," she said. "But at least I can give the kids some first aid skills. I'm taking the class seriously. I'm not just there to be nosy."

"I expected nothing less. You never do anything halfway."

She looked down at her hands—fingers long and delicate, the nails trimmed short and painted pale pink. "I hope that's meant as a compliment."

"One of the things I've always admired most about you is your dedication and loyalty," he said. "If you do a job, you give a hundred percent. If you love someone, you'll do anything for them. Even when you were furious with me over what happened to Gary, I knew it was because he was your brother, and you would do anything to protect him."

"I wouldn't lie," she said. "I always told the truth about him. That's what upset me the most. My alibi for him wasn't enough."

Aaron sighed. How could he make her understand? "We were wrong," he said. "I can say that now. I didn't see it for a long time, though. We were trying to find a killer and on paper—from our skewed point of view at least—Gary looked like the only suspect."

"I've done some reading," she said. "About confirmation bias. Apparently, it's something people don't even realize they're doing."

"I'm glad Gary was released," he said. "And I'm sorry for the hurt I caused you both."

"I wish you would have had the courage to speak up for Gary. To point out how wrong it was to single him out."

They were hard words to hear, but he didn't dodge or excuse the accusation. "I wish that, too," he said. "But at the time I didn't see it."

The silence stretched between them. Was she thinking about how he had pointed out Gary to the sheriff when Olivia disappeared? Could he make her understand that if the sheriff had learned after the fact of the prior accusations against Gary, it would have been a black mark against Aaron's own professionalism?

"As a law enforcement officer, we have to view everyone connected to a case as a potential suspect," he said. "Part of our job is to rule people out. Even though it took a while, the system worked for Gary. There wasn't solid evidence against him and he was released. I know that doesn't happen every time, but it did this time. And here in Eagle Mountain, the sheriff saw right away that Gary wasn't connected to Olivia. Waiting to be ruled out isn't pleasant for anyone involved, but most of the time, the system works."

Are you ever going to forgive me? he wanted to ask, but he couldn't bring himself to beg.

She stood. "I haven't eaten all day. Are you hungry?"

"Yes. We could go out."

She was already removing things from the refrigerator. "I'll cook. Just don't expect fancy."

"When have I ever?"

She turned on the burner under a pan. "Tell me how you ended up in Eagle Mountain."

"You know Bethany moved here first."

"She and her fiancé canceled their wedding," Willa said. "I remember."

"The rest of the family came to visit her after she had been here a few months," he said. "The Jeep tour business where she was working was for sale. My parents decided to buy it and they and the twins all moved here."

"Right. I remember you talked about how beautiful the place was. I think that's why the name of the town caught my eye when I saw the ad for a nurse."

"I came down a second time to help with the move, after you and I broke up, with no intention of staying. But then

I learned there was an opening with the sheriff's department. I interviewed on a whim and they offered me the job."

"Look at you, being impulsive," she said.

"I thought a fresh start might be good." Everywhere he went in Waterbury was filled with memories of her. He thought getting away from that might help him move on with his life. And the change of scenery had helped—until she showed up in town.

Her expression sobered. "Starting over in a new place is hard. But I feel like I'm finding my footing here. Search and rescue has helped. It's good to be part of something bigger than myself."

"Law enforcement is that way, too. The sheriff has a good team here."

She nodded, but said nothing, and focused on cooking.

"Can I do anything to help?" he asked.

"You can get plates from the cabinet and fill glasses with ice water."

Setting the table felt like old times, when he had spent so much time in her home he knew it as well as his own. They had talked of moving in together, and he had planned to propose, when the time felt right.

She served salad topped with grilled chicken, cheese and bacon. "It's delicious," he said.

She laughed. "You always were easy to please."

"Anything you do pleases me."

He hadn't intended to say the words out loud. They had simply slipped out. But he didn't take them back. He looked at her steadily, watching the color bloom on her face, the pupils of her eyes darken. Her tongue darted out to wet her lips.

"Aaron," she said, her voice a little breathy.

I never stopped loving you. But he didn't say it. That would be going too far. Expecting too much.

"I'd like us to be friends," he said instead.

She hesitated, then nodded. "I don't want us to be enemies. But I can't do more."

"I know." Some wounds were too big to get over. He believed that. They finished the meal in silence. When his plate was empty, he stood. "Thanks for dinner," he said. "I'd better go. Let me know if you run into any problems."

"I'll call and let you know what I find out from the kids."

She walked with him to the door. He turned, and started to kiss her good-night, the way he had so many times when leaving her place. Instead, he brushed his lips to her cheek. Not exactly the way he would have kissed his sister, but close enough she couldn't object.

Then he slipped out the door, a picture fixed in his mind of her standing there, one hand to her cheek, staring after him—almost as if she regretted him leaving.

Chapter Twelve

Mrs. Mason greeted Willa when she arrived at camp Friday morning. "Mr. Sprague is sorry he can't be here," she said. "The poor man is spending all his free time searching for Olivia. He's running himself into the ground, he's so worried about her."

"It's an awful situation," Willa said.

"You'll need to sign these." Mrs. Mason handed her a sheaf of papers.

Willa read and signed the documents, which indicated she was not being paid for her services and agreed to comply with a long list of rules for interacting with the children and other camp policies, such as no smoking and no alcoholic beverages. Paperwork complete, she followed the older woman to an open pavilion, where a dozen girls sat at picnic tables.

A counselor, Veronica, sat with the girls. "I can help with anything you need," Veronica said. "I was a life guard in high school and had to take CPR and stuff."

"Thanks." Willa turned to face the children. She had suggested starting with the oldest children first, which meant Olivia's group. She had learned that children older than thirteen attended a sister camp across the lake. "First, I want to learn all your names."

The children took turns introducing themselves, each

saying her name and where they were from and if there was anything in particular they wanted to learn. Most didn't have much to say in this regard, though one girl—Kenya—announced that she wanted to learn how to bandage people like a mummy.

Juliet, in her purple cast, was there. And Stella, Olivia's closest friend in the cabin, her ankle no longer wrapped, her brown hair pulled back in a ponytail. Stella wanted to learn how to stop people bleeding. Was this because of the wound of Olivia's that had left blood on her shirt?

Willa began by passing out some basic first aid supplies and letting the girls examine them—bandages, slings, splints and ice packs. They talked about the kinds of accidents they had encountered in camp—burns, cuts, sprains and breaks. "Rodney Carpenter fell face-first on the rocks and knocked out three teeth," one girl volunteered.

"Accidents can't always be predicted," Willa said. "But some can be prevented. The best first aid is the kind you never have to give. What are some of the things you can do to avoid being hurt?"

The girls shared their ideas, from watching where you were going to listening to adults when they told you not to touch things like hot stoves and knives.

"I think we can agree the best way to avoid being hurt is to stay out of dangerous situations," Willa said. "That includes things like wearing a seat belt, not crossing a busy street against the light and wearing a helmet when riding a bike. But it also includes learning to recognize people we should avoid."

"Like people playing with fire and stuff," Juliet said.

"My mother told me if I have a bad feeling about someone, I should stay away from them," Stella said.

"Your mother is right," Willa said. "Not everyone is a

good person, so if someone makes you uncomfortable you should stay away from them. And tell an adult you trust."

"If you tell, the bad person might hurt you," Stella said.

"If you tell a person you trust—like your mom and dad—they'll protect you," Willa said. What had prompted Stella to say this? How could Willa find out?

"Can we practice with the bandages now?" a girl asked.

"Yes. I want to be the patient," someone else shouted.

"I want to be the doctor," another girl said.

Willa had to let the moment pass. But she kept a close watch on Stella as the girls took turns fastening slings or trying out the flexible metal splints. Was the girl speaking from personal experience, or remembering things Olivia had told her?

She didn't have a chance to speak to Stella again before her time with this group was up. Willa spent the rest of the morning repeating the experience with younger groups of girls, finishing up with a class of six-and seven-year-olds who had a loud discussion about how awful shots were and the importance of washing your hands after you touched boys because of cooties.

The last session ended at twelve thirty and Mrs. Mason presented Willa with her own green Mountain Kingdom T-shirt and thanked her for coming. Willa headed back to her car. She was passing the mess hall when the back door opened and a small figure with a tail of brown hair darted out, then disappeared behind a tree.

Willa looked around. No one else appeared to have seen the girl, who she was sure was Stella. Moving cautiously, hiding behind trees as much as possible, Willa hurried after the girl, whose figure she could just make out ahead of her.

Willa ended up breaking into a run to keep up with the swift little girl. She leaned against a tree and tried to catch her breath, watching as Stella tucked something in the crotch of a tree. She made sure her offering was secure, then turned and raced back toward camp.

And collided with a waiting Willa. The little girl looked up, wide-eyed, then burst into tears.

Willa knelt and patted Stella's shoulder. "It's okay," she said. "You're not in any trouble. I just wanted to make sure you were okay."

Stella continued to sob.

"What's wrong?" Willa asked. "What has you so upset?"

"My friend is hurt and lost and I'm so worried about her." The little girl leaned into Willa, sobs shaking her slight frame.

"Do you mean Olivia? Were you leaving something for her in the tree?"

"I put part of my lunch there." She looked up, expression pleading. "Please don't tell anyone. I'll get in trouble. Mr. Sprague caught me coming out here one day and I had to miss afternoon swimming as punishment. He said I was wasting food and that was wrong."

"Does Olivia come after you leave and get the food?" Willa asked.

"I don't know." Stella scrubbed at her wet eyes. "Sometimes when I come back the food is gone, but I don't know if Olivia gets it or an animal. I hope she gets it. I don't like to think about her hungry."

"Do you know where Olivia is hiding?" Willa asked.

"No. I promise I don't. If I knew, I would tell you. I'm worried about her."

"Do you know why Olivia ran away?" Willa asked.

Stella toyed with the friendship bracelet on her left wrist. "She didn't tell me. And I didn't know she was going to run away, either. If I had, I would have told her not to."

"But she said something? Something to let you know she was upset?"

"She said she saw something she shouldn't have. And she said she was afraid."

"What was she afraid of?"

"She said if she told me I might get hurt, too."

Too. "Had someone hurt Olivia?" Willa asked.

"I don't know." Stella looked doubtful. "Maybe? I never saw her hurt. But then they found that shirt with her blood on it…" Her voice gave way to fresh sobs.

Willa waited for the sobs to subside. She searched for something to distract the girl. "Did you make your bracelet?" she asked. "It's pretty."

"Olivia made it." She held out her wrist, the show off the chevron pattern of pink, purple and green threads. "I made one for her." Fresh tears welled in her eyes. "A deputy showed me a bracelet they found in the mud. It looked like Olivia's. They wouldn't say, but I think maybe they found it with the shirt."

"How did you know about the shirt?" Willa asked. Surely no one had told the children.

"Mr. Sprague told me. The day he caught me with half my lunch wrapped in a napkin. He said I needed to stay close to camp or the person who had done that to Willa would hurt me the way they had hurt her."

She began to weep again. Willa held her tightly, and cursed Scott for frightening the child this way. "When did Olivia tell you these things?" she asked.

"The night before she left. The next day she seemed okay, and when I asked her how she was feeling, she said she was fine. But then, after dinner that night she was acting upset again. She didn't want to talk about it and told me not to worry, but how can I not worry when I don't even know where she is?"

Willa nodded. Olivia clearly needed help, but so did Stella. "When do you see your parents again?" she asked.

"Not for another month. When camp is over."

"Do you talk to them on the phone?"

"On Sunday afternoons. I told them last Sunday that I don't like it here anymore and I want to go home, but they said I had made a commitment and it was important that I keep it."

"Stella, look at me." Willa studied the girl's face. "Has anyone threatened to hurt you?"

She shook her head no.

"Has anyone done anything to make you uncomfortable?"

"No. Not how you mean."

"What other way is there?"

"I didn't like missing swimming that afternoon, but that was because I broke a rule. Not because anyone was bullying me. We studied about bullying in school, so I learned about that." She pushed away. "I need to get back to camp before somebody misses me. You won't tell anyone about the food, will you?"

"No, I won't. Not anyone at camp. I might tell another friend of mine, but he's very good at keeping secrets. And he'll make certain you don't get in any trouble. And wait just a second." She dug in her purse and pulled out a pen and a receipt. She turned the receipt over to the blank side. "What are your parents' names and their phone number?" she asked.

Stella's eyes widened. "You're going to call my parents?"

"Only if I need to. I might suggest they let you come home early, if that's okay with you."

Stella bit her lip, then nodded, and gave Willa the information. "Don't make it sound like I'm in trouble," she said.

"I won't. I promise."

Stella looked at Willa a long moment, then turned and raced away. Willa stood and walked to the fork of the tree. Half a dozen potato puffs, a corn dog and one broken cookie were wrapped in a napkin. Willa started to wrap the food again and return it to its hiding place when she saw the note in the corner of the napkin. Written in tiny letters, in pencil, was Stella's message to her friend: "Olivia, please come home."

I have to talk to you, but not at the sheriff's department, and not at my house.

Aaron stared at the message from Willa, heart racing, then replied, Did you learn something at the camp?

I'll tell you when we meet. Mount Wilson trailhead?

Why there? But he would find out when he saw her. He texted, I could be there at 3:30.

See you then.

He changed out of his uniform after his shift ended at three, and drove to the trailhead. Willa's Toyota was there, and she climbed out of the driver's seat when he pulled up beside her. She wore jeans and a lacy top, and carried a small pack.

"We don't have time to do the whole trail," she said. "But let's walk up to the first overlook."

"All right." He grabbed his own pack and followed her up. She was a strong hiker, with a confident stride. By the time the trail leveled out after the first half mile they were both breathing hard from the exertion. "What did you want to tell me?" he asked, unable to pretend patience any longer.

"Olivia's best friend at camp, Stella, was in my first class of the morning," Willa said. "She said some things that piqued my interest, but I didn't get a chance to ask many questions. Then I saw her right before I left and she had a lot of interesting things to say."

"Does she know where Olivia is now?" he asked. "Does she know why she ran away?"

"She doesn't know either of those things, but she said the night before she disappeared, Olivia told Stella she had 'seen something she shouldn't have,' and that she was afraid. Olivia wouldn't elaborate, and said she couldn't tell Stella anything else because she was afraid Stella might be hurt, *too*."

"Had someone hurt Olivia?"

"Stella said Olivia didn't look hurt. But maybe it was something Stella couldn't see."

"Or maybe what Olivia saw was someone hurting someone else."

Willa started walking again. The trail was wider here, and Aaron fell into step beside her, matching his stride to hers. "Stella said she didn't know Olivia was planning to run away," she said. "When she found out Olivia was gone the next morning, she was really afraid."

"Why didn't she say anything to us when we questioned her?" Aaron asked. "Or to one of the counselors?"

"Because she was afraid," Willa said. "She didn't know what Olivia had seen or who was involved so she kept her mouth shut. A pretty smart decision, considering."

Maybe it *was* smart, from a frightened child's point of view. "And she really doesn't have any idea where Olivia is now?"

"She says she doesn't and I believe her. She's really worried about her friend. She's been saving back part of her lunch every day and leaving it in a tree in the woods for Olivia."

"Does Olivia come to get it? Maybe we could hide and wait for her."

Willa shook her head. "Stella said sometimes when she comes back the food is gone, but she doesn't know if Olivia is taking it, or animals. I think it's probably animals. The tree where she's leaving the food is still in the camp. If Olivia is as frightened as Stella made her sound, I'm not sure she would risk coming that close."

"Does anyone else know about this?" Aaron asked.

"Stella said Scott caught her carrying part of her lunch outside the mess hall one day. He told her she needed to stay close to camp or the person who had hurt Olivia would hurt her. He told her about the bloody shirt they had found." She glared at Aaron. "What kind of person frightens a child that way?"

"One who wants her to stay close, no matter what," Aaron said. "What did he do then?"

"He made her stay in her cabin and miss afternoon swimming as a punishment for wasting food."

"He obviously didn't frighten her enough to make her stop leaving food for Olivia," Aaron said. "I still think it would be worth staking out that tree to see if Olivia shows up."

"If you do that, you can't tell anyone about Stella," Willa said. "I promised. And if someone at camp is the person who frightened Olivia away, I don't want to risk them going after Stella." They reached a small sign for the overlook and turned onto a short side trail. Thirty yards later the trail opened up to a view of the landscape below.

"I wanted to come up here and see this," Willa said.

Aaron moved in close beside her. Not touching, but close enough to smell her floral shampoo, and see the gentle rise and fall of her chest as she breathed. "I think Olivia is down there somewhere," she said.

"If she would come out of hiding, we could keep her safe," Aaron said.

"She must not believe that. Not yet."

"What could she have seen that has her so frightened?"

"Whatever it was, it was at the camp," Willa said. "You're going to have to dig deeper there."

He put a hand on her shoulder. She didn't pull away. "You need to tell all of this to the sheriff," he said.

"I promised Stella."

"Travis Walker is a good man. He's not going to endanger a child. But he needs to know about this. He's the only one who can authorize any kind of investigation at the camp."

She bowed her head. Her hair fell forward, revealing the nape of her neck, pale and vulnerable. As fragile as a child hiding food—and secrets—for her friend. Or another child, hiding in the wilderness. Or any human heart, so easily broken and difficult to mend.

"I'll talk to him," she said. "But only if you come with me."

"Of course." He put his arm around her and she leaned back against him. The position was so familiar, but he had never thought he would feel this closeness again. He didn't dare hope it would lead to anything else, but it meant a lot that she trusted him enough in this moment to lean on him, however briefly. Neither of them said anything for a long while, then she turned and walked back down the mountain, him following behind.

Chapter Thirteen

Willa had seen Sheriff Travis Walker around town, on search and rescue calls and during the search for Olivia. With leading-man good looks and a solemn, reserved demeanor, he had attracted the attention of more than one lovestruck tourist who had gone on to learn he was a happily married father of two. But it wasn't his looks or his attitude that intimidated Willa. As she sat across from him in his cluttered office at the sheriff's department, she was all too aware that he was a man with the power to put an innocent man—like her brother—behind bars. And the power to dismiss the concerns of someone like her.

"Aaron tells me you have some information that may help us in our search for Olivia Pryor," he said after Aaron had formally introduced them. Aaron sat in a second chair next to Willa, a silent, encouraging presence.

"I gave a first aid class at Mountain Kingdom Kids Camp this morning," Willa said. "The girls from Olivia's cabin were in my first class and one of the girls, Stella, told me Olivia confided in her that she—Olivia—had seen something she shouldn't have. She was clearly frightened, but she wouldn't tell Stella what she had seen or what had frightened her. She said she was afraid that Stella would be hurt, too. And the next night, Olivia ran away." Did summarizing the story this way made it sound trivial? "Stella was really afraid for Olivia. Whatever Olivia saw must have been bad. If we could find out what that was, maybe that would help us find a way to bring Olivia home safely."

"Tell me the timeline," Travis said. "When did Olivia see this event that upset her?"

"The night before she disappeared," Willa said.

"That would have been Saturday night," Aaron said. "The night of the bonfire."

The sheriff nodded. "Olivia was reported missing on Monday. We believe she ran away Sunday night."

Five days ago. For five days Olivia had been out there in the wilderness. Alone. Afraid. Hungry and thirsty. Cold.

"Stella has been leaving food for Olivia in a tree at the edge of camp," Willa said. "She doesn't know if Olivia is coming at night to take the food, or if animals are eating it. She swears she doesn't know where Olivia is now, and I believe her."

"We'll talk to her," Travis said.

Willa leaned forward. "Please be careful. Stella is terrified. She knows about the bloody shirt you found and she's afraid whoever hurt Olivia will come after her. I'm afraid of that, too. I think she needs to go home, away from the camp."

"We'll need to get in touch with her parents," Travis said. "Do you know their names?"

"I have their names and a phone number." Willa opened her purse and took out the receipt on which she had written the information and passed it across to Travis. "Try not to frighten her more. The poor girl is miserable, between worrying about her friend and being afraid."

Travis picked up the handset of his phone and punched in the number. "Mr. Ireland?" he asked. "This is Sheriff Travis

Walker in Eagle Mountain, Colorado… Your daughter is fine. I'm calling because we would like to talk to her about the disappearance of her friend Olivia, and we would like you and your wife present when we do so… Stella is not in any trouble. We understand she's very upset about her missing friend, and we believe she may know some small details that could help in our search for Olivia Pryor… It's very important that you bring her in as soon as possible… Tomorrow morning would be good. I know Stella will be happy to see you. One thing I have to ask is that you don't tell the camp or Stella ahead of time that you're coming. Simply show up and bring Stella here to the sheriff's department. We're on Second Street in Eagle Mountain… The camp might object, but they can't keep you from your daughter. If they give you any trouble, call me. I'm going to give you my direct number." He recited a phone number, then repeated it. "Thank you. I really appreciate your help."

He ended the call. "They're bringing her in tomorrow," he said.

"That was good, telling them not to contact the camp ahead of time," Willa said. "Will you tell them after the interview that Stella needs to go home with them? I'm afraid if someone at the camp did hurt Olivia, they might go after Stella, too."

"I'll tell them."

He thanked her again for coming in and she walked with Aaron to his truck. He had offered to drive her to the interview and she had gratefully accepted. "I don't want to go home yet," she said as he started the engine. "Gary is there and he'll ask about the interview. I'm not ready to talk about it yet."

"Where would you like to go?"

"Someplace quiet and private."

He considered this a moment, then shifted into gear and pulled out of the parking space. She didn't ask where they were going, merely stared out the window, her expression pensive.

AARON DROVE TO his house and pulled into the driveway. "Is this all right?" he asked as he shut off the engine.

Willa studied the A-frame, with its fading paint and ragged yard. It wasn't that different from her own rental. A comfortable place to stay, but not yet a home. "This is fine," she said, and got out of the truck.

She was waiting at the door when he came up behind her to open it. The living room was as she remembered from her visit three nights ago, cluttered and comfortable, dust motes drifting in the sunlight that arced through floor-to-ceiling front windows.

"I can make coffee," he said, shutting the door behind them. "Or tea."

"Let's just sit for a minute." She sat on the sofa. He started to take the chair across from her—the one she had chosen the other night—then shifted to sit beside her. Close, but not touching.

"Sorry the place is such a mess," he said, following her gaze to the shirt draped across the back of the chair and the empty glass on the coffee table.

"It's better than the place you were living in when we met," she said. "There were boxes everywhere."

"I had just moved and wasn't unpacked yet," he said. "It got better."

She angled toward him, smiling at the memory. "Do you remember the first time I saw it? The first time we went out?"

"The day we met. I remember."

She put a hand to her cheek, which felt hot. "I still can't believe how fast I fell for you. You brought in that prisoner to be stitched up and we started talking and the next thing I knew I was agreeing to have dinner with you. That night."

"I couldn't believe my luck," he said. "The minute I saw you I was just…bowled over. I knew I was completely monopolizing your time but I couldn't stop talking to you. I was sure you were going to think I was the biggest fool you had ever met."

"I didn't think that. I was just…mesmerized."

He laughed, from nerves as much as amusement. "No one has ever said that about me before."

"I don't know what it was about you," she said. "It was like…we had so much to say to each other. I didn't want you to leave, and I couldn't wait to see you again."

"When I asked you back to my place after dinner, I was sure you'd turn me down," he said. "I was already planning to ask to see you the next day. And I knew I'd call you the next morning, but you said yes."

"I had never done that before—gone back to a man's place when I'd known him less than twenty-four hours. Even as I was saying yes, I couldn't believe I was doing it." She fell silent, remembering what else she had done that evening—falling into bed with him as if they had known each other for months instead of hours. It was as if they had come down with a fever that left them only able to think about each other.

"That was a good night," he said. "A special night."

He slid his hand into hers and the warmth of him wrapped around her. That hadn't felt rushed or tawdry or any of the things she might have imagined sex with a man she scarcely knew would be. It just felt…right. She looked down at his hand. She would have denied she ever believed in love at first sight, but looking back, she could see she had started falling in love with Aaron during that first conversation, while she cleaned the cut hand of a bleeding prisoner and they talked about the phenomena of emergency rooms being busier during the full moon.

She closed her eyes against sudden tears, the pain of missing him overwhelming her. How had something so right ended so badly?

"Willa?" He stroked her hair, and turned her toward him. "What's wrong?"

She opened her eyes and looked at him, his features blurred but familiar—strong jaw, thick eyebrows, dark lashes any woman would envy. "I loved you so much," she blurted.

"I know."

His lips on hers were firm, not hesitant or doubting. *This is what I want,* the kiss said. And everything in her echoed, *This is what I want.*

She reached for him, sliding her fingers around the back of his neck to the warm, soft place beneath a tickling fringe of hair. She opened her mouth and more warmth flooded her as his tongue tangled with hers, every sensitive nerve alive to his touch. He slid his palm up to cup the side of her breast and she knelt on the sofa cushion beside him, then crawled into his lap, straddling him, hands gripping his shoulders while his fingers dug into the curve of her hips.

They began to undress each other, not talking. Not needing to talk. She pushed back his shirt and the cool metal of the St. Michael medallion brushed against her palm. He lifted his hips and she tugged off his jeans, then straightened so that he could pull her top over her head. She stripped off her jeans and underwear with no self-consciousness. She had been here before, with this man, and she had never felt safer.

Her fingers moved without her having to think, rediscovering territory that had once been as familiar to her as her own. His skin was firm and warm, taut over a muscular chest and arms. There was the mole on the left side of his ribs, and the perfect whorl of dark hair centered between his nipples. There was the lopsided indentation of his navel, and the small silvery white scar from the appendectomy he had had at age twelve. She pressed against him, and felt the rigid heat of his erection, and the answering flood of warmth within her.

He gripped her bottom and settled her more firmly against him, then kissed her long and hard until she was dizzy and breathless, trembling with need.

"Condom?" she asked, no longer capable of full sentences.

In answer, he gently shifted her off of him and stood, then took her hand and tugged her upright. She let him lead her down a hall to a bedroom—comforter pulled up over pillows, a single lamp casting a pool of light over the right side of the bed in the gloom of drawn curtains.

"I'll be right back," he said.

She lay back on the bed, the thrill of anticipation washing over her. She didn't allow herself to think—didn't give doubt time to take hold. Aaron returned in moments, a foil packet in his hand. The bed dipped as he lay beside her, and when he pulled her close she surrendered everything, no longer fighting what she had needed for so long.

AARON HAD DREAMED of making love to Willa again—tortured dreams after which he woke frustrated and grief stricken. There was no grief now, only the joy of knowing she was just as he remembered—just as beautiful. Just as passionate. Just as able to make him feel so much better than he deserved.

He wanted to take his time—to reacquaint himself with every inch of her. But neither of them could wait for that. When she whispered for him to hurry, the urgency in her voice sent a tremor through him. He unwrapped the condom and slid it on, then moved toward her. She moaned as they came together, and that was almost his undoing. Nothing had felt this right—ever. When he began to move, she moved with him, and smiled up at him, his own delight reflected in her eyes. Then she laughed, and he laughed, too, increasing the pace of their rhythm, wanting to memorize the incredible feel of her—of them together.

Then the intensity of the moment silenced them both, and they communicated only with a shifting of hips or the nudge of a hand. His heart pounded, and when he rested his palm between her breasts he felt the thud of her heart, too. Her face was flushed, her eyes glazed, and he knew she was close to the edge. He slid his hand down between them to touch her and felt her convulse around him, a tension that triggered his own release, powerful and overwhelming and humbling.

They lay together for a long while afterward, thin bars of white light showing around a gap in the curtains in the otherwise dim room. She rested her head in the hollow of his shoulder, one thigh draped over his thigh, her skin soft as satin, the perfume of her hair mixed with the musk of sex, taking him back to other bedrooms they had shared, as if scarcely a day had passed since they had last been together, instead of almost a year.

"I hope that wasn't a mistake," she said, breaking the silence.

"It wasn't a mistake," he said. The words hadn't alarmed him. He had known she would think this, even if she didn't say it. Willa had lost so much in her life she lived with the fear of loss even in the midst of bounty. He had tried to be that bounty for her. That he had failed still haunted him, but he was not one to dwell on the past. He could only look forward, and try to prove she had nothing to lose with him this time.

She shifted, and raised her head to look at him. "It can't be like before between us. I can't be that…consumed… again. I can't lose myself that way again."

"I never wanted you to lose yourself." He stroked her arm, the fine hairs soft against his fingers. "I don't want to own you or monopolize you or do anything but love you."

Her eyes met his, her gaze as open and honest as he had ever seen it.

"I'm scared," she stated.

"I know. I'm scared, too. Scared of screwing up. Scared of losing you again. But isn't it better to be scared together than apart?"

She lay down again, curled against him. "Yes," she said. "Yes, it's better."

He rested his hand on her back, and felt her relax and fall asleep. But he lay awake a long time. Being with her was better than anything else. But he didn't know if he could survive losing her again.

Chapter Fourteen

Saturday morning shortly before noon, Gage, Aaron, Jake and Ryker reported to the main office of Mountain Kingdom Kids Camp with a warrant to search the property. Other deputies waited outside for the order to begin combing through the various buildings on the property.

"Mr. Sprague isn't here," Mrs. Mason said. "I can't allow you to look at the files without his permission."

"We have a warrant, ma'am," Gage said. "We don't need his permission."

He stepped past and she watched, hands clutching a copy of the warrant, as the deputies filed into the office.

"What are you looking for?" she asked.

"Everything," Gage said. "It would be best if you waited in your office while we're here. We don't take any more of your time than necessary."

She pulled out a cell phone and punched in the number, listened for a moment, then hung up. "Mr. Sprague isn't answering his phone."

"Where is Mr. Sprague?" Ryker asked.

"I imagine he's where he always is these days," she said. "He's searching for Olivia Pryor. But I need him here. We've already had a set of parents show up and withdraw their child early from camp. I'm sure it's because of all the bad publicity about Olivia Pryor. But it's not our fault if one headstrong girl decides to run away."

Stella and her parents had met with the sheriff this morning at nine o'clock, and Stella's statement about Olivia seeing something that had frightened her, plus the sheriff's argument that it was possible Olivia was being held prisoner somewhere on the property, had resulted in a judge granting a warrant to search the camp once more—including the office, all outbuildings and the Sprague residence. These had been searched before, but with the cooperation of everyone involved. Camp employees and Scott himself had accompanied deputies as they searched for the missing girl. This time, they would also be looking for any evidence of a crime that might have involved Olivia, or that she might have witnessed.

They started with staff records. "We're looking for any kind of disciplinary action for inappropriate behavior with a child," Gage said. "Also any records of theft or vandalism. Maybe what Olivia saw was someone breaking the law."

The records search took very little time. With less than a dozen employees and very few records on them, going through all the files took less than an hour. "Everyone here is squeaky-clean," Ryker announced when they were done. "Either Scott has been very lucky with his hires or the records are lying."

Interviews with the staff revealed nothing, either. "We've got a really great bunch of people here," Wade Lawson told Aaron and Ryker. "Most of us have been here two or three summers, at least."

"You're telling me that all summer, nothing has turned up missing?" Ryker asked. "No one's gotten into any trouble at all?"

"The only trouble was when my brother died," Wade

said. "I still don't know what really happened that night, but I can't believe anyone here had anything to do with it. Everyone really liked Trevor."

"This is leading nowhere," Ryker said as he and Aaron walked back toward the lodge.

They detoured when Gage hailed them. The sergeant was coming out of Scott's house. "Find anything?" Ryker asked.

Gage shook his head. "The man lives like a minimalist. No photos, very few books, one file drawer full of personal papers. Nothing incriminating."

Aaron looked back at the log home, straight out of the 1970s, or '50s, or even '30s. "Didn't his family own this camp for years? Maybe his grandparents started it?"

"That's the story," Gage said. "But there's not one family heirloom in the place, unless you count a toaster that probably dates from the 1980s."

"Sarge!"

They turned to see Jake jogging toward them. He held out a small evidence bag. "Found this in Mrs. Mason's apartment."

Gage examined the plastic pouch, which contained a prescription bottle. "Seconal. The prescription is made out to Phyllis Mason."

"She said it was prescribed last year, when she was going through a difficult time. She didn't elaborate on what was wrong, but said she hadn't taken the pills in months."

Gage shook the bottle. "How many are in here?"

"Three. But she can't remember how many were left when she stopped taking them. She swears no one else has been in her apartment."

"Where is the apartment?" Gage asked.

"Upstairs, over the dining hall."

"Anything else of interest in there?" Gage asked.

"Nothing," Jake said. "I asked her if she knew Trevor Lawson. She said she had met him when he filled out the employee paperwork but she never spoke to him afterward. He had only worked part-time at the camp for about a month when he died."

"We'll see what we can get from this." Gage handed back the evidence pouch. "But lots of people have prescriptions for sleeping pills. It doesn't mean there's any connection to Trevor."

"Trevor died the night before Olivia disappeared," Aaron said. "Stella said Olivia was upset about something that happened the night before she ran away. Could she have seen something to do with Trevor Lawson's death?"

"Stella also said Olivia had been 'sad' for a couple of weeks before that," Ryker said. "I read that in one of her first interviews. I think that means whatever upset Olivia wasn't something new."

"All right, but what if she was sad about something—maybe homesick, something like that?" Aaron asked. "And then the night Trevor died, she saw something. Maybe she saw who killed him. That might have frightened her enough to run away."

"Trevor Lawson committed suicide," Gage said. "He drove his car off Dixon Pass."

"He was legally drunk and had Seconal in his system," Jake said. "But his brother swears Trevor didn't drink to excess or do drugs. And there were indications Trevor had been in a fight before he died."

"Maybe someone made sure Trevor wasn't in any shape to drive before he got into his car to go home that evening," Aaron said.

"They couldn't have been sure he would go off the road," Ryker said. "I've stopped plenty of drivers with blood alcohol levels higher than Trevor Lawson's who weren't showing any signs of being drunk."

"Still, what if Olivia saw something to do with Trevor's death?" Aaron said.

"You're going to have a hard time proving it," Gage said.

"Maybe. But if someone did do something to Trevor and they knew Olivia saw them, it would explain why she was frightened enough to run away."

"It could also explain the blood and the ripped shirt," Ryker said. "I can't help wondering if Olivia ever left this camp. There are a lot of places to hide a body around here."

"And we're searching them all," Gage said. "We've got a cadaver dog coming on loan from Mesa County tomorrow. Meanwhile, let's get back to work."

They trudged after him to take apart the storage shed and the kitchen, while workers huddled in the empty mess hall, casting hostile stares their way and muttering among themselves. No one liked disruptions to their routine, and everyone thought the deputies were wasting their time.

Aaron couldn't help thinking the same thing. They were missing something here. He had felt that way with other unsolved cases. If they could only discover the one missing piece of the puzzle, everything would shift into focus and they would find the guilty party. But all this searching wasn't turning up anything, and with a little girl's life at stake, they were running out of time.

GARY STOPPED BY the medical clinic a little after noon on Saturday. Willa spotted him coming in the door and rushed into the waiting room. "Gary! What are you doing here? Are you all right?" She searched him for any sign of injury or illness.

"I'm fine. The camp sent me home early."

"Why? What happened?"

He glanced around the empty waiting room. "The sheriff's deputies are at camp searching everything," he said, keeping his voice low. "From attic to basement. They came this morning with a warrant. Mrs. Mason was in a tizzy and Scott was nowhere in sight. He showed up two hours in and I thought he was going to stroke out, yelling at the cops to stop what they were doing. They went right on emptying drawers and going through files, as if they hadn't even heard him. About that time, Scott ordered all the kids confined to quarters and all nonessential personnel—meaning everyone but the counselors—to go home. He also told us not to talk to anyone, but I figure that's an order he can't really enforce."

The door buzzer sounded as a woman and a little boy entered.

Willa took Gary's arm. "Come back here where we can talk." She led him to the back of the building, and the small break room. "What are the deputies looking for?" she asked.

"They didn't say." He helped himself to a doughnut from a box someone had left on the counter. "You should ask Aaron. Maybe he'll tell you. He was there today. I saw him shifting boxes of canned goods in the storage shed. He didn't look too happy."

She turned away, praying she wasn't blushing. She couldn't claim she hated Aaron anymore, after the night they had spent together. But she wasn't ready to declare they were a couple again.

"Anyway, I stopped by to tell you a couple of the kitchen staff and I are going hiking along a stretch of the river near camp to see if we can find any sign of Olivia. We want to find her, but we don't want to find her, if you get what I mean."

She nodded. "You want to find her, but you don't want to find her body."

"Yeah. Anyway, don't wait up."

"You're a grown man, Gary. You don't have to check in with me."

"I don't have to, but if I don't, you'll worry."

"I can't help that."

He squeezed her shoulder. "I know. I hated it when I was a teenager and I'd come home and you'd be sitting there, waiting. But later on, I could admit it felt good, after Dad died, knowing I had someone looking out for me."

"We looked out after each other," she said.

"I was fifteen when Dad died. I could hardly look after myself, much less you. And I barely remember Mom. You were the one who washed my clothes and nagged me to clean my room and did all the mom stuff." He shook his head. "It's wild, when you think about it. You were only, what, nine or ten when she died? And I remember Dad was a mess for a while after that. You were the one who kept us together."

"Dad looked after us. I just did what I could to help." She still remembered the panicky feeling of coming home to an empty house, dust on the furniture and nothing waiting for dinner—as if her parents had simply walked out the door and forgotten to return. Forgotten they had two children to care for. She had done what she could to make sure Gary never had that feeling. And when their father had died when she was twenty, she had carried on looking after Gary. He was the only family she had left.

"Be careful," she said. "It's rough country out there."

"If it's rough for us, imagine what it's like for a little girl. Let's hope she's a tough kid, like you were." He patted her back and left.

I wasn't tough, she wanted to tell him. *I just didn't know what else to do.*

Maybe it was the same with Olivia. She had been frightened and had run. Now she was just hanging on—for what, Willa didn't know. She sent a silent message to the girl: *Keep fighting.*

AARON WAS WAITING by Willa's car when she emerged from the clinic that evening. He was exhausted from searching through the Mountain Kingdom camp all day, his uniform dirty from crawling through attics and moving aside boxes in storerooms. He probably had spiderwebs in his hair. It wasn't the most attractive picture to present a woman, but if he had taken time to shower and change he would have missed Willa. He wanted to see her, to reassure himself she hadn't changed her mind about him after last night. He didn't want to pressure her to spend more time with him or to sleep with him again—though he would have welcomed both of those things. He just wanted to see her. To know things were good between them again and that was one less weight to carry.

"Aaron, you look awful," she said as she approached. "Are you okay?"

"Just tired. I'll go home in a few minutes and take a shower, I just wanted to make sure you were okay."

"Why wouldn't I be okay?"

"I was worried you were regretting last night." He searched her face, trying to read her emotions. "I'm not," he added.

"No, I'm not regretting that." She moved closer, and touched his shoulder. "You look exhausted. Gary told me you were helping to search the camp. Did you find anything?"

"We didn't find Olivia, or any sign of her. I don't think we found anything else, either."

"I guess it's good that you didn't find her body, but how could she have simply disappeared?"

"It's easier than you might think, out here. Every few years a hiker goes missing. Some are never found."

"I've been learning about that in my search and rescue training. It's still hard to imagine." She took a step back. "Go home and rest. Maybe there will be better news tomorrow."

"I have to be back at the camp tonight. I was hoping you'd come with me."

"Why?"

"It's bonfire night. A camp tradition, every Saturday night."

"Is the public invited?"

"Not usually. But the sheriff told Scott he wanted to put some officers there to see if they could spot anything suspicious. Last Saturday was the night before Olivia went missing—the night when, according to Stella, she saw something that upset her. We're hoping we'll spot something to give us a clue what that something might have been."

"It was also the night Trevor Lawson died, wasn't it?" she asked.

"You made that connection, too?" He nodded. "Trevor was at the bonfire. He was supposedly fine then, but now I'm really curious to see what goes on at this thing, if it managed to upset two different people. Will you come with me to the bonfire?"

"Are you really supposed to take a date if you're working?"

"You'll be another set of eyes. And the kids like you."

"Did Scott agree to have a civilian there?"

"You'll be part of my cover. We agreed to come in plainclothes so we don't upset the kids. The story is, Scott has invited some guests from town. He's done it before—usually parents or big donors."

"The campers have seen deputies at the camp all week," she said. "They're bound to recognize some of you."

"Probably. We'll do our best not to alarm them."

"All right. I'll come with you." She linked her arm with his. "I won't think of it as a date. I'll think of it as helping the police with their inquiries."

Chapter Fifteen

Willa and Aaron arrived at the camp just after sunset. The bonfire on the shore of the lake sent sparks into the sky, the wood snapping like twigs underfoot. They heard the buzz of conversation as they crossed the grass toward the shore, high children's voices soaring in the clear evening. The scent of woodsmoke perfumed the air, and a cool breeze raised goose bumps on Willa's bare arms, making her reach for the sweater she had brought.

"Did you go to camp when you were a kid?" Aaron asked.

"No."

"Did you want to?"

The memory came to her clearly—a summer when her two best friends were going to a sleep-away camp for two weeks. While she stayed home.

"One year I wanted to go," she said. "But it wasn't possible. I didn't even ask my dad."

"Because you knew he couldn't afford it?"

"I have no idea. But if I left, who would cook dinner for him and my brother, or do the laundry, or pack his lunch?" She shook her head. "Looking back, I can't believe I saw my father as so helpless. Surely he would have found a way to look after himself and Gary while I was away. But I took that on as my responsibility and I couldn't let it go."

"He let you take it on."

"He had a hard time after my mother died. It was probably easier to let me handle some of the things he didn't have the energy to do." She didn't want to think about that sad time, or about how things might have worked out differently. "What about you?" she asked. "Did you go to camp?"

"Boy Scouts. Camp Walla Walla or Winemuka or something like that. Two weeks of canoeing in deep water, archery with arrows with sharp points and dangerous crafts involving leather and sharp knives. All in the hands of preadolescent boys to which everything was a potential weapon. I'm amazed we all survived."

She laughed. "I think Mountain Kingdom is tamer than that. I didn't see a single sharp knife or arrow with a point in my visits here."

They reached the edge of the bonfire. A trio of girls were roasting marshmallows. Willa recognized Juliet, her purple cast covered with scrawled signatures.

"If you want a marshmallow, you have to ask Veronica," Juliet said. "She won't let you help yourself."

"Because some people take too many," a second girl, with black braids, said.

"Boys take too many," the third girl, a pixie-cut blonde, said, and all three dissolved into giggles.

Aaron touched Willa's shoulder. "I see someone I need to talk to," he said.

"Fine. I'm going to get a marshmallow."

He headed toward a cluster of cabins and she walked over to a folding table where Veronica sat, looking bored.

"Could I have a couple of marshmallows, please?" Willa asked.

Veronica handed her a bent coat hanger with two marshmallows impaled on the end. "I thought you were a nurse," she said. "Are you a cop, too? They told us there would be some cops here tonight."

"I'm friends with a cop." She glanced toward Aaron, who stood halfway between the bonfire and the cabins, talking with another counselor, a young man with wire-rimmed glasses.

Veronica followed her gaze. "Lucky you," she said. "He's hot. I noticed him yesterday, when they were searching the place."

"Did they find anything?"

"You tell me." She shrugged. "I don't think there's anything to find. This place is beyond dull. Olivia probably ran away because she was bored out of her mind."

"Were you her counselor?"

"One of them. And before you ask, I already told the cops she was normal as could be before she ran away. No tears. No moping."

"I heard she was sneaking out of her cabin for a while before she disappeared."

Her expression grew sullen. "I don't know anything about that. I'm not these kids' jailer. And I have to sleep sometime."

"If you had to guess, who do you think she was sneaking off to see? Did she have a boyfriend?"

"I never saw her so much as talking to a boy. Some of these girls, they're regular flirts. They hit on the male counselors, even—guys who are four and five years older."

"Did Olivia do that?"

"No. She was still a little girl. Which is a good thing, you know? She was kind of a tomboy. Athletic. Not afraid of spiders and stuff. She was having a lot of fun at camp. I don't know why she left."

A pair of boys approached, demanding marshmallows, and Veronica turned away.

Willa returned to the fire. She held her marshmallows over the blaze. Within seconds, one burst into flames. She blew it out, then popped it into her mouth—one side scorched, the interior half-melted, the other side cold and pillowy. Exactly as she remembered.

She roasted the other marshmallow and ate it, then looked around for something else to do. Aaron had disappeared, though she spotted a couple of other deputies, conspicuous by their alert attitudes and watchful gazes, despite their civilian clothing.

She scanned the crowd for anyone else she knew and her gaze came to rest on a girl who stood by herself on the edge of the firelight. The girl's stillness made Willa look more closely. She had the air of someone waiting for something—but not necessarily something good. She was tall and thin, growing too fast to have yet filled out, shiny brown hair hanging straight to the middle of her back. She wore a green Mountain Kingdom T-shirt and khaki shorts, and scuffed green sneakers. A boy ran up and said something to her, laughing. She scowled and slapped at him and he ran away, still laughing.

Then something caught the girl's attention from somewhere in the darkness. She looked away, then back, then darted off, disappearing quickly into the shadows.

Was she meeting someone? Another boy? Or had something else attracted her? Could it be Olivia, signaling a friend to meet her and bring food or a message or something else?

Heart pounding, Willa hurried after the girl. She had lost sight of her in the darkness, then she heard soft footsteps, moving toward one of the pit toilets. She slowed. Maybe that's all the girl had been doing—going to the restroom.

Unlike the other pit toilets, this one didn't have a light

over the door. Why purposely choose one in the darkness? Willa stood next to a thick-trunked tree and waited. The door to the toilet didn't open, but the shadows to the side of the little building thickened as the girl stepped into them.

There was a scuffling sound. A sharp "no!" Willa started. There had been fear in that one word, and she felt an answering fear grip her throat.

She started to turn away—to go for help. Then another sound, like weeping. Willa still held the coat hanger she had used to roast the marshmallows. It wasn't much of a weapon, but it would have to do.

She rushed toward the pit toilet. "Hey!" she shouted. "What's going on back there?"

More scuffling, and one high-pitched scream. Footsteps raced away—someone young and light. The girl. Then strong arms grabbed Willa.

"What do you think you're doing?" a low voice growled, but before she could answer, a hand clamped over her mouth.

"WAS IT LIKE this last week when your brother was here?" Aaron had spotted Wade Lawson and pulled him aside.

Wade glanced back at the bonfire—a five-foot wide, four-foot high blaze encircled by a double stack of rocks, the flames licking several feet into the night air. Kids crowded close, waving marshmallow sticks, talking, and laughing.

"Yeah. It's the same every week. Bonfire, kids, singing, marshmallows. Later one of the counselors will play guitar and lead a sing-along. Someone will tell a scary story. Then we've got scared kids hyped up on sugar that we have to take back to the cabins and try to settle down."

"About what time did Trevor leave?"

"Early. Maybe an hour in."

Aaron checked his watch. "It's seven o'clock. Did he leave before or after that?"

"About that, I guess. Maybe a little after? It was just getting dark. When the sun gets below the mountains, it gets dark fast."

"And you say he left here and headed for the pit toilet?"

"Yeah. That direction." Wade pointed to their left. "And I never saw him alive again. He was fine and definitely sober, yet you people tell me he got wasted, got in his car and drove off the pass. I can't even wrap my head around that." He grabbed at his hair. "It's like you're talking about somebody else."

"I'm sorry," Aaron said. "It must be tough being here, so soon after it happened."

"It sucks, but I don't have a choice. I've got a cabin full of kids to look after." He glanced over Aaron's shoulder. "I have to go. Malcolm! What did I tell you about burning holes in your shirt with that coat hanger?"

Aaron looked toward the row of pit toilets clustered under the trees. Three log-sided sheds, painted green, each with an LED light over the door.

Wait. There was a fourth. The light over this one was burned out. Something moved beside this one—a big shadow. A man-size shadow, struggling with something. Aaron started toward the scene, walking at first. Then he heard a scream and broke into a run.

WILLA GRABBED AT the hand clamped over her mouth and tried to pull it away. Whoever had hold of her was big. And strong. He jerked her off her feet and started dragging her, one arm clamped over her throat, cutting off her air. She continued to bat at him feebly, until he struck her with his fist. She reeled, vision blurring, but concentrated on keeping her wits about her. She remembered she had the coat hanger in her hand. With all the concentration she could muster, she gripped the coat hanger near the end, then waited until she felt the man's thigh against her leg. She reached back and plunged the wire end into his leg with as much force as she could muster.

The man swore, but not loudly, and kept his hold on her. But he loosened it enough she was able to slide down his body, out of his grip. He grabbed her shirt and she heard it rip as she lunged away from him. Then she was running, into the darkened woods, ducking and weaving and praying she wouldn't run over a cliff or into a tree.

AARON ALMOST COLLIDED with Scott as the camp owner staggered around the side of the pit toilet.

"Deputy!" he exclaimed, and clung to Aaron. "Did you see which way he ran?"

"Who?" Aaron helped Scott stand. The camp owner was red-faced and breathing hard, his hair disheveled.

"There was a girl. One of the campers. I saw her over here by the pit toilets. By herself. That's not safe. We tell the kids to always go to the pit toilets in pairs, especially at night. Then I realized she wasn't alone. Someone had hold of her. She was struggling. I ran up and yelled and the guy let her go and lunged for me. He stabbed me."

He looked down and Aaron saw the trickle of blood down Scott's thigh. He pulled out his radio. "We've got a bleeding man over here by the pit toilets near the bonfire," he said.

Jake responded that he would be right there, echoed by someone else.

Aaron stowed the radio. "What happened to the man who attacked you?" he asked.

"He ran off," Scott said.

"Which direction?" Jake asked.

"Up toward the lodge, I think."

Jake jogged up to them, Jamie close behind. "What's going on?" Jake asked.

Aaron gave them a quick recap of Scott's story. As he was talking, Scott interrupted, "Now that I'm thinking more clearly, I don't think the camper was a girl," he said. "It was a boy. A little boy. It can be hard to tell when they're little, but I'm sure now it was a boy."

"What happened to the boy?" Jamie asked.

"He ran off," Scott said.

"Which direction did he go?" Jake asked.

Scott looked around. "I'm not sure. Back toward the bonfire?"

"Do you know the boy's name?" Jamie asked. "Which cabin he's in?"

"I'm sorry, I don't. It all happened so fast." Scott put a hand to his head. "I'm not feeling so well." He carefully lowered himself to the ground and buried his face in his hands.

"The ambulance should be here soon," Jamie said.

"I don't need an ambulance." Scott looked up. "I just need to rest a moment and I'll be fine."

"The paramedics are on their way," Jamie said. "You can let them check you out."

"I'm going to look for the guy who stabbed him," Aaron said, and headed toward the lodge, leaving them to deal with Scott.

The grounds of the camp were deserted, with all the campers and staff at the bonfire. Aaron slowed to a jog, then a walk. The lodge was bathed in floodlights, but he didn't see anyone up there. Scott's attacker could be hiding in the shadows.

Aaron thought better of running into trouble and keyed

the mic again. "I'm up here at the lodge, where Scott said his assailant headed," he said. "I don't see anyone, but it might be a good idea to get a few people up here."

"We're headed your way," Gage replied.

Aaron settled in the shadow of a tree, where he hoped he would be invisible to anyone watching. After a moment he keyed the mic again. "Scott said something about one of the campers who ran away. Someone should look for him—or her, Scott seemed confused on that point—and make sure they're okay."

"Jamie's already on it," Gage said. "Sit tight until we get to you."

He leaned against the tree and stared up at the lodge. He hoped someone would tell Willa what was going on. He would text her when he got the chance, but didn't want to light up his phone, in case someone was watching. She would be all right, he told himself. She had always been good at looking after herself.

Chapter Sixteen

Willa ran until her sides ached. As her eyes adjusted to the darkness she could make out more of the terrain, bathed in the glow of a moon that was three-quarters full. She pressed up against the fat trunk of a ponderosa pine and waited for her breathing to slow, listening for the sounds of footsteps following her.

She could no longer see the lights from the camp, or hear the children singing or any sound but the pounding of her own pulse and her still-ragged breathing. Not so much as a bird disturbed the darkness, which felt thick and black, despite the moonlight. She had lost her bearings in her flight, and wasn't even sure which direction she needed to go to get back to the camp. She reached for her phone, but couldn't find it. She checked every pocket, then realized it must have fallen out, either while she was running, or during her struggle with her attacker.

Her attacker. Who was he? She had the impression of bulk, and strength, but it had been impossible to see him in the dark, and he had held her from behind. Was it the same man who had attacked Olivia? Renewed fear gripped her at the idea. The man who had held her had meant to hurt her; she was sure. Had they all been wrong from the beginning of the search in thinking that Olivia was still alive, either lost or deliberately hiding in the wilderness? Had she died that first night, her body hidden where they would never find her?

He had been trying to hurt another camper when Willa had interrupted him. She had to get back to camp and tell Aaron and the others so that they could stop him. She looked around her, but could make out little in the nighttime gloom. Even though her eyes had adjusted to the dimness, and moonlight outlined the trunks of trees closest to her, nothing looked familiar. Which way was the camp?

She tried to remember what her fellow search and rescue team members had said about navigating in the wilderness. But the only lesson she had had so far was in using a compass and noticing landmarks. Then there was the standard advice to stay put if you were lost. But was that a good idea when someone might be coming after you? She didn't think she had wounded her attacker very seriously. He was bound to be furious, and determined to get even.

She started walking in the direction she thought would lead her toward the camp. The trick would be finding Aaron or another deputy before her attacker found her.

She hadn't gone far before something caught at her foot and she fell, hard. She cried out as she hit the ground, and rolled onto her side, gasping. After a moment, the pain subsided and she sat up. She tried to stand, but pain shot through her and her leg gave way. She sat down, waiting until the throbbing subsided, then gingerly ran her hands down her leg to her ankle. She was able to squeeze it, then rotate it gently. Not a break. Just a slight sprain.

She tried again to stand, gritting her teeth, and this time was able to remain upright. But she wasn't going to go far or very fast like this.

Then her heart slammed against her ribs as she heard footsteps approaching. She bit her lip to keep from crying out, and tried to gauge where the sound was coming from. Ahead of her, and to the right. If she stood very still, maybe whoever it was would pass her by.

"Don't be afraid," a soft voice said. "I'm not going to hurt you."

A slight figure emerged from the shadows—a girl with a backpack, a stout walking stick in one hand. Her face was dirty, her jeans with a rip in one leg, but she looked healthy.

"My name is Olivia," she said. "Have you been looking for me?"

Hannah Gwynn was one of the paramedics who responded to the call for assistance at the camp. She and her partner, a reedy young man named Henry, met Deputy Declan Owen in the camp's parking lot and hiked to the scene by the pit toilets, where Scott remained sitting on the ground. But at the sight of the paramedics, he tried to struggle to his feet.

"Remain still, Mr. Sprague," Jamie urged. "Let them examine your leg."

"I can't leave the camp while there's someone here who's attacked one of my campers," Scott said, though he remained sitting.

"Can you describe the attacker?" Jake asked.

"I didn't see much in the dark. It was a man. Big. And he stabbed me."

Hannah knelt beside Scott and directed the beam of a flashlight at his thigh. "It looks like the bleeding has stopped," she said. "I'm going to need to cut away your pants to get a better look." Before he could protest, she started cutting the cloth where a rusty streak of blood trailed down the khaki fabric. "It looks like a puncture wound," she said when the injured area was exposed. "Not a knife. Something small. Maybe an ice pick? Or a pen?"

Jake emerged from the other side of the pit toilet. "I found this behind the outhouse," he said, holding up something in a gloved hand. "I think it has blood on it."

He moved closer and they studied the item he held. "It's a bent coat hanger," Jamie said. "The kind the kids are using to roast marshmallows."

"Were you attacked by one of the campers?" Jake asked.

"Of course not." Even in this dim light, they could see his face redden. He was a big man. Even armed with a coat hanger, a child wouldn't have much of a chance at overcoming him.

"I'm going to look for the camper who was supposedly being attacked," Jamie said, and set off toward the camp.

Jake leaned forward to take a closer look at Scott's face. "Are those scratches on your cheek?" he asked.

Scott put a hand to his face. "I must have scraped it on a branch. We need to have the trees trimmed. Those low-hanging branches are a hazard in the dark." He winced as Hannah flushed the wound on his thigh with saline.

"I don't think you're going to need stitches, Mr. Sprague," Hannah said. "Are you up to date on your tetanus vaccine?"

"Yes," he said. He shoved to his feet. "I'll be fine."

"You need to be careful of infection," Hannah said.

"I promise I'll put some antibiotic ointment on it when I get to my office." He looked down at his torn trousers. "I need to change."

"Are you sure you don't have any other injuries?" Hannah said. "Let me check your blood pressure. You look very pale."

"I'm fine," Scott said with more force. Then more weakly he continued, "Thank you for your concern, but I really need to take care of my campers."

"No," Jake said. "You need to come to your office with us."

"I don't have time for that now," Scott said. "And you need to find the man who attacked that child and injured me."

"We're looking for the camper. In the meantime, we need you to answer some questions."

"I've already answered your questions. Over and over again," Scott said. "None of them are helping you find Olivia. Or stop people like this man who attacked me."

"We have some different questions now," Jake said. He took Scott's arm as Declan moved in on the other side. "These are about what really happened here tonight."

AARON, GAGE and two other deputies searched all around the lodge and found no one.

"It doesn't even feel like anyone has been here," Gage said when they reconvened in front of the lodge. His phone beeped and he pulled it out, "It's Jake," he said, after glancing at the screen. "Yeah?" he answered. He listened for a moment, then ended the call. "I have to go," he said. "The rest of you, get back to the bonfire. You're looking for an upset kid who may or may not have been attacked by the pit toilets an hour or so ago."

"The kid Scott saved?" Aaron asked.

"Supposedly," Gage said. "We need to talk to them and find out what really happened."

Aaron pulled out his phone and texted Willa:

Sorry I went awol. Something came up. Headed back to the bonfire now.

She didn't answer, but who knew if she could even hear her phone, with all the noise around the fire now. Someone was leading a sing-along, complete with shouted choruses and fits of laughter. He circled the firepit, alert for Willa's blond hair or the pink of the sweater she had been wearing.

Halfway around, he met Shane, who was also searching. "Have you seen Willa?" Aaron asked him.

"No. I'm looking for one of the campers. Tall, thin, long brown hair. Her name is Kelli, one of the older girls. Another girl said she saw her headed toward the pit toilets right before all the commotion with Scott."

"I thought Scott said it was a little kid he rescued—a little boy," Aaron said.

Shane shrugged. "I don't know about that. But if this girl was near the pit toilets about the time the attack happened, she might have seen something."

"Okay. I'll look for her, too." He had an uneasy feeling in his stomach. Maybe Willa had gotten angry that he had ditched her and decided to go home. She could have called Gary to pick her up, or caught a ride with someone else. He tried texting her again.

Sorry I was such a bad date. We thought we had something.

He stared at the screen, willing her to answer. But there was no reply.

"Have you two seen anything?"

He turned to see Jamie walking toward him. "I found another girl who said she saw Kelli running toward her cabin about half an hour ago," Jamie said. "She said Kelli looked really upset."

"Which cabin?" Shane asked.

"Pine Cabin—the same cabin Olivia was in. Can one of you come with me to talk to her?"

"I'll go," Aaron said. Anything to distract him from worrying about Willa.

He followed Jamie across the campground. "There are a lot of dark hiding places out here in the woods," Jamie said. "I'm thinking a girl wouldn't venture out here alone unless she was really upset about something."

"Being attacked by a stranger would qualify as upsetting," Aaron agreed.

Light shone through the front windows of the cabin, a rectangular log structure with green shutters. They knocked on the door. After a moment, the door eased open and a slender girl with long brown hair looked out. Her eyes widened when she saw Jamie and Aaron.

"Did you catch him?" she blurted.

"Catch who?" Aaron asked.

"You two are cops, right?"

"We are," Jamie said. "Can we come in and talk to you for a minute? I'm Jamie and this is Aaron. Are you Kelli?"

She looked past them. "There's no one else with you, is there?"

"No," Jamie said.

The girl held the door open wider and stepped back to let them pass. She moved over to a bunk and sat on the edge of the mattress. "Where's Mr. Sprague?" she asked.

"Mr. Sprague is with some other deputies," Jamie said.

Kelli gnawed at her thumbnail. "Are they, like, arresting him?"

"Do you think we need to?" Jamie asked, her voice gentle.

Kelli burst into tears. Jamie moved to her side. Kelli leaned into her, sobbing. Jamie patted her back.

"If Scott has done something to hurt you or anyone else, we will arrest him," she said. "You don't have to worry about him hurting you again."

Aaron sat opposite on another bunk, feeling helpless in the face of this child's obvious pain.

"Aaron, could you get us some tissues?" Jamie asked.

He found a box of tissues on a table by the door and brought them to her. Kelli pulled out several and blew her nose.

"When you're ready, could you tell us what happened?" Jamie asked.

"Yes." Kelli's voice was stronger than Aaron had expected, tinged with anger. She blotted her eyes and raised her head. "I want to tell you what happened. I want him to get everything he deserves."

"We want that, too," Jamie said.

"Mr. Sprague is a creep and a perv," Kelli said. "He pretends to be all concerned about us campers but really he's just waiting for a chance to grope one of us. I even fell for his nice act, then, a couple of days ago, he cornered me on the way back from evening assembly. He said he needed help with something in his office. The next thing he had me in there and he was trying to feel me up and stuff."

"That must have been terrifying," Jamie said.

"It was." She looked at Jamie with pleading eyes. "At first I was just, too grossed out to even move. Then I kind of woke up and tried to fight him off, but he said no one would hear me. There isn't anybody in that part of camp at that time of evening. Everyone is back here at the cabins, getting ready for bed."

Fresh tears welled in her eyes. Aaron fought down a rage that squeezed his chest.

"Did Mr. Sprague threaten you if you told anyone?" Jamie asked.

Kelli nodded. "Yes. And not just me." She bowed her head, her fingers shredding the tissue. "I have a little sister. She's eight. She's in Willow Cabin. Mr. Sprague said if I didn't do what he wanted—everything he wanted—he would hurt her." She began to sob again.

Jamie's expression remained neutral, but Aaron sensed the anger radiating off of her. "Thank you for telling us," she said. "I know it's not something that's easy to talk about. What happened tonight?"

Kelli sniffed and blotted her eyes. "He sent me a message this afternoon. He said I needed to wait by the bonfire and when he signaled, I was to meet him by the pit toilets—the one with the burned-out light. I didn't want to do it, but I didn't have a choice. I couldn't let him hurt Emma."

Jamie handed her more tissue and waited until once more her tears subsided. She looked at Aaron. "You'd better notify Gage."

Aaron moved toward the door to step outside to make the call, but before he could open it someone knocked.

Declan stood on the top step, a plastic bag in one hand. "I found this on the ground by the pit toilet," he said. "It might be the girl's phone. It keeps buzzing, but I couldn't figure out how to unlock it."

Aaron stared at the phone. Flowered case, with a purple stick-on socket on the back. "That looks like Willa's phone," he said.

"What would Willa's phone be doing behind the pit toilet?" Declan asked.

Aaron took out his phone and punched in Willa's number. The phone in the bag vibrated.

He took the bag and turned back to Kelli and Jamie. Even though he knew the answer, he asked Kelli, "Is this your phone?"

She looked at the phone in the bag. "No."

He kept his voice even. "Was there anyone else there at the pit toilets tonight, when you went to meet Mr. Sprague?" he asked.

"No." She wet her lips. "I mean, not at first. He was waiting for me and he...he tried to kiss me. I tried not to struggle, but he was holding me so tightly, he was hurting me. I cried out, and I scratched at his face. He didn't like that. He slapped me. And then someone shouted at us."

"Who shouted at you?" Aaron asked.

"A woman. I didn't get a very good look at her. She had blond hair, and she ran toward us. Mr. Sprague let me go and I ran. I ran all the way back here." She looked at Jamie. "Did I do something wrong?"

"No. Of course not." Jamie patted her hand and sent Aaron a questioning look.

"I'm sure this is Willa's phone," he said. "I think she was the blonde woman who shouted at Mr. Sprague."

"Willa is the nurse who gave the first aid class to campers yesterday," Jamie said. "Do you think this woman was her?"

"I don't know," Kelli said. "It was dark and I didn't get a good look. I just wanted to get away."

"I've been searching for Willa and I can't find her," Aaron said. "After Kelli left, Scott would have attacked her. He would have wanted to stop her from telling anyone what she had seen."

Aaron was a cop. He had been in scary situations before. Once a burglar had held a razor to his throat, the sharp blade nicking him and drawing blood. He had talked down drunks armed with broken beer bottles, and done traffic stops with semitrucks whizzing by inches from his back. But never had fear hit him the way it did now—clutching his throat and threatening to pull him under.

Jamie studied him, then pulled out her radio. "We need to talk to Gage," she said. "And we need to talk to Scott."

Chapter Seventeen

"You have to bend down kind of low to get in here, but I promise it's all right." Olivia put her hand on top of Willa's head and urged her to crouch down farther to squeeze into a narrow opening between two boulders. Willa did so, crawling on hands and knees through a short passage, gravel digging into her knees. Just when she was sure she couldn't go any farther—the opening was too narrow—she felt fresh air against her face, and popped out into a wider space.

Olivia scooted in after her. She took something from her pack, then switched on a little LED light and set it on a tree stump. Willa looked around at a circular space, about four feet across with a floor of smooth sand. She raised her eyes to the ceiling, dark and flat. "That's a tarp up there," Oliva said. "I stole it from a wood pile at camp. I don't think anyone has even missed it yet. The outside has about a foot of leaves over it. You'd have to dig down to even see it. It took me most of a day to construct it, but once I had it in place I didn't have to keep moving."

There was no missing the pride in the girl's voice.

"I'm impressed," Willa said truthfully. "Did you make the brush shelter in the national forest, too?"

"I did. But I only spent one night there before a hiker found it. I left to take a look around and when I came back,

I saw a woman nosing around. I knew I had to have someplace better. Someplace closer to camp, so I could keep track of what was going on." She knelt and opened her pack again. "Would you like some tea? I have a little stove and I can heat water. I only have one cup but we can share."

"Tea would be good." Willa sat with her back against the wall, knees bent, and watched the girl unpack a single-burner stove, like the kind used by backpackers. Olivia turned the knob and hit a striker and the stove lit. Then she filled a small metal cup from a bottle stowed in the side of the pack and set it over the flame to heat. She took a bag with what looked like shredded leaves in it and carefully sprinkled some in the cup. She looked up and caught Willa watching her.

"It's just dried mint and some clover. It tastes better than you might think." Olivia sat back and they waited for the water to boil. "How's your ankle?" she asked after a moment.

Willa had forgotten all about her ankle. She felt it. Only a little puffy. "Not bad."

"Did you hit your face when you fell?" Olivia asked. "Your lip is all swollen, and I think you're going to have a black eye."

Willa touched the corner of her mouth and winced. She patted the puffiness around her eye. "Someone attacked me," she said. "By the pit toilet. He was... I think he was molesting a girl. One of the campers. I yelled at him and he let her go and went after me."

"Oh God." Olivia buried her face in her hands, and her shoulders began to shake.

Alarmed, Willa crawled to her. "What's wrong? What did I say?"

Olivia raised her head and wiped at her eyes. Then she

leaned forward and switched off the burner. "That will need to steep a minute." The only sign that she was still upset was the way her hand trembled as she pulled it away from the stove. She took a deep breath and looked at Willa. "I'll bet it was Scott Sprague who hit you. He hit me, too. But he killed Trevor. Or, I'm pretty sure that's what he was doing when I saw him. That was why I had to run away. As long as he's still walking around free I can't go back."

"Mr. Sprague killed Trevor Lawson?" Willa asked.

Olivia nodded. "I think so."

"But why?" Willa asked.

"Because Trevor interrupted Mr. Sprague when he was feeling me up behind the pit toilet, just like you interrupted him today. It was what Mr. Sprague did. He took girls back there on bonfire nights—and other times, too—and kissed you and fondled you and…and other things. If you cried too loud or threatened to tell, he would hurt you even more. He said if I told anyone what he did he would say I lied and no one would believe him. He said he had done the same thing before. I knew he was telling the truth because I had heard that the year before some girl accused him of molesting her and he called her a liar with a sex addiction and her parents believed him and not her. I figured the same thing would happen to me. Everyone knew I had been sent to camp because I was seeing an older boy. But the thing is, Jared and I never actually had sex. Nobody believed that, either."

She leaned forward and picked up the cup and passed it to Willa. "It should be ready now. Sorry, you kind of have to strain out the leaves with your teeth."

Willa tested the tea, more out of politeness than anything else. "It's not bad," she said.

"It would be better if I had sugar, but I forgot to take any of that. I have a couple of cookies, though." She dug in her bag and pulled out a bundle wrapped in plastic. "Stella left them for me a couple of days ago. She didn't know I was the one taking the food she left but she really helped me out. She didn't leave anything today, though. I hope she didn't get in trouble."

"You eat the cookies," Willa said when Olivia offered her one. "I ate at the bonfire."

"Smores!" Olivea groaned. "What I wouldn't give for one of those."

Willa set aside the tea. "How did you learn to do all of these things?" she asked. "The shelter and the tea and everything."

"From books, mostly. I like to read adventure stories. And some of the stuff I just figured out on my own." She popped a piece of cookie into her mouth and chewed, then swallowed.

"Did you make the trap in the woods?" Willa asked. "The pit with the branches over it?"

"You know about that?" She rose up on her knees, her expression excited. "I made that after I saw Mr. Sprague sneaking around the woods, looking for me. I was really hoping he'd end up in that hole, unable to get out, and nobody around to hear him yell. Too bad it didn't work."

"Someone else fell into it," Willa said. "A man who was searching for you. He broke his leg and a couple of ribs."

Olivia looked stricken. "Oh no!" She flapped her hands. "That wasn't supposed to happen! I didn't think anyone else would be out there. Oh gosh, I'm so sorry. Is he going to be okay?"

"He'll be okay. But why would you make a trap like that?"

"I just saw the hole and thought it would be perfect." She groaned. "I really only wanted to get back at Mr. Sprague. I didn't think about anything else. What happened to the trap?"

"Sheriff's deputies marked it so no one else will fall in."
"Good."

"Are there any other traps in the woods we should know about?" Willa asked.

"None, I promise."

"How about other shelters or hiding places?"

"None of those, either. Once I fixed up this place, I didn't need anything else." She sighed. "It was almost fun, at first, figuring things out and building stuff. But it's getting old."

"So many people were searching for you," Willa said. "How did you keep from being found?"

"It wasn't as hard as you might think. Big groups of people in the woods make a lot of noise. Most of the time I could hear them coming from a long way away. I doubled back behind them and hid in places they had already looked." She frowned. "The dogs were harder to avoid. I did a lot of things like walking in streams or across rocky places. I climbed trees and walked along fence rails. It was kind of a game. I think they did pick up my scent a few times, but they always lost it. As miserable as the rain was, I think it helped destroy my scent."

She rested her chin on her upraised knees. "I saw Mr. Sprague looking for me a couple of times. He was alone, sneaking around. He was right by one of my hiding places one time and I thought I would die before he finally left—I was so scared. I knew if he found me, he would kill me." She lowered her voice to a deep, nasal timbre, not unlike the camp owner's. "Poor little Olivia, she had an accident in the woods. Isn't it terrible?"

"I'm glad you're okay," Willa said. She hesitated, then added, "Do you mind telling me what happened with Trevor?"

"I don't mind. I planned all along to tell someone, as

soon as I was sure I was safe from Mr. Sprague." She sat back, considering. "Last week, at the bonfire, Trevor came around the corner of the outhouse and his flashlight lit up the whole scene—gross Mr. Sprague leaning over me, trying to stick his tongue down my throat, him with his pants already undone. I screamed and Mr. Sprague turned around. I ran away, but then I had to stop and look back. I was hoping to see Mr. Sprague on the ground, being beaten to a pulp by Trevor, who wasn't a really big guy, but he wasn't little, either, and he was a lot younger and stronger than Mr. Sprague. Instead, I saw Mr. Sprague punch Trevor, and Trevor went down like a fallen tree. Then Mr. Sprague dragged him over to this cabin nobody uses anymore. A night watchman used to use it, I guess, though now the kids just make up stories about how the watchman hanged himself there and the place is haunted. That didn't really happen, did it?"

Willa shook her head. She had no idea, but she didn't want to interrupt the flow of Olivia's story. The girl finished her cookie and picked crumbs off her lap. "After Mr. Sprague hauled Trevor to the cabin, I sneaked up and watched through the window. He'd switched on one of those LED lights we all carry around, like this one." She nodded to the light on the ground between them. "Mr. Sprague tied Trevor to a chair, then left for a little bit. He locked the door behind him. I tried to break the lock but I couldn't, and I had to run hide again when I heard Sprague coming back. Trevor was awake by that time, and throwing himself around, trying to break free. Mr. Sprague pulled out a really big pistol and put it to Trevor's head. I thought I was going to die right there. If he had shot Trevor, I might have—not died, maybe, but I bet I would have passed out. Instead, Sprague handed Trevor this big bottle of whiskey and made him drink it. He held the gun there until Trevor had drained about half of it. Then Mr. Sprague pulled his head back and forced something down his throat. Maybe pills or poison or something. Then he made Trevor drink some more."

She bowed her head and fell silent. Willa waited a moment, then prompted, "What happened next?"

Olivia blew out a breath. "I stayed there watching a really long time, until Mr. Sprague untied Trevor and led him to the parking lot and helped him into his car. I thought everything would be all right then. He was letting Trevor go. So I sneaked back to my cabin and went to sleep."

"And the next day you found out Trevor had died?"

She nodded. "Yeah. I saw his brother, Wade, out by the boat house. I could tell he'd been crying. I asked him what was wrong and he told me about his brother. I wanted so bad to tell him Trevor didn't commit suicide—that Mr. Sprague had gotten him drunk and poisoned him. But then Mrs. Mason came up and told me I needed to get back to my cabin. Everybody knows she's Mr. Sprague's stooge, so I couldn't say anything with her standing there."

"What do you mean, Mrs. Mason is Mr. Sprague's stooge?"

"Oh, she's got this huge crush on him. You can tell by the way she moons over him. She does anything he tells her, and she's always spying on us and reporting back to him, even though he either ignores her or orders her around like his personal servant. But if any little rule gets broken, he'll end up hearing about it, and we know she's the one telling him. I'd feel sorry for her if it wasn't so gross."

"Why did you have to run away?" Willa asked.

"Because Mr. Sprague sent me a note to meet him Sunday night. He did that sometimes. I had to sneak out and go or something horrible would happen. I know it wasn't smart or brave of me or anything, but that man scares me. So I went and let him do his nasty thing and kept my mouth shut. I figured camp would be over in a few weeks and I'd never have to see him again."

She fiddled with her shoelaces. Willa wanted to reach out and pull her close, to tell the girl that none of this was her fault. But would those words from a stranger mean anything?

Olivia looked at Willa again, determination in her eyes. "When I got word that Mr. Sprague wanted to see me that night, I was terrified. I figured he would kill me, the way he killed Trevor. He knew I could tell everyone he was the last person who had been with Trevor, even if he didn't know I had seen what he had done in that cabin. It would be a lot harder for him to make people believe I was lying about something like that."

"So you decided to leave instead?"

"Yeah. I took what food I could from dinner and stuffed it in my pockets, then took an extra blanket and some water and camped out in the woods. The next day I decided I could do better and took a sleeping bag and a pack and more food from the shed. I had to break into the building but it wasn't that hard. That door is really old and kind of flimsy."

"They found a shirt," Willa said. "With your blood on it."

"Oh yeah, that." Olivia made a face. "I really wanted the cops to take a good look at Mr. Sprague. I knew I wasn't the first girl he had bothered, so I thought if they started asking questions, someone would say something. So I took one of my old shirts and ripped it up and put that blood on it."

"You put your own blood on it?" Willa couldn't keep the horror from her voice.

"Gross, right? But we had a first aid class and I remembered one of the things they said was that head wounds bleed a lot, even if they're not serious. So I stabbed my forehead with a pair of scissors." She pointed to an inch-wide cut on her forehead, already almost healed over. "It hurt so bad! And I felt pretty stupid. But it did bleed a lot, and I wiped it all up with that shirt and shoved it under the edge of Mr. Sprague's house. It was raining so hard I just hoped the rain wouldn't wash all the blood away before someone found it. But then they did find it and they didn't even look at Sprague."

"So many people were searching for you," Willa said. "Why didn't you go to one of them and tell them what happened?"

"Because I figured the first thing they would do is take me back to camp, where Mr. Sprague would make a big deal about me being a runaway juvenile delinquent who made up lies because I didn't want to get in trouble. And then when all the cops left he would strangle me in my sleep or something."

"They're going to be looking for me now," Willa said. Aaron would be looking for her. He would know she wouldn't leave without an explanation.

"I know." She picked at the frayed hem of her jeans. "But they'll believe you. You're an adult. So then maybe they'll believe me, too."

"They'll believe you," Willa said. She slid over until she was next to the girl and put her arm around her. Olivia had done a good job of surviving on her own, but for all her maturity, she was still a little girl.

She laid her head on Willa's shoulder. After a while, she said, "It was fun at first, hiding from everyone, making this hiding place and stealing food. But I'm really tired now, and I think I'm ready to go home."

"Do you know how to get back to the camp from here?"

"Yes. But we need to wait until morning. Trying to get anywhere in the dark is dangerous. I fell into a gully one evening and it took me hours to climb out."

"Promise you'll go with me back to the camp in the morning," Willa said.

"I promise." She yawned. "If I spread out my sleeping bag, we can both sleep on it. It's better than the hard ground. And I have the blanket from my bunk."

They made their bed and Olivia turned out the little lantern. Soon she was sleeping, breathing evenly next to Willa. But Willa lay awake, staring into the darkness, praying for morning to come soon.

KELLI AGREED TO come with Aaron and Jamie to speak with Gage. "I figure I'm safer with you guys than here in this cabin by myself," Kelli said.

"We won't leave you alone until we're certain you're okay," Jamie said. "But Sergeant Walker needs to hear your story so we can take Mr. Sprague into custody. Aaron and I can tell him what you said, but it will be better if he hears it from you. And he may have more questions for you."

"I can talk to him." She stood, then hesitated. "Can I make sure Emma is okay, first? I mean, what if Mr. Sprague was so mad after I ran away that he went after her?" All color drained from her face and Jamie reached to steady her. "I just now thought of that."

"I'll find Emma," Declan said. "Do you know where she is?"

"If the bonfire is still going, she'll be with the younger girls. Their counselor is a woman named Sage. Or they'll all be in Willow Cabin. It's the cabin farthest from the lake and closest to the parking lot."

"We'll be up by the lodge," Jamie said to Declan. "If you could bring Emma to us."

Aaron called Gage and let him know they were bringing Kelli to speak with him. "Scott is in his office, with Ryker watching over him," he told the others after the call ended. "Gage is going to meet us outside the lodge."

Gage was waiting outside when they arrived, the overhead security light casting ghastly shadows over his features.

"Sergeant Walker, this is Kelli," Jamie introduced the girl. "She needs to report a crime."

"Yeah. A crime." Kelli lifted her chin. "Mr. Sprague has been molesting girls at the camp. He molested me, and threatened me, and I think he did the same with Olivia. That's probably why she ran away."

Gage glanced at Aaron, who nodded. "You have a statement about all this?" he asked Jamie.

"Yes, sir. It wasn't a stranger who attacked a camper behind the pit toilet tonight. It was Mr. Sprague."

"Did you stab Mr. Sprague with a coat hanger?" Gage asked Kelli.

"Is that what happened to him?" Kelli shook her head. "I didn't do it, but I wish I had."

"I think Willa stabbed Scott," Aaron said. "She heard Kelli cry out and went to investigate. She shouted at Scott to stop and that startled him enough that Kelli was able to get away. But now Willa is missing. Declan found her phone behind the pit toilet." He held up the evidence bag with the phone inside.

"Where is Scott now?" Jake asked.

"He's in his office," Gage said. "Ryker is keeping him there. His story about rescuing a camper who was being attacked by a mysterious stranger didn't add up to me."

"Don't believe anything he says," Kelli said. "He lies all the time."

Gage's radio crackled and he answered the summons. "Sergeant, I've over here at Willow Cabin. Emma Agnew is fine. No sign of Scott."

Gage sent a questioning look to Jamie, but Kelli answered him. "Emma is my little sister. Mr. Sprague threatened her if I didn't do what he wanted. I asked the deputy to make sure she was okay."

"You say you think Mr. Sprague was molesting Olivia Pryor?" Gage asked.

"I don't have any proof," Kelli said. "But he didn't start bothering me until she was gone. And why else would she run away? If it hadn't been for Emma, I might have tried to leave, too."

"We need to contact your parents," Gage said. "Where do they live?"

"Pennsylvania," Kelli said.

Gage checked his watch. "It's after midnight there."

"I can contact them, sir," Jamie said. "Kelli can speak with them. I'm sure they'll want to come down as soon as possible."

"What do I do until they get here?" Kelli asked. "I don't want to stay here at camp."

"We'll speak with your parents," Jamie said. "But if it's all right with them, you and Emma can stay with me and my husband. He's a law enforcement officer, too. My sister and our infant daughter live with us. You'll be safe there."

Kelli smiled. "It will be like having two bodyguards."

"Speak with the Agnews," Gage said. "I'll see to Sprague."

"There's a side parlor we can use to make the call, over there." Kelli pointed to a doorway to their left.

When Jamie and Kelli had left, Aaron turned to Gage. "I want to talk to Scott," he said.

"What about?" Gage asked.

"I want to ask him about Willa. What happened when she interrupted him and Kelli?"

"He may not tell you anything."

"I still want to ask."

Gage nodded. "Come with me."

Ryker stepped aside to let them into the office. Scott was seated behind his desk, fresh scratches on his face glowing red in the bright overhead light that bleached the rest of his skin the color of a puffball mushroom.

"I've telephoned my lawyer and I don't have to say anything else to you," he said.

"All I want to know is where is Willa?" Aaron asked.

Scott frowned. "Who is Willa? We don't have a camper by that name."

"She's not a camper," Aaron said. "She's a nurse. Her phone was found behind that pit toilet. Where you were fighting with your alleged assailant."

"There is no 'alleged' assailant. I was attacked."

"How's the leg?" Gage asked. "I'll bet it hurts."

"No thanks to you."

"You could have gone to the hospital with the paramedics," Gage said.

"I don't need a hospital."

"I don't know." Gage peered over the desk at Scott's leg. "Those marshmallow roasting sticks probably aren't the most sanitary things."

Sprague glared at him, then rose. "I'm going to bed."

"First, would you like to tell us about Kelli?"

"I don't know any Kelli."

"She's a camper here," Gage said. "Long brown hair. Twelve years old. She says you were molesting her behind the pit toilet when Willa Reynolds interrupted you. She ran away. You struggled with Willa and she stabbed you with a coat hanger used to roast marshmallows."

Scott's expression remained impassive. "I don't know what you're talking about. And that's all I'm saying until I see my lawyer."

"Fine." Gage turned to Ryker. "You and Shane take him to the station and book him."

"Book me for what?" Scott roared. "I've done nothing wrong."

"Mr. Sprague, you're being charged with sexual assault of a child by one in a position of trust, for a start. There may be other charges forthcoming. You have the right to remain silent…" Gage recited the full Miranda warning while Scott gaped at him.

Ryker moved forward and cuffed Scott's hands behind his back. Scott remained silent, though he glared at them all, eyes dark with rage.

Chapter Eighteen

While other deputies took Scott Sprague to jail, Aaron, Jake and Declan stayed behind at the camp to search for Willa. Aaron started by calling Gary. As he listened to the phone ring, he paced, hoping to hear that Willa had found her own way home and was sleeping peacefully. She might be upset with Aaron for deserting her, but she would be safe.

"Hello?" Gary answered. He sounded groggy.

"Gary, this is Aaron. Is Willa there?"

"Why are you asking me? Why not call her? And aren't you supposed to be with her?"

"There was a problem here at the camp and we got separated. She must have dropped her phone, because we found it, but I can't find her. I was hoping she got a ride home with someone else."

"Let me check her room."

Shuffling noises, then a long silence. Aaron began to wonder if the call had disconnected when Gary's voice came back on the line. He sounded wide-awake now. "She's not here. Her bed hasn't been slept in. What's going on? What kind of problem at the camp? Where are you now?"

"I'm still at the camp. Have you heard from Willa at all tonight?"

"No. Not since she left to meet up with you. She said you

were going to the bonfire at the camp to snoop around for more evidence about what might have happened to Olivia. Why isn't Willa with you?"

Aaron blew out a breath. He didn't want to upset Gary, but clearly the man was already upset. "Scott was caught with a camper, one of the older girls, behind one of the pit toilets tonight," he said. "Willa interrupted them. The camper got away and Scott has been arrested, but we can't find Willa."

"Wait—Scott was with a camper. Like—how was he with her?"

"We believe he was molesting her."

"Oh, wow."

"Were there ever rumors about that kind of thing among the staff?"

"No." Aaron pictured Gary shaking his head. "I never heard anything like that. You're saying Willa interrupted them—what happened?"

"We're not sure, except that the camper got away and Willa dropped her phone. There may have been a struggle, but we're not sure."

"What does Scott say?"

"He's not talking."

Gary swore under his breath. "Let me come down there. I can help look for her."

"No. I need you to stay there in case Willa shows up or tries to contact you."

A long silence. Finally Gary said, "All right. But you promise to call me as soon as you know anything."

"I promise." He ended the call and turned to the others. "Her brother hasn't heard from her. Let's go."

But finding their way in the darkness, especially after clouds moved in to cover the moon, proved more difficult than Aaron had imagined. They could detect no indication of which way Willa had gone. After Declan fell on the rocks and Jake got tangled in a stretch of barbed wire fence, they halted.

"We need to wait until daylight," Jake said. "We can get Anna Trent and her search dog, Jacqui, out here, plus we can call in search and rescue to assist. All we're doing now is risking ourselves and possibly obscuring the trail more."

Aaron kicked at the dirt, frustrated. "You're right," he said.

Jake clapped him on the back. "Remember—we caught Scott minutes after Willa surprised him with Kelli. He didn't have time to spirit her away. And there was no blood at the scene but Scott's own, so it's unlikely he hurt her badly."

"Then where is she?" Aaron asked.

"We're going to find her," Jake said. "Tomorrow."

Aaron let them persuade him to get in his truck and leave, but as soon as they were out of sight, he turned around and went back to the camp parking lot. If this was as close as he could be to Willa right now, then this was where he would stay. He pulled a sleeping bag out from the back of the vehicle and spread it on the front seat and crawled in.

He didn't sleep. He didn't even try. Instead, he sat and stared out the windshield, going over the events of the last few hours. How had they missed that Scott was responsible? They could have at least asked the campers if any of the staff had behaved inappropriately toward them. True, there had been no evidence pointing them in that direction, but if they had dug deeper, would they have found some? Was he a bad cop because he hadn't figured this out?

He had so many questions, none of them with answers. But the one that hurt the most kept repeating in his mind: Would Willa forgive him for failing her again?

WILLA WOKE, stiff from sleeping on the floor of the rock shelter, and checked her watch: 6:30 a.m. She sat up, and Olivia stirred beside her.

"What time is it?" the girl asked.

Willa told her and Olivia groaned and pulled the blanket over her head. "I want to get back to camp before everyone wakes up," Willa said. "We can call the sheriff's department before Scott knows what's going on."

Olivia pushed off the blanket. "You're right." She sat up. "I can heat water for tea, but there's nothing for breakfast."

"I'd rather wait until we get to camp." Olivia's herb tea was a poor substitute for real coffee.

Olivia yawned. "Then I'll pack up and we'll get started."

Five minutes later, the girl had the blanket, sleeping bag and little stove shoved into or strapped to her pack. She led the way out of the shelter, pushing the pack in front of her.

Pink streaked the sky as they set off through the woods. Willa pulled her sweater around her in the early-morning chill. Olivia didn't seem to notice, though she slowed her own brisk pace when she noticed Willa limping.

"I forgot about your ankle," Olivia said. "Does it hurt much?"

"Not that much," Willa lied. "I'll be fine once we get to camp." Though she had spoken confidently about the unlikelihood of running into Scott Sprague at this early hour, her memory of the story Olivia had told her about Scott's violence toward Trevor Lawson sent tendrils of fear through her.

"It's not much farther," Olivia said. "I lucked out, finding that hiding place so close to camp. It made it easier to slip over here to steal food and supplies, and keep an eye on Mr. Sprague. And I figured no one would expect me to be so nearby."

A few moments later, they reached a barbed wire fence. Oliva halted and waited for Willa to catch up with her.

"When we cross this, we'll be on Mountain Kingdom property," Olivia said. "Where should we go? Not the office. I don't want to risk seeing Mr. Sprague."

Willa took her hand. "I'm not going to let him hurt you." Though realistically, she knew she couldn't stop him by herself. "We'll avoid Scott, though, and find someone else to help us." Someone who would contact the sheriff's department.

"I'm really nervous about going back," Olivia said. "Mr. Sprague is really evil, and he knows a lot of important people."

"The sheriff and his deputies don't care how important someone is if they've done something wrong." Aaron believed that, and he had said the sheriff was a good man. She took the girl's hand. "And I'm not going to leave you. Not until I'm sure you're safe."

Olivia squeezed her hand. "Thanks." She faced forward again, and took a deep breath. "I'm ready now. Let's do this."

Olivia slipped through the strands of wire, and waited for Willa to follow.

They set out at a faster pace now. "This is my favorite time to come here," Olivia said. "No one is around. You could walk away with half the camp and no one would know."

They made a wide berth around Scott's cabin, then passed the remains of the bonfire, the smell of woodsmoke still hanging in the air. Olivia detoured to grab a partial bag of marshmallows someone had left on a bench in the boat house. She offered the bag to Willa, who declined, but Olivia stuffed two in her mouth.

"Why don't you have a phone?" Olivia asked after she had swallowed the marshmallows. "I just now thought of that. I'm so used to no one around here having a phone, since we all have to give them up when we get here. But you could have called for help."

"I lost it, either when I was struggling with Scott, or when I ran away."

"How did you get away from him?"

"I stabbed him in the thigh with a bent coat hanger I'd been using to roast marshmallows."

Olivia clapped her hand over her mouth to stifle a laugh. "Oh, that's perfect. The only thing better would be if it was still hot—and if you could have aimed a little more toward the center."

Willa smiled, and looked toward the parking lot, then stopped.

"What is it?" Olivia moved in close beside her. "Did you see someone? Is it Sprague?"

"I see someone, but it's not Scott." She took Olivia's hand. "Come on. This is one of the good guys."

Aaron had just climbed out of his truck when he saw them walking toward him. He didn't run, just waited, but when they were close enough, he moved forward and enveloped them both in a hug. Then he stepped back and looked at the girl.

"You must be Olivia."

She nodded.

"I'm Aaron," he said. "Deputy Aaron Ames. We arrested Scott Sprague last night."

Olivia began to sob. Aaron and Willa moved in to hold her, letting her cry until she had no more tears left.

When the girl had quieted, Aaron looked at Willa.

"You're hurt." He started to touch the side of her face, then drew back.

Willa hadn't seen her face, but she could feel the swelling of her lip and around her eye. "Scott hit me pretty good. But it will heal."

"She sprained her ankle, too," Olivia said. "But not before she stabbed Mr. Sprague with a marshmallow roaster."

"That was one of the things that made us suspicious of his story that he had chased off a stranger who was attacking a camper," Aaron said.

"I'm glad you didn't believe him," Olivia said.

"Are you sure you're okay?" Aaron asked Willa. "Do I need to call someone?"

"It's not too bad, really," Willa said. At the moment, the joint was throbbing, but she didn't care. That, too, would heal. "You don't need to call anyone. We just need to get away from here."

"Then let's go." They got into Aaron's truck, Olivia in the back seat, and he headed away from the camp.

Aaron called the sheriff directly. Travis was awake, though he wasn't at the sheriff's department yet.

"What have you got?" the sheriff asked when he answered the phone.

"I have Olivia with me," Aaron said. "And Willa."

The sheriff's relieved sigh was audible down the line. "Are they all right?"

"Willa has a sprained ankle and a few bruises. They're fine otherwise." He gave Olivia a questioning look.

"I'm hungry," Olivia said. Then more softly she added, "And I'd really like to see my parents."

"I'll call your parents," Travis said. "Meet us at the sheriff's department."

Aaron started to protest that Willa needed to see a doctor, but she laid her hand on his.

"Let's take Olivia to her parents," she said. "I'll be fine." She smiled. "And I'm hungry, too."

Mr. and Mrs. Pryor were waiting in the sheriff's office when Aaron, Willa and Olivia arrived. Sylvia Pryor burst into tears and Olivia started crying, too. The others looked on at the touching reunion.

Aaron moved closer to the sheriff. "Where is Scott?" he whispered.

"He's in the jail in Junction," Travis said. "I'm going down there later today to question him, after his lawyer gets here from Denver."

"Do you think he'll tell you anything?"

"Probably not, but we don't need his statement. Between what Kelli has told us and what Olivia will tell us, we shouldn't have any problem proving the charges."

The Pryors finally released their hold on the girl. "I know you're all anxious to be done with this ordeal," Travis said. "But we're going to need a statement from Olivia." He glanced at Willa. "And from you, too."

"Can I at least have breakfast first?" Olivia asked, a plaintive whine edging her words.

"It's on the way," he said.

Aaron wondered what restaurant had agreed to cater breakfast at this hour, but voices rose and the door opened to admit an attractive brunette, followed by office manager Adelaide Kinkaid and two toddlers.

"I hope you like waffles," the younger woman called as she passed.

They followed the women and children into the conference room at the end of the hall, where they began unloading a bin full of food dishes—waffles, scrambled eggs, sausages, hash browns and biscuits.

"This is my wife, Lacey," Travis introduced the younger woman. "And our office manager, Adelaide Kinkaid."

"And this is Casey and Kelsey." Lacey put a hand on the top of each toddler's head. The two children grinned up at them.

"I love waffles," Olivia said. She eyed the spread hungrily. "Thank you."

Aaron realized that he, too, was suddenly ravenous. They all filled their plates, then ate without saying much for the next fifteen or twenty minutes.

Finally, Olivia pushed away her plate. "That was so much better than leftovers and granola bars," she said.

"Is that what you've been eating?" her mother asked.

"It wasn't so bad," Olivia said.

"I don't understand any of this," her mother said. "Would someone please tell us what happened?"

"I'll let Olivia do that," Travis said. "When she's ready."

"I'm ready," Olivia said. "I want to tell you everything."

"Then come with me." Travis stood. Olivia and her parents followed him down the hall to an interview room. "Wait until we're done here," he instructed Willa and Aaron.

They sat alone in the conference room, amid the remains of breakfast. For a long time, neither said anything, too weary or stunned or overwhelmed to speak.

Finally, Aaron turned to her. "I don't have words to describe how glad I was to see you this morning," he said. "I spent the night telling myself you were probably all right, but it's hard not to think of the worst." He stilled as a thought struck him. "You should call Gary. He's probably worried sick."

"I don't have my phone," she said.

"We'll have to get that for you later." He handed her his phone and she called her brother and reassured him she was all right.

"I'll tell you all about it later," she said. "Right now I'm waiting to give a statement to the sheriff." She glanced at Aaron. "Yes, he's with me. I'm using his phone... I will, I promise."

She ended the call and returned his phone. "Gary says hello. A friend from camp already called to tell him Scott was arrested. I told him I'd fill him in on more details later."

"I want to hear everything, too," Aaron said. "But I won't ask you to go through it twice."

"What happened with Scott?" she asked. "How did he end up in custody?"

"The girl he was with when you interrupted his attack on her told us how he had targeted and threatened her. And she told us about you making it possible for her to escape Scott's clutches. She didn't know who you were or what happened after she ran away, but after we found your phone behind the pit toilets we put two and two together. I wanted to believe you had run away and were safe, but we just didn't know. We tried to search for you in the dark, but it's impossible in that rough country." He frowned. "Where were you all night?"

"I was with Olivia. She had a pretty comfortable hideout fixed up in a space between two boulders. She's a remarkable girl."

He glanced down. "How's your ankle?"

"It hurts." She reached down and slipped off her shoe. "I'm sure it's just a sprain, but I should wrap it and keep it elevated."

"Let me see." He beckoned and after a moment's hesitation, she lifted her foot into his lap. He began massaging very gently, his hands warm and soothing. She closed her eyes and sighed. He watched the tension leave her face and his throat tightened as he thought of how close he had come to losing her.

Behind them, someone cleared their throat. Willa opened her eyes and pulled her foot from his lap as he turned to see Adelaide frowning at them. "The sheriff is ready for you now."

Aaron stood. "Thanks, Adelaide. And thanks for the breakfast."

"Yes, thank you," Willa said as she and Aaron slid past her into the hallway.

"OLIVIA'S PARENTS ARE taking her to the hospital to have her examined," Travis said when they joined him in the interview room. "She's a strong little girl." Though he had dark circles beneath his eyes, the sheriff looked energized. They all probably felt that way. After so many days and nights of searching, Olivia had been found safe, and they had a man who had hurt a lot of people behind bars.

"Olivia is amazing," Willa agreed. "I was stumbling around in the dark, lost, and she found me and took me to her hideout, gave me tea, offered to share her food and promised to lead me back to the camp in the morning. While we've all been worried sick about her alone in the wilderness, she was doing a pretty good job of taking care of herself, though she admitted the novelty of the situation was wearing off and she'd be glad to get back to her parents."

"Did she tell you her story?" Travis asked.

"Yes. Does it fit with what you know about Trevor Lawson's death?"

"It does."

"What about Trevor Lawson?" Aaron asked.

"Why don't you tell us what you know." Travis nodded to Willa.

She spread her hands flat on the table in front of her. How to tell everything she had learned in the past twelve hours, without talking for half a day?

"The night before she disappeared, Olivia says Trevor caught Scott molesting her and they fought," she began. "Scott tied up Lawson, made him drink a bottle of whiskey and forced pills down his throat, then walked him to the parking lot. Olivia didn't see anything after that. It sounds like Trevor got into his car, tried to drive home and in his intoxicated state was unable to keep the car on the road."

"Or Scott followed him and made sure he ran off the road," Aaron said.

"That last may be difficult to prove, but we'll investigate it," Travis said. "Maybe someone spotted Scott's car on the road behind Lawson." He turned to Willa once more. "Now let's hear what happened to you."

She told her story, from the moment she spotted Kelli waiting for someone by the bonfire until she and Olivia reunited with Aaron that morning. "After hearing Olivia's and Kelli's stories, I wonder how many other children that man has harmed," she said.

"We'll put out a plea for other current and former campers who may have information to come forward," Travis said. "That may result in more charges." He stood. "Go home, both of you. Get some rest. We'll be in touch if we have further questions."

Aaron rose. "I start night shift this evening," he said. "I'll be in then."

She and Aaron left together "Do you think Olivia is going to be all right?" he asked when they were in his truck, headed back to Eagle Mountain.

"I think so. She's been through a lot, but she's a very resilient girl. And she'll have her parents. They'll get her the help she needs." She shifted toward him. "What about Scott? What's going to happen to him?"

"Some of it depends on how many other girls he molested, and who will testify against him. And on what charges he faces in relation to Trevor's death."

Gary met them at the front door and pulled Willa into a tight hug. When he stepped back, her eyes were shiny with unshed tears. "Did Scott do that to your face?" Gary asked.

She nodded. Gary made a growling sound. "I made coffee," he said. "Come and tell me what happened."

They followed him into the kitchen and sat around the table, and the two men listened as Willa retold Olivia's story of witnessing the torture of Trevor Lawson, and about Sprague's habit of abusing girls.

"Just as well I didn't know that about him," Gary said. "I'd have been tempted to ruin some tools on him."

"With the evidence of the two girls and what we know about Trevor's death, I think Scott will be locked up for a very long time," Aaron said.

Gary wrapped both hands around his coffee mug and studied them both. "Are you two friends again?" he asked.

Aaron looked at Willa, awaiting her answer. She took his hand in hers. "I never stopped loving you," she said.

"Ha! I knew it," Gary said.

Aaron looked at him. "What I can't understand is why you don't hate me," he said. "You almost went to trial for a murder you didn't commit. Even so, your life was pretty much ruined because of the accusations against you."

"I didn't go to trial." He drained his coffee mug and set it down with a thump. "The DA knew a bad case when he saw one. And my life wasn't ruined. I like it here in Eagle

Mountain. The only thing I hated was how miserable Willa was. She was upset about what happened to me and all the harassment, but what she really missed was you."

"I never stopped loving you," he told her. "And I'll never stop apologizing for what I did to tear us apart."

She raised their clasped hands and kissed the back of his. "I'm as much to blame as you are," she said. "So let's forgive each other. We both came to Eagle Mountain to make a fresh start, so let's do that."

"Together."

"Yes, together."

Gary stood. "I'm outta here. Have fun kissing and making up."

He left, and Aaron pulled her to him. "I like the way your brother thinks," he said, and kissed her.

She took his hand and pulled him toward her bedroom. "We have a lot of catching up to do," she said.

Aaron followed willingly. They would never get back the months they had lost, but they had years to build a love that would last.

Epilogue

New Evidence Leads to Killer

Waterbury police announced today that they have charged Albert Wayne Terriot with the murder of Rachel Sherman two years ago. Rachel was abducted from Deer Hollow Youth Camp and her body was later found in a nearby creek. She had been strangled. Though police had identified several persons of interest in their initial investigation of the murder, they were never able to find proof of the real killer. A review of the case by the department's newly formed Cold Case Squad this year led to the discovery of previously untested items found at the crime scene. This led to the construction of a DNA profile that was eventually linked to Terriot. The now-fifty-eight-year-old Terriot was never on law enforcement's radar as a suspect before this new DNA evidence linked him to the crime.

Police Detective Darrel Green said law enforcement now believe Terriot was the mysterious vagrant living in the woods near the camp that several campers told stories about at the time. Law enforcement was unable to find any proof of the vagrant's existence at that time and dismissed the story as something children invented to scare each other.

Terriot was convicted of an attack on another minor child in Chester, Vermont, last year and is currently serving a fifteen-year sentence for that crime. Washington County District Attorney Randall Freed says he expects Terriot to be tried for Rachel's murder some time next year.

"Do you feel like a big weight is off your shoulders?" Willa asked Gary when she met him for lunch the day after Aaron sent her a link to the story about Albert Terriot's arrest.

"Yeah," Gary said. He traced a line of condensation down his water glass with one thumb. "I told myself I was past all that, but knowing they'll never come back and try to pin the crime on me is a big relief."

"For me, too," she admitted. "I always worried about you."

"I'm good. What about you? Things going okay with Aaron?"

"They are. We're good together." She glanced down, unable to stop admiring the sapphire solitaire he had recently given her, two months to the day after she had moved in with him.

"So when's the wedding?" Gary asked.

"We're waiting to schedule it until after Bethany's wedding. We don't want to take any attention away from her. What about you? You're not too lonely in the house without me there?"

"I like my privacy. Always have. And it's easier to sleep during the day without someone else there."

She made a face. "How long will you be on night shift?"

"Don't know. Until they hire someone with less experience than me. But I like it. Emergency dispatch isn't as busy at night around here, so it's a good way to ease into the job."

"But you still like the work?" She tried to keep the concern out of her voice. Gary didn't like it when he suspected her of babying him.

"Yeah, I do. It's not something I ever thought I'd be doing, but it's really interesting. And I'm helping people, which is good, too." He pointed a french fry at her. "I'm pretty sure I only got the position because Aaron recommended me. But he won't admit it."

"He still feels guilty about accusing you of murder."

"That's in the past now. It all worked out. And I'm happy you're happy."

"I am." Happier than she would have thought possible. "He's a good man," she said.

"He is. And he's lucky to have you."

"What about you?" she asked. "Are you seeing anyone? There's a new nurse at the clinic…"

He shook his head. "Don't go there," he said. "I'll find my own dates, thank you very much."

"All right. All right." She would never stop wanting to look after her little brother, but she was willing to relax, for now. Gary seemed to be doing well, and she wanted to focus on her own life, and the future. With Aaron, and, if things worked out, their children.

"You've gone all dreamy-eyed again," Gary said. He laughed. "It's good to see it."

She only smiled and nodded. Life was good, and she wasn't going to take that for granted for a single moment.

* * * * *

KILLER ON THE HOMESTEAD

NICOLE HELM

For baseball fans.

Chapter One

Duncan Kirk stood in the front yard of his childhood home while his dad chattered on about the improvements they'd made to the old foreman's cabin.

He would have rented a car and driven himself, or hell, bought one, but he'd only just gotten cleared to move from an immobilizer to a soft sling for his shoulder. The drive would have been too long and too painful on his own.

He could have hired a driver, but no matter how much money he had to spare, his parents would have seen it as an insult.

So his father had picked him up at the airport and driven him…home.

Funny to think of Bent County, Wyoming, as home when he'd barely spent more than a handful of holidays at his family's ranch since he'd left for college.

But it was home, all the same. Because baseball had been home for these odd fifteen years, and now it was gone. Duncan hadn't really thought about or missed the ranch or Wyoming in all this time, but now that he was here…

It was surprisingly comforting.

The house didn't look the same. Nothing really did. Bent County had expanded and grown, and his parents' ranch had come along with the times.

But still, it was nothing like his house back in LA, his *life* in California. The life he was returning to was nothing like the world he'd been living in for almost half his life.

Six months ago, he'd been pitching in front of a sold-out crowd in Dodger Stadium. World Series. Game seven. The moment every little kid who loves baseball dreams of. It was supposed to be his crowning achievement. Oh, he'd thought he had a few years left in him, but he knew he was reaching the peak of what he could do.

Age would take him eventually, but not yet. Or so he'd thought.

He'd gone through his normal warm-up, been amped and buzzed at the noise of the home crowd. He'd visualized a complete-game shutout, obviously. He wasn't too greedy to think of a perfect game. He'd have been happy with anything that resulted in a win, but in the pregame, it was all about seeing the end. Knowing it was within his grasp.

He'd taken the field. Stared down the intimidating lead-off hitter known for his power *and* speed. Then he'd thrown one pitch, felt a terrifying *snap* in his shoulder that had sent a numbness down his entire arm, and watched the ball sail over the catcher's head.

He'd come out of the game. His team had lost.

And his career was over.

Really over. The doctors had made that clear. He might get his shoulder back to functioning in a somewhat normal capacity, with lots of work and years of healing, but not the kind of shape that could throw a ball over eighty miles an hour, and with the kids coming up these days topping triple digits, he didn't have a prayer.

Everything he'd worked for since he could remember was gone. It was always coming for him, that inevitable end. He just wished he'd had some *say* in the when, and the how.

Instead, he was back in Wyoming. Still a young man, all things considered, but feeling old and wrung out.

When his mother opened the front door and stepped onto the porch while drying her hands on a dishrag, a wave of love and nostalgia swept over him strong enough to make him smile and forget the dull pain in his shoulder.

He walked up to the porch as she walked down the stairs. She enveloped him in a tight hug, though she was careful about his left shoulder. "Welcome home, sweetheart."

For a moment, he just stayed there. He didn't know what the hell to do with his life without baseball, but his steady, stable parents and the sight of the ranch that had been in their family for well over a century reminded him that he'd figure it out.

He pulled back, smiled down at his mother. "Good to see you, Mom."

"You would have seen me sooner if you'd let me fly down for your surgery," she said, swatting him with the dish towel. "Come on now, dinner's waiting."

It was four o'clock in the afternoon, but he wouldn't say no to his mother's cooking. He walked inside, Dad trailing behind and bringing in his bags, even though Duncan had told him he'd handle it.

It was going to take some getting used to, being back with his parents who did as they pleased. But at least he wasn't staying in the main house. None of them would survive that. The cabin that had been built for a foreman generations back would suit. A lot smaller and more rustic than he was used to, but that was fine.

He took a seat at the dining-room table Mom had already set. He let her fuss, mostly because she liked it and partly because his shoulder was killing him. It was time for another painkiller, but he needed to eat before he took the pill.

And to not take it around his parents. His mother would fuss no matter what, but he wanted to keep the fussing to a minimum. If she knew he was still in a lot of pain...

Well, he'd be back in his childhood bedroom, and that wasn't going to fly.

They ate together much like they did when he came home for Thanksgiving or Christmas. Dad talked about the ranch. Mom caught him up on the goings-on in Bent County, though he only remembered half the names she mentioned. The Youngs still lived next door, though Tim had died and Joan had moved to Florida. Their daughters ran the ranch now, though mostly the oldest, Audra.

He remembered Audra as a serious girl with serious eyes, a year or two behind him in school. The younger sister, Rosalie, had been the polar opposite. He remembered, with some fondness, when she'd punched one of his high-school teammates for trying to cop a feel on the bus.

She was a private investigator, according to Mom, at some place in Wilde. Duncan wasn't surprised at that. The main things he remembered about Rosalie Young were her red hair and the way she always liked to stick her nose into trouble.

Mom told him about an issue with a cousin of theirs not too long ago, and even bigger trouble a while back, when the mysterious Hudson family disappearance had been solved after years of being a cold case. Which had led to the gruesome discovery of years of dead bodies in a cave in the state park.

Mom claimed she'd told him about all this already, but he didn't remember it. In fairness, he didn't pay attention to much aside from baseball when the season was in full swing. Or in the offseason, when he was already planning on the next season.

Now there was nothing to plan for.

He really thought he'd moved a little closer to acceptance in the past few months of doctor's appointments and discussions of options, then surgery and the inevitable bad news, but something about being home was like finally fully admitting defeat. Even more so than the retirement announcement he'd had to make.

He was *not* going to deal with that horrible sinking feeling at his parents' dinner table. He'd wait until he was alone in the cabin, tucked away for the night.

Dad's phone chimed, and Duncan was surprised to see his father check it without one admonition from his mother. They shared a look and Dad scooted back in his chair.

"I've got to go check on some things. I'll be back."

Duncan watched his father go, then looked at his mother, who was staring very hard at her plate.

"What's wrong?" Because he could think of no other reason his mother would accept anyone reading a text at her dinner table *and* then leaving, unless it was an emergency.

He watched his mother consider her answer. Then look over her shoulder as if to make sure Dad was gone. "It's nothing."

Which was clearly a bald-faced lie. "Mom."

She sighed. "He won't want me to tell you." She looked over her shoulder again. "He's already mad at me for being pushy."

"Pushy? You?"

She scorched him with a mean look in response to his sarcasm. "We've had some cows disappear is all."

"Disappearing? How do cows disappear?"

Mom waved away the question. "Dad'll figure it out." She smiled, but there was some worry in the new lines on her face. "Except…" She sighed. "You have to pretend I didn't tell you."

"Scout's honor."

"You weren't a Scout, Duncan," she said, but she almost smiled at the old joke. "It's just strange. In all our years of ranching, we've never seen such a thing. Because cows just don't go *missing*. Not one by one like this."

"Is someone taking them?"

"That's one theory."

"If someone's stealing them, why hasn't he called the police?"

"We don't know for certain anyone's stealing them. It may be a bad spot in the fence. Or maybe some silly prank." She sighed. "Dad talked to Sheriff Hudson, but that's Sunrise, and we're unincorporated. Bent County is who Dad would need to file a report with, and he's stubborn. Doesn't like their new 'modern' sensibility. I guess they hired a detective from Denver, over that good-for-nothing cousin of his's kid." Mom shook her head disgustedly. She had no fondness for some of Dad's extended family.

But Duncan wasn't interested in old family feuds. "So what's he doing about it then?"

"Worry himself to death," Mom said with a scowl. She sighed, leaned close and lowered her voice, even though Dad was long gone. "He's afraid he's getting old and forgetful. He even went to the doctor of his own accord."

Duncan was surprised at how hard that hit him. Once Dad had broken his arm and refused to go to the doctor for *days*. Until Mom had threatened to knock him out and drag him to the hospital herself.

"Nothing came back, except a bit of high cholesterol, go figure. But he's still embarrassed that something's going on under his nose. Worried. Blaming himself. I've tried to get him to call Bent County. I've talked to the ranch hands, tried to get them to convince him to call, but… Well, you know your father."

"Stubborn is an understatement."

She smiled fondly. "He certainly didn't pass that trait on."

Duncan grunted.

"I did have one idea, but he'd be so angry with me if I butted my nose in even more than I already have."

"I've never known you to care about getting Dad's temper up," Duncan said. He meant it as a joke, but Mom didn't smile, laugh, or have any of her usual responses.

He suddenly *felt* the years he'd been away. And the fact that no matter that he'd always come home for holidays, or flown his parents out for a visit and a game, it was a lot different than living under the same roof. Or even in the same state.

Mom looked down at her hand. Her left hand, where the simple wedding band she'd worn for almost forty years had always been. "It's weighing on him, and it's weighing on us," she said very quietly.

Quiet enough that Duncan's whole stomach knotted and knotted hard. The idea that his parents might have marriage problems was just…

God-awful.

She inhaled deeply, then looked up at him with her usual smile. Though he thought he saw a shininess in her dark eyes, which made the knot of dread in his gut tighten. His mother didn't *cry*. At least not in front of people.

"But you know, his only child, freshly moved home. Well…he might not be so angry at him."

Duncan blinked. He didn't particularly like the idea of crossing his father either. "You want me to…do what exactly?"

"Talk to Rosalie."

He wrinkled his nose. "The neighbor girl?"

"She's not a *girl* any longer. She's a private investigator with a company in Wilde, like I just told you. Maybe she could look into this without Dad knowing. Sheriff Hudson said there hadn't been any other missing cattle in the area, but maybe Rosalie could just…look into it. *I* can't ask her to do it—it would get back to Dad—but *you* could."

Normally he'd balk at the idea of getting involved. Usually, he'd talk to his dad himself. But everything about this conversation had him unsettled and he just wanted to make everything easy and right.

"Sure, Mom. I will. Don't even worry about it. I'll handle everything."

He didn't have baseball anymore, so maybe this was his new thing to focus on.

Duncan woke up late, the sunlight streaming in through his window. No doubt Dad would have a few comments about *that*, but he'd probably spent more of last night awake and in pain than sleeping.

Duncan pushed himself up in bed and cursed the dull ache in his shoulder. Cursed a lot of things on his way to the tiny kitchen of the cabin—his new *home*. He had the presence of mind to set up the coffeepot last night, so all he had to do this morning was press a button and wait for it to brew. Mom had stocked the pantry and fridge, including some breakfast sandwiches he only needed to pop in the microwave.

Bacon, egg, and cheese with a homemade biscuit. Not exactly the kind of food that he usually allowed himself. He'd always been so determined to stay in the best physical shape he could—exercise, diet, limited alcohol.

Fat lot of good that had done, he thought grumpily.

But once he'd eaten, sucked down two mugs of coffee and taken his pain pill, he felt better and more like taking on the day. He could unpack, but that sounded horrible. He doubted he'd be much help around the ranch with his shoulder in a sling. The thought of riding a horse like this had him wincing.

So he figured the best option for his day was to drive out to Wilde and see about Rosalie Young and private investigators.

He texted his mother that he was taking her car—she'd given him an extra set of keys. Maybe he'd take a detour to Fairmont and see if the car dealer there had anything that'd work for him long-term. None of the cars he'd kept in LA would survive ranch life, so he'd sold them off.

He drove off the ranch. It was a cloudy spring day, and rain started to spit from the sky about halfway to Wilde. He preferred that to sunny blue skies, which reminded him of summers at the ballpark.

Wilde was still little more than a postage stamp of a town. Duncan didn't know how they managed to have an actual private investigator's business here. He supposed the historical tours that started here and wound around Bent County might help with that, but it wasn't like they had much else to offer.

He pulled into a parking spot along the street. The office was in some kind of historical building, and had no doubt been something else in the past. Maybe a bank? He jogged inside to avoid as much of the rain as possible.

Inside, it smelled like fresh paint, and there were a lot of pretty feminine touches. There was a woman behind the big counter, but he wouldn't say *feminine* as a descriptor quite fit her.

She looked…tough. Wild. Pretty, no doubt, but not like she'd been the woman to arrange the flowers on the counter or put potpourri out on tables. Then again, looks could be deceiving.

The woman glanced up from whatever she was typing into her computer, but her gaze was distracted. "Be with you in a second." She immediately looked back down, then stilled, sneaking a glance at him. He watched as the recognition crossed her face. Then, with some amusement, watched as she decided how to handle it.

He was used to it, to an extent. He didn't like the new layer of *embarrassment* that went with people recognizing him, but still. He'd been a young phenom with plenty of attention, then a young man with a record-breaking contract, and he'd lived the high life in LA when he'd wanted to. So he got noticed.

But it was still weird back here, where he felt more like a kid with big dreams than the adult who'd achieved them. Then lost them.

When she addressed him, her smile was bland, and any reaction she'd had to recognizing him was hidden behind an easy smile. "What can I do you for?"

"I don't suppose Rosalie Young is here?"

"You know Rosalie?" the woman replied, studying him carefully.

"Sort of. We're neighbors. Or were, growing up."

"Huh." She shrugged. "Rosalie's out, but I can leave her a message for you."

Duncan considered. Would leaving a message get back to Dad? Bent County itself wasn't a small town, it was a large, sprawling county made up of ranches, mountains, and a handful of small and almost medium-size towns, but he knew the way information snaked through those places. One to the other.

"Do you know when she'll be back?"

The woman looked up at the wall behind him, so he did too. There was a big old clock up on it. "Sometime this afternoon."

"Maybe you could give me her phone number."

The woman's expression hardened a little. "I can give you her extension. You're welcome to leave a message on her work line."

Duncan considered that. It would be private if it was her own extension. But before he could decide what to do, a bell on the door tinkled. He turned and watched as a redhead whirled into the lobby.

"If that lousy SOB had talked instead of giving me the runaround, I wouldn't be caught in a damn downpour," she muttered as she wiped her boots on a mat by the door.

Sure, she wasn't the only person in the world with red hair and blue eyes that leaned toward violet, but he knew it was her.

And that on an adult woman all those little details landed…differently, in a kind of *jolt*. Because she didn't have skinned knees and falling-out braids any longer. She was dressed in tight jeans, heavy boots, and a black T-shirt. He didn't know much about guns that weren't meant for hunting, and even then, he'd never been into it. But he knew she had one strapped to a holster on her hip. She was short, with a medium build, but something about the way she carried herself gave the aura of someone taller, someone who could kick ass.

But her face somehow looked delicate on that tough package. Maybe it was the raindrops in her hair and on her face that seemed to tease out the little smattering of freckles across her nose.

Something about the whole of her was surprisingly *attractive*. Not that he had the time or presence of mind to be noticing just how attractive. Even if it *had* been a while in that department, and he—

No. He was here to help out his parents. Not flirt with the neighbor girl.

Who, as his mother had pointed out, was not a *girl* anymore.

He saw the recognition on her face right away, and in the slight pause in her stride. But her expression didn't give away much more than that. Just that she recognized him.

He didn't know what possessed him then. He hadn't seen her in something like fifteen years, and it wasn't like they'd been friends or even enemies. They'd been neighbors. Their parents had been friends. And they'd had to take the same interminable bus ride into school for the years they'd been going at the same time, which was quite a few since the bus ran ranch kids in kindergarten all the way up to seniors in high school.

But an old memory struck him, of someone calling her Rosie, and her coming unglued. And no doubt it was a *bad* instinct, but he leaned into it anyway.

"Heya, Rosie. Long time, no see."

Chapter Two

Rosalie Young stared at the outrageously handsome man standing in the lobby of Fool's Gold Investigations and didn't let any of the feelings rambling around inside of her show on her face.

His dark hair looked a little windswept, and longer than he kept it during the season. He'd grown a beard, but she wondered if that was more because of the sling his arm was in rather than any choice in the matter. His dark eyes were focused, intelligent, and a little amused. His mouth... Well, his mouth was an interesting mix of all sorts of things that might have normally had her offering a flirtatious smile.

But this was Duncan Kirk. Hometown boy turned baseball superstar.

Even though she'd watched his career with interest—who wouldn't cheer on the hometown kid?—she still had the mental picture of him as the grumpy little cuss who'd lived on the ranch next door.

Maybe grumpy wasn't fair, she could admit, with years of growing up under her belt. She didn't know much about professional sports, but she knew for anyone to get out of a ranch in the middle of nowhere Wyoming and become a professional athlete took a lot more than luck.

Maybe he hadn't been so much *grumpy* as focused, she had amended a few years back.

Still, she preferred thinking about a grumpy teen as opposed to when she'd last seen him. On a TV screen. Along with a lot of people in Bent County, shoved into Rightful Claim, ordering beers and ready to cheer on the hometown kid.

Only to watch him all but collapse in pain after one pitch.

It was hard to be ticked that he'd called her *Rosie* when she remembered that, and all the subsequent stories about a man's amazing career being cut short. Especially when he was wearing a sling, which was the same color as the T-shirt he was wearing, so it *almost* blended in.

But not quite.

"Duncan," she offered. She looked at her boss, Quinn, who ran Fool's Gold. Quinn shrugged like she didn't know why he was here either. "Having some trouble you need investigated?"

"Actually..." Duncan looked back at Quinn. "Maybe. You got somewhere to talk in private?"

"Sure." She moved past him, and ignored the little jolt to her system when, underneath the flowery smell of potpourri that Quinn's sister put out in the lobby, she caught a hint of piney aftershave and afternoon rain.

Whatever. Rich guys *should* smell good. She didn't tell him to follow her, or gesture him to, but he did all the same. She led him into her office. Only she and Quinn were full-time employees right now, so they both had their own offices. There were two other rooms with doors off the lobby that part-time investigators could use to talk to clients, interrogate witnesses, or whatever else was needed.

Maybe she should have taken him into one of those rooms, she thought as he moved into her space and started studying her array of desk pictures, but it was too late now. He was already staring at the newest addition. A picture from her second cousin's wedding last month. Vi looked pretty as a picture in her simple white dress, holding her one-year-old. Thomas Hart, her husband, was handsome in his suit, the jacket hiding his own sling after he'd been shot trying to save Vi just a few weeks before the wedding.

Audra, Franny, and Rosalie fanned out next to them in their spring dresses, smiling at the camera, the Young Ranch and mountains spread out behind them.

It had been a good day. A healing day. Rosalie wanted to remember it always. But there was something about Duncan Kirk looking at that moment captured in the picture, knowing some of the players, but not all, that felt…weird.

She closed the door, took one quick second to settle herself, then turned to look at him. He'd stopped staring at her pictures and was studying her.

"We tend to lean toward helping women," she began. Which wasn't the kindest way to ask him what he was after.

"Well, in a way you would be, since it's my mother who sent me."

She raised an eyebrow as she moved behind her desk. "Your mother is not the kind of woman who sends someone else to do her dirty work."

"No, she isn't."

He didn't offer anything else. She sat and motioned for him to do the same on the other side of her desk.

He looked at the chair, the desk, the picture, then sighed and took a seat. She couldn't quite read him. So she waited for him to explain.

She tried very hard not to fidget when it took a lot longer than she considered *polite*. "I don't have *all* day, Duncan."

"Right. There's been some trouble at my parents' ranch.

Some missing cows. I don't suppose you've heard anything about it?"

"I can't say that I keep up with the ranch gossip. That's Audra's department." Which still left Rosalie feeling guilty. She loved the ranch, but as an abstract. As a home. Not as a business to see to.

Which meant all the nuts and bolts of running that ranch fell on her older sister's tough and capable, but way overworked, shoulders.

"I guess, one by one, cows have been disappearing from the ranch. Dad was worried he was just getting…forgetful. He talked to Sheriff Hudson in Sunrise, but he hadn't heard of any found cows. I guess he doesn't like some detective from Denver being at Bent County, so he doesn't want to call there."

"Yeah, Beckett ruffles some feathers, but he's not all bad," Rosalie responded. She worked with a lot of the deputies and detectives in Bent County. Or harassed them into giving her information. Copeland Beckett wasn't her favorite, but watching him work on her cousin's case last month had softened her a bit in that department. That and the fact that Vi's husband worked with and trusted him.

Still, it read fishy to her that Mr. Kirk didn't want to call the actual cops, who might be able to help him.

"My mom's worried," Duncan continued. "About him. About the missing cows. She just wants someone to look into it. See if it *could* be someone purposefully taking those cows."

"Problem with that theory is a few months back, Audra found some of your dad's cattle on our land. Looked like a fence had just been left open. Nothing nefarious. The cows were returned."

"Maybe this is different."

"Maybe." But in her experience, cattle rustling wasn't much of a money maker around these parts. One cow at a time didn't exactly scream criminal plot. "Any ranch hands suspect?"

"Mom didn't think so, but I don't really know the players. Except my father."

"And it's not possible that it's an honest mistake?"

Duncan's mouth firmed. The slight flicker of anger and the ticking muscle in his jaw were far more attractive than they had a right to be.

Yeah, she had issues. She knew it.

"No," he said firmly.

"Look, this isn't the type of case I usually take on. I'll do it for your mom. But I like my clients to know they might not like the answers they want me to find. That sometimes, the most obvious answer we don't want *is* the answer."

"My dad isn't rustling his own cows, and he's not careless."

Rosalie shrugged. "It'll be my job to determine that myself. You need to be prepared for it to be either of those things."

"My father's the most honest man I know."

It left a pang in her heart. She would have said the same about her dad. But hero worship was a hell of a thing. It blinded a person to…everything. She pushed aside all that buried past.

"Look, I'm not saying I won't take the case."

He scowled. "For a price."

She didn't mind the hint of bitterness in his tone. She was too sure of herself and what she did to be hurt by someone else's opinion of it. "It's my job, Ace. And last I checked, you could afford it."

"Yeah, when was the last time you checked?"

There were a lot of ways she could take that question. A lot of ways she could answer it. But in typical Rosalie fashion, she took the one that hurt. Besides, he *had* called her *Rosie*, and no doubt remembered that she hated that nickname. "Y'all had a heck of a postseason run."

His expression became guarded. She'd somehow known it would. "Something like that."

"You pitched a hell of a game one. Four wasn't bad either."

Now he scowled. "I know it."

She didn't mind putting that scowl there any more than she minded the pride, and maybe ego, that went into the *I know it*. First, because she was a little perverse and found a pissed-off man hotter than she should. Second, because she needed him to understand she wasn't doing a favor, and this might not go the way he wanted. *She* certainly wouldn't be putty in his hands like he was no doubt used to.

"I'll dig around a little, see if there's anything fishy going on. You only have to pay me for my time. I won't hose you, even if you can afford it."

He huffed out a bit of a laugh. "I guess we'll see."

ROSALIE CURRENTLY HAD two cases going. One was simple enough. A woman had hired her to prove her husband's philandering ways. The other one was a little bit more complicated, as it involved a very *careful* stalker who knew his victim had gone to the cops. It was a pretty full plate, and she shouldn't take on Duncan's case, but...

Mrs. Kirk had been more than kind to Rosalie and her family. Especially after Dad died. Natalie Kirk had even tried to convince Mom to stay. Rosalie knew the Kirks helped Audra a lot on the ranch side of things and never made it seem like a big deal or an inconvenience.

Maybe the current facts pointed to Mr. Kirk, in Rosalie's estimation, but she supposed if she found that out, the Kirks could deal with it. They'd have to.

She knew all about uncomfortable truths.

On her way home, she decided to stop by Bent and kill a few birds with one stone. She parked her truck in the Bent County Sheriff's Department lot, locked her gun away, then went inside.

Thomas Hart was manning the information desk. He looked up as she walked in. Normally a detective, he'd been shot in the line of duty last month, so he was chained to his desk for a while yet.

"Hey, Hart."

"Hey, Rosalie."

"How's the arm?" she asked, leaning against the counter of the desk.

He scowled. "Horrible."

"How's the wife?"

Said scowl turned into a grin. "Amazing. I am a well-fed man."

She glared at him. Because his wife, *her* second cousin, had once lived on the Young Ranch with *her* and used her considerable cooking skills to feed Rosalie. "Bragger."

"I aim to be when it comes to Vi and Mags."

And since the simple sweet *love* imbued in each of those words made her itchy, she got to the point. "You got a copy of that police report on the property damage I requested?"

He swiveled in his chair, pulled out a file folder, and handed it to her. "No leads. Not sure how that's going to help your case."

She shrugged, flipped through the file to make sure everything she requested was there. Hart was okay to work with, but some of the deputies sneered at what she did. She figured they were jealous she could bend the laws they had to enforce to get her perps. "We'll see." She closed the file, looked at Hart.

"You heard of any cattle rustling going on?"

His expression immediately changed to one of concern. "Something happen at the ranch?"

She shook her head. "Not at our place. This is Fool's Gold business."

He leaned back in his chair, blew out a breath. "Haven't heard anything that I can think of off the top of my head, but I'll ask around. Let you know."

"Thanks. How many more weeks you got back here?"

He grunted. "Got a doctor's appointment next week. Hoping to wheedle some clearance out of him."

"Good luck, then. See you Sunday."

"Vi's bringing rolls and pasta salad."

"Thank God," Rosalie said, and meant it. "Audra can bake, but she can't cook for a damn."

"You should tell her that."

"Ha. Ha." Rosalie left the sheriff's department and drove back to the Young Ranch, out closer to the small town of Sunrise. She pulled off the highway onto a side road, then onto the gravel road that would lead her home.

There was a sign under the arch that read *Young Ranch, Established 1908*. She loved this place. In her bones. She didn't care a whit about raising cattle, the price of beef or hay. She wanted nothing to do with the accounting books or inventory, but she *loved* the place. The feeling of ancestry and history and just…home.

Even if her parents had turned out to be the opposite of everything she'd thought, it didn't tarnish the love she felt for this *place*. For roots.

And it had been nice, really, just her and Audra and their

cousin, Franny. Three twentysomething women living together, kicking Wyoming ass together. They'd helped Vi out of her terrible situation, gotten to help raise Magnolia before Vi had moved in with Thomas. Life was good.

Good.

She heard voices the minute she walked into the main house. The welcome smell of meat sizzling in the kitchen—which meant Franny had cooked, thank goodness. She dropped her bag, took two steps, then wrinkled her nose and turned back to hang it up on the hook, as Audra preferred.

Sometimes she liked bothering her older sister. Sometimes she lived for it. And sometimes Audra's long-suffering self-sacrifice made Rosalie feel like a guilty slob.

Once her bag had been hung up acceptably, she moved into the kitchen. Audra and Franny were already sitting at the table, plates full.

They greeted each other and Rosalie went straight for the food and began to pile her plate high. There was nothing better than a home-cooked meal after a day of work. Especially when Franny was making it.

"I heard someone talking about Duncan Kirk being in town," Franny said in between bites as Rosalie slid into her seat at the table.

Audra nodded. "Natalie told me he's planning to stay indefinitely. They even fixed up one of the cabins on their property for him."

"That's next *door*. Do you think we'll see him?" Franny had grown up in Seattle with Audra and Rosalie's aunt and uncle, but they'd always made the trek out to Wyoming for holidays. Audra and Franny especially had kept in touch as teenagers, and when Franny's writing career had taken off, she'd moved out to Wyoming to live with them for a bit. For *inspiration*, she said.

Rosalie thought about Duncan Kirk in her office this afternoon. He would be one hell of an inspiration. "*I* saw him," Rosalie volunteered. "Talked to him even."

Both Audra and Franny whipped their gazes to her. "You did?"

Rosalie realized that even telling them he'd come to Fool's Gold was a little too close to ruining the client privacy she worked very hard to keep. "Yep. Ran right into him on the street."

"You talked to him?" Audra asked.

"Is he as hot in person as he is on the TV?" Franny demanded.

Rosalie grinned at Franny. "Hotter."

"Impossible."

Rosalie shook her head, kind of enjoying herself. "Swear it. His hair's a little shaggy. He's got a beard going on."

"Not a beard." Franny groaned and put a hand to her heart, making Audra and Rosalie laugh.

Conversation turned to *other* hot guys with beards—locals and celebrities. Franny told them some about her newest book idea—with details she'd gotten from pumping Hart for detective stories. Once they were done eating, Rosalie took her chore of cleaning up the dishes while Audra packed up the leftovers.

"You were nice, weren't you?" Audra asked.

Rosalie frowned at her sister, irritated she knew just what Audra was talking about. And tried not to feel guilty for kind of making it sound like Mr. Kirk might be his own problem. "What's that supposed to mean?"

"It means I know you. The Kirks have been so good to us. I just want to make sure you remember that. Even if Duncan hasn't been around, he's a Kirk."

"I'm not a total jerk, Audra."

"That's not what I'm saying," Audra replied. But she didn't say *of course you're not a jerk, Rosalie.*

Which probably shouldn't grate as much as it did. And it only grated because she *was* kind of a jerk. She liked to think she'd earned it, and it kept people from taking advantage of her, like they did with Audra when Rosalie wasn't around to run interference.

But Audra, with her impeccable eldest-sister abilities, knew just how to twist an unintended knife.

Rosalie spent half the night looking into the Kirks' cattle operation.

Chapter Three

Duncan spent the next few days getting settled into his new life. He bought a truck. Bought some new clothes more suited for life on the ranch. He unpacked one box, but that was depressing as hell, so he ignored the rest.

He ate dinner with his parents every night. He hadn't been planning on that, but Mom seemed to expect it, and he couldn't deny he was worried about his parents. It didn't sound like any more cattle had disappeared, and he hadn't heard from Rosalie at all.

But he'd thought about her. And not in an is-she-researching-missing-cattle kind of way. More like, is she single and is this too complicated?

He had a demanding life, or he'd *had* a demanding life, so he was very well versed in what he liked to call *risk management* when it came to women.

Rosalie was intertwined in his parents' life. That one fact was reason enough to keep his thoughts to himself. But thoughts—and fantasies—never hurt anyone, did they?

When Dad said he was going back out to check the fences with a couple of his hands before sundown, Duncan offered to help Mom with the dishes even though it was usually Dad's job.

If he cast back among all his memories of his parents, it was that simple after-dinner routine that made him feel the most centered, the most...*home*. Dad sitting on a stool at the sink, rinsing off dishes and putting them in the dishwasher while Mom put the leftovers away and cleaned up the cooking debris.

"I don't suppose you've heard anything from Rosalie about the cattle?" she asked as he dutifully put plates in the dishwasher.

"She said she'd look into it."

"It's been days."

"Maybe it takes days to look into stuff." Though he supposed he could call her tomorrow. Test the waters.

The *investigation* waters. Nothing else. He tossed the detergent pod into the dishwasher and closed the door. When he turned to his mother, she was holding out a paper grocery bag.

"Why don't you go on over to the Young house. Take this over. That Audra runs herself ragged. It's always my pleasure when I can send some extras her way."

Mom had already packed up a bag of their dinner leftovers—leftovers they only had because Mom no doubt had made enough to ensure there was food left to take to the Youngs. She shoved it at him. He grabbed it with one arm, his other arm throbbing. He considered using it as an excuse, but before he could, Mom looked at his sling. Considered.

"Well, I suppose I can do it. I'm supposed to lead the church meeting tonight, but…"

"I'll do it," he grumbled, not letting her take the bag back.

"Only if you're sure you're up to it. I'm sure driving with the sling isn't comfortable and—"

"It's fine."

"That's my boy." She patted his cheek. "I'm going to go wash up. You run that out to them before they eat."

He knew he'd been maneuvered when she bounced off like she'd never had a care in the world about his arm. He was going to have to relearn how to fend off his mother's machinations.

But for this evening, he took his punishment and the food and drove the access road from the Kirk house to the Young house, cursing his shoulder every time he hit a bump, or when he had to get out and open and close the gate.

It hurt like hell, but at the same time it felt better than those first few weeks when he'd just been moping around his place in LA. Something about fresh air, sunlight, and mountains, maybe.

Or maybe it was just being home.

He drove onto the gravel lane that wound up to the Young place. Unlike his childhood home, their house looked exactly as he remembered it. A little on the small side, with a big rambling porch. Mountains rose up in the distance, like guarding sentries looming over everything.

Two redheads sat on the porch swing, heads bent together. One—Audra, he was guessing—had her legs crossed and was sitting upright. The other—Rosalie, definitely—was lounging, using her bare foot, which was on the porch railing, to move the swing back and forth.

They watched as his truck approached, then him. Rosalie was drinking a beer out of a bottle, and Audra had a glass of something. They didn't look a heck of a lot alike, except for their coloring. Both were redheads, though Audra's ran closer to brown. Both had those too-blue eyes, though Audra's were smaller and closer set than Rosalie's. Audra was tall and willowy, he noted as she got to her feet.

Then swatted her sister when she didn't do the same.

"It's good to see you again, Duncan," she offered politely, as she walked over to the top of the stairs. Rosalie stayed on the swing and said nothing.

"You too, Audra." He held up the bag. "Hope you guys didn't eat yet. Mom sent me over with leftovers."

"Thank *God*," Rosalie said under her breath, earning her a scolding look from Audra.

"*You* could learn to cook," Audra said to her sister as she took the bag from Duncan.

"Can't. No patience," Rosalie replied, and it was clearly an old argument without much heat. But she flashed a grin at Duncan as she said it that made a disconcerting bolt of lust go through him.

Disconcerting because her sister was right there, and because she was connected to his family in a weird kind of way. And with the cow-investigation thing, it certainly wasn't smart to be distracted by a quick smile and pretty eyes.

But even with those alarm bells ringing, it was kind of a relief, because it had been a long time since anything—including a woman—had distracted him from his laser-beam focus.

"Thank your mom for me, Duncan," Audra said. "We really do appreciate everything she does for us."

"She likes it, or she wouldn't do it, but I'll tell her."

"I'll just go put this away. And I'll warn you to run out of here rather than spend even a second in small talk with my feral hog of a sister."

"*Hog?*" Rosalie huffed. "Rude."

Audra just smirked and went inside. He watched her go, noting more differences in the sisters. Audra didn't have that...*swagger* Rosalie wore like a second skin.

Rosalie cleared her throat, and he turned his attention to her, but she didn't say anything. So he did.

"Y'all should have a guard dog."

"Franny's allergic."

"Who's Franny?"

"Oh, our other roommate. Our cousin on our mom's side. Besides, who needs a guard dog when we're all carrying and excellent shots?" She grinned at him, all sharp angles and implied threat. "Audra wins sharpshooting trophies on the regular."

Maybe there was something wrong with him that he was very interested in every last one of her implied threats.

She finally got up off the swing and walked over to the steps. "Sorry I haven't been in touch. Had another case get hot. I did do some initial looking into everything though. I haven't forgotten about you. Just haven't found much to go on. Except I did run background checks on some of your dad's ranch hands. He's got a newer one. Owen Green. He had a few brushes with the law when he was a minor."

"I'm not saying it's not worth looking into, but most of the younger guys who work for my dad are his brothers' or cousins' ne'er-do-well kids. Mom calls it Norman's Camp for Wayward Boys."

Rosalie chuckled. "Yeah. I've heard the complaints. I didn't realize this one was one of his though."

"Pretty sure Green is a North Dakota cousin. But by all means, look into him. I don't trust them any more than my mom does."

"Will do, boss."

"So how much do I owe you? Or do you just bill me when you're done? And make sure it's me. I don't want Mom seeing the cost."

She lifted a shoulder. "Free of charge."

"I thought I could afford it."

"Audra lectured me about how great your parents have been to us since…" She trailed off, never finishing that sentence.

But he knew. Maybe he hadn't remembered all the details, but Mom had been filling him in. When Tim Young had died, it came out that he'd been having an affair for quite a few years. He had a whole second family out in Cheyenne no one had known about. Then his actual wife had left the girls with the ranch, not wanting to be around anything that reminded her of Tim.

Including her daughters.

Apparently the Young girls—*women*, he had to keep reminding himself—had tried to make some overtures with their half siblings in the time since, but that hadn't worked out.

Audra popped her head out of the door. "Duncan, have you eaten? You're more than welcome to come in and join us."

"No, I ate. Thanks. Enjoy the food. I'll see y'all around." He gave a bit of a wave, and one last glance at Rosalie, then turned back to his truck. He was about halfway there when Rosalie spoke.

"Hey, one more thing." She hopped down the stairs and took a few strides toward him. Then, when she was out of earshot of the front door, she spoke quietly. She pointed a finger at him. "You check out my sister again and I'll castrate you."

He supposed he should take that as the warning it was meant to be. He *supposed* he should let the comment slide and get out of there. But she was standing there, chin lifted, arms folded over her chest. The falling sunlight made her hair look especially…fiery.

He supposed a lot of men were intimidated by her. Maybe he should be. But he couldn't seem to find it in himself. "What if it was you that I was checking out?"

He watched her wrestle with something, hoped at least a *little* of that mischievous sparkle in her eyes was humor, not castration plans.

"Audra's got too soft a heart. Me? Mine's titanium. I can handle myself against the likes of you."

"That feels like a dare, Red."

This time, she couldn't quite stop herself from smiling, though he watched her try. "I'll be in touch, *Ace*," she said, then turned on a heel and strode back inside.

And, yeah, he checked her out the whole way.

HE'D BEEN FLIRTING with her. Not uncommon. While Rosalie intimidated some guys, some took her attitude as a challenge. Duncan seemed to be the latter.

But damn, he was so unfairly good-looking. She didn't mind a good flirt. She didn't mind other things. She wasn't looking for anything serious, ever, but she liked the male species on a very superficial level.

Maybe Audra had dreams of roses and white dresses. Maybe Audra *and* Franny looked at Vi and Thomas and Magnolia a little wistfully.

Rosalie most decidedly did not.

Maybe it was a cliché, maybe it meant she needed therapy, but learning her dad had a whole secret family after he'd died had killed absolutely any trust she held in the male species.

Or at least any trust in her judgment of it. Because Hart was okay, and so clearly in love with Vi. Maybe it wasn't that she didn't believe in love, but more that she didn't trust her own take on it.

Either way. She wasn't looking for anything, and she doubted Mr. Superstar was either. But even a flirtation was complicated with the ways their families overlapped, and the fact she was helping him look into some missing cows.

She didn't mind some complications. A person couldn't in a small community like Bent County. Not if she wanted to get laid on occasion. And she *did*.

But Duncan? Nah, too complicated.

Really, *really* hot though.

She shoved away thoughts of Duncan, or tried to, and ate a delicious meal prepared by his mother with Audra and Franny. Most days, it felt like enough, but some days…usually after a night like last night when they'd had Vi, Hart, and Mags over, it felt a little lonely.

She refused to wallow in that though. She enjoyed her dinner, watched a terrible movie with Franny, then went to bed.

In the morning, she figured her first order of business once she got to work would be to look a little deeper into Owen Green, the ne'er-do-well cousin from North Dakota.

She headed downstairs, lured by the smell of coffee and the sound of voices. Audra was pouring her coffee into a thermos, while Franny rested her head against the table.

"What happened to you?"

She lifted her head. "I was up practically all night."

"Writing?"

"In a matter of speaking," she said around a yawn.

Which meant she'd likely spent her entire night either following some research rabbit trail, or watching Taylor Swift conspiracy-theory videos. Or both.

Rosalie grabbed her own thermos from the cupboard. She filled it, but before she could grab a power bar for breakfast, Audra was shoving a bag at her.

"On your way out, can you return all this Tupperware to Natalie?"

Rosalie looked down at it. She really didn't want to, but that was childish. "I guess."

"I was texting Chloe last night, and I mentioned how Duncan was back. She told me to invite him to the engagement party. So, if you see him, can you do that?"

"Invite him to our friend's party?" Rosalie returned. Chloe was a friend of Audra's going way back. Rosalie worked with Jack's sister at Fool's Gold. And a million other connections that happened in a small town.

"Duncan's new to town, kind of, and it'll give him an opportunity to meet, or remeet, people his age."

"He was a famous professional athlete for *years*, Audra. I'm sure he can meet people on his own."

"Here? This is a different world than LA. He might feel out of place. A casual engagement party is the perfect place to reacquaint himself with old friends or meet new ones. I'm sure Duncan knows Jack."

They were around the same age, so probably. But Rosalie didn't know why it fell on *her* to do the inviting. She almost said it, but she saw the way Audra was moving around the kitchen. Too fast because she had too much to do.

"Everything okay, ranch-wise?"

Audra waved her off. "Sure thing. But it'd help me a lot if you took care of that."

"Yeah. Sure." She glanced at Franny, who was still lying on the table, possibly sleeping. "Why don't I bring home a pizza tonight instead of having anyone cook?"

"Sounds good to me but let us know if you're going to be late."

Rosalie nodded, took a few steps toward the kitchen's exit. Then turned to face her sister.

"You're not like…trying to flirt with him, are you?"

Audra blinked, cocked her head. Her expression was blank enough Rosalie couldn't tell what she felt about that question.

"Why?" she asked, sounding casual even if her gaze was considering. "Would that bother you?"

"Why would it bother me?"

Audra shrugged. "I don't know. But you didn't ask it like 'are you trying to flirt with him?' You voiced it as a negative. 'You're not, are you?'"

"No, I didn't."

Audra looked at Franny, whose eyes were open again. "Didn't she?"

"She did," Franny agreed.

"Traitor," Rosalie muttered, then whirled out of the kitchen. It didn't bother her in the least. Not that she was going to let some puffed-up baseball player touch her sister, but if Audra wanted to flirt, she had every right.

Every right, Rosalie repeated to herself as she got in her car and drove over to the Kirk Ranch house. Not at *all* in a foul mood, because she didn't care about Duncan Kirk or parties or *anything*.

When she pulled up in front of the house, a lot more recently modernized than the Young house, where they scraped by year after year thanks to her selfish parents, she was *not at all happy* to see Duncan standing on the porch.

That leap in her chest was definitely irritation. She got out of the car, grabbed the bag of Tupperware, and marched it right up the stairs.

"Your mom here?"

"No, she went to town for some errands already apparently," he said, holding up a Post-it. "Which is suspicious because she told me I could come by this morning and grab some more coffee. I'm out. I didn't even bring my keys with me." He jiggled the knob in frustration.

"Audra insisted I bring this stuff back this morning," Rosalie said, holding the bag out to him. With a frown, he took it.

"Where am I supposed to put it?"

Rosalie shrugged. "How am I supposed to know? I've got to get to work." But since he was here, she could tell him about the party and then not have to see him until she had something to do with the case to talk to him about. *Professionally.* And if she handled this, she could maybe handle making sure her sister's heart didn't get stomped on by this—this…

Whatever he was. "And…she also wanted me to invite you to this party."

"Party?"

"A friend's thing in a few weeks. It's for an engagement, but really informal. Outdoor backyard barbeque type thing. A bunch of us are going, and Audra thought… You know, since you haven't really lived here for a while, you might want to meet or get reacquainted with someone your age. You probably know the host anyway. Jack Hudson?"

"I played T-ball with Jack."

"See? So you should come."

"Because Audra wants me to?"

Rosalie tried not to growl. "She's just being *nice*. Don't let it go to your head."

His mouth quirked up on one side, a kind of boyish, mischievous smile that had butterflies kicking up a racket in her stomach.

"I like nice."

Butterflies officially grounded. She stepped forward. "You touch nice, I'll—"

"Yeah, I remember the threat. You know, I think much better about invitations when I've had my coffee. Want to go up to Coffee Klatch with me? I've been told a lie that their coffee doesn't taste like gas-station dregs anymore."

Rosalie blinked. She couldn't remember the last time she'd been caught so off guard. Before she could decide what to do with *that* invitation though, she heard a scream.

Both she and Duncan moved toward it simultaneously as a young man came scrambling toward them from the barn, waving both arms.

"Call nine-one-one. Call nine-one-one, now!"

Chapter Four

Once they moved, the excitable ranch hand, whose name Duncan couldn't think of though he was sure he was a relation of some sort, started running away from them, like a dog alerting people to danger. So he and Rosalie followed. Rosalie had her cell out, no doubt already dialing 911.

Running jolted pain through his arm with every step, but the frantic terror in the ranch hand's voice meant he couldn't stop.

Until he saw a body in the pasture. Then he came to a skidding halt, even as Rosalie shoved the phone at him and rushed forward. She went right up to that bloody body and kneeled down next to it. She was careful, but she didn't recoil. She reached out and touched his neck.

Another unrecognizable person, except this time not just because he didn't know anyone anymore, but because the head of the very, *very* still body was covered in blood.

"He won't move!" the ranch hand yelled, not fully running up to the body on the ground. He looked from Rosalie to Duncan. "I kept shouting his name, and he won't move."

"What is your emergency?" Duncan heard vaguely from the speaker, jolting him back to his body—not some far-off place of shock. He lifted the phone to his ear. "Sorry. It seems... Someone's been hurt."

"We've already dispatched police and an ambulance. What kind of injury has the person sustained?"

"I'm not...sure." Duncan didn't want to look, but he couldn't help himself. "There's blood."

"Is the person conscious?" the dispatcher asked with a kind of detached calm Duncan envied. He felt jittery and outside his body. Because Duncan didn't think consciousness probably had much to do with anything right now. When Rosalie's gaze lifted to his and she shook her head slowly, he knew it didn't.

Duncan had to clear his throat to speak. "I don't think he's alive."

The dispatcher had him stay on the line and answer questions. Rosalie tried to calm the ranch hand who'd found them, but the kid just kept repeating the same information.

I called his name. He wouldn't move. Why won't he move?

As they waited, a few more ranch hands appeared, and Rosalie somehow managed to corral them all in the same area. She was about a foot shorter than all of them, but she had a kind of stature and calm in the face of all *this* that had every single person obeying her without question.

Duncan heard the blaring sirens before he saw the vehicles approaching. The police cruiser appeared first, followed by an ambulance. Both vehicles came to a stop on the drive, close to where they all stood.

Even as the paramedics rushed forward, Rosalie was walking past him, right for the uniformed cop who was striding toward the body. He couldn't make out exactly what she was saying, but her tone was confident. Authoritative.

And it was clear, the cop didn't like it. So Duncan moved over to her, not sure what he thought *he'd* do about anything. Only knowing he didn't like the scowl on the cop's face.

Rosalie didn't acknowledge his approach, but she must

have noted it because she held out her hand. "Give me my phone, Duncan. I've got a phone call to make."

"You can go crying to your friends in the bureau, but that's not how this works," the cop told her. And not kindly.

"It's a free country, Stanley, which means it's how *I* work." She jammed a finger onto the screen of her phone and whirled away from the police officer.

Who was now studying him. "Name?" he demanded.

For a full minute, Duncan could only blink at the guy. "What?"

"Your name? You're not Natalie or Norman Kirk, so I need to know your name and reason for being on the property."

Duncan supposed he shouldn't be offended. Not everyone who knew his parents was going to know who he was, especially by sight, but the guy's tone *grated*. Everything about this guy grated.

"I am *a* Kirk. I'm Duncan Kirk, their son. So I'd say I know *Natalie and Norman* pretty well and have a pretty damn good reason for being on the property."

The guy looked taken aback for maybe a second, then went back to big-chested bluster. "Where are your parents then?"

"Mom's running errands." But he wasn't sure where his Dad was. With her? Somewhere on the property? But if he was around, shouldn't he have heard the commotion and come running?

Duncan's entire body went cold. Oh *God*. What if...? The phone in his pocket buzzed just as the fear of something awful befalling Dad gripped him.

It was a text from his dad.

What the hell is going on up there?

Duncan thought his legs might fully give out, just from relief alone. We've got a situation. Come on up to the north gate. Then he shoved his phone in his pocket and tried to find his strength again.

"My dad is on his way," Duncan told the cop. Then, before the guy could ask any more questions, Duncan turned away from him. He felt weak-kneed from that bright bolt of terror.

So he walked until he didn't. Until he found Rosalie. She didn't look at him, but she began speaking, and he could only figure it was *to* him.

"I called a detective at Bent County. He's rounding up the coroner, though the paramedics hopefully already put that call in. I don't know why Stanley has to be such an ass about it." She scowled over her shoulder at the guy, who was now talking to the ranch hand who'd gotten them. "You said your mom's out running errands. You better give her a call. No doubt if *anyone* noticed emergency services turning into the ranch, they're already calling her to ask what happened."

Duncan swore inwardly. "Dad texted asking what was going on. I just told him to come on up."

She nodded. "Call your mom, or text her, if she'll read those. Tell her you're okay."

"Why wouldn't I be okay?"

Rosalie shrugged. "Small-town gossip isn't always *true* gossip, Ace. You should know that. Text your mom."

Duncan sighed. He didn't like taking orders from anyone, but particularly this slip of a woman who was only a little more than a stranger to him. But he still pulled his phone out of his pocket and texted his mom.

Come home. I'm okay. Before he hit Send, he quickly added that Dad was okay too, then slid the phone back in his pocket just as yet another car he didn't recognize came to a stop next to the police car and ambulance, followed by a truck.

A guy dressed far too nice for ranch work, with expensive sunglasses, got out of the car. A woman who looked vaguely familiar got out of the truck. The woman headed for the paramedics, while the man made a beeline for Rosalie.

He approached, surveyed Duncan with a flicker of recognition, but he didn't say anything about it. "How'd you get roped into this?" he said by way of greeting to Rosalie.

"Long story," Rosalie returned, shading her eyes against the quickly rising sun.

"Well, Bent County will take it from here." He held out a hand to Duncan. "Detective Copeland Beckett, Bent County Sheriff's Department."

Duncan shook the offered hand, still feeling fully out of his body. "Duncan Kirk."

"Yeah, I know."

"It's his parents' place," Rosalie explained. "By the way, I don't want Stanley on this case."

The detective sighed. "You don't have a say," he replied with a shrug. And then, as if he realized it was not in his best interest to fully piss her off, he added, "Besides, he won't be investigating. I will."

Rosalie let out a huff of a breath. But once the detective walked away, toward the possible *murder* scene, she muttered something that sounded suspiciously like "so will I."

Which eased some of Duncan's tension, whether it should or not.

ROSALIE HUNG AROUND while Copeland asked questions, poked around the murder scene, conferred with the coroner. No matter how many times Copeland tried to shoo her away, she stuck close. She observed, kept a tally of questions and answers, and a mental note of everything she overheard. Once she had some time, she'd sit down and write it all out while the information was still fresh.

Copeland Beckett was a fine enough detective. She trusted him to do his due diligence, even if some of the people involved were incompetent.

Xavier Stanley was at the top of *that* list.

But this was too close to the Young Ranch, and until Rosalie knew why someone had murdered this guy, she wasn't about to back off and let anyone else handle the case, even if she trusted them.

Until she knew why that guy was murdered, and by who, she was working this case.

The body was removed, evidence sealed and packed away, pictures taken.

Rosalie snuck a few of her own on her cell phone when Copeland and Deputy Stanley weren't looking.

When the coroner was making the move to leave, Rosalie sidled up to her. Gracie Cooper was older than her, so they hadn't gone to school together and didn't really know each other socially, but that never stopped Rosalie from trying to press an advantage.

"You'll share that report with me, right?"

Gracie let out a sigh, the long-suffering kind. "Rosalie. You know better."

"It's for a case."

"Uh-huh." Gracie glanced at Duncan, gave Rosalie a *look* that implied things Rosalie would *not* acknowledge. "Some case."

Rosalie scowled, but she didn't argue with Gracie because she knew all about protesting too much.

But she did find herself looking back at Duncan. He stood with his parents, was about two inches taller than his dad and a few more than his mom. All three were looking at Deputy Stanley, and if the scowl on Duncan's face was anything to go by, he didn't like what he was hearing.

Duncan had been out of his element for a bit there. Hard to blame him, though Rosalie would have if he hadn't snapped out of it once his parents arrived on the scene. She'd watched him very carefully put all his *what the hell* away behind a demeanor that was firm and authoritative. He didn't let Copeland start asking questions until he was sure his parents were ready. He hadn't let anyone run roughshod over them.

She didn't care for the fact that she respected it.

"No reason for you to still be here."

Rosalie looked at Copeland, who'd come to stand next to her. He was clearly about to leave too. "The Kirks are friends of mine."

"The parents or the baseball player?"

"Both, thank you very much."

"Small towns," Copeland muttered with some disgust. Because he was Mr. Big City Hotshot. Except he'd landed here and stayed. So far. "I'm headed back to the department to put some stuff together. Stay away from my murder scene."

She smiled at him, batted her eyelashes. "Well, of *course*, Detective."

Copeland muttered curses all the way to his car. But he said something to a uniformed deputy—*not* Stanley, thank God—and Rosalie knew he'd leave someone posted until they were sure they had all the evidence and pictures taken they needed.

But she could get access to anything she needed. If not through Copeland, then through Hart. Oh, his loyalty would be to the Bent County Sheriff's Department, but with the right familial pressure, she could get what she wanted.

With that knowledge tucked away, she walked across the yard to Duncan. He was standing alone now, his gaze on where the body had been. Caution tape now marked the spot, and a lone deputy who stood watch.

Duncan turned that dark gaze to her when she approached. He offered a wry smile.

"How are they holding up?" Rosalie asked, nodding at the house.

"Mom's...upset. Dad's...upset. I guess that's really all there is to say. They'll feel responsible because it happened on their property, even if it had nothing to do with them."

Rosalie's heart twisted. What a terrible thing. "Was it one of your cousins?"

Duncan shook his head. "No, I guess this was a friend of one of the second cousins. Had some trouble back in North Dakota, so came here to get his life straightened out with Owen. That's the cousin."

"Maybe trouble followed him?"

Duncan nodded. "Sounds like. Owen talked to your detective. I imagine they'll look into that."

Rosalie nodded. "Mind if I talk to Owen?"

Duncan studied her. "He's been through a lot, but... Well, I don't know that detective. And neither do my parents. But they know you. We trust you."

Odd that he included himself in that *we*. Odd that it should make her feel something flutter inside of her. Like pressure, when she didn't believe in pressure.

Because Rosalie Young always got her man. "Good, because I intend to look into this."

"Whatever the fee, I'll pay it."

Rosalie shook her head. "No need. My sister and my

cousin live just across that access road. I'm working on this for my own peace of mind over their safety."

"What about you?"

"What do you mean 'what about me?'"

"You live there too. You should be safe too."

"Yeah…" She knew she wasn't invincible. And she knew Audra and Franny weren't weaklings. It was just…

She was the protector. Always had been. Always would be.

"And I thought you all were armed and knew how to shoot. Wasn't that the warning you gave me?"

She scowled at him. "Sure, but… Well, that's all true, but that doesn't mean I'm not going to worry about a murderer lurking about. I protect my own."

Duncan looked back at the house, where his parents had gone inside. His expression was deadly serious. "So do I." Then he turned that serious expression onto her, and that *fluttering* was back, with a full set of *jittering* to go along with it. "I'm no detective or investigator, but I want to help. I'm *going* to help."

"How?"

"You tell me."

Chapter Five

Duncan wouldn't say he'd caught Rosalie off guard with his intention to help, but she didn't have a quick answer for that. In fact, when she did speak, it was with a question of her own.

"Where'd all the ranch hands go?"

"The detective said they could go back to their bunks, but no one is supposed to leave the property. They'll be back in a few hours with more questions."

"More questions and search warrants, I imagine. They'll want to go through all the buildings. Bunks, stables, the house. I don't know how long it'll take Gracie to determine time and cause of death."

"Gracie? Gracie Delaney?" He knew he'd recognized the woman. They'd gone to high school together. Though he couldn't remember much else about her besides the name and the vague look of *Delaney*—the family that had run Bent, more or less, back then.

"Gracie Cooper these days," Rosalie said offhandedly. "She's the coroner."

Coroner. Death. *Murder.* "I'm guessing the cause of death had something to do with the way his head was blown to hell."

Rosalie slid that pretty, blue gaze to him. "Noticed that, huh?"

"Hard not to." And yeah, it was going to haunt the hell out of him for a very long time, no matter how tough he tried to act.

"They'll want to find a murder weapon. It was a gunshot wound to the head, so they'll do what they can to identify a murder weapon, get search warrants and the like for anything that might match."

"You don't think one of the other ranch hands did it, do you?" The thought filled him with different kinds of dread for all sorts of reasons. The toll it would take on his parents. The danger they all might be in with a murderer running around.

What on earth had he come home to? At least he *was* home. This was the first time he was truly grateful for the timing. Because his parents would need him.

"Impossible to say just yet," Rosalie returned. She surveyed the crime scene, the rest of the ranch. "Let's go talk to Owen. See what he had to say about his friend."

Duncan hesitated. The poor kid had just stumbled upon his murdered friend and already answered a bunch of questions from the police. Should he let Rosalie pile on?

"Look, Duncan, you can either spare everyone's feelings or you can find the truth, but let me tell you from experience, you can't do both."

She said it kindly enough, but he felt *judged* all the same.

"Let's get the truth."

She nodded, then started striding away from the house. Since it was in the direction of the bunkhouse, he figured she knew where she was going. Though he wondered *why* she was so well-acquainted with the layout of the ranch. He followed her.

"Your shoulder holding up okay?" she asked pleasantly enough as they walked. She wasn't even looking at him, but he knew it wasn't a casual question. She'd noticed him wincing or something. And now she was slowing down, like he needed someone to slow down for him.

He focused on walking without showing any pain, and walked faster just to prove all was well. "I'm fine."

"Not what I asked."

He supposed it wasn't, and he didn't particularly care for her calling him out on it. So he grinned at her. "Worried about me, Red?"

She snorted, shook her head. "I'm worried about *murder*, Ace."

He blew out a breath. He was still trying to live in denial about *that*. "Yeah."

Once they got to the bunkhouse, Rosalie waited for him to knock. The door opened, and an older ranch hand stood in the opening, crossing his arms over his chest. Blocking the entrance.

Terry Boothe had been on the ranch since Duncan had been a kid, and Duncan was pretty sure he remembered Dad saying Terry was foreman now.

"Duncan," Terry greeted. He looked at Rosalie with suspicion and did *not* greet her.

"We just want to talk to Owen," Duncan said, hoping to offset some of the suspicion and distrust Terry was aiming Rosalie's way.

"Didn't he already—"

"I know he answered the detective's questions," Rosalie said, in a clear, polite tone that Duncan was sure he hadn't heard from her before. "And I'm sure he's broken up about this, but I have some questions that might help us figure this out that the cops aren't going to ask."

Terry's suspicion didn't lift. "What makes you better than the cops?"

"Not better. Different," Rosalie said, in that same even tone. "I'm a private investigator. Licensed, mind you. I've got rules and laws to follow, but I don't have a whole county with its bureaucracy breathing down my neck. The sooner we get to the bottom of this, the safer we all are. And Owen will be able to grieve fully."

Terry moved his hard gaze from Rosalie to Duncan. "Your parents okay with this?"

"Yeah," Duncan lied. He hadn't run it by them, but he couldn't imagine them having a problem with Rosalie helping. "Rosalie's a friend of the family. She just wants to help."

Terry grunted but he led them inside. The first room was the kitchen and dining area, open and wide, with a few tables. No one was in there right now, but Terry gestured them to a table. "I'll get him. You wait here."

They did just that, but Duncan noted that Rosalie was looking around the room like she was filing every detail away, like every dirty plate or can of soda was something that might answer a very simple question.

Who killed Hunter Villanova?

When Owen shuffled in, the poor guy was red-eyed and clearly overwrought. But he still walked over. Rosalie pushed a chair out for him, and he slumped into it.

Rosalie smiled at him, her look soft and reassuring. "Hi, Owen. My name's Rosalie Young. I live on the ranch just across the way. You probably know my sister, Audra, if you do anything with the agricultural society."

Owen seemed to struggle to take that all in, but eventually he nodded. "I know Audra."

"I don't want to take up too much of your time. I just want to ask some questions about what happened today."

Owen looked down at the table and nodded.

"I know some of what the detective already asked you, and I know it's frustrating to tell different people the same thing, so if you don't want to answer, you just go on and tell me that. No harm, no foul."

Owen blinked, looked up at her. Something like hope and trust flickered over his face. "Yeah, okay," he said, almost eagerly.

"Hunter and you came here from Bismarck?"

"Close enough. My mom and Mr. Kirk are related somehow. Mom said I had two choices. Get out of her house and make my own way or come on down here and work. I was getting in some trouble, and she was tired of it. Hunter…" He sucked in a breath, and it hitched. "I just don't understand what happened." He looked up at Rosalie, like maybe she could explain it to him.

"Can you tell me some things about him?" Rosalie asked gently. "Whatever you think might be important."

Duncan watched in fascination as Rosalie was…really, really sweet with Owen. She let him babble, and carefully would bring him back around to the main point—which seemed to be who would want to hurt Hunter, and what kind of people he was mixed up with. She didn't write anything down, like the detective had, but somehow Duncan knew she was filing every last point away.

Like the fact that Hunter had brothers who sold drugs. Which *seemed* like petty criminal nonsense, but he supposed with murder in the mix, you never knew.

When Owen started to get emotional again, big fat tears sliding down his cheeks, Rosalie rubbed her hand up and down the kid's back and offered to call his mom once she was done asking questions.

"Nah, Aunt Nat was going to do it for me." Owen looked

up at Duncan. "I know he was trouble, but he really did want to get out of it. It was his idea to come with me. He wanted to get away from it."

Duncan nodded, wanting to reassure this guy he didn't even really know in some way. Just like Rosalie was doing. "I'm sure he did." He wasn't sure at all, but it seemed the right thing to say to this devastation.

"Thank you, Owen. I really appreciate it, and I'm going to do my best to help the detectives get to the bottom of it. They're going to keep asking you questions, and it's going to be hard, but you're going to get through it, because every answer is a chance for making sure whoever did this to Hunter pays."

Owen nodded as a few more tears fell. When Terry came back into the room, Rosalie gave Owen's shoulder a squeeze as she got up, then followed Duncan out of the bunkhouse and back into a shockingly sunny early afternoon.

They walked onto the pathway that led to the main house. Almost in tandem, they let out slow breaths and took deep ones of the summer sunshine.

"Hell, I feel old," Duncan muttered. "Back when I was twenty-two, I thought I was such an adult. Now I look at him and think what a kid he is. Shouldering all this."

"Yeah, we've all got things to shoulder. Life doesn't discriminate much, does it?"

"Guess not."

"Besides, you are old," she offered, with some forced cheer he knew was meant to be an attempt to lighten the mood.

And since he figured they both needed it, he went along with it. "Too old?" he replied, flashing a grin.

"Obviously," she replied, but she was smiling. Nah, not too old.

She sighed. "I'm going to head to my office, do some paperwork on this. When Detective Beckett comes back with search warrants and questions, I want you to pay attention. What the search warrants are for, what questions they ask. Record what you can if you don't have a good memory."

"I've got a good memory."

"Excellent. I'll be in touch." She started to march toward her truck, those short legs eating up the distance in quick time. A completely different person than she'd been back there at the bunkhouse.

Or was it different? Because she was taking on a case no one would pay her for. Out of concern for her sister, maybe, but she'd treated Owen like… Well, like he figured anyone would want to be treated in such an awful situation.

Duncan couldn't have managed that on his own.

"Rosalie."

She stopped, looked at him somewhat suspiciously.

He didn't know how this would have all gone down if she hadn't accidentally been here. Certainly not as smoothly. "I'm glad you were here."

There was just a *second* where she went completely still. An arrested expression crossed her face, then she shrugged and stalked away.

Duncan couldn't think about her reaction to that, or his. He had to go inside and deal with his parents.

ROSALIE TYPED IT all up. Her fingers moved *almost* as fast as her mind. She found in her years of working at Fool's Gold Investigations that people talked a lot more when you weren't taking notes or recording things. They gave information more freely when it felt like a conversation, like you cared about them as much as the case.

Owen Green was telling the truth. Rosalie knew that not because she believed she had some amazing ability to tell truth from lie, or that she didn't believe people could act. She'd learned her gut instincts *could* be fallible and *some* people didn't need a reason to lie—they just liked it.

But poor Owen was overwrought. Hurting. Grief was one of the few emotions she'd never seen someone fake well. When people were faking it, they just acted sad, or maybe they'd maneuver in a little anger. They cried a lot, yelled a lot. They didn't know that with grief always came a helpless undertone of shock, and guilt. No matter how old or young the deceased, no matter how peacefully they might have passed, grief and guilt held hands for those who'd loved the person they lost.

Rosalie muttered a foul curse under her breath, because she didn't want to be thinking about *grief*.

She focused on this case for the rest of the day. Well past dinnertime she was sending emails, making phone calls, and putting together what disparate details she could. Quinn popped in to say goodbye, and still Rosalie stayed at her desk and worked, only taking a quick break to tell Audra she wouldn't be home with pizza any time soon.

Later, she heard the faint sound of a knock and looked up, but she couldn't see the front door from where she sat in her office. Her gun was still holstered at her hip, so she put a hand to it as she stood and carefully moved to the doorway.

The front blinds were drawn for the night, but there was a little window at the door, and in the window, she saw a recognizable face.

Duncan.

Why that made her feel nervous she couldn't quite figure out. He was an easy enough guy to deal with. It was no doubt about work, so there was absolutely no reason for her heart to skip a beat.

She moved forward and opened the door. It was dark outside, though she saw a flicker of lightning in the distance and could smell the rain with it as well.

Which was the only reason she let him step inside, the threat of that storm in the distance.

So it was just her and Duncan alone in this old, finnicky building, with the lights dimmed for the night.

A strange tension wound itself into a tight ball in her chest. Not discomfort, not anything she fully recognized, and that left her feeling off-kilter. Unable to find her usual brash way through without her normal footing.

"Why are you here?" she asked, sounding far too grumpy and demanding.

He eyed her with some humor, which put her even more off balance. Who met rudeness with humor?

"Cops finally left. You said you wanted to know what they did and said."

"Yeah, I do, but you didn't have to come all the way out here."

He shrugged. "Mom's already planning the funeral—I guess Hunter's family wasn't interested. She had me run some errands for it, and I was in the area, so I thought I'd stop by and tell you. Be easier here, anyway."

Rosalie remembered then, with a clear detail she didn't want, how Natalie had stepped in and walked Mom through funeral preparations for Dad even as their entire foundation had crumbled around them.

The Kirks did what needed doing, and maybe she figured the hotshot baseball player who'd barely been home wouldn't follow suit, but clearly he did.

"We don't have to do it here if you're..." He trailed off. The humor didn't leave his expression. "Uncomfortable."

She barely resisted a scowl. "Why would I be uncomfortable?"

He gave a little shrug, still standing close to the doorway. "I'm a big guy. You're a small woman. It's late, and I assume we're in this building alone. I wouldn't blame you for feeling...intimidated."

She wasn't sure if he meant that to be a challenge, or if he was just an arrogant SOB. She patted the gun on her hip. "I'm armed." Because she wasn't *intimidated.* Rosalie Young didn't do intimidated. Never had.

But his amused smile stayed put. "Noted."

"And you're not that big," she continued. Childishly, she knew, but she just hadn't been able to stop herself. Because, of course he was *that* big. He had to be pushing six-five, and she was fairly certain there wasn't an ounce of body fat on that tall, muscular frame.

The way his mouth seemed to take its time unfurling into an upward curl, the way his dark eyes danced with humor, had unwanted and unfamiliar fireworks going off inside of her. Rosalie *hated* feeling knocked off her axis. She associated it with the aftermath of her father's death, and even if this was a kind of...an almost pleasant knocked-off-her-axis feeling, she still didn't trust it.

Or him for bringing out unfamiliar feelings.

"So run me through it," she said, brusquely turning away from him and marching back into her office.

He followed her into the room, took the seat across from her desk that she gestured to. When she looked at him again, the humor and smile had both melted away.

Back to murder and questions. She almost regretted it. Except this was her job and this was why he was even here.

"They came back with search warrants for the house and the bunks. They were really interested in gun safes and who owned what, the licenses everyone had. That sort of thing. Makes sense, I guess."

Rosalie nodded. That was about what she'd expected. "They'll be back once they know what kind of gun killed him. They'll compare what guns they first inventoried, make sure none mysteriously disappeared. They'll have more questions as they carefully and methodically build a case."

"Against who?"

"It'll depend on the guns. It'll depend on if they think they've found a motive. An investigation like this... It's all layers. They'll work hard, but unless it's easy answers, it'll be slow going."

Duncan clearly didn't like that answer, and Rosalie couldn't blame him.

He sat forward, balancing his elbows on his knees as he looked at her intently. "The thing is, if everything Owen said was true, Hunter was trying to get on the straight and narrow. He left the bad stuff behind in North Dakota. Why would it follow him all the way here? Why would it end in murder?"

"I've put some feelers out, as no doubt Detective Beckett has, to the authorities in North Dakota to see if we can get an idea of the trouble he'd been in, and who else was involved."

"What if it's nothing?"

"No point crossing that bridge 'til we come to it. First, we've got to find the nothing."

Duncan made a frustrated grunting sound. "I'm worried about my parents. Not just their safety, but the mental toll of all this. They were already worried about the missing cows, now this. If it drags on... I don't want it to drag on."

Rosalie's heart twisted at the genuine concern in his tone and on his face, but the cows…

Missing cows. Another unexplained bit of weirdness going on at the Kirk Ranch. "Could it be connected?" she wondered aloud, trying to work out *how*.

Duncan just stared at her for a full minute. "A murder and missing cows?"

"Neither make much sense, so maybe they don't make sense together. Did your parents or you tell the detective about the missing cows?"

Duncan was quiet a moment, clearly reaching back and remembering. He shook his head. "No, I don't suppose it occurred to any of us that the murder would have anything to do with something so…mundane."

"They should tell Detective Beckett. As soon as possible. Someone needs to bring it up. I'll corroborate you came to me before the murder. It'll help."

"Help what?"

"Duncan…" She hesitated, which was rare for her. She believed in being a straight shooter, and she left softening blows to people better suited to it. But the concern he felt for his parents was palpable and she didn't want to add to it.

It was the right thing to do, though. "If there's anything it looks like they're hiding, that's going to… It's going to draw attention to them."

"To… My *parents*?" The pure, unadulterated shock on his face made it clear that Duncan Kirk had never known a day of truly *unfair* in his life. "You can't be serious."

She wanted to resent his naivete, but… Well, Natalie and Norman Kirk were good, honest people. Why shouldn't he be offended on their behalf? "Duncan, you know your parents. I know your parents. The Bent County Sheriff's Department? They don't. At least, the lead detective doesn't.

So he's going to treat them like facts on paper—and that might grate, but it's his job to do that. His job is facts."

Duncan stood up, somewhat abruptly. She thought maybe he was going to leave, but he just stood there, looking thunderous and...

Hot.

So not the time.

"If anyone so much as insinuates that my parents could have possibly had something to do with this murder—"

Rosalie stood, skirted the desk, and against her better judgment, reached out and put a hand on his arm.

He winced a little instead of finishing his sentence, and she realized her grip was on his bad arm.

She pulled her hand back. "Sorry," she muttered, feeling stupid for too many reasons to count. "Listen. You have to put your personal feelings away, okay? I know that's asking a lot, but if you get mad, then *you're* in the line of fire."

"So what?" he demanded. "I'll hire a passel of lawyers to drown their asses."

"Or," she returned evenly, "you could just tell the truth, Duncan. You could give the detectives everything they need to hopefully find a murderer. Put your pride aside, put your..." She hated to admit that she understood this was more than some rich guy's pride and pettiness. He wanted to protect his parents.

And that understanding made her softer than it should. "Put aside wanting to protect them. I get it. I really do. I'd protect my sister at any and all costs, but take it from someone who knows their way around a police investigation. If you take it upon yourself to protect—and keep the police at arm's length—you're only making everything worse."

He stood there, breathing a little hard, eyes blazing with a pointless anger she understood too well.

Damn it all to hell, the last thing she needed was to *understand him*.

"All right. I'll trust you on this, Rosalie." His gaze was hard, but she couldn't quite fight the shudder that jittered through her at the way he said her full name. "But you better be right."

Chapter Six

Duncan made it through the next few days on little more than caffeine and worry. His arm throbbed, because he never seemed to have anything to eat on hand to take his pain pill with. His head ached, both from too much caffeine and not enough sleep. And the worry that had tied its way around his entire body got tighter every day, not helping any with sleep or the ability to eat.

Mom took too much on her shoulders. Dad seemed like he was somehow disappearing in front of Duncan's very eyes. It reminded him too much of a time he only barely remembered, because he'd been five or six, when his grandmother had been sick and dying. The stress, worry, and grief had clung to the ranch then. As they did now.

He hated it. He didn't know what to do about it. Except volunteer for every errand, every ranch chore he could manage one-armed, more or less, and so on and so forth. Trying to take some of that weight away. *Any* of the weight.

Three days later, on a pretty afternoon, they held a small graveside funeral in the small cemetery in Sunrise for a young man almost no one had actually known.

The ceremony was small and depressing. Apparently poor Hunter Villanova didn't have much in the way of family.

No one had wanted his remains, so Mom had taken it upon herself to secure him a plot and a stone here in Sunrise.

The entire group was made up of Duncan, his parents, Owen, and a handful of the ranch hands, including Terry. It would have just been Kirk Ranch people, but Rosalie was there.

With Audra and their cousin—Duncan couldn't quite remember her name—but he mostly just saw Rosalie and the way the afternoon sun glinted off her red hair, and the way a little breeze teased the tendrils around her face.

And maybe, most of all, the way she held herself. A little stiff. A lot formal. Like there was something she was bracing herself against. Not a weight, exactly, but something akin to one.

When the funeral ended, and Audra and the cousin drifted over to a section of the cemetery where the name *Young* seemed to dominate, Rosalie didn't follow. She stood a ways back, staring ahead at seemingly nothing without blinking.

It was then Duncan finally realized that she was likely bracing herself against grief. Because her dead were buried here.

But she didn't go pay them any respects, and that struck Duncan as…sad. Twisted something in him, so he stepped away from his parents—who were thanking the minister for handling the small, brief ceremony—to approach Rosalie.

"Afternoon," he offered in greeting, coming to stand next to her. He looked straight ahead too, trying to determine what she might be staring at.

"Audra thought it would do your mom some good if more than just Kirk Ranch came."

"She's right. It eased her heart some."

Rosalie sighed, and Duncan thought he should understand

that sigh, but he couldn't quite reason it out. Or the almost wistful expression on Rosalie's face.

"Any news on the investigative front?" he asked, even though he figured he knew the answer. He doubted she'd keep information from him. They'd told Detective Beckett about the cows, as Rosalie had advised, but since then, nothing had really come to light.

"Not much," she said, and he could hear the frustration in her voice. "Anyone been back out to search the guns?"

Duncan shook his head. "Detective Beckett came out to talk to Terry yesterday, but I don't know what they talked about. I assume he told Dad, but Dad... He doesn't like to talk about it." And Duncan couldn't bring himself to press. "I told Beckett about the cows myself the day after I talked to you. He didn't have much interest in a connection."

Rosalie frowned a little at that, but she didn't offer anything else.

"I don't think anyone thinks we're in any immediate danger. It seems the consensus is that whatever Hunter had been mixed up in back in North Dakota followed him here. And if it had anything to do with cows, it was primarily coincidental."

"That would make the most sense, I suppose," Rosalie said, sounding less than convinced. Which Duncan had to admit, eased some small portion of the worry on his shoulders.

He looked over at his father. Pale. And in a strange kind of daze neither Duncan nor his mother seemed to know how to get through. "But Dad is taking it personally. Someone being hurt on his land."

Rosalie nodded slowly. "It's a desecration of something holy."

When Duncan stared at her, because that was exactly it and beautifully said, she shrugged in a jerking motion.

"To him," she said somewhat defensively.

"To him," Duncan agreed, surprised to find his throat a little tight. He understood that his parents lived in a tight-knit community. He tended to think of small-town life as one of gossip and a slow pace of running errands, but in the past few days, he'd been reminded of this.

It wasn't just community—nosiness and pettiness existed here just as assuredly as they did everywhere—but it was people who understood why some virtual stranger who had no family to bring him home might mean something to his parents.

Because the land was holy, and someone had desecrated it.

"I'm going to stop by the sheriff's department after this," Rosalie said into the heavy silence. "Rattle some cages." She offered him a pathetic attempt at a smile. "If there's anything of note, I'll let you know."

She started to move, but Duncan moved with her. He didn't know what he was going to do if he stayed here. He couldn't keep standing still, trying to hold everything together with just one working arm. He needed to…do something.

"Let me come with you," he said, on a whim, without thinking it through.

But when she looked at him with a kind of condescending refusal, the idea took root.

"Duncan," she said, shaking her head. "No."

He wasn't taking no for an answer. "Why not?"

"Because I'm a licensed private investigator off to do my job and you're…" She looked him up and down, no doubt weighing how mean she was going to be.

He kind of wished she'd be really mean. It'd give him something to fight against.

But in the end, she just said, "...some guy."

"Let me come with you," he insisted. He could follow her, either way, but it'd be better if they worked together. "I've got to *do* something."

He didn't know why it was that sentence that got through to her, but something about it had her relenting.

"Fine," she muttered. "You need a ride?"

He nodded. "I came over with my parents. But I'll let them know I'm hitching a ride with you. Unless you need to drop your sister off?"

Rosalie shook her head, even as her gaze darted over to where Audra stood next to a newer-looking stone.

"We came separately," Rosalie said firmly. She turned her back on Audra. "I'll meet you at my truck."

Duncan wasn't sure what was going on there, considering how close it seemed the sisters were when he'd dropped by their place. He made his way back to his parents so he could tell them he was heading into town. But before he made it to them, he took a little detour so he could see the name on the gravestone Audra had been standing next to before she and the cousin had moved over to talk to Mom.

Tim Young was carved clearly in stone.

Audra and Rosalie's dad.

Duncan glanced back at the parking lot, where Rosalie stood outside her truck, her back to the graves.

It wasn't any of his business, but he wondered what made one sister grieve and one sister turn her back on a memory.

Audra was still talking to his mother when he approached, but they both immediately stopped talking once he was in earshot and beamed similar smiles at him.

Why it felt suspicious, he couldn't fathom.

"I'm going to head into town for a bit. I'll be back at the ranch later," he told his mother.

"You didn't bring your truck."

"I'm going with Rosalie," he offered, somewhat reluctantly, because both Audra and Mom were already looking in Rosalie's direction. He didn't want to say it was about the investigation, because they were in a graveyard. He didn't want them thinking it was something else, because clearly they *were* thinking that.

Then he figured it would really annoy Rosalie if Mom and Audra thought that he and Rosalie were off doing something *together* together, so he just went with it. Let them think it. He sure hoped Audra asked Rosalie about it later today. Wished he could be there.

He said goodbye to his parents, then walked back to Rosalie. She climbed in the truck when she saw him coming, had the engine going by the time he managed to leverage himself up into the passenger seat.

"Here's the deal. I'm going to the station to see what I can find out that Detective Beckett doesn't want to tell me. So when we get into the detective's office, you let me do the talking. We'll use you as a potential distraction."

"How would I be a distraction?"

"Oh, I don't know. Hey, everyone, look, the famous baseball player is lurking about. Ask him for autographs while I take a tour of Beckett's desk."

He wriggled the hand hanging from his sling. "Not much on signing these days."

"Fine. We'll line the women up and you can smile at them. Maybe have a few swoon so Beckett has to do something."

"Are you calling my smile distracting, Rosalie?"

She rolled her eyes, but there was some humor to it. And that felt like such a relief, he wanted to lean into it.

"I think my mom has some suspicions. Audra too."

"Suspicions about what?" she asked, backing out of the cemetery parking lot.

"Why we're headed off together."

"You didn't tell them it was for the case?"

He looked at her, all feigned innocence that clearly irritated her. And amused him even more. "Should I have?"

She gave an injured sniff, focused on the road, and held the steering wheel just a touch too tight, if the white in her knuckles was anything to go by. "I'm sure they know," she said stiffly.

"Yeah," he replied. "I'm *sure*."

Her knuckles got even whiter as she drove.

ROSALIE STILL HADN'T decided how to handle Duncan. She figured the flirting was just for fun, or maybe even just part of his personality. Normally, that sort of thing didn't bother her any because it was usually *her* MO.

But something about Duncan really scrambled things up. Or maybe it was the *murder*, which he should care more about than scrambling her up.

Of course, she'd seen the way he'd looked at his parents. So full of worry. She saw the way the last several days hung on him, almost as much as it hung on his dad. Their color was off, and they both managed to look…gaunt.

Maybe that was the scramble. She didn't know this guy, not on any deeper level, but she saw things she recognized in him.

And she didn't *like* it. Any more than she liked his big frame taking up space in her truck. Or that pinched look on his face when they hit a bump and his arm in the sling bounced a little and clearly hurt him.

Or the fact it made her drive slower.

She pulled to a stop in the parking lot at the sheriff's department, then led Duncan inside.

She waved at the admin at the front desk, didn't bother to sign in because she knew Vicky wouldn't say anything to anyone about it, and made a beeline for the detective's office.

Copeland wasn't in it, and neither was the third Bent County detective, Laurel Delaney-Carson, but Hart was.

"Hart. How's it going?" Rosalie greeted, gesturing Duncan to follow her into the room.

"Going," the guy grumbled before glancing up. His gaze stopped on Duncan, clear recognition sweeping over him, but he didn't linger. He moved his eyes back to Rosalie. "Something I can do for you?"

"No, came to bother Copeland. Hart, this is Duncan Kirk. His parents own the ranch where the murder was. Duncan, Thomas Hart is a detective when he's not waylaid. Hey, look at that, you guys practically match." She pointed to both their slings when Thomas stood in greeting.

"I'd shake your hand, but as Rosalie so helpfully pointed out, I'm a bit stuck as of yet," Thomas said wryly.

"You're both old. You probably went to high school together," Rosalie offered, earning her scathing looks from both men. She smiled sweetly.

"I don't think we did. At least we didn't run in the same circles," Thomas said. "But it's nice to meet you, Duncan. Big fan."

"I don't suppose you blew your arm out throwing a ball," Duncan offered with some humor.

Hart smiled kindly. "Not quite."

"He got shot saving his wife's life," Rosalie said, because she knew somehow it would make them both uncomfortable. "Real hero stuff, our Thomas."

Before the conversation could continue, Copeland stormed into the office. His eyes were narrowed, and Rosalie figured he thought she was pumping Thomas for info. As if she'd do that here. She'd visit Vi if she wanted to secretly hound Thomas.

"I'm not giving you—either of you—any information you don't already have," Copeland said, pointing at Rosalie, then Duncan.

When Rosalie looked over at Hart, Copeland immediately stepped in her line of sight. "And none of that. You can't use your cousin's connection to Hart as some sort of leverage."

"Sure I can," Rosalie replied good-naturedly. "Vi marrying Thomas has been quite the boon for my business."

Copeland looked disgustedly at Hart, who shrugged. "I tell my wife everything. Don't plan to stop. Maybe you need yourself a wife, Cope."

"I'll chew my own arm off first," he muttered, returning his annoyed gaze to Rosalie. "I don't have anything for you."

"Maybe I have something for *you*." She didn't, of course, but he might slip up if he thought she did.

Copeland opened his mouth, no doubt to argue, but his eyes narrowed. He studied her. "You don't."

She lifted a shoulder. "Guess you'll never know."

His suspicious gaze turned to Duncan. "She doesn't."

But Duncan, clearly in the spirit of messing with Copeland, just shrugged.

"You don't have a lead on the murder weapon," Rosalie said, wanting to poke at him until he gave something up. Since she really didn't have a gosh darn lead at the moment.

Copeland didn't react. So she kept poking.

"You don't have a hint of a suspect," she said, ticking the points off on her fingers. "You don't even know where to start looking for one."

"The victim was messed up with some dangerous stuff back in North Dakota," Copeland growled. "The most likely answer is something from his past caught up with him. We're looking into it. Along with all other leads that have been brought to us, including a rash of missing cattle."

But she saw it, in Copeland's thinly veiled frustration. In that blank way he delivered the information. He wasn't *hiding* anything.

"You really have nothing."

"We're investigating," he said stiffly.

But Rosalie felt deflated instead of victorious. She'd been certain Copeland would have caught wind of something she hadn't. He had more resources than she did, even if she could bend the rules a little bit.

And if he had all those resources, all these *detectives*, and he had nothing... It made her chest tighten. Like she was failing everyone.

She whirled out of the office and started marching back outside. It was just a setback. The cops had nothing, which meant she had to find something. She *had* to.

"It seems like my dad was right," Duncan said, following along easily enough.

"About what?"

"Some city detective doesn't belong here. No leads? What the hell is this?"

He didn't *sound* mad, but the take was an interesting one. She didn't blame Copeland's background on no leads, but... "You just moved back after living the high life in LA and you think you know more than a detective?"

"No, but I grew up here. I know ranching. That Detective Beckett probably doesn't know a bull from a cow. How would he know if anything Hunter was mixed up in had something to do with the ranch?"

Rosalie considered that. She didn't fully agree, but there were little true points hidden in his not fully correct one. And the thing was, Thomas might be from Bent, even Detective Delaney-Carson was *from* here, but they weren't ranchers. They might have an idea about things just from proximity, but they didn't have the full picture.

"You're right," she said, everything clicking into her head in the way she liked. In the way that prompted action, so she could follow one tiny little clue to the next.

"I am? Hey, say that again. I get the feeling I'm going to want to live off that admission for the next five years."

She ignored him, focused on the *point*. "They're detectives. They're not ranchers. Hart might be from here, but there's no ranching blood there. But me? I'm both. Sort of. Come on."

"Where are we going?"

"Back to your place, Ace."

She had a plan.

Chapter Seven

She drove like a mad woman, and though Duncan's heart leaped into his throat approximately four different times, he refused to show it. A woman like Rosalie would see clutching the door handle as a weakness.

Besides, he couldn't clutch a damn thing with his bad arm anyway.

She took a side entrance on the Young side of the property line, but cut over closer to his cabin where there was no real road or path.

He eyed her. "Been mapping out ways to come find me, Red?"

One side of her mouth curved up—amusement in spite of how badly he knew she didn't want to be amused by him. It eased something inside of him, this very simple human interaction that didn't have any weights to it. Even when his life had been baseball, every relationship had been full of weights—responsibility to his team, his manager, his agent. How he was representing the team, himself. His *brand*, as his agent liked to say.

And he loved his parents, with everything he was. There wasn't a weight there he didn't take on gladly and with enough humility to know the weights went both ways. Because when you loved people, you worried about them.

When people supported your dream, you wanted to do right by them in every way you could.

And he wanted to fix this stress for them, this hurt. This *desecration*. So that was a weight.

But with Rosalie, she was just…a friend. Helping him with a problem. And there were no weights.

For a minute, that felt just as disorienting as it did freeing. Especially when she pulled her truck to a stop in front of his cabin, then got out with a little hop and started marching right for the cabin. Up his porch, like she was coming inside with him and that…felt a little more like panic than ease.

He hurried up to the door, which he'd locked, so it wasn't like she could get inside. Still, he felt the need to bar the door with his body.

"I haven't unpacked yet."

She waved that away with the flick of a wrist. "I'm a slob. Won't bother me any." She gestured for the door. "Let me in or I'll assume you're hiding a murder weapon and a bunch of dead cows in there."

She smirked at him and since he genuinely didn't know what else to do, he let her inside. The curtains were drawn, so the room was dim. He could turn on the lights… He could do a lot of things, but exhaustion was poking at him. Pain— in his shoulder, his head. Since she wasn't explaining what was up, he took a seat on his couch. For just a moment, he closed his eyes and let out a long, slow breath.

"You're in pain." She said it like an accusation.

"You're not living if you're not in pain."

"That's the stupidest thing I've ever heard anyone say, and I deal with criminals on the regular."

When he opened his eyes, she was standing in front of him, hands on her hips. She was wearing a simple little black dress. It wasn't the right color for her at all, but he didn't mind the view of her legs. Which he took his time enjoying before meeting her gaze.

"It's the way of life for a professional pitcher. The older you get, the more it hurts."

She stared down at him, those violet eyes flashing with a restrained annoyance that never failed to amuse him. Or maybe *arouse* him was the more apt word, even if he was trying to ignore how much he liked being in her orbit. "Got any aspirin around here?" she demanded.

"For you or for me?"

She sighed at him as if he was a difficult toddler. "For you."

"I've got a pain pill I can take, but I need to eat something with it."

She marched right into his kitchen, poked around in the fridge and the little pantry. He almost told her to stop, that he'd handle it, but she just…moved around the space that he didn't think she'd ever been in and made him a sandwich without asking any questions. She filled a glass with water, brought both over, and set them on the coffee table in front of him. Then she put a little orange bottle there too.

"Eat. Take the pill. And learn this lesson pretty dang quick—you can't take care of the people in your life if you don't take care of yourself." She said this firmly, with enough conviction that he studied her.

"You do a lot of taking care?"

Her gaze skittered away from his. "I give it a shot every now and then. So here's what we're going to do." She was pacing in front of him now, but if he stopped eating, she'd stop, and glare at him until he did.

So he ate, while she laid it out.

"We're going to map it out, the missing cows. The cows Audra found on our land last year all the way to the last one.

Map it out by location. Mark it down by calendar. We're going to follow every last step from a ranching perspective and see if something jumps out and connects to a murder perspective."

He liked that it sounded like something, but it didn't sound like finding a murderer. "And if this has nothing to do with the murder?"

"We'll have figured out one mystery at least." She tapped her fingers on the table. "Listen, maybe this is the deadest of ends, but we're already at one. And so are the cops. If they won't follow this line, we have to. Because we've got ranch eyes, or at least I do."

"I've got ranch eyes," he muttered, feeling defensive because…yeah, he didn't have a clue. For the past fifteen years, he'd only been on this ranch on holidays. But there'd been a time—before high school, because even then his parents had let him focus on baseball—in the early part of his childhood when his life had been about setting him up for taking over the ranch someday.

He'd never…wanted that, but he'd been raised in it. So he wasn't ignorant. He wasn't going to let himself feel like he didn't belong right here. Like he didn't know more than those detectives who'd never dealt with calving or branding season and everything after and in between.

"Okay, so we use our inherent understanding," Rosalie said firmly, not arguing about his *ranch eyes*. "And maybe it's the wrong direction, but sometimes when you scale a brick wall, you get to the other side and realize it didn't lead you where you wanted to go at all. But other sometimes, that's an answer all on its own, or it leads you to a place you'd never have thought of otherwise. We need a map of the ranch."

Duncan nodded. "I can get my hands on a map."

"Then we need dates. More than just that list of cows your mom gave you. What was going on that day, who was working what jobs. Maybe you could talk to Terry about it. Or I can."

"I'll do it," Duncan said. "Not sure Terry's my biggest fan. Pretty sure he sees us both as outsiders, but he'll be more careful with you. If I get Mom behind me, he'll tell me everything."

"Okay. So I'll leave it up to you. Gather all that information, and we'll go from there. Tonight, I'll talk to Audra about everything she remembers when the cows ended up over at our place."

"Sure, I—" He was interrupted by a vibration in his pocket. He pulled out his phone and saw his agent's name. He could avoid it, but then he'd be distracted, and he still wanted to talk to Rosalie about Owen. "Can you wait here? Just a second. I have to take this, but… Just give me one second."

She eyed him suspiciously, but she nodded, so he walked deeper into the cabin and went into his bedroom. The last thing he wanted was Rosalie's eyes on him while he talked to Scott about baseball things.

ROSALIE WATCHED AS Duncan moved stiffly down the hall and into a room she suspected was his bedroom. He shut the door.

She'd never seen that look on his face before. A kind of hard-edged annoyance. Not quite as pissed off as she'd seen him get over things with the case. No, there was something too resigned about it.

Rosalie forced herself to survey the cabin instead of continuing to mine thoughts about Duncan's *facial* expressions. But there was something she had no compunction about mining.

Since he was occupied, Rosalie poked around his living room, which was indeed full of unpacked boxes. She'd been a private investigator too long not to take liberties when she had the opportunity. She nudged open a box in the corner, then just stared at it.

It was full of…trophies and awards. Somewhat haphazardly packed. None were wrapped up carefully, but a few sheets of bubble wrap were stuffed here and there. She didn't reach out and touch one, but she read the engraving on one that she could see. *Cy Young Award.*

It sent a strange wave of sympathy through her—which didn't make much sense, because he had an award she knew was incredibly important and amazing in his sport. He was loaded. He had gone out into the world and lived his dream. So why should she feel any sympathy for that, even if it had ended on a sour note?

But he'd been at the top of his game. A bona fide star. Now he was back in Wyoming and in constant pain, it seemed. With missing cows, murders, and worry about his parents.

And that was the foundation of where any sympathy came from. She could see it on his face, the way he wasn't taking care of himself. He worried far more about his parents than about his old awards, or life, or even his pain.

He'd been going around today hurting, all because he hadn't taken the time to eat something and take a pain pill.

She was just soft enough that she couldn't quite harden her heart against that. Which didn't seem fair at all.

"Did it ever occur to you some of that might be private?"

Rosalie refused to jump or startle. She glanced over at him and smiled, not bothering to close the box. "Of course it occurred to me. That's why I looked."

Maybe she expected him to be angry about it. Maybe she

hadn't really considered his reaction. But she sure wasn't prepared for that grin of his, and the way it shot through her like fireworks.

"You want to go through all my awards, Red?" he asked in that slick way he had that she really, *really* wished didn't affect her the way it did. "You'll be here all night."

Something about him saying *all night* poked holes in all her usual smarts. Because she should have let that go. Stepped back and away from the *danger, danger* of it all.

She didn't. "Well, if that's the most entertaining thing you can think of to do all night, no wonder you're back to living with your parents."

The air felt charged then. *All night* hanging around them like a storm that rolled in out of nowhere. Which just kept happening. Every time she was around him.

It's not going to stop.

No, it wasn't. Not when he moved closer, and she was not someone who retreated, even when she should. She stood her ground. She fought any threat head-on and with relish.

Except this one. She took a step back, and then another, until she found herself backed against a wall.

A place she had never found herself in all her life.

"That wasn't an invitation to prove yourself," she said, but she didn't sound like her normal, in-control, haughty self. She sounded winded.

Particularly when he stood in front of her, all tall and broad and so handsome it hurt.

He raised an eyebrow, leaned closer. "No?" he asked, reaching out. She thought he'd touch her face or something, something she should stop him from doing. But he only smoothed a big hand over her hair.

Still that almost touch skittered through her like the sizzle of a lightning strike that hit close enough to worry about. "N-no."

"Did you just stutter?" he asked, too much amusement in his tone as he leaned close enough that she could feel his breath against her cheek. He smelled like clean, crisp winter. A hint of pine.

But she did *not* stutter. Wouldn't. Her scoffing laugh was high-pitched even to her own ears. But he was so *close*, and he was so damn *tall*. His eyes felt like magnets. Like entire solar systems that sucked her into their orbit.

She knew better than to be sucked in, than to get mixed up in anything that wasn't light and easy. Anything she wasn't in complete control of, and boy, was she not in control of this.

It was just…she could almost imagine it. His hands on her. His mouth on her. She could imagine it so well she was having a hard time reminding herself why she shouldn't let it happen. There was a reason.

Wasn't there?

"Rosalie." He said her name in a way she couldn't even describe. It was low, almost…pained. Like he felt even half the two polarizing things tearing her apart. She could *feel* his dark eyes searching her for some explanation, some answer, because for whatever reason there was this *question* between them, an unknowing she wanted an answer to.

And at the very same time, didn't want at all.

"Let's just see," he murmured. "Let me."

It wasn't a question. There was no answer she was supposed to have. It was almost an order, not that she ever took orders.

Ever.

But she *let him* anyway.

His mouth touched hers, the lightest, nothing touch. His

eyes were still open and on hers. An answer to a question she didn't understand, because there were too many layers to it. To him. To her.

That would have been enough to have her stepping away, but it was like he sensed it. Her closing in and up, and he didn't let her. He deepened the kiss instead, bringing his hand up to cup her head and pull her in.

It was like being catapulted into a carnival ride. All spins, and dips, and a strange weightless joy. He didn't taste like cotton candy though. No, there was an edge to him, a danger at the periphery of all that summer sweetness.

And Rosalie had always been a little too intrigued by danger, the rush of it all. Because danger was simple, and temporary. It destroyed in little ways.

It was secrets, and time, and believing too much that destroyed in big ways. And that was what seemed to twist inside of her now. It was too big, too…something.

But the kiss was like a drug, even knowing it was a bad idea, she shouldn't do it, and it would be terrible for her, she sank into it, and him, and the sweet twining of want and need.

He eased his mouth away, his hand still cupped around her head, keeping her close. Too close. She blinked up at him, not altogether certain she was breathing. His dark, intense gaze just held hers, with a seriousness she couldn't *bear*.

What the hell was she doing?

"I have to go." She ducked out from his light grip, didn't look back. She had never been a coward in her life. Not once. But she needed to be one now. "You get all that information. Call me when you do."

Maybe he said her name, maybe she imagined it. But she got the hell out of Dodge while she could.

Chapter Eight

Though Duncan was tempted to follow her, he didn't. She'd looked…rattled, and he couldn't say he loved seeing rattled on steady, sturdy Rosalie Young.

He liked everything else he'd seen. The blush in her cheeks, her blue eyes shaded toward violet, that catch in her breath.

Did he know what he was doing? Hell no. He wasn't sure where to slot that kiss. He'd never once dipped his toes in complicated waters, because since he'd been twelve years old, and a coach had taken his parents aside after a Little League game and told them he had a *gift*, his one true love and passion had been baseball.

Sure, there'd been women, but there hadn't been relationships. He didn't have the time or inclination for complications, even in the offseason.

He didn't have to be in a relationship with Rosalie, or even know her all that well, to know there was no way to do casual in this world he found himself in.

So it was best that she'd run away.

But he looked around at his new life. Sans baseball—because just before this little interlude, he'd told Scott once more that he had no plans to attempt a comeback, take a coaching job, or anything remotely related to broadcasting.

He was terrified it would feel empty.

But he had his family now. His roots. His legacy. Things he'd let fall by the wayside for far too long.

So why should he balk at exploring something that might be deeper than a one-night stand in a hotel room?

When a knock sounded at the door, Duncan's eyebrows raised. Was she back? Now that would be something.

But it was not Rosalie.

"Mom." He glanced out at the yard. Would she have seen Rosalie rush out of here? Drive off? He didn't know how he felt about that. There was something like an echo of old teenage embarrassment, except she didn't say anything.

Which he was almost certain meant she hadn't seen anything. Mom didn't hesitate. She called him out. Always.

"Everything okay?" he asked, then shook his head. "Stupid question. Come on in."

Mom stepped inside. "Your dad is out running himself ragged. I thought maybe you could ride out and help him. I tried, but he's tired of me pecking at him. You two are excellent at sitting in silence."

He almost managed a smile at that.

"You don't have to go right away. He'll figure I sent you if we don't give him *some* alone time. But maybe in an hour or so you could hunt him down?"

He didn't ask why she'd come down to his cabin to ask that, because he could see as she moved restlessly around the front room, eyeing the boxes with a mix of frustration and zeal, that she was looking for things to do, to manage. That was how Mom dealt with stress.

"Sure. I'll track him down. Give him a run for his silent money," he said, hoping to make her smile.

She did, but it was small.

Because he couldn't joke or pester her out of this horrible

reality they found themselves in. So maybe that was what he could do. Find answers.

"Rosalie wants to follow a theory about maybe this connecting to the missing cattle. I told her I could get a map of the ranch, and some more information about the times cattle have gone missing."

Mom frowned. "Of course," she said. "I'll get you a map. I… Don't tell your father, but I wrote down little details about the cows every time it happened. If I ever got him to go to the police, I thought it'd help. I'll give the notes to Rosalie. Or you."

"You've got enough on your plate. You get it to me, I can handle it."

Mom glanced at the door, something Duncan couldn't quite read in her expression. "You know, if you… You don't have to always be here, Duncan. You don't always have to be helping. Your father and I will muddle through."

He couldn't quite understand what she was trying to say, but he went for light and teasing. "Trying to get rid of me?"

"No, I just thought maybe you'd… Well, you don't need to focus on only this case, honey. You're home for good. You should…"

"I should what?"

"Settle in. Meet people. Connect."

He heard every silent word in between the words his mother spoke. *Grow up. Get married. Have kids.*

"Mom. Someone was murdered in your front yard just last week."

"Yes, and it's awful and tragic. But isn't that reminder enough? Life doesn't promise us anything. Might as well find some good in the midst of all that bad." She looked at the door again, considering. "Rosalie's a sweet girl."

Duncan snorted. *Sweet?* No, that was not what Rosalie

was. But she *was* something. "What's any of this got to do with Rosalie?"

She gave him a look then. "Come now, let's not play dumb. You've got your eyes all over her."

Duncan felt that old teenage embarrassment creep in, but he pushed it away. He wasn't going to be a coward just because this woman was his mother. "She's nice to look at."

Mom smiled at that. "She's nice, period. Had a rough go. She looks right back, you know."

His mouth curved in spite of himself. "I know."

She rolled her eyes, despairing of him and loving him in equal measures, as she always had. But her expression immediately sobered, her hands clasped and wringing the way they only did when she was really upset about something.

"I just… Something about that young man dying. What a waste. What a loss. Because there's nothing else he can do now. It's just over. I know you felt like losing baseball was…a death of sorts, and I'm not saying it isn't, or you can't grieve it. I just don't want you grieving it at the cost of life. Because you still have that."

He was rendered speechless for a moment. His mother wasn't afraid to wade in and say anything. Ever. But they didn't really have heart-to-hearts very often. He realized this really was stemming from poor Hunter's murder. Since it was, he tried to be honest with her, instead of doing what he wanted to do, which was fend her off.

"I'm not grieving it at the cost of anything, Mom." That was the truth of it, even if he hadn't really thought of it in those terms. "Maybe I was, but… I'm glad I came home, Mom. To help deal with this, but also because… It feels like life here."

"And I suppose you'll tell me Rosalie has nothing to do with that and I should butt out."

He studied her, knowing he shouldn't say it, but it'd get a smile out of her if he surprised her. "Maybe one of those things. I'll let you pick which one."

ROSALIE GOT HOME LATE. She'd forgotten the pizza she'd promised to make up for last week. She was a mess. She'd be smart to go upstairs, take a long shower, and sleep.

She hunted for Audra instead. Found her in her little office, going over accounts, no doubt. Rosalie hesitated. She didn't want to interrupt Audra, who was already overworked, but...

Audra looked up.

"You got a few minutes?" Rosalie asked reluctantly.

"A few." Audra pursed her lips, studied Rosalie. "Have you eaten?"

"I'll scrounge up something in a minute. I've just got to finish this up. Can you tell me about when you found the Kirk cows on our property? Let me record it?"

"Okay." Audra leaned back in her chair, closed her eyes. "It was back in December. In fact..." She trailed off, got up, and went over to her sturdy stack of filing cabinets. She opened one, pulled out a little top spiral notebook. She hummed to herself as she flipped through the pages. "'December fourteenth. I found three of Norman Kirk's cattle in the east pasture. Returned by nightfall.'"

"Do you remember anything else?"

"We couldn't figure out how they'd gotten over to my place. I helped him and his foreman, and a couple of his hands, search fence line. Tried to retrace their path. It didn't make any sense, but poor Norman was distracted. That was around the time Duncan was having his second surgery, and I know they were just worried sick about him refusing to let them come down to California."

Rosalie tried to remember it, but she didn't really. She didn't pay attention to the ranch, and as nice as the Kirks were, she hadn't paid attention to them. She remembered the story Audra had brought home vaguely because she tended to file mysteries away.

But she hadn't thought about how that affected anyone. Not the Kirks, who were already dealing with worry about their injured son. Not Audra and how much she had on her plate, not just at their ranch, but at the agricultural society, and with neighbors.

Not the neighbor who'd had his whole life upended by some tendons snapping.

She refused to feel sorry for a millionaire who'd achieved his dreams, except she couldn't seem to help herself. What would it be like to devote your entire life to something that you always knew would end? Then it ended, not because of any choice you made, but because of bad luck?

"Rosalie. You aren't paying any attention."

Rosalie blinked back to where she was, what she *should* be thinking about. "Of course I am." Besides, it didn't matter if she'd been thinking of something else, because she was recording what Audra was saying. She could go over it in detail a million times.

"What's up with you?" Audra demanded.

"Nothing."

"Nothing?"

"Nothing."

Audra rolled her eyes. "The minute I mentioned Duncan, you went somewhere else."

She could lie to her sister. It wouldn't be the first time. She wanted to lie. She *planned* to lie, but when she opened her mouth the truth just sort of escaped. "Duncan…kissed me."

Audra beamed at her, all smiles and excitement. "That's fantastic."

"Why the hell would it be fantastic?" Rosalie demanded. "He shouldn't have done it, and I have no plans to repeat it."

Audra's expression fell. Then her eyebrows drew together and she leaned forward, and almost on a whisper, asked, "Was it bad?"

"Of course it wasn't *bad*. My God. He's handsome as a devil and knows it." And apparently knew other things. Like how to make a kiss twist and linger. So that even hours later, steeped in work, and worry, and exhaustion, it still felt like her lips were someone else's.

"Rosalie… There's nothing wrong with…" Audra sighed heavily. "Duncan's a nice guy from a nice family who seems to have an interest in you. You've got to stop pushing guys away just because…"

"Just because our father was a lying, cheating bastard?" Rosalie supplied for Audra. "Weirdly, that doesn't endear me to the gender as a whole."

"Dad was one guy," Audra said, almost defensively. Because she still dreamed of wedding days and happily-ever-afters, even though she kept herself on this stupid ranch, working too hard, giving too much to everyone but herself.

Rosalie looked at her sister then, wondering if after all these years she could actually get Audra to understand. It wasn't just what Dad had done… "You never saw him the way I did." Audra hadn't worshipped their father. *She'd* seen his shortcomings. Rosalie used to think Audra was just being mean, but she understood now. "And I'm glad you have sense when it comes to that sort of thing, but *I* clearly don't."

"Oh, honey." Audra reached out and Rosalie sidestepped

because she didn't want Audra's *sympathy*. "You don't really think that, do you?"

"It doesn't matter. I don't want that stuff. Why don't *you* go kiss Duncan?"

For a moment Audra was so still, so quiet. "Is that what you want?"

The thought of Duncan putting his hands on Audra made her want to crumble into dust. She *hated* the stab of jealousy, hated everything about this.

"There is nothing wrong with liking him," Audra said gently, when Rosalie couldn't manage a response.

"There is. And I don't. He's hot, sure, but so what? I'm a grown woman with a job to do. So that's what I'm going to go do." She moved to leave, but Audra blocked her way.

"We need to talk about Dad. And Mom, for that matter."

They had been avoiding this conversation for three years. Rosalie didn't know why Audra wanted to rehash it now, but Rosalie wasn't about to do it. Certainly not because of Duncan Kirk, of all things. "I don't have time, Audra."

"You do. If you're blaming yourself for thinking better of Dad than I did, then we need to have a talk. A real talk."

Rosalie's phone beeped. She had a text message. Even though Audra was scowling at her, Rosalie read it. Her heart rate picked up. "I've got to go." She nudged Audra out of the way.

"Rosalie."

"Duncan just texted me. The cops are at his parents' house, seizing a gun. I have to go."

Chapter Nine

"You're not taking anything before we get a lawyer," Duncan said, or maybe he'd yelled it. Panic was like a living thing inside of him, inside his parents' cozy living room. The front door was open, and two uniformed cops stood on the other side of the storm door on the porch behind Detective Whoever. The one Rosalie wasn't related to by marriage.

"We have a search warrant, Mr. Kirk," the detective said with a disdainful look at Duncan, like he was falling into every rich-guy stereotype, and maybe he was.

He didn't care.

When headlights cut across the drive, everyone turned to watch the approaching truck. Duncan didn't miss the way the detective and deputies' hands fell to their weapons. Then released them when Rosalie hopped out in the yellow glow of the porch light.

Detective Beckett looked back at Duncan with a hard expression. "Last time I checked, she wasn't a lawyer."

But Duncan didn't have to respond, because Rosalie was shouldering her way past the two cops on the porch. She opened the storm door herself and stepped into the living room, glaring at the detective.

"Come on, Copeland. You can't be serious."

"Can. Am. Look, if everyone is innocent, then it doesn't matter. The tests will prove it. We have a search warrant. I'm trying to be nice here, but I don't have to be."

"The ballistics report came back?"

"Isn't that the kind of thing you should already illegally know, Rosalie?"

"There isn't anything illegal about my investigations, Copeland. If there was, no doubt you'd arrest me. Now, you've gotten the report back, and matched it to a gun the Kirks own? Is that right? Because if you came out and told them what was going on, things would go a lot smoother."

"I can have you removed, Rosalie."

She ignored him and turned to face Duncan's parents. Who looked pale and anxious.

"There's nothing wrong with letting the police do their job," she told them gently. "Even if it's a waste of everyone's time," Rosalie continued, smiling at his parents.

She didn't *look* at Detective Beckett, who was scowling at her, but Duncan figured she knew it was happening.

"I'll get the key," Mom said quietly.

"I'm afraid I'll have to go with you, ma'am."

"Like hell—"

"Stand down, boys," Rosalie said cheerfully to both Duncan and Dad, because apparently they'd been saying the same thing. "You two sit. I'll handle it." She gave Duncan a pointed look, and realized she was putting on that cheerful, breezy demeanor for his parents' sake.

And since she was, he nodded. Then he nudged his dad into a seat at the kitchen table while Rosalie, Mom, and the detective moved deeper in the house to get to the gun safe.

"What the hell is happening?" Dad muttered, looking at his hands. They suddenly looked old to Duncan, and his heart lurched. The amount of anxiety and stress this was putting on his parents was too much. It just wasn't fair.

"I don't know, Dad, but Rosalie will get to the bottom of it."

Dad took in a deep breath, then let it out. "She's a smart girl," Dad said, squeezing his hands into fists then spreading his fingers wide. "I don't trust that detective, but I trust Rosalie."

Duncan nodded. On that, they agreed. But when Mom, Rosalie, and Detective Beckett reappeared, Duncan's entire body went ice-cold.

The detective carried two guns. He wore gloves, and instructed one of the deputies on the porch to put his on before he handed the guns to him. Duncan could only stare in utter shock.

When he looked back at Rosalie, her expression was grave, but she immediately wiped that away into something more blank once she knew he was looking.

Which scared the hell out of him.

"Who has access to this gun cabinet, Mr. Kirk?" the detective asked.

"Myself."

"And?"

Dad shrugged, looked away. Not because he wanted to lie, Duncan knew, but because he wanted to *protect*.

Since Duncan wasn't about to let Dad take the fall for *anything*, he continued the list. "Me."

"Duncan," Mom said disgustedly. "You couldn't find the key if I handed it to you on a silver platter."

"I know where you keep the key," he insisted. Lying, but he'd lie. He'd do whatever.

"Prove it, Ace," Rosalie said. Why the hell was she putting him on the spot? Why wouldn't anyone let him…protect? He remembered what Rosalie had said about letting the cops do their job.

It didn't soothe him any, but he figured... Well, like Dad said. Rosalie was smart. They trusted Rosalie. He tried to breathe through the anxiety riding high in his chest, and though he was going to try to move forward with cooperation, he scowled at Rosalie, then his mother, for not letting him tell a little protective lie. "Okay, I don't know where it is, but I could have asked. I could have found it. Anyone could have—"

"You didn't," Mom said firmly. Then she turned to the detective. "There are two keys. Norman and I keep one at the house, and only we know where. The second key is with Terry Boothe, our foreman."

The detective looked at the uniformed officer behind him, the one without the guns, gave a nod. The guy took off. No doubt to round up Terry.

"Now, don't go harassing my boys in the middle of the night," Dad said, pushing to his feet and pointing at Detective Beckett. "That's not how things are done around here."

"That's how they're done in a murder investigation, Mr. Kirk. Two guns registered to you could be the murder weapon. We have a search warrant and the authority to confiscate them so tests can be done. We'll head down to talk to Mr. Boothe, then we'll be on our way. I know I don't have to repeat myself, but it'd be in everyone's best interest if they stayed put, if they cooperated with the deputies. We all want the same thing, don't we?"

Duncan figured his answer was *no*, because at the moment, he wanted Copeland Beckett to rot in hell. But even he knew he shouldn't voice that. Though it took biting his tongue not to.

"I'm going to be straight with you all. I could arrest you,

Mr. Kirk, or Mrs. Kirk, or both, if I had any reason to believe you'd be behind something like this, even without the tests. But I don't see any motive, any reason. *Yet*. So please, if you really want answers, forget that I'm an outsider, drop the small-town, circle-the-wagons, tight-lipped merry-go-round, and let me do my *job*."

His parents didn't say anything to that, and Duncan couldn't really either. It didn't endear the detective to him any, but the idea he *could* arrest his innocent parents, and wasn't...*yet*... It was some kind of relief. Some kind of hope that... That no matter what anything looked like, the truth really was the goal.

But he still didn't like the guy.

"We'll be in touch," the detective said before pushing out the door. He headed down to the bunkhouse to question Terry. And put the whole ranch up in arms.

But Duncan knew that if either of the guns they'd confiscated connected to the murder, it implicated someone on this ranch.

IN THE WAKE of the police leaving, the silence was a heavy weight that reminded Rosalie of times in her life she didn't wish to revisit. Stress, worry, shock, and that horrible *what do we do*. So she took charge of the situation.

"Mr. Kirk, it would be quite a feat for someone to sneak into your house, steal your gun, kill that boy, then put it back," Rosalie told him. "Not impossible, but quite a feat. If it comes back that one of those guns is the murder weapon, I don't think the suspicion would be on you. It'd be someone who works for you."

"No one who works for me would do such a thing," Norman said, offended.

But Rosalie watched as Duncan shared a look with his

mother. Maybe they didn't love the idea that one of the ranch hands could *murder*, but they both knew Norman was too kind when it came to all those troubled distant cousins.

Rosalie didn't argue with him though. No point to it. She had researched all of them. There weren't any violent offenders, but she'd keep digging on each of them. "You've got a detective bureau and an investigator looking into it. I know I can't tell you not to worry, but I'm determined to help get to the bottom of this. Keep cooperating with Detective Beckett. As much as his bedside demeanor leaves something to be desired, he's right. Shutting him out just because he doesn't know us won't help. But I'm not going to let what he doesn't know—about Bent County, about ranching, about you all—affect you. That's a promise."

Mrs. Kirk rose, walked over to her, and enveloped her into a warm, motherly hug that smelled like cinnamon and felt like an old memory Rosalie certainly wasn't going to indulge in right now.

She awkwardly patted Mrs. Kirk's back before the woman released her. "Thank you, Rosalie." Her eyes were shiny, but she didn't cry. She turned to her husband. "Come on, Norman. Let's get some sleep. Duncan can lock up."

Rosalie watched them go, wishing there was more she could do. Wishing she could see something in this case that Copeland and Bent County didn't see. *Wishing* for faster, better answers, and maybe a time machine to just erase this.

But those were never useful thoughts or feelings.

"Thanks for coming," Duncan said.

She should say "you're welcome" and leave it at that, but... Well, sometimes she really couldn't help herself. "You've got to stop trying to play hero, Duncan. We're all on the same side."

His expression hardened. She looked away before she

cataloged too many things about the way his eyes darkened, or lines bracketed his mouth, or how her stomach did an entire gymnastics routine if she spent too long looking at him—whether he was smiling or scowling.

"Not if they let my parents think, for even a second, they might be implicated."

Her response was a little curt, and not because he deserved it, but because she didn't like the thing going on in her chest. "They're adults. It sucks, but they can handle it."

"*I'll* handle it."

She rolled her eyes. *Men*. "Are you always this frustrating?"

"Yes," he said firmly. But his demeanor changed. Lightened. "Come on. I'll walk you to your car. And I can already tell you're opening your mouth to say I don't need to, but if you say that, I'm going to assume you're scared to be alone with me."

"Nothing about you scares me, Ace." *Wow, Rosalie, could you lie any harder?* Since she recognized the lie, instead of settling into the denial like she wanted to, she walked for the door. And she didn't argue when he followed, when he walked her out to her truck. She just marched on ahead and told herself that once she was in her driver's seat, she'd feel in charge again.

Except, when she turned to give him one last warning about trying to protect his parents, she was effectively caged against her truck. He wasn't *touching* her, and she wouldn't need to even use self-defense to get out of this, but she stayed there all the same. Back to the truck door. Front to him. A *him* who was far too close.

"What do you think you're doing?" she demanded, glaring up at him. But that was the only weapon she wielded.

She didn't try to push him away. She didn't draw attention to the gun at her hip. She just glared.

While Duncan's small, tired smile curved up. "Looking."

"Well, stop."

"All right." But he didn't back off. Instead, he lowered his mouth to hers. Not like back at his cabin. With a pause, with a softness.

No, he swooped in. Just like... Like they were doing this thing. Like he had any right to just lean in and kiss her. Like his mouth was made for hers and everything she ever thought she knew about how to handle a guy was a joke, because there was no handling *this*. This twisted-up, dizzying feeling he brought out in her.

But *God*, he was good at it. All those arguments she held very near and dear to her heart seemed to turn to ash and scatter on the wind. All that self-control she was so proud of disappeared somewhere.

A kiss wasn't a vow, she told herself as she kissed him back. It was just a kiss, and kisses were fun, she reminded herself, even as his arms came around her and pulled her flush with the long, muscular frame of his body...one arm holding on a little tighter than the other.

And because it did, because she wanted to fix that injury for him in spite of herself, she wrapped her own arms around his neck and held on tight with her two good arms.

His big hand smoothed down her back, and this kiss eased, ended. But he pressed another one to the corner of her mouth, then her jaw, her neck. Soft, almost reverent, and that slowdown had alarm bells trying to sound in her head.

Her heart was vibrating in her chest. She wasn't sure she could walk straight if she had to. She didn't understand what was happening to her, but she knew she couldn't trust it. She knew she had to hate it.

"I'm not starting anything with you, Duncan." Because that was what this all felt like. A start. And just the *thought* had tears she refused to shed springing to her eyes. Almost like she was painfully, wistfully, desperate for some kind of *start* with him.

Not in the cards.

Except he made a noncommittal kind of sound, then pressed his mouth to hers again. Soft, a little needy, like a man seeking comfort. And she might have resisted that, she told herself she would have had that strength because needy was dangerous, but then he spoke against her mouth. "Thank you for coming."

"You already said that," she returned, not pulling away from him. The fact that he kept saying it warmed her in ways it shouldn't. In ways she didn't like. Didn't *want* to like.

"I really mean it," he murmured, still there against her mouth. Like they were fused, connected, *right*.

"I have to go." But she wasn't pushing him away, was she? No, she let his arm stay wound around her, she let his mouth stay on hers.

"You don't *have* to go."

Tempting. Damn it, why was he so tempting? "You want me to solve a murder or you want to talk me into bed?"

"Why can't it be both?"

She shouldn't laugh, but she couldn't help herself. Nothing was funny about this, and she wanted to accuse him of not taking it seriously. But she'd seen him in there with his parents, how he tried to shield them.

She'd said she protected her own and he'd said "so do I" like it was a vow.

But she wasn't his, and she wasn't about to fool herself into thinking there was any way for this to work out. She gave him a nudge, and he went. She refused to acknowledge that his expression, only dimly illuminated by his parents' porch light, was one of amusement as he let himself be nudged away.

But he didn't let her go without a parting shot.

"I've got a thing for you, Rosalie."

"Keep that *thing* in your pants," she muttered, even knowing that's not what he meant. She turned her back to him so she could unlock her truck and jerk her door open.

"You can play that game if you've got to, but I don't."

She heard it, that hard edge of warning in his tone. She didn't take the warning. "Last I checked, you played a game for a living."

"Past tense, as you well know. I'm home now. New life. New…everything. And I'm happy to be patient, to focus on murder investigations. For a time. But only a time."

"You'll be sorely disappointed."

"Why, Rosalie Young, what makes you think I'd be disappointed in a thing about you?" He said it with a grin, but his eyes were serious. He backed away, then slowly turned, and headed back to his parents' house.

Leaving her there, blinking after him. Rocked to her core.

Because of course she wasn't disappointing. That wasn't what she'd meant.

But it felt like he'd lanced her through just the same.

Stay away from this man, Rosalie. Far, far away.

She repeated that mantra all the way home.

Chapter Ten

The next morning, Duncan blearily drank his coffee while looking over everything Mom had given him. A map of the property with the cow losses marked. Her copied recollections about what had happened each day.

He couldn't say he'd slept well. He was churned up about too many things. Murder and that kiss...*kisses* with Rosalie. Which he'd much rather concern himself with, but he couldn't deny the murder was more pressing.

He sighed.

Last night, he'd considered staying up at the cabin with his parents, but figured the separation was good for all of them. Pretend things were normal, even when they weren't.

He had moments of worry but he couldn't think of a single reason his parents would be targets. Even if the murderer ended up being one of the ranch hands, Dad had been nothing but kind and giving. Mom too, even with her reservations about some of them.

Besides, he'd hired a security business in Bent to come out and install a security system today. He knew it didn't solve *every* threat, but it would ease his mind considerably at night. He'd set the alarm himself every night if he had to.

He ate some breakfast, then headed up to the main house and met the installers. Mom would be volunteering at the

Sunrise library until dinnertime. Dad would be out working until about then too. So Duncan had a few hours to get into town and deal with Rosalie and the case before he had to be back to explain the new system to them. And figure out whatever tricks in the book he had to pull out to make sure they used it. Mostly guilt.

With that sorted, he packed up what Mom had given him about the missing cattle and drove out to Wilde to hand the information over to Rosalie.

She'd tell him he didn't need to bring it up to her. She'd be frustrated with him in her office space.

Which made it all the more enticing. It was good to move. Good to do. Good to think about something that felt like life instead of death. Just like Mom had said.

Duncan parked in front of the old building. Since it was during office hours, this time the front door was unlocked. He pulled it open and step into the cozy lobby.

A young girl, middle or high school—he wasn't good with ages—jumped to her feet from a chair. He noted there was a softball glove clutched in her hands and eager excitement in her eyes. "Hi," she greeted exuberantly.

The woman who'd been here the first day he'd come in strode out from back in the office somewhere and rolled her eyes. "Down girl," she muttered at the teen. "Sorry about her. My niece. Once she heard you'd been in the office, she wouldn't stop hounding me. I told her she could pick one day to come in, and if you happened to show up, she could pester you." The woman looked dolefully at the teen, then back at Duncan. "You picked the wrong day."

"I'm Sarabeth," the girl interjected.

"Hi, Sarabeth. I'm Duncan."

"I know. Duncan Kirk. I know all your stats. Want me to recite them?"

"Uh, no. I'm…good." Back in LA, he'd been used to this kind of thing. Had dealing with fans, especially eager kids, down to a science. But something about being home, about the way Rosalie's boss was studying him, made his usual ease with excited kids less than *easy*.

"You, uh, play softball?" he asked, gesturing at the glove she was clutching.

Her face fell a little at that. "I play softball *and* baseball," she said, not *quite* with a sneer, but close. Eagerness seemed to take over any affront though. "Fall's for softball. Baseball is in the spring—I'm the first and only girl on the Bent County High School baseball team. I pitched a shutout last week. Struck out eight." Her grin was one of easy teenage pride—he recognized it, felt some echo of himself in it. "All boys," she said smugly.

"How'd they take that?"

She grinned at him, hazel eyes alight with mischief. "Like babies." She practically bounced on her heels. "We're going to our conference playoffs this week. I'm starting again. Will you sign my glove for good luck?" She held it out to him.

He took it. It was almost like rote muscle memory. Take the glove. Sign the glove. Smile and compliment.

But his shoulder was in its sling, and it twinged in pain as he tried to hold the weight of the glove in it. He couldn't do the usual, because… "You did see my arm explode on national television, right?"

"Sure. But I'm not old yet. I figure it'll be lucky 'til I am."

He laughed in spite of himself, met Quinn's amused gaze as she tried to hide her own laugh. Quinn handed him a marker.

He balanced the glove as best he could with his good arm, fought back a wince as he signed the heel of her glove and handed it back to her. "Mow 'em down, kid."

"I will. Thanks. Thanks a lot! It's tomorrow night at Bent County High School at seven o'clock if you want to come."

"Hell, Sarabeth. I'm taking you home, you menace. Rosalie!" she called out. "Going on my lunch. I'll be back."

Rosalie appeared in her office doorway. He watched as her quick gaze took in Sarabeth, the glove, him. "Sure, Quinn. I'll hold down the fort." She nodded at him. "Duncan."

She looked wary, so he grinned at her.

She didn't grin back. She was guarded again, trying to hold him off with cool indifference. But he saw the faint hint of pink at her cheeks. There was no way she wasn't reliving—at least a little bit—that kiss from last night.

And that put him in quite the good mood.

ROSALIE DIDN'T WANT to have Duncan in the close quarters of her office, cowardice or not. Especially the way he was grinning at her, like he could read her mind. Or her memories.

She still hadn't been able to shake that damn kiss. *Kisses*.

So she stayed where she was, leaning against her office doorframe, while Quinn and Sarabeth said their goodbyes and left.

"I'd apologize for them, but… Sarabeth's a special kid. She's been through a lot. Deserves a thrill of a lifetime, no matter how misguided she is for thinking your signature is a thrill."

Duncan, of course, didn't take offense to her little jab. His grin didn't die. He just kept *looking* at her and moving toward her. Normally, she'd refuse to retreat, but she had a bad feeling if she let him get within touching distance, she wouldn't have the presence of mind to stop whatever he would do.

So she turned her back to him, moved into her office, and sat down in her chair behind her desk. To create a nice boundary between them. She refused to acknowledge the amusement on his expression as he took the seat across from her desk.

"I've got what I call character sketches of all the ranch hands," she said, jumping right into business. "Terry, obviously, is going to garner the most attention from the detectives since he had a key. So I want to let the detectives handle that, and I'll put my attention elsewhere. Cover all our bases."

Duncan nodded. "I've got the map. Mom's recollection of what happened on the days the cows went missing." He put the folder she hadn't seen him carrying on her desk.

Rosalie opened it. She was most curious about the map. She wanted to picture everything, visually. Get a sense of the space of the whole timeline of events. She spread out the map on her desk, then stood so she could see it better.

"The red circle is the general area they think the cows disappeared from. *Xs* are where they found dead cattle—just the one time. Hash marks are where the rest of the herd was, approximately. It's dated here, and the dates match up to Mom's recollections."

Rosalie didn't want to look at the recollections or dates just yet. First, she wanted this sense of place. The missing cattle didn't cluster. There was the first incident—the missing cows found on the Young Ranch.

She wouldn't call what she noticed a pattern exactly, but it was movement.

She pointed it out to Duncan. "They move. Slowly. Closer and closer to the west side of the ranch. First, you had three end up on our property." She put her finger on the map, slid it over. "Then you had two disappear, and a cow found dead here. Seemingly two different problems, but maybe not." She moved her finger again. "One disappears here. Two weeks before the murder."

"Doesn't this kind of follow the pathway you drove me on the other day?"

Rosalie nodded. She didn't like that. Didn't like the proximity to Audra and Franny and their own herd.

Duncan pointed to a spot on the map. The pasture where Owen had found Hunter.

"If you include the murder, it follows the movement."

"But not the path," Rosalie murmured, considering all the different angles.

"No, but there's a cut-through right here." He pointed again, slid his finger from that point to the pasture. "Or there was when I was a kid. I haven't paid close attention, but when I go back this afternoon, I'll check it out. Back when I was a kid, we used it as a cut-through. Ranch hands, dogs, horses, whoever and whatever if we didn't want to take the service road around but needed to get up to the house."

"Or maybe, in this case, the pasture."

Duncan nodded grimly. "But what does it mean?"

"I'm not sure yet. I'll go through your mom's recollections. I might go over it with Audra too. How she got the cattle back to your dad." Rosalie had been avoiding Audra since last night, and wanted to continue to do so, but eventually she'd have to face her. Might as well be for work.

"In the meantime, I want you to go over these write-ups I put together on the other ranch hands besides Terry. Add your own interpretations, and ideally, your mom's. Unless it'll be too tough on her." She got out the papers she'd printed out earlier, stapled them together and handed them across the desk.

"No, she'll want to help. And she'll be able to give Dad's

real opinions on them too—not just the no-one-would-murder one he gave the cops."

That was good. Rosalie didn't see any reason for it not to be a Kirk ranch hand, even *if* the guns confiscated weren't the murder weapons. Someone on that ranch had to have helped.

If she hadn't heard from someone at Bent County by dinner, she'd head down to the department and see what she could irritate out of Copeland. If that didn't work, maybe she'd stop by Vi's on the pretense of catching up and playing with Mags and see what she could pump out of Hart.

"You've been hard at work," Duncan said, skimming over what she'd put together about all the ranch hands.

She had indeed been hard at work, and not just to avoid all the things she was hoping to avoid. She didn't like the way this case nagged at her. Like there was a very clear piece she was missing, when, of course, nothing was clear, or Copeland and Bent County would have figured it out by now.

"Go out with me."

She didn't stiffen at those words, at the calm, casual way Duncan threw them out. She didn't let herself react outwardly. She just carefully raised her gaze to his. "We're working, Duncan."

This did not deter him. "I heard there's a hot-ticket, high-school baseball game tomorrow night at Bent County High."

That shocked her enough to forget about keeping her guard up. He wanted to go to Sarabeth's baseball game? "You want to take me to a high-school baseball game?"

"Sure. Why not? We'll see what that kid's got in the tank," he said, clearly referring to Sarabeth. "She seemed pretty sure of herself. Turns out, I like sure of herself."

It really was no wonder she liked him, because that simple summation of Sarabeth, and whatever interest he had—

real or feigned—would make that kid's day, and that made Rosalie far too warm and fuzzy.

But she just couldn't…trust this. *Him*. What was she going to do? Go out with him? Sleep with him? Then what?

There was no *then what* in her future. Why couldn't he get that through his thick skull? Well, it probably wasn't his *skull* that was making his decisions, was it? And he'd been away enough to forget that small-town liaisons tended to bite you in the ass. If he really stayed, they were going to be neighbors for the rest of their lives.

"There's a murderer running around," she told him firmly. And ignored the fact she didn't say the simplest thing, which would have been no.

"You have the lamest excuses, Rosalie."

She didn't want to laugh. Damn it, it wasn't funny. But the sound bubbled up inside of her anyway.

He was grinning back, but then sobered some, in his eyes. "I set up a security system at the house this morning. Mom… Before the cops came out last night, she… Well, she's worried about so much. Murder at the center, but me in the fringes. It'd help, I think, if she thought I wasn't flinging myself into murder investigations like some kind of distraction."

"So you're only asking me out to keep your mom happy?"

"Sure, if that's what it takes to get you to say yes."

She didn't know what to say to that. She was torn between being insulted and that horrible, creeping warm feeling. It was terribly sweet, and she didn't want him to want to date her anyway. So why shouldn't it be about his mother?

Because it's not, and you know it's not.

"What security company did you use?" she asked, hoping maybe she could work her way around the entire subject. Hoping this somehow just…went away. Which had never been her MO in her entire life, but it felt like the only way to survive one very charming Duncan Kirk.

"Some company in Bent. Run by a Delaney."

"Cam Delaney. We used him ourselves at the ranch a few years back. Does good work. A security system can't cover a whole ranch, though."

"No. We talked about some solutions there, but I knew my parents would flip if they thought I was going overboard. I can get away with the house. Use guilt and all that, but the whole ranch? Dad'll put his foot down there. Until I wear him down. Hopefully we'll have everything solved quickly so I won't have to wear him down."

Rosalie wanted to smile at the fact Norman Kirk was the most quintessential kind of Wyoming rancher, but nothing about this felt *quick* enough to suit her. She looked back down at the map. She couldn't make sense of the cattle missing from a pattern of places along a path and a cut-through. But the pattern of it all wasn't a comfort. It was an annoying and painful hangnail. A puzzle she *should* be able to solve, but couldn't.

"Come to the game with me, Rosalie." He said it in that same straightforward, calm way he'd said "let me." An order, wrapped up in something that left room for her to say no.

Except deep down, she didn't want to, and she supposed he knew that, and it's why he said it that way.

Wanting aside, she *should* say no. She needed to keep her eyes on the map—because if she looked at him, she'd forget all about *no*. She'd forget about too many things.

But she looked up at him, because it was hard to be a coward. That too-handsome face, that cocky smile. But there was something soft under all that. His connection to this place, his parents. His wanting to solve this murder to ease their worry. He would have grown up on that solid Kirk foundation, and as much as she wanted to believe that all his years away, all his fancy, high living could have—*would* have—changed him, she knew they hadn't.

He was a damn good man, and that was a damn big problem.

Problems had always been her weakness. "All right."

Chapter Eleven

Duncan had given Rosalie space after that. He had a bad feeling if he was around her too much, she'd change her mind.

So he'd taken her little biographical sketches on the different ranch hands back home. He'd gone over them, added his own notes to the margins. Tried to draw some conclusions and come up empty.

He'd gone up to his parents' for dinner, both to help them learn the new security system, and to get their take on Rosalie's sketches. But by the time he'd finally talked them into actually *using* the security system, and they'd sat down to dinner, he could only see how pale and *off* his father was and figured the sketches could wait.

He'd talk to Mom in the morning after Dad headed out for chores. She seemed sturdy enough to handle it, even if she was worried sick over Dad. So he'd made sure the security system was set, headed back to his cabin, then taken a pain pill and gone to bed. He'd actually slept well, and it had been a while on that front.

He supposed he'd taken Rosalie's advice from the other day and tried to take care of himself so he would be able to take care of his parents.

In the morning, he considered not wearing his sling. His

arm still ached, but wasn't it time to move on? He drank some coffee, choked down a protein bar, and took a pain pill while he considered it. In the end, he slid it on. He'd wear it today, leave it off tonight, and hope that there was some kind of progress there. And that he didn't have to remind himself and everyone else at a *baseball* game what had happened to him.

He drove up to the main house, which was empty as he walked through it. Empty and not locked up. He was going to be mad about that, but he spotted his mother from the window that looked out over the backyard. She was attacking her garden. And Duncan knew his mother and her moods well enough to know this was a stress-filled planting morning.

So he went out back to help. He approached as she ruthlessly hoed a line of dirt.

"What can I do?" he asked by way of greeting.

Mom wiped her forehead with the back of her forearm. Her gaze dipped to his arm in the sling. "I've got it handled, honey."

"You have to let me help, because I'm not going to be around tonight." He probably couldn't hoe much with his left hand, but he could plant. So he crouched next to the line of seedlings and started dropping them where he knew they belonged. He felt like a kid again, but in a kind of nostalgic, nice way.

"Where will you be tonight?" Mom asked, going back to the task of hoeing rows.

"I'm taking Rosalie to the Bent County High baseball game."

Mom sent him a doleful look. "That's not very romantic."

"First, I wasn't trying to be *romantic*. Second, baseball is very romantic, Mom."

"I went to every one of your high-school baseball games, Duncan. There is nothing romantic about a bunch of sweaty boys—and girls, Sarabeth *is* the talk of the county, aside from you being back—throwing a ball around."

It made him laugh in spite of himself. "Trust me. Rosalie wouldn't have agreed to dinner or much else. This is… we'll call it an easing-in."

"Mmm." Mom studied him. "Are you at least going to bring her flowers?"

"I'm going to bring her more information for our case," he replied, dropping the last plant for this row. It hurt a little, but he began to scoop the dirt over the roots.

Mom sighed heavily. "Duncan. Honestly."

"She won't trust flowers." Though it was tempting, just to see the narrow-eyed suspicion on her face. But since she was actually going out with him, he didn't want to rile her up too much. There was a fine, careful line with Rosalie that required some…finesse.

Luckily, he'd spent most of his adult life learning the fine art of when to finesse an off-speed pitch and when to blast one right down the middle.

When it came to Rosalie… "She doesn't trust much."

"No, I don't suppose she would." Mom's sigh was sympathetic this time. "I could throttle Tim Young for what he did to those girls. If he was alive. Joan too, for that matter. But make sure you understand, just because Audra got all the sweet, and Rosalie got all the sour, doesn't mean she's not tender under all that bite."

He glanced up at his mother. Her cheeks were a little red from how hard she'd been working, and she scowled down at him like he'd done something wrong.

"You warning me off all of a sudden?"

"No, I'm not warning you *off*." She puffed out a breath.

"Haven't I been the one…? Oh, never mind. My point is… That girl is so busy looking out for everyone else, including us, by looking into this murder, even though she doesn't have to. I just want you to understand, you should be looking out for her."

It amused him that's how his mother looked at it, that it would annoy Rosalie to be *looked after*, that it was exactly what he wanted to do anyway. He'd spent most of the past fifteen years—longer maybe—not being selfish, necessarily. The last few years he'd mentored some rookies, he'd given back, but that had always been about baseball. And sometimes that bled over into the personal if a teammate was making some bad choices off the field, but he'd never had the time, *taken* the time, to take care of anyone who mattered to him just because of who they were.

His parents. A friend—romantic or not—that didn't connect to a baseball uniform.

Even though he wished it wasn't *murder*, he was glad to be here, taking care where he could. Whether Mom, Dad, or Rosalie liked it or not.

"I do understand that," Duncan said, getting back to his feet and brushing off his dirty knees with his good hand. "And you know why I do?"

"Because she's got a pretty face?"

"Because my mama raised me right." Being back home gave him a new perspective on how everything he'd managed to build as a professional athlete had been built on the foundation his parents, and this ranch, had laid.

She made a scoffing noise, but her mouth curved. "I should hope so. We'll see how long that sweet talk lasts when I task you with my next favor. I don't suppose you can think of a way to follow your father around this morning without making him think we're trying to babysit him?

I'd rather you do that than ruin my garden by continuing to plant my cowpeas too close together."

"I'll see what I can do," he said, ignoring her old complaint. She used to joke she'd put him in T-ball just so she could plant her garden right.

Then both his parents had sacrificed a whole hell of a lot, all because he'd fallen in love with a game. And he wanted to pay them back the only way he thought they might accept. By figuring this damn murder out.

"But first, I want you to tell me more about Owen."

Mom blew out a breath and squinted out toward the bunkhouse. "I didn't have much interaction with the boy before the murder. I remember the first week he was here, Terry had some complaints about the both of them. Lazy work. Bad attitudes. Dad, of course, asked Terry to be patient."

"Was he?"

"Always," Mom said loyally. "Kept complaining for quite some time, but no threats to turn them out. It takes time to work the lazy out of boys who've never been given a chance."

"And when do you think they worked it out of them?"

"Your father would have a better grasp on timing." Her eyebrows drew together, as if she was trying to think back. "I can't remember when the tide really turned. Sometime after Christmas I'd have to guess."

"So they've been model hands these past few months?"

"Model? No. Efficient? Not really. Better? Yes. Improvement. I had high hopes for Hunter. Less for Owen, but that's probably how I feel about your father's family coloring my perspective." She glanced toward the bunkhouse again. "Poor boy has been nothing but grief-stricken since. I asked him if he wanted to go home, be with family, and he begged me to stay. Said he'd worked twice as hard, enough for him and Hunter. Just begged me not to send him away."

"Something back home scares him?"

"I don't know about that. I just don't think anyone cares about him back there, poor kid. And not that Terry *cares*, but he takes good care of those boys. So does your father. This is a good place to be."

That sentiment stayed with Duncan as he went about his day. Helped with a few ranch chores he could do one-handed, talked with some of the hands, shared a sandwich with Terry at lunchtime. He tried to poke into Owen, and Hunter for that matter, without being too obvious about it.

Not one of them, Dad included, would give the two compliments on their work ethic, but the consensus among the hands matched up with Mom's. They'd been improving.

This is a good place to be.

Except someone had been murdered. Right there, in his own front yard, and the cops hadn't found any answers yet.

So if they wouldn't, he and Rosalie would have to.

IT WASN'T A DATE. Rosalie told herself that as she debated for far too long about what to wear. It was a high-school baseball game. So jeans and a T-shirt and she needed to stop overthinking *which* T-shirt.

But she considered about ten different options, told herself to wear her ratty old Bent County High School T-shirt, and ended up pulling on the form-fitting V-neck the color of her eyes. She considered her hair next. She should just throw it up and slap a hat on it, but she didn't. She took time—too much time—curling the careful strands she pulled out of the ponytail. Then putting on makeup—ridiculous, just ridiculous—with a deft hand to make sure it didn't look like she was wearing any.

When she was done with that, irritated with herself, irritable with the situation, so damn nervous she thought she'd be sick, she marched herself downstairs.

"It's just a baseball game," she muttered to herself. But just as she got downstairs, the front door opened and Audra stepped in.

Rosalie had been hoping to escape before Audra was done for the day. But there was no way around her sister, standing there in front of the door. "Hey," she offered.

"Headed out?" Audra asked, innocently enough, nodding toward the purse Rosalie carried.

"Yeah." Rosalie let the silence stretch out. Maybe Audra would hear it through the grapevine, maybe Rosalie would feel like talking about it *after*, but she was not about to let Audra think she was going out on a date with Duncan.

Because she wasn't.

"You've been avoiding me," Audra said.

There was no point in denying it, and it was better than talking about Duncan. "Yep."

"You can't forever."

"You'd be surprised."

"Rosalie."

"I can't talk about our parents tonight, sis," she said brightly. "I'm going to the baseball game. You know…" It dawned on her, quick and perfect. "You and Franny should come."

Audra's eyes narrowed. "On your date with Duncan?"

"It's not a date," she immediately snapped. Then stopped short. "How did you know I was going with Duncan?"

For a moment, Audra stood there with a kind of surprised look on her face that Rosalie couldn't figure out. Then Audra shook her head, but her cheeks were turning red. "Natalie mentioned it in passing," she said with a shrug.

"Why are you acting guilty?"

Audra made a dismissive noise, then cocked her head. "Is that him?" She opened the door behind her, and there was Duncan's truck bumping up the gravel lane.

Nerves seemed to full-on explode in Rosalie's chest, and she didn't know what the hell to do with that feeling. The only time she ever got nervous was when something at work went south, but even that she usually brazened her way through.

All of her brazenness wasn't enough to get through Duncan Kirk. But she could do it, would do it, if she had company. Support. *Distraction*.

"Look, just because Duncan's driving doesn't mean you and Franny can't come. It's not a date. It's just…a get-together. To support Sarabeth and our alma mater."

"Franny didn't go to Bent County, and I've got things to do. You're going out, have fun." Audra grabbed her by the arm and pulled her to the door. "And if you end up not coming home tonight, you just make sure to text me so I don't worry."

Rosalie had never been embarrassed about sex. In fact, she liked to flaunt it in Audra's face, because Audra was usually the one being a little prudish about it. But this was… different. Why was everything about Duncan different? "I am coming home tonight, Audra," she said firmly. Because it was *just* a baseball game.

"Then you don't have to text me. And we can have a nice long talk about our parents when you get back."

She blinked at her sister. "Are you trying to blackmail me into having sex with Duncan?"

"If it helps." Audra gave her a shove out the door as Duncan pulled to a stop. He got out of his truck, offered a wave with his good arm.

"Hi, Duncan," Audra called with a return wave. "You two have fun. I won't wait up." Then she closed the front door behind her, and locked the door, as if Rosalie didn't have her own key.

But there was no going back now, because Duncan was here. Looking like he always did. Casual jeans, work boots that looked a little on the new side, a plain navy blue T-shirt, and a baseball cap, also plain. No doubt because he didn't want to draw attention to the fact he was Duncan Kirk, former professional baseball player. She also noted he wasn't wearing his sling.

"You got a doctor's note?" she demanded, pointing at his arm, trying to determine if he was holding it more awkwardly than the other one.

"You going to tell on me?"

"Maybe."

"Uncool." But he grinned at her. "I'm allowed to take it off for a few hours a day. I'm taking my few hours. You ready to go?"

She nodded, hoping it didn't come off as jerky as it felt. She moved in his direction, reminding herself it wasn't a damn date. She climbed up into his truck. It still smelled like new, and that did nothing to ease these knots inside of her. Because it all felt new, when it damn well shouldn't.

"I can drive if it's bad on your arm."

"I got it," he replied easily, and he did seem to have it. He turned around and drove down the lane, then toward the highway without any winces that she could see as she studied his face, waiting for one.

"I brought your list of ranch hands with some added information," he said, eyes on the road. "In the back seat, if you're interested."

She reached back and picked up the pieces of paper. She

skimmed through the sloppily written additions. "Am I supposed to be able to read this chicken scratch?"

"Sorry. Bad arm. I can read it to you. Some of it is stuff I knew, some of it is stuff I got out of people today. But I just keep coming back to Owen and Hunter. The detectives haven't come up with anything that ties Hunter's former life to here, but there's got to be something there, doesn't there? They were in trouble in North Dakota. There was no trouble here. Then all the sudden, he's dead. And Owen's not."

"You suspect Owen?" Rosalie asked, surprised. She hadn't thought he would.

"I don't know. It just seems too much of a coincidence. I talked to Mom and Dad today, about Owen and Hunter. How they were lazy whiners when they first arrived, but slowly over time got a little less whiny. But still lazy."

"Makes sense."

"I guess. But Dad told me when he thought they kind of started to turn things around in the helpful department. And it seems weird as hell to me that their slight changes of heart coincide with the first cow's death."

Rosalie turned that over with everything she knew. Did it connect? They had to look into everything, she supposed. She thought about Owen that day when he'd yelled for help. And after, when she'd questioned him. "He was genuinely grieving." Though that didn't mean anything, but she wanted to hear how Duncan would argue his theory.

"I think so too. But people can grieve things, even when they have something to do with the end result."

Wasn't that the truth? "Did Owen have a way of getting into your parents' house?"

Duncan's gaze slid to hers. "I'm not sure, but I'd bet he would. You heard from the cops about those guns?"

She shook her head. "No. Tests will take a few days, I

imagine. They probably had to send them away. They're still working on expanding their crime-scene-investigation unit, so not everything can be done in house, and then you gotta wait."

"It doesn't make sense to me that Owen would go through all that trouble, then have us find the body. Seems a stretch. But there's just something about those two that doesn't add up."

Rosalie couldn't help but agree. She read through Duncan's sloppy notes again. "We'll keep digging," she said, as much to him as herself.

The truck came to a stop and Rosalie looked up. They were in the high-school parking lot.

Duncan shifted the truck into Park, then turned to face her. "All right. No more shop talk. Just baseball and hot dogs, Red."

It was easy, she told herself. Just two people at a baseball game. So she hopped out of the truck and walked with him toward the field. A decent crowd for a high-school baseball game. He bought the hot dogs from a bored-looking teen at the concession stand and they walked toward the bleachers to find a seat among the crowd.

"That's the Sarabeth cheering section," she said, pointing to about half of the bleachers. She waved at Quinn as she led Duncan forward. "There are six Thompson brothers, and one of them married Sarabeth's mom. The rest are all married and half of them are procreating. Makes for quite a racket. Hope you're ready."

"I played in Dodger Stadium, Rosalie."

"Such a big shot." She was going to rib him some more, but she spotted Sarabeth waving wildly. She pointed over to the dugout. "Your biggest fan has spotted you."

Duncan turned, gave Sarabeth a wave. She beamed at him, clutching her glove to her chest.

"There's no accounting for taste," Rosalie muttered, but she was smiling in spite of herself, because… Oh, she was a big, dumb softy.

They found a place in the bleachers, and Duncan maneuvered himself in first. "Here. Sit on my right side."

"Why?"

"So I can do this." He casually rested his arm across her shoulders.

She should push it off.

But she didn't. She settled in and watched Sarabeth pitch while the crowd went wild around them, and Duncan watched with avid interest. So much interest, she found herself watching *him* a little too much. The way she could see the wheels in his head turning with every play, the way he got into it, whistling and cheering on Sarabeth just like her family was.

She felt it, deep inside, the slow, horrible unlocking of her heart. She would have tightened it up, added fifty more locks, thrown away every last key, if she thought it'd do any good.

But sitting next to him like this, watching him enjoy himself, it just felt inevitable.

Inevitable doom.

Chapter Twelve

Duncan had forgotten how much he loved baseball. As a spectator. It wasn't just that he'd been good as a kid—he'd loved the game. The intricacies of it. The teamwork required. That feeling of being in a crowd holding their breath while everyone waited for the next pitch.

It's a good place to be. His mother's words kept echoing in his head. Because it *was*. Bent County wasn't perfect. Hell, even the Kirk Ranch wasn't perfect. But there was a community, a teamwork to it. Just like baseball.

Maybe Owen Green had come from a not-so-nice place. Maybe that explained why his demeanor had changed slowly, as had Hunter's, over their first months of being here.

He hated that even in the middle of the fun, and a date with Rosalie, his mind kept trailing back to Owen and Hunter. A dead body. A distraught young man.

Two outsiders.

When the game was over, a close and tense win for Bent County High, what Duncan really wanted to do was disappear, but he couldn't quite bring himself to do it.

Maybe he didn't really know Sarabeth from any other kid around here. They weren't kin, and as far as he knew his parents weren't acquainted with the Thompsons. But he couldn't forget who he'd been out there on the field, and if a major league player had come to one of his games?

Hell.

"Go on, Ace. Give 'em a thrill," Rosalie said, giving him a nudge toward the dugout, where the coaches were talking to the kids, but all eyes were on him.

The excitement was palpable as he approached—from both kids and coaches alike. It was a different staff than when he'd played here, so he didn't recognize any of the coaches. He introduced himself to the head coach, and then he was essentially engulfed.

He gave compliments. Signed balls, gloves, and bats. Answered a zillion questions. Politely declined a job assistant-coaching…three times. Then, in an attempt to escape, had to shake what felt like a million parent hands until his arm was throbbing.

Eventually the crowds began to dissipate a *little*, but Duncan had officially had enough. He searched the area for Rosalie, found her underneath a tree, watching him with amusement.

Save me, he mouthed at her.

She grinned at him but pushed off the tree and sauntered over. Smooth as could be, she extracted him from a small group of overzealous adults without making either of them look like jerks.

"You're a real pro," he said. "I'd have hired you back in LA."

She shook her head at that. "You're too nice to those people."

"Can't really have it getting around town that LA changed me and I'm some snooty SOB now. My mother would have my neck."

It got a good laugh out of her, and since they were back

at his truck, in the shadow of it and a tree, and most of the parking lot had cleared out, he went ahead and followed the path of that laugh.

Because his life had been ruled by discipline for so long, there was something freeing and irresistible about following an impulse, a temptation.

So he pressed his mouth to hers, caging her subtly against his truck, the size of his frame no doubt obscuring her from any straggling crowd members.

He half expected her to push him away, but she didn't. She melted into him like wax. When he wrapped his good arm around her back and pulled her tight against him, she raised her hands to clasp around the back of his neck.

Maybe it was the location, maybe it was Rosalie, but there was a kind of sweet nostalgia to it all. But underneath that sweetness, and the smell of baseball, and a crisp Wyoming night, was the sharpening edge of need.

The throb in his shoulder twinged with the drugging pulse of pleasure. A strange, potent mix of feelings wrapped up in the faint strawberry scent of her.

She didn't push him away, but she did ease back. He could only barely make out her face in the dark. "We're in a parking lot, Ace."

But her breath came out on a little sigh, and her hand was still curled around his neck.

"Yeah, we are. Did you ever make out in this parking lot after hours back in your day?"

She looked around—the baseball diamond was dark now. The school behind them was dark. "A lady never tells." Then her eyes narrowed. "What about you?"

He put a hand to his chest in mock outrage. "A gentleman never tells either."

She snorted.

And because she did, and because she hadn't taken her arms down from around him, he lowered his mouth again. This time with a little more of that urgency he was starting to feel, and a nip against her bottom lip.

"Come home with me," he murmured against her mouth. Not charming, he knew, but she pulled something out of him. A directness. A straightforward need. Like a bright new light, after quite a few months of existing and maybe even wallowing in the dark.

He could feel the inner battle going on inside of her. But he was getting the picture that her internal battles weren't about him specifically. They were about stuff going on in her life.

Still, when the battle ended, and she said, "Maybe for a minute or two," he considered it a win.

IT DIDN'T MEAN she was going to sleep with him.

Rosalie told herself this, over and over again, as his truck drove down the highway and a mournful country song twanged around them in the dark of the truck's interior.

But if she *did* sleep with him, then it might eradicate this...*this*.

Like something had wrapped around her lungs, tight and with thorns. A bramble bush inside of her chest.

It went away when he kissed her. Everything did, except the delicious lick of heat. Her lungs could expand when he kissed her. She didn't *worry* when his arm banded around her. All those doubts and concerns just evaporated.

So it could just be sex. She could handle just sex. A little fling with the hot neighbor guy. She was good at flings and handling men. She was a *pro*.

Even as he pulled onto the service-road entrance to his family ranch, rather than the main entrance that would lead to his parents' house. Even as he pulled up to his cabin at the back of the property. Even as he turned off the car and hopped out, she told herself it was just a bit of fun.

And once they got a little bit of fun out of their systems, they could just…move on. No harm, no foul.

She slid out of the truck as he did, still not saying anything. She met him at the front of the truck in the little porchlight that barely illuminated the little patch of yard they were in. He was so tall, so handsome, there in the moonlight.

So much potential harm, she knew, as her heart lurched, and beat unsteadily in her chest as they stood there just staring at each other. She managed to swallow, to look away, up at the stars to steady herself.

It was a riot of stars, universes up there, bright and vast. She had only ever lived here, looking up at *this* sky, without light pollution, without an entire world out there that Duncan had gone out and experienced.

"Miss this out in LA?" she asked, and maybe she meant it as a little dig aimed at his time away, but really, she was curious. What had he missed about home while out in California living his dream?

"Yeah. Yeah, I did. I used to lay out under the stars after every game here—win or lose—and picture myself under the lights of a professional ballpark. People chanting my name."

"And you got it."

"I got it, and then there was nowhere to lay outside and watch the stars. I mean there was, but it wasn't home. I never regretted it. I don't, even now, even when it didn't end in a nice little bow like I wanted it to. But that doesn't mean I didn't miss this as much as I enjoyed that."

It was somehow the perfect answer. A blend of understanding how lucky he was, without losing sight of where he'd come from. Why did that lodge in her chest like physical pain?

At least until he moved closer, drew her into his arms, and kissed her. Soft and sweet at first. A kiss meant for starlight and the chill of a Wyoming night she didn't feel because his body gave out warmth and stirred up some inside her as well.

But the angle changed, the grip. Everything got a little deeper, hotter, needier, and that was exactly what she needed. Ride the wave, forget about all the messy emotions cluttering up inside of her. She'd deal with those later, alone. Pick them apart, set them away.

They moved toward the cabin, arms wrapped around each other, mouths on each other. A laugh when they tripped, a shuddery exhale when his hand slid under her shirt, spread out on her back. Hot, big, rough.

They somehow managed to stumble up the stairs to his door, and he opened it without even taking his mouth from hers. She would have told him it was impressive, but he nibbled at her bottom lip, taking away all rational thought. He pulled her in, backing them into his living room.

She heard something *crunch* under her shoe. Confused, she blinked her eyes open even as Duncan's mouth took a very interesting tour of her neck.

But the sensual haze faded into cold fear as she saw the room around them. "Oh my God."

"If you think that's impressive..."

She choked on a half laugh, even in the midst of the mess. "No, Duncan." She pushed at his chest. "God. Your place is trashed."

He turned then and saw what she saw. His face went utterly blank.

All his boxes had been upended. Trophies—some broken, some shattered. Clothes strewn about, drawers opened and emptied.

"What the hell?"

"We need to call the police, Duncan," she said sharply. She felt a bubble of panic try to burst free, but she pushed it back down. Because this wasn't murder. They didn't know what it was, but things could be replaced, so it wasn't *murder*.

But because there *had* been a murder, it was more terrifying than just a break-in.

When Duncan didn't move, Rosalie pulled out her own phone, irritated that her hand shook. She hesitated for a moment, not sure what decision to make, then went ahead and dialed Copeland's cell.

Maybe this didn't relate to the murder, but how could it not?

"Do I even want to know why you're calling my personal number and not Bent County?" he answered, as she tried to push away from Duncan.

Who held on to her. Tightly.

"There was a break-in at Duncan's cabin," Rosalie said without sounding panicked. She hoped. "Someone broke in and trashed his place."

He grunted. "Call the emergency line then."

"Copeland."

The long, world-weary sigh on the other end was dramatic. "Yeah, yeah, I'm coming. I'll handle it."

The line went dead, and Rosalie put the phone back in her pocket. She surveyed the room again. "Duncan..." She felt helpless and strange, and that wasn't *her*, so she dug deep for some kind of control. "We should wait outside," she decided. No contaminating a crime scene. "We should... Duncan, you're going to have to tell your parents. When the police come up the drive, they'll see."

"Call the detective back. Have him cut through. I'll..." Then he cursed and took off, back out the door and into the dark night. She realized, only a second or two after he did, what he might be worried about. So she took off after him.

She ran after him—he was a quick shadow in the dark—across fields. She even had to hop a fence and wondered how he'd done it with his bad arm. The main house was fully dark in the distance. His long legs, and maybe the whole being-a-professional-athlete thing, meant he made it to the front of the house before her. He was peering into the window on the front door when she caught up, lungs burning and eyes watering.

"Everything looks fine from here. The security system is set." He was breathing heavily. She could tell he was in pain, but he didn't reach up and grip his shoulder.

She hated to say it, but she knew she had to. "You're still going to have to wake them up," she said around panting breaths. "You don't want them to wake up to cops coming up the drive. They'll think something worse happened."

He inhaled deeply, let it out slowly, evening his breathing quicker than she was able to. "Yeah. Why don't you call Audra. Have her pick you up?"

She was surprised that the words landed like little stabs of pain. That damn bramble being yanked out of her heart. But she managed to keep her tone even, light. "Is that what you want?"

He stared at her there in the dim glow of the ranch's security light. "No," he said, and with enough heft and weight that those little brambles dug right back into her heart.

She swallowed it all down. "Then I'll stay."

Chapter Thirteen

"Let's go over this one more time. You don't know if the door was locked or not?"

Duncan sighed. He was in all kinds of pain, but the cops wouldn't let him into his cabin to grab a pill. Rosalie had somehow, after quite a while, convinced his parents to go back up to the house and try to get some sleep, so there was *that*.

He knew they wouldn't sleep, but at least they wouldn't stand out in the increasing cold and worry. They could worry comfortably and inside.

"I've told each and every one of you," Duncan said, trying not to be irritable. "I locked the door before I left. When I got back, I was distracted." He'd settled on that word about the third time they'd asked this same damn question. "I unlocked the door, but it's not like I tested the knob. I just jabbed my key in and twisted, and assumed that's what unlocked the door. Until I stepped inside to all that."

There were cops crawling around his cabin, all the lights on and blazing. He wanted to be grateful they were taking this seriously, but he was in some serious pain, and worried about his parents and what this *meant*.

Detective Beckett approached him and the uniformed deputy that had been asking the *same damn questions*.

"We've taken pictures. The guys are working on trying to lift some prints right now. You'll need to go through and see what's missing, but as much as some of that stuff might be a gold mine, most of it is personalized and unique enough, selling would come back on the seller. They were no doubt looking for easy items. Cash. Guns."

"I don't keep a gun down here." His shoulder ached. A migraine had started drumming at his temples. Rosalie's hand rubbed up and down his back, but he barely felt it. "If I had cash, it was nothing major."

"Can't one of the deputies bring him out one of his pain pills? Some water?" Rosalie demanded.

"Why are you here again?" Copeland asked her.

"To ruin your life," she replied, and almost, *almost* made Duncan smile. "He's in pain, Copeland."

The detective huffed out a breath. "Where do you keep them?"

"Cabinet above the stove."

Detective Beckett grunted, then stalked back to the cabin. Rosalie didn't stop rubbing Duncan's back.

"Getting prints is good. We saw the mess they left. They'd have touched something, and there's no way they had the sense to wipe it all down with a mess like that."

She was surprisingly comforting when she wanted to be. "And then what?"

"And then we see if it connects to the murder. If it does, this might be a real big break."

God, he hoped so.

Detective Beckett came back a few minutes later, but there was nothing in his hands. His expression was grimmer than it had been.

"Well, I think we figured out what they were after, or

at least what they took. Bottle's empty. No chance it was empty, and you just forgot?"

Empty... Duncan shook his head. "No. No possible way."

"How many do you think you had left?"

Duncan blew out a breath. "Most of the bottle. I only take them sporadically. I'm not sure I could give an exact count, but I could get close if I sit down and think about it."

"You do that. Once we clear you to go in, you make a list of anything that's missing in as much annoying detail as you can manage." He glanced at Rosalie with a little sneer. "Have her help. She knows what we're looking for."

She smirked at Copeland. "Flatterer."

He rolled his eyes and strode away, back into the cabin, which was swarming with deputies. Well, it wasn't *really* a swarm, it just felt like that.

"How about some ibuprofen or something. Will that take the edge off?"

"If I take a whole bottle," he muttered irritably. "Listen. Hell, it's late, and I'm not fit to be around anyone. You should head on home. I'll drive you—"

"Are you going to go up to your parents and sleep there if you drive me home?"

He surveyed the strange landscape in front of him. His cabin. His things. Cops everywhere. "No, I won't be able to sleep until I go through everything. See what they took besides my damn pills."

"Then I'm staying with. Detective's orders, remember?"

"You don't have to, Rosalie."

"Who said anything about having to? I'll have you know, I don't do anything I *have* to. Except pay taxes maybe."

It surprised a little laugh out of him, unbanded the tiniest bit of tension in his chest. He pulled her to him, rested his chin on the top of her head. "Thanks, Red." For a minute, he was almost able to relax a little bit.

But then the detective came out of the cabin and walked over to them. "You can go in and clean up."

Duncan watched as Copeland seemed to take notice of his arm around Rosalie.

"Get me that list as soon as you're able." Then he stalked away. Not angry, exactly. Just purposeful. The deputies were leaving the cabin too. Getting in cars, talking to each other as they did.

Duncan found that all of a sudden he didn't want to go inside. Didn't want to see or even begin to think about cleaning up or sorting through what he might still have, and what he might not.

So he focused on the little niggling thing that settled in his brain whenever Rosalie and Copeland were around each other.

"You ever have a thing with the detective?"

Rosalie looked up at him, and even in the dim light, he could see confusion on her face. Followed by amusement. "Define *a thing*?"

He scowled at her. "The point is the lack of definition. *Thing* could be anything. That's my point."

"Does it matter?" she asked, her expression sober, even as amusement danced in her eyes. She *liked* making him uncomfortable, and that should be some kind of turnoff. But it wasn't.

"It doesn't *matter*," he replied, calmly if he did say so himself. "I'm just curious."

"Curious or jealous?"

He looked down at her, matched her smug expression with one of his own. "Does *that* matter?"

She held his gaze for a minute, then shook her head on

a sigh. "I don't mind jealous. I don't mind curious. Never looked in that direction. Actually kind of hated him until a few months ago."

"What happened a few months ago?"

"He worked on a case involving my cousin, Vi. Hart's wife. She was kidnapped by her abusive ex." Rosalie shuddered, and he found it was his turn to rub a comforting hand up and down her back. "Anyway, Copeland worked his ass off to help us find Vi. Hard to keep hating the guy after that. Though he tries to make it easy."

Duncan chuckled. But it died, because...

"We can keep avoiding it, Ace, but it's still going to be there."

"Yeah," he agreed, stepping toward the cabin with her. Avoiding it wasn't going to change anything. And at the very least, he had a *we*.

ROSALIE WAS DRAGGING, and she knew Duncan was too. She'd tried to clean up as they went along, particularly the shattered glass, and he tried to remember what he had packed away in boxes that might be missing.

She'd coaxed him into taking some ibuprofen as they worked, but even after hours had passed, he hadn't come up with anything to add to the list of missing items to go along with his pain pills.

When he'd stood in the same place for a good two minutes, just staring at some fancy engraved plate in his hand, she crossed to him, took it out of his grasp, and placed it in a box. "Come on, Ace, you're beat. Let's take a break, get some rest."

"I'm pissed," he corrected. He flung his good arm toward the front of the cabin. "It would have taken someone who knew their way around to get back here without passing by the main house."

"Maybe," Rosalie said, considering the layout of the Kirk Ranch. "Or they could have turned off their headlights. Used Neutral to cruise down the drive to your place. They could have known about the cut-throughs because they've been ranching these parts for years. There's a lot of explanations."

"They would have to know this cabin was back here, and that there might be something valuable in it. Because *I'm* in it. It wasn't random, or they'd burglarize Mom and Dad's, which makes me sick to think about."

She rubbed a hand up and down his arm. "It wouldn't take much for someone to know all that, Duncan. I bet all of Bent County knows more of your business than you'd ever be comfortable with."

He scowled at that. "Down to my pain pills?"

"Afraid so." She could tell that *really* didn't sit well with him, but it was true. Maybe Bent County was a big place geographically, but interesting tidbits spread through all the small towns like wildfire.

He sank onto the couch. "Maybe other things are gone, but if they are, they're small, inconsequential things I don't remember. All my awards are here. I couldn't tell you if they slipped out with a jersey, or ball or bat, or whatever the hell. There's just nothing of any value that's gone, I don't think."

She settled next to him on the couch. "Well, like Copeland said, the awards are too specific. No resale value. What about watches or… I don't know, what do rich guys buy?" She was hoping to get a little bit of a smile out of him, but his scowl didn't budge.

"Cars. Nice houses. All of which I got rid of when I moved home. I didn't even bother to keep expensive suits or shoes. Why would I?"

"Okay, fair enough, but someone who knows you're a professional baseball player wouldn't necessarily know that. Maybe they came looking for cash, couldn't find it, and bailed."

"Just stumbled upon the pills?"

"Maybe."

He looked over at her then. Shadows in his eyes, mouth downturned showing off grooves bracketing his lips. Beat clean up. She wanted to reach out and smooth the tuft of hair that was sticking up where he'd raked his fingers through it, but it felt like an intimacy that bordered too close to a bunch of things she just wasn't sure about yet.

"You don't sound convinced," he said, and because he sounded so damn distraught, she didn't resist the urge. She reached out, smoothed her hand over his hair. And it felt good. To reach out and soothe.

"I would be convinced. If not for the murder," she said gently. She kept her arm around him. "Coincidences happen all the time, but this feels like a stretch to think they aren't connected considering your parents haven't had criminal issues at the ranch before, except the missing cows. Which I still think might be connected." A lot of connections, but no answers. Still, that was an investigation. Steps, connections, and little threads, until you found the thing that bound them all together.

Connections, but not obvious ones. She looked around the trashed room. Silly just to do for some pain pills, but… "Maybe whoever did this was looking for something specific if they didn't take anything."

"They took the pills."

"Yes, but surely someone capable of murder is capable of scoring their own drugs without creating this mess. What about weapons?"

"Like I told the cops, I don't have guns down here."

"Maybe they didn't know that. Maybe they were looking for something else."

"I thought everyone knew everything."

She sighed, feeling nothing but sympathy for him. "You're getting grumpy."

"No shit."

"Get some rest, huh? I'll call Copeland and tell him you know how many pills you think were stolen and that's all we found. If you think of anything else, we'll let him know, but you need some rest."

She started to get up, but he grabbed her arm. So she stood by the couch but couldn't step away because he held her hand firmly.

"You've been up as long as I have."

"Yeah, but I haven't had my shoulder recently reattached, so I'm just a little tired, not exhausted and in pain."

"I took some damn ibuprofen."

"Yeah, it really helped. Come on, you big baby, I'll tuck you in."

He raised an eyebrow, and she laughed in spite of herself.

"Mind out of the gutter." She pulled him up, making sure it was his good arm before she yanked. He got to his feet.

"My mind doesn't have much juice left to find itself in the gutter, but I could work on it."

She pushed him gently to the bedroom. "I'm sure you could, but not tonight. Or this morning, or whatever it is." She nudged him into a sitting position on his unmade bed. There hadn't been any broken glass in here, just upended drawers and a trashed closet. "Take off your shoes," she told him.

He grunted, then toed off the shoes.

"Lay down," she ordered, waiting for him to balk at being

told what to do. But he really *was* tired, because he did as he was told. And he held out his good arm.

"Lay down with me, Rosalie," he said, in the same kind of authoritative tone she'd used on him.

She didn't like the idea of him sleeping alone in this place that didn't have a security system. That had been violated in some way. Maybe it wouldn't make sense for a burglar to come back, but none of this made much sense.

So she moved over to the opposite side of the bed. She didn't pull any covers over her, but she lied down on her back, staring up at the ceiling.

But Duncan reached over, snuck his good arm under her, and pulled her close to him. She might have balked at it, but she could *feel* him relax. The tension leaked out of him as he exhaled.

Which somehow made her worry worse. Because this felt too good and there was nothing good about what was going on. "Once you've gotten some rest, we're calling Cam Delaney and getting a security system for this place."

"Are we?"

She could feel him falling asleep almost immediately, so she didn't say anything else. Just lied there.

While she stayed awake, protecting them both.

Chapter Fourteen

Duncan woke up with a curse on his lips as a sharp zing of pain shot from his shoulder down his arm. Grumbling irritably, he blinked his eyes open. Everything about last night came rushing back at him and made him want to close his eyes and go back to sleep.

But Rosalie wasn't here and he wanted to know where she went, so he forced himself to sit up. He scrubbed a hand over his face while his opposite shoulder throbbed. Just throbbed.

It was to be expected. It wasn't a career-ending injury and two surgeries for nothing. But he was damn tired of it, and he didn't have a real pain pill to take the edge off. Because someone had trashed his stuff and stolen his pills.

Rosalie was right that it had to connect, but that it didn't make much sense in the grand scheme of things. Missing cows. Murder. Missing pills.

He scrubbed a hand over his face again. Coffee. He smelled it, and he needed some. Then he and Rosalie could sit down and plan out what to do next.

But when he moved into the kitchen, it wasn't Rosalie in his house. It was Mom. She was wiping down his kitchen counter and Rosalie was nowhere to be seen.

She looked up at him, surveyed him in that way she had

when he'd been sick as a kid and insisted he was well enough to go to baseball practice anyway.

"She had to go into her office," Mom said, even though he hadn't asked about Rosalie. "I'm not sure she slept, poor girl. But she's as stubborn as you are."

"More."

Mom shook her head with a tiny smile. "Impossible."

"What about you? Any rest?"

"I tried. Slept in snatches, I suppose." She rinsed out the dishcloth, folded it neatly over the faucet.

"How's Dad holding up?"

Mom didn't look at him and didn't speak right away. That's how Duncan knew it was bad.

"He was out before dawn. Calving season is in full swing and we're down a hand. He's got lots of work to throw himself into. For good or for ill."

"I wish I could be more help."

"Next year you will be."

Duncan smiled. It was a nice enough thought. To know he'd be here next year and the year after. That he'd be in better physical shape to really help Dad out. But he sure as hell hoped they weren't dealing with any of this next year.

Still, he didn't say that to Mom. He just nodded in agreement and took the mug of coffee she offered him.

"Rosalie left you a list of things to do."

"Did she?"

Mom held out the paper, and in an only kind of legible chicken scratch there was a bulleted list.

- *Call your doctor get prescription refilled.*
- *Call Cam Delaney. Security system installed TODAY.*
- *Eat something and take care of yourself.*

Nothing about the case. Which no doubt meant she'd gone into her office so she could work on it alone.

Wasn't going to happen.

He was tempted to crumple the list, but she wasn't wrong about the first two things. Getting a security system up and running for his cabin would be necessary if he was going to have more pills on hand and wanted to feel safe about it.

But he hated the idea of Rosalie down at her office, investigating this case that involved everything he held dear without him.

"I've got a favor to ask you, Mom."

"Anything, honey."

"I've got a few calls to make. If I get an appointment set up for the alarm install, can you be here for it?"

"Where are you going to be?"

"I'll probably have to go into Fairmont to pick up my pills."

"And you can't plan that around a security install?"

He supposed there was no point trying to hedge with Mom. Even if she didn't figure it out, someone would see his truck in Wilde and no doubt tell her. "Okay, fine, I'm going to stop by Fool's Gold and talk to Rosalie." He looked down at the list with a scowl. "She's not shaking me off of this."

"Investigating is her job, her expertise. Is she shaking you off or is she just doing her job?"

Duncan didn't know quite how to respond to that. Mom wasn't wrong, but this was… It was a unique circumstance. Her job involved *him*. This ranch. His family. "You want me to just sit around and stew?"

"I want you to be safe."

Guilt was a sharp pang in his heart, but he didn't let it take over what had to be done. "I'm not in any danger. This all happened while I wasn't here. The murder happened when no one was around. Whatever's going on doesn't connect to us. You don't have to worry about me being safe. We're all safe."

"Duncan."

He hated the way his mother sounded. So...beaten down. Distraught. That just wasn't her. She had endless patience and optimism that everything could work out with enough hard work.

She sighed. "I want to believe some stranger came in and did both these things. I know that's what your father believes. And I'm trying so hard, but..."

He knew what she was going to say, and he hated it, but he felt that way too. "But it feels like an inside job."

Mom nodded. There were tears in her eyes, but they didn't fall. "It's one of our own. I just know it."

ROSALIE KNEW THE reception from the detectives wouldn't be positive, but maybe that's why she went. She wanted an argument. She was itching for a fight. Why not have it with Copeland?

Not smart when she was riding on the fumes of sleep deprivation, but she didn't want to be smart or patient, or depend on any of her usual investigative techniques. *Usually* the job itself kept her in line.

Except when the client mattered personally to her. Then her lines got a little blurry.

She wanted action and answers, and for this damn thing to be over. Because all she could seem to think about, worry about, *obsess* over, was how bereft Mr. and Mrs. Kirk had looked. How beaten down and exhausted Duncan was.

Even in sleep, when she'd slid out of bed maybe having dozed for less than an hour herself, he'd looked beat up, lying there, breathing evenly. Handsome as a devil but beat *up*.

Police investigations were full of waiting. Full of time ticking. Funny how easy that was to understand when she didn't really know the victim, and how impossible and unfair it felt when the crime was mixed up with people she knew and cared about.

And because she did *care* about Duncan in uncomfortable ways, she was going to throw her whole self into getting answers *fast*. Better than dealing with all that care.

She strode into the sheriff's department with a grim smile on her face. She made a beeline for the detective's office and was gratified to find all three of the detectives in there. Clearly having a little meeting.

Before she could even open her mouth for an obnoxious greeting, Copeland was snarling at her.

"Get the hell out of here, Rosalie."

"You guys busy?" she said, ignoring him. "Did you get a match on the prints you pulled from Duncan's place? Matches to the murder weapon?"

Copeland didn't respond. He jerked his chin at Detective Delaney-Carson and she nodded. She left the room, Copeland followed with little more than a glare in Rosalie's direction.

She waited until both detectives were out of the room, then turned to Hart, who was sitting at a desk. Expressly not making eye contact with her.

"Where are they going?"

He studied her with that pinched-cop look she hated. Especially from Hart, because unlike Copeland, he had an excellent bedside manner. Which meant it felt like he was *pitying* her, and she'd rather spar with Copeland than be *pitied* or treated gently by her cousin's husband.

"There's movement on the case," Hart said with careful *cop* language.

"What kind of movement?"

"The kind I can give you a general debrief on, because you'll find out soon enough once you talk to the Kirks. But I need you to promise to keep clear of it for a little bit while we sort out some logistics."

"Why would I promise that?"

"Because otherwise I'll make you go get the information out of the Kirks. I know I can't stop you, Rosalie, but I can slow you down."

She scowled, but figured he would do just that, and she didn't want to be slowed down because there was movement. Besides, she didn't have to keep any promises. Not if it meant helping.

"I know you'll keep your word if you promise, Rosalie," Hart said gravely and seriously.

Oh, damn him and his guilt tactics. "Fine, I promise I won't get in the way *this* morning. So just tell me."

"We didn't get a match on the prints in Duncan's place yet. We're still waiting on the report for the murder weapon too. It's a process, full of red tape. You know this."

"Yeah, I do. So, what's the movement then?"

"There was an emergency call out at the bunks at the Kirk Ranch not too long ago. One of their hands was unresponsive, had clearly taken a large number of pills. Ambulance got out there and transported the patient to Bent County Hospital."

Oh God. Pills. It had to be Duncan's pills. It just had to be. One of the ranch hands had… "Owen." He'd been so distraught over Hunter. It made the most sense that it was Owen who'd done it.

Hart's expression was grim. "What I can confirm is Owen Green was transported to Bent County Hospital. The first responders confiscated the remaining pills they found on the scene, and we can confirm they are the same type of pills Duncan Kirk reported stolen last night."

Owen had stolen Duncan's pills. Trashed his cabin. But why? Just to hurt himself? She might have believed that if he hadn't made a mess of Duncan's whole place. That he'd just been looking for oblivion.

But the scene of the crime didn't make sense if all he wanted was some pills. There were other ways to get drugs around here, no doubt. It just didn't add up, and worse, it made her heart hurt, the whole of it. She rubbed at her chest, trying to determine her next move. "But… Owen's alive?"

"So far. We haven't been notified of a change in his condition. We will be, either way, and if he wakes up, we'll need to question him on the pills."

She hated the thought of it. Of Owen stealing from Duncan. Making that mess in the cabin. She just hated all of this. She really hadn't pegged him as capable of it.

"Rosalie, I know you're close with the Kirks, and I'm not sure they realize what the next step of this is going to be."

For a minute, she was confused. But it connected, and quickly, just what the next steps the detectives would need to take.

They were going to try to connect Owen to Hunter's murder. Because how could the burglary, the murder, and a suicide attempt in this short of time on the same ranch not connect?

"I need you to let us do our job, Rosalie," Hart said, trotting out his no-nonsense detective voice that brooked no argument. "Trust us to do our job. You're a hell of an investigator, but this is a big deal, and we need to make certain our case doesn't have any inconsistencies."

"Owen didn't kill Hunter, Thomas. Hunter was his friend." All she could think about was him crying at that table in the bunkhouse. Maybe it was guilt. Maybe a response to killing, but...

She just couldn't believe it of him.

"Unfortunately, when you add drugs to the equation, nothing is as cut-and-dried as *friend*," Hart said gently. "But if there's no evidence he did it, then that's going to tie our hands."

Rosalie wanted to argue with Hart about drugs and murder, but what was the point? Hart was right. Drugs complicated everything, and both Owen and Hunter had a history of being involved in them.

But that didn't make Owen a murderer. And there was no evidence, so... "You're still waiting on the reports for the Kirk weapons Copeland confiscated?"

Hart nodded. "Yes. Looks to be a few more days yet."

Slow and frustrating. "Do you know if the Kirks are at the hospital?"

"I'm going to ask you to stay away from the hospital."

She shook her head. "No go, Thomas. If they're there, I'm going to stop by and make sure they're taking care of themselves."

"If I thought that's all you'd do, I'd be okay with it. But I know you, Rosalie. You're going to try to push your way into Owen's room, and if he's awake at all, you're going to try to push your way into our investigation."

"I'm a licensed investigator. What I find out will hold up in court."

"You're too close to this case. You're a liability. Stay away from the hospital. Okay? Don't put me in an awkward position at home."

More guilt. She wanted to hate him for it, but how could she? The fact he was even being kind about this was because he was married to her cousin. Otherwise he'd tell her to get lost and threaten to arrest her if she went to that hospital.

But she didn't need to go to the hospital to help. "Fine," she muttered. "Can you at least let me know if he wakes up?"

"I'm sure the Kirks will."

She wanted to roll her eyes, but instead she just left the office without so much as a thanks or goodbye.

Halfway through the parking lot on the way to her car, her phone rang. She pulled it out of her pocket.

Duncan.

She closed her eyes, took a deep breath. Answered.

"Hey," he said, his voice sounding rough and tired. She wondered how much sleep he'd gotten. "I've got some... alarming news."

"I'm at the police station, so I just heard. What can I do?"

"Mom and Terry are at the hospital with Owen. I convinced Dad to stay behind, but he's distraught. It's a hell of a mess."

"Yeah, it is." And she couldn't break it to him that the detectives were going to lean on the Owen theory now. But there were things they could do. She *was* an investigator, and if Hart was so dead set on keeping her away from the hospital, she'd take another angle. "I'm coming out."

"You don't have—"

"I'm coming out so we can do some investigating of our own. Can your dad clear out the bunkhouse for a bit?"

Duncan was quiet for a minute. "I imagine everyone will be getting back to work soon enough."

"Good. Meet me by the bunkhouse. Make sure it's empty." She was going to find *something* to prove that Owen hadn't killed his friend.

Chapter Fifteen

Duncan couldn't remember the last time he'd felt so god-awful, but he looked at his father and knew that he'd suffer through a hundred days more of his god-awful if he could take even one weight off his father's shoulders.

He'd forced Dad to eat some breakfast, drink some coffee, then walked down to the stables with him. He tried to think of something to make small talk about, but every topic Dad cared about felt like a minefield.

Mom was better at this kind of thing, but she was also better at hospitals. At logistics. So waiting for Owen's prognosis there with Terry made more sense, but that didn't magically allow Duncan access to the tricks of the trade to keep Dad busy.

They were walking the fence line between the Young Ranch and Kirk property, checking out gate locks, when Duncan's phone chimed. A text from Mom. He read it then relayed the information to Dad.

"Owen's stable. He'll be all right."

Dad nodded slowly, took a few more steps, then came to a stop. He rested an elbow on the fence post and looked over the ranch that stretched out in front of him.

"I called his grandmother. My cousin." He looked so damn grave, Duncan didn't know what to say to that. "You know, I don't take those kids because their parents want them out of trouble," Dad said, staring at the horizon. "I think if that's all it was, your mother would put her foot down. But she knows, I took those kids because their parents don't care about their trouble, and someone should."

Duncan stared at his father for a full minute in absolute stunned silence. He'd never considered... He always assumed Dad's relatives called him up and begged them to fix their kids, and because Dad was a softie, deep down, he couldn't say no.

It had never occurred to Duncan that Dad took it upon himself to help.

And it should have, he realized here in this quiet moment. Mom handling Hunter's funeral should have made it clear to him. These *cousins*, or friends of cousins, or whoever Dad had taken in over the years hadn't needed straightening out so much as a soft place to land.

And Dad had found a way to give that to them. Completely and selflessly, simply because he couldn't stand the idea that someone wasn't cared for.

"I called his grandmother," Dad continued. "My own cousin. We used to spend summers together right here, the lot of us running around while my grandmother and grandfather kept us whole and busy and *loved*. I called his own damn grandmother, and she... She basically said it was the boy's own choice. Like he ever had a choice with parents who didn't care. Grandparents who didn't care." Dad shook his head, and Duncan didn't know that he'd ever seen his father so upset, except maybe at his own mother's funeral.

"That boy could have died, and not her nor his parents gave half a damn. Despicable, is what it is. Far worse than anything Owen's gotten himself messed up in."

Duncan had always known his dad was probably the

best man he knew, but he'd never actually *thought* about it. Comprehended what that meant.

And now that he had, he had to say *something*. "I hope you both know how much I appreciate you. The both of you. Everything you sacrificed for me over the years. I've never thanked you, but I've always appreciated it."

Dad grunted, shifted from foot to foot, clearly uncomfortable with the gratitude and naked emotion. Which Duncan supposed was why he'd never vocalized it before.

Dad squinted, shaded his eyes. "Looks like Rosalie's truck is coming on up," he said, not engaging with Duncan's comment at all.

"She wants to take a look through the bunks. I don't imagine you could make sure no one comes back while we do that?"

Dad nodded grimly. "I'll make sure. Everyone's out, either in the south or north pasture, and Terry is at the hospital. I'll keep an eye out for anybody returning and give you a call if I see someone headed that way."

"Thanks." He hesitated a minute, because leaving Dad alone seemed like a bad idea.

"You go on. I want to get to the bottom of this, before another boy winds up dead or this close to it. You go on up and meet her there. I won't crumble apart."

"No, you never have." So Duncan couldn't allow himself to either. Duncan patted his father on the shoulder, then walked toward Rosalie's approaching truck. They'd get to the bottom of it. If anyone could, it was Rosalie.

Once he reached the truck, she rolled down the window and leaned out, so he headed to the driver's side.

"Hop in," she greeted. "I'm going to park down at your cabin. Then walk up to the bunks. The less chance of someone noticing me poking around the bunkhouse, the better."

It was a good thought, so Duncan followed her instructions. He climbed into the passenger seat, then looked over at her as she drove. She'd put on a little makeup, but he figured it was just to hide how tired she looked.

She pulled to a stop in front of his cabin, but he didn't get out right away. He reached across the center console, swept his thumb under her eye. "You ever going to sleep, Red?"

She studied him for a minute, neither of them leaning into the touch or away from it. Almost sizing it up, deciding what to do about it. But she didn't react either way. Just kept still and fixed him with her own stern look.

Which was a lot different than *last night*. Before everything had gone off the rails. But he thought of his dad, torn up about Owen and the people who didn't care about him, and knew he needed to focus on getting to the bottom of this.

Not figuring out him and Rosalie.

"You ever going to not be in pain, Ace?" she finally asked him after all those beats of silence.

He sighed in spite of himself, dropped his hand, and rotated his bad arm a little. "Feels like the answer is no, but it just takes time. The pharmacy said it might be a day or two before they can get the prescription filled."

"You're telling me a millionaire can't get himself some pain pills before a few days?"

He scowled a little, because there probably were strings he could have pulled, but he didn't like pulling them here. It felt...embarrassing.

"I'll be just fine."

"No doubt. You need your sling? Something to take the edge off?"

He glared at her. "You babying me?"

"If you need babying, look somewhere else."

"Yeah, you like to pretend you're real tough, Rosalie, but you know what's clear to me?"

"What?"

"You're a big old softie."

She snorted. "You're a little delusional there, Ace," she said, hopping out of the truck before he could reply.

But he knew he wasn't. There were people she had a soft spot for, and somehow, he happened to be one of them. It didn't hurt his ego any that she seemed frustrated about it or in denial about it. She'd get over it at some point.

But first, they had some mysteries to solve.

THEY WALKED UP to the bunkhouse. Rosalie considered bringing up last night. Laying down some ground rules. Like maybe that it was a one-off.

But she knew she'd be lying to herself and him if she said any of that, and since now wasn't the time or place to try to dig into a lie—especially after the *softie* accusation—she decided not to mention it at all.

And if she was irritated *he* didn't bring it up, didn't even mention it or try to pursue a line of conversation about it, well… She'd deal with that later. When he wasn't accusing her of being a *softie*.

It grated for a wide variety of reasons because it was both untrue and…true. When it came to certain people, she couldn't keep her defenses up and hard outer shell in place. Certain people, like *all men*, had always been easy to harden herself against.

But she couldn't seem to manage with Duncan.

Which was going to get her hurt, and she knew it. So she wanted to *avoid* it because she wasn't a masochist.

Apparently, except when it came to him.

He didn't try to make conversation on the walk over to

the bunkhouse, and she told herself she was grateful for it. Silence was great for thinking, and she needed to be thinking about what she was looking for.

Something... *Something*. Anything that might give her even half an idea to go on. Because this was just getting more and more confusing as more terrible things happened.

Duncan unlocked the front door and gestured her inside. She'd been in this room before, when they'd talked to Owen the day of the murder. So, that wasn't what she'd come for today. "You know which room is Owen's?"

"No, but I might be able to figure it out." He moved through the common area, back to a long hallway with lots of doors. Only one of them was open. Duncan gestured to it. "This would be my guess."

Rosalie brushed past him and stepped inside. It was in disarray. There were muddy boot prints from more than one person—probably the paramedics and cops. So, yeah, Owen's room. There were two beds in it—one on either side. "Did he share a room?"

"Not sure, but I can find out."

"Probably with Hunter, if he did," she said, more to herself than to Duncan, trying to get in the right frame of mind. Because investigating was her job, and she was damn good at it. She'd searched plenty of rooms before. She'd found evidence of theft, affairs, abuse.

She had to keep an open and agile mind. She had to think like the person she was investigating.

"What exactly are you looking for?" Duncan asked.

"I'm not sure. The police confiscated the pills. I'm sure they searched the area. Took pictures of what they found so they can connect it to your case. I don't know that I can magically unearth something they didn't, but I want to look. Get a sense of things." She pulled a pair of latex gloves out of the cross-body bag strapped to her chest and began to pull them on.

Since Duncan was giving her a funny look, she gestured around the room. "Don't touch anything. The police might come back to take prints, like they did at your place."

"Fingerprints," Duncan said, frowning. "Right."

"Having second thoughts, Ace?"

He sighed. "No, but I can't say that means I'm comfortable with all this."

"You can always leave me to it."

He shook his head, but he stayed there, hovering closer to the door than anything else. Rosalie started on one side of the room. She studied walls, baseboards, furniture. There wasn't much. Even the little closet just housed some clothes, a few pairs of boots, and little else. Nothing really personal.

It made her feel even more sorry for Owen in the hospital. Hunter, dead without ever having a chance to have a life that was more than this…impersonal holding pattern. She went through a nightstand, but it was empty. Hunter's likely, because the police would have confiscated any of his personal effects for their investigation.

She moved to the next nightstand and found more items in there. A few receipts—from a gas-station convenience store for what looked like a fountain drink and some snacks, a Rightful Claim bar tab from before Hunter's murder, and some fishing bait. Nothing that stuck out as important, but she made sure to commit it all to memory so she could transfer it to her notes later.

There was a book under the receipts. A bible. Suspicious, Rosalie lifted it out of the drawer, flipped through it, then held it over the bed, pages down, and shook.

A little square of paper tumbled out of the book and onto

the bed. Rosalie set aside the bible, picked up the paper, and began to carefully unfold it.

It was a map of the ranch. Boundaries were marked, and there were little hash marks where the different cattle herds were.

It was similar to the one Duncan's mother had made, but not identical. Which meant it was Owen's own map, outlining exactly what Rosalie had wanted outlined to see if they could connect the murder to the missing cattle.

Rosalie's heart sank. She shouldn't have any feelings about it, but she felt…bad. Bad for poor Owen. Bad for Hunter. Just a bad sign that maybe, just maybe, all her instincts about this case were wrong.

She moved over to Duncan and showed it to him. His expression went very hard.

"That doesn't look too good for Owen, does it?"

She shook her head. "No, it doesn't look good." She looked around this little room. Why would he have this? Why would he have anything to do with the cattle? Murder was one thing, but the missing cattle?

But then again, why would he steal Duncan's pills and take most of them himself? There were a lot of ways to hurt yourself when you were distraught. Stealing Duncan's pills had required quite a bit of effort. None of the answers to any of those questions made much sense.

"Are you going to take that to the cops?" Duncan asked, not showing any emotion regarding how he might feel about either answer.

She should take it straight to the cops, or even just call Copeland to come out. She wasn't even concerned about explaining how she'd come across it. She was a private investigator with the landowner's permission to search. She had Duncan as an eyewitness.

But… "I don't like this. Something doesn't feel right." Still, she refolded the paper, then slid it into a little evidence container she'd put in her bag. Then slid both into the bag. "Let's search the rest before we decide what to do with it." She moved past him and back into the hall. She went through room after room. Some guys had more items than others, some more personal than others, like they'd made this their home, their life.

But nothing that seemed to connect to the missing cattle, the murder, or the pills. She reached the final room at the end of the hall, but before she could reach for the knob, Duncan stopped her.

"That's the one room I know who it belongs to. It's Terry's room. I don't know how I feel about his privacy being violated. Owen is one thing, but you're talking about the guy who's been my dad's right-hand man for over a decade."

"If it offends your sensibilities, go away. I'm finishing the job."

He scowled, but he also moved out of the way.

Rosalie tried to turn the knob, but it didn't open. "It's locked."

"Makes sense. Each room is each man's living quarters. It's private."

Rosalie rolled her eyes at the censure in his tone. "No one else had theirs locked. And if he's innocent, what does it matter? Avert your eyes, Ace, I'm about to break the law."

This wouldn't be admissible in a court of law, but if it gave her something to go on, to investigate, she could do that. She would do that. She pulled her keychain out of her pocket, assessed which tool would be best, then stuck it into the keyhole.

After a few minutes of teasing it out, she finally managed to unlock the door and push it open. She didn't look back at Duncan to see how he felt about it. It didn't matter.

She expected Terry's room to be more…cluttered. He'd been here the longest. A long, long time. A man in his fifties, no doubt planning to stay.

But it was…a lot like Owen's. Sparse. Not personal. There were no pictures, no knickknacks, no books. Just clothes and hats, a few toiletries, and some notebooks and pens on a tiny desk.

She flipped through them. All blank.

Rosalie really didn't know what to make of it. "Why doesn't Terry live in the cabin you're in? Back when we had a full crew, our foreman lived in his own place, separate from the bunkhouse. A pecking-order kind of thing."

"Dad offered years ago when Terry got the promotion. Terry declined. Said he preferred to live with the men he was leading."

A good sentiment for a foreman to have. It showed a loyalty she was no doubt not repaying by poking around his things. But still, something…prickled at her neck. A kind of investigative sixth sense, but she couldn't find the center of it, the reason for it.

What was she missing here?

Duncan's phone chimed, interrupting her thoughts. She looked over at him as he studied the screen.

"It's Dad. A couple hands are on their way back. They'll stop with their horses at the stables first, but we better get out of here if we're wanting to keep this on the DL."

Rosalie gave one last quick look around. Nothing. Nothing stuck out to her, and the police would have searched the entire bunkhouse after Hunter's murder. She was just…desperate for answers, sadly.

She pulled off the gloves as they walked out of the bunkhouse. She shoved them into her back pocket. She blinked against the bright afternoon sky, as she walked side by side with Duncan back to his cabin.

"So what's next?"

Rosalie knew the answer, but that didn't mean she liked it. "I guess I'm going to take that map to the cops."

"You don't want to."

"No, I don't. Something about this doesn't feel like the whole story. But unfortunately, without police help, I don't think we can find the whole story." She didn't say the rest of what she thought: She wasn't even sure they'd find it *with* police help.

"Let me grab my keys."

"You don't have to come, Duncan. I can—"

"Let me grab my keys," he repeated firmly, striding over to his door.

She could leave without him. Handle this on her own. She didn't need a partner. She didn't need his input.

But she waited for him all the same.

Chapter Sixteen

Duncan wasn't surprised to be met with Detective Beckett's creatively crude curses when Rosalie strode into the little office the detectives shared.

Because the man who'd been introduced as Hart was standing in a corner—he also wasn't wearing his sling anymore. Then there was a woman. Blond and blue-eyed, dressed in slacks and a Bent County polo shirt. Midthirties, or maybe pushing forty. Cop, *clearly*, so maybe a third detective. She looked vaguely familiar, but Duncan couldn't place her and didn't have the energy to try.

"We're too busy to deal with you two," Detective Beckett said disgustedly.

"And apparently too busy to do your job," Rosalie returned, none of that fake cheer she usually used on Beckett. She was just straight pissed.

She slapped the bag with the map in it on the desk. "I found that in Owen Green's bible."

"Don't BS me, Rosalie," Beckett said disgustedly. "There was nothing in that damn bible, and what the hell were you doing poking around Owen Green's room?"

Since Duncan didn't care for this guy's entire demeanor, he waded in. "She had the property owner's permission."

Detective Beckett's angry gaze moved to Duncan. "Last time I checked you weren't the property owner."

"Yeah, but my father is. He knew. He was okay with it. You can verify that."

"Your parents should reconsider just who they're so free and easy with giving permissions to," Beckett replied.

"Why don't we all take a breath," the female detective said, pushing into a standing position from behind the desk. "I understand this is stressful and heated. We have an unsolved murder, a burglary, and a suicide attempt. This is serious, but sniping at each other certainly doesn't solve anything."

"My case," Beckett said, crossing his arms over his chest and continuing to glare at Rosalie. "I like sniping."

"Your case, your screwup," Rosalie retorted. "That map was in that bible. You didn't search it hard enough," Rosalie insisted, clearly ignoring the other detective.

"You can make a stink all you want, but you're not a cop. You're not a detective. Go private investigate all you want, but this is my case, and I don't need you screwing it up with lies brought on by whatever this is," he said, gesturing at Duncan. "I searched that bible. I've got bodycam footage to prove my point—not that I need to prove it to *you*."

Bodycam footage. Duncan frowned. Beckett had to be lying. It didn't make any sense otherwise. "I watched her do it," Duncan said. "I watched her upend the bible and the map fell out. It happened. So explain that with your bodycam."

The detectives somehow all shared a look. A beat of silence.

"It wasn't there this morning," Detective Beckett said, sounding more in control of his irritation. More concerned and considering than offended now. "Not only did I shake out the bible, I flipped through every page. There's not a stone I didn't turn over in that room. So if it was there *after...*"

"Someone *else* put it there," Rosalie said, finishing for him.

Duncan didn't like that *if* still hanging out in Beckett's sentence, but Rosalie didn't seem offended. Like Beckett, she seemed to have turned frustration and irritation into concern with the case at the drop of the hat.

It was enough to give a normal guy emotional whiplash.

"Which means that map isn't Owen Green's and he didn't put it there," Rosalie said. "Because Owen was in the hospital in between the police search and mine."

Even with the whiplash, Duncan kept up. "So was Terry. Terry Boothe, our foreman," Duncan clarified for the detectives, though they probably knew all the players. "He went with my mother to the hospital to wait on word about Owen's prognosis after the ambulance left."

Detective Beckett nodded thoughtfully. "I guess that's three people we can mark off the list. Who else has access to the bunkhouse?"

"It'd be the same list we gave you after Hunter's murder. Nothing would have changed."

"No. Nothing would have changed," Beckett agreed, but his gaze of suspicion was pinned on Duncan. "I don't recall your name being on that list."

Duncan blinked in surprised. "*My* name?"

"You have access to that bunkhouse, right?" Beckett asked, sounding somehow casual and deadly serious all at the same time.

Accusing him. Him. When he'd had his place trashed, his painkillers stolen. The detective was standing there throwing suspicion on him? "Yeah, I've got access," Duncan replied, anger coursing through him.

Detective Beckett shrugged casually. "Seems to me you're the new person in all this. You own any guns you haven't told us about, Mr. Kirk?"

It was…absolutely ludicrous. Duncan had never been a guy with much of a temper. All his feelings, all his passion, had always been centered on baseball.

But something hot and dangerous erupted inside of him now. He took a step toward Beckett. "Seems to me—"

But Rosalie grabbed his arm—his bad arm—and squeezed. Hard enough he couldn't get a word out because pain zinged through him.

"See if you can get some prints off that map," she said, interrupting whatever else Duncan might have said.

"You don't run this investigation, Rosalie. And you might consider your partner a liability until you know for sure…"

But Rosalie was dragging Duncan out of the office, and he didn't hear the rest of the detective's sentence.

"Look, I get that you're pissed and you have every right to be," she said in a low, seething voice, still pulling him along by his bad arm. "But if you assault an officer of the law, we'll have big problems. Let's cool off somewhere we're not so likely to get arrested for assault."

"We?" he demanded. Because she seemed a hell of a lot more in control of herself than he felt of himself.

"Yeah, *we*. Accusing you is a jerk move for no good reason except to get a rise. We won't give him what he wants. So we walk away before we start swinging."

The idea of her starting to swing, the picture of it in his head, was enough to soothe some of the roiling anger. But that didn't make this something he could swallow.

"How do you do all this?" he asked as they strode out of the police department and into the sunny afternoon.

"All what?" she asked, still moving at a quick pace toward her truck.

"Deal with an ego like that?"

"You know what's funny? I'd bet money on the fact that back in that little office of theirs, they're having a conversation about how they handle dealing with me and my ego."

Duncan didn't have a quick retort to that, because he imagined it was true. He just didn't happen to find Rosalie's ego damn insulting.

They reached her truck, but Rosalie didn't unlock the doors. She stood at the bed and sighed, squinting up at the sky. "Bottom line? We're all good at our jobs. We all want the same things. But we have to go at it in different ways. Which means we butt heads and things get heated. Outside that heat, I can tell you, Copeland and I are a little too much alike and that's probably half our problem." She wrinkled her nose. "I'd have done the same in his position—needle you, see what came out. As little as I like to admit that we go about things the same way, we do."

"That's very diplomatic of you," Duncan replied, because even if some of his anger had cooled, he didn't feel like being fair or diplomatic when it came to Detective Beckett.

"Yeah, well, if I couldn't find that diplomacy deep down on occasion, I'd have been arrested a long time ago." She smiled at him, but it wasn't her usual flash of personality. There was something sad behind it.

Because they could be annoyed at Beckett or the detectives, or any number of things, but it didn't change the very clear facts of the matter.

"Someone on that ranch is the problem," Duncan said quietly.

"Yeah."

A problem. A murderer. Someone who had access to

Owen's room. Someone right under his parents' nose had killed a man. And was trying to make Owen look responsible. It didn't feel like trouble brought with them. It felt like trouble right there in his home.

"Whoever killed Hunter wants Owen to look guilty. Wants to tie the whole thing to these damn missing cows, or that map wouldn't have been planted. But that was their first mistake. Planting that map *after* the detectives means we *know* there's a frame job happening."

"No one knows you looked today," Duncan said. "Not yet."

Rosalie seemed to consider that. "So who were they hoping *would* look? And when? Did they think the detectives were coming back?" She shook her head. "More questions and no more answers."

"That isn't true. We can cross Owen off any suspect list."

"Except your burglary," Rosalie said. "Unless… What if he didn't steal those pills? What if he didn't voluntarily take those pills?"

"Is that a leap?"

"Maybe. But it's one I want to look into. The fact of the matter is someone was already murdered. Whoever was behind that isn't above hurting people, so it isn't a leap to wonder if they forced Owen to take those pills. To frame him for all of this."

Duncan wasn't sure. This all felt like a stretch, but it was reality. A dead ranch hand. Stolen pills. Missing cattle. "Too bad we don't have a security camera on the bunkhouse."

Rosalie clapped her hands. "But we can. We absolutely can, and no one has to know."

ROSALIE DROVE WITH more determination than caution, and though Duncan didn't outwardly react, she didn't miss the way his good hand gripped the door like it would save him.

She supposed it made her a bad person, but it amused her. So she didn't slow down. She drove fast and only a *little* recklessly to Fool's Gold headquarters.

Because these little things that didn't add up were all steps. Maybe she couldn't see the top of the staircase yet, but she was building it.

She parked in her spot behind Fool's Gold HQ. She noted there were a couple of vehicles in the lot. Quinn's truck, and a car she didn't recognize. Brand-new, it seemed.

"We've got a lot of surveillance equipment. I'll grab what I want, and then we'll head out to the ranch. Do you think everyone will be out of the bunks tomorrow morning?"

"What about tonight?"

"I can put the outside surveillance up tonight without raising any eyebrows, but I don't think I can get anything inside as long as people are there. We'll just have to chance giving it some time. This only works if no one knows we're on to them."

Rosalie unlocked the back door, gestured Duncan inside, then led him down the little hall toward the equipment room. She heard voices, so she popped her head into the main office area where Quinn was standing with Anna Hudson-Steele, who wasn't working, considering she had her toddler on her hip.

They both looked over at her, or probably at Duncan hovering behind her.

"Just came in to pick up some surveillance equipment. Anna. That your new car out there?"

"Yeah. Had to upgrade." She patted her stomach. "And be relegated to desk duty again for a while."

"Aw. Congratulations. You and Hawk make cute babies."

"That we do. That your new partner back there?" Anna asked, eyeing Duncan.

Rosalie didn't scowl, though she wanted to. "Anna, this is Duncan. Duncan, Anna's one of our part-time investigators. You probably know some of her older siblings. She's a Hudson."

"Guilty as charged," Anna said with a grin, bouncing the toddler on her hip. "I heard you're having problems out at your folks' ranch. You have our sympathy there, but Rosalie'll get to the bottom of it. Stubborn is her middle name."

"Pot. Kettle."

"I have mellowed in my old age and motherhood era," Anna replied loftily.

"My butt," Quinn muttered, making Anna laugh.

"Well, congrats again. But we've got to get to work." Since Duncan was right behind her, and there wasn't room to move in this tight part of the hallway, she pointed down the hall. "Door at the end."

Before she could follow him, Anna called out.

"Hey, Rosalie?"

Rosalie popped her head back in. Anna pointed out where Duncan had gone down the hall, then pretended to fan herself, and Rosalie rolled her eyes and walked away, amused in spite of herself.

She went down to the storage room, unlocked it and led Duncan inside. Duncan was quiet and frowning, clearly working something over in his head while Rosalie gathered what she thought she'd need.

"What's on your mind, Ace?" she asked once she was sure she had everything.

"The Hudsons. Their parents went missing all those years ago. For years, no one knew what happened."

She studied him for a minute. Worry. But it wasn't for himself, or even the truth. He was worried about his parents dealing with unknowns for years, and she couldn't give him a hard time for that, or let it stand. "Yeah. But there were no bodies. They disappeared. It's different, Duncan. We're going to get to the bottom of this."

His gaze moved from the door to her. "Because stubborn is your middle name?"

"Because, as little as it might seem right now, we've got plenty to go on. So let's get on it." They walked back out to her truck, and she drove to the Kirk Ranch with her radio on, trying to discourage conversation.

She needed to think. About camera placement. About how to untangle these strange twists and turns.

About literally anything but *him*.

It was dark when they arrived back at the Kirks', which was good because she'd need dark to hide a surveillance camera outside the bunkhouse. She parked down at his cabin again. People would just think…

Well, she didn't need to consider that. "You can stay here," she told Duncan, maybe a little tersely, as she hopped out. She opened the back door of the truck, pulled out the equipment she'd need for an outdoor camera placement.

He came over to her side of the truck.

"I'm going with you."

"Look, it'll take maybe fifteen minutes when I get up there, and it's less suspicious or noticeable if it's just me wandering around in the dark."

"That's a lie and you know it."

She stopped what she was doing and glared at him, though it didn't matter. It was dark and the light on his porch didn't reach all the way out here.

"You're not wandering around in the dark with an unknown murderer on the loose, Rosalie."

"Because you're going to save me with your wounded arm even though I'm the one carrying?"

He sighed at her. "Because you'll be focused on putting up the camera, and you need someone watching out to make sure no one happens upon you doing it."

She couldn't argue with that, even though she wanted to. But she was being prickly and petty for no good reason, and that irritated her too.

So she let him tag along. They crept across the ranch in the dark, and Rosalie was used to this kind of thing, but Duncan must have still known the ranch pretty well despite all his time away because he didn't take any stumbles or make any noise.

There were a few old trees around the bunkhouse, and Rosalie had already decided on hooking her camera up to the one that faced the front door. If anyone noticed it, it could easily be played off as a trail camera meant to catch glimpses of wildlife, not people.

"I've got to use some light, so situate yourself in front of me where your body should block most of it from anyone looking out from the bunkhouse. But make sure you've got a good view of the door and the driveway."

Duncan followed instructions, but unfortunately, he was right. With his eyes watching, she could focus on the work rather than worrying if anyone was spotting her. She wished she could get into that bunkhouse, hide a few cameras in strategic places, but she had to believe tomorrow morning would be soon enough.

What would happen in there tonight with Owen in the hospital? She didn't think much of anything. She hoped to God nothing.

Once she was sure the camera was connected and she

could access it from her phone, she tapped Duncan on the shoulder. "Good," she whispered.

They didn't say anything, just started walking back to his cabin. Once they were closer to his cabin than the bunkhouse, Duncan spoke.

"What about actual surveillance? Like following guys around? Watching what they do?"

"Even if you hired out all of Fool's Gold, we wouldn't be able to follow everyone. Maybe if we just watched who came and went, but even that's a tall order considering most of these guys only leave the ranch sporadically."

"Well, we don't have to follow Terry. Maybe we can do it like that. Narrow down who it could have been."

Rosalie nodded. "See if your dad knows where everyone was over the course of the morning. Anything we can rule out helps us focus in."

"He'll be in bed by now, and he hasn't been sleeping, so I don't want to interrupt on the off chance he is. I'll talk to him in the morning, see what he can tell me. Maybe talk to Terry. Even if he was at the hospital all morning, he would know what everyone was supposed to be working on."

"Good idea. I know Terry's not on our list, but we need to be careful what we tell him, so he doesn't inadvertently let on to whoever is doing this something we don't want spread around. No matter who we think is innocent, we have to be careful what we say to them."

"That's depressing."

"That's murder investigations for you."

He didn't say anything to that as they approached his yard. But before she could break away and head for her truck, he grabbed her hand.

"I'm sure I've got leftovers in my fridge. Come in and eat some dinner."

She studied the cabin. There was one light on inside, the porch light beaming at them like some sort of welcoming beacon.

Last night, she'd said yes. This morning she'd snuck out of his bed, and out of his cabin, without anything having happened last night. They hadn't spoken about it all day. Hadn't acknowledged it in any way. They'd focused on what was important.

She'd been given a reprieve. Time to screw her head back on and not be dazzled by him. She needed to take that save.

"I better not." She pulled her hand out of his. "I'll see you around, Ace."

He frowned at her, but she turned away from him. Started walking to her truck. The sensible thing was to cut this off at the pass while she still could. If they focused on this case, then they didn't have to deal with whatever aberration last night had been.

It was the smart, sensible, *safe* thing. And maybe that wasn't her usual MO, but it had to be when it came to Duncan Kirk.

"Hey."

"Hey what?" she asked, turning around. She'd barely gotten the *what* out of her mouth when his lips touched hers. His good arm wrapped around her waist, pulling her close and into this... *Vortex* was the only word for it, because everything else disappeared.

Over the course of the day, focusing on work and not mentioning last night at all, she'd almost convinced herself that the memory of kissing him was an exaggeration.

But it wasn't. Nothing could be. She didn't understand how one man could kiss her in a way that made every other kiss that came before stupid and pointless. Weak and pitiful compared to this wallop of a sensation. His mouth on hers, his arms around her. A *vortex* she couldn't fight.

Didn't want to, damn it.

He eased his mouth from hers, but he didn't let her go. His gaze was direct and intent. "This murder mess may take precedence, but this isn't going away. *I'm* not going away."

Rosalie found herself utterly and uncharacteristically speechless. Her heart hammered, and it wasn't just the kiss. The chemistry. It was the way he looked at her that seemed to unearth her foundations she thought were so steady.

He ruined them so damn easily. Made her want to melt when she knew all the disastrous ways believing in someone ended.

"Still going home?" he asked, one eyebrow raised.

She should, just to prove that she could. She should, because she was a smart woman who knew how to guard her damn soft heart.

But she shook her head and followed him inside.

Chapter Seventeen

Duncan rolled over to find a naked, sleeping woman in his bed, and figured he could pretend there weren't murderers wandering around for about five minutes to enjoy Rosalie Young sleeping in his bed.

He thought she'd try to sneak out sometime in the night, or early in the morning, like she had the night before. But exhaustion must have caught up with her, because her eyes were closed, her breathing deep and even.

So Duncan slid out of bed, narrowly biting back a hiss at the throbbing pain in his arm. He moved as quietly as he could manage into the kitchen, got the coffee going, then grabbed a banana his mother had no doubt stocked yesterday. He scarfed it down with the express purpose of taking a few ibuprofen with something in his stomach.

He decided to consider it progress that the over-the-counter stuff was helping to take the edge off.

Owen using those pills—or someone using those pills against Owen—really made Duncan reluctant to replace them.

When Rosalie came out of his bedroom, her hair was a mess and she looked bleary-eyed and still half-asleep. She was wearing one of his T-shirts, which nearly went down to her knees.

His heart did one painful roll in his chest, and something inside of him seemed to say "this is it. Right here."

But he hedged on admitting to himself what that *it* was. "Morning, sunshine," he greeted instead.

She just grunted, shuffled over to the coffee maker, saw it hadn't brewed a full cup, then grunted again.

It was amusing to watch. She was usually so put together, so...*vibrant* and in control of herself. She made it look like she was all instinct and wild, but there was a careful note to Rosalie hidden underneath all that bluster.

He liked her bluster. He liked the hint of something softer underneath. He liked her, plain and simple. No doubt if he didn't, it would have been easy enough to let her leave last night.

He wrapped his good arm around her from behind to pull her closer. She stiffened a little, but then she relaxed. It was starting to irritate him. The push and pull. It'd be one thing if she had no interest. If she flat-out rejected him, but she hadn't.

"Look, Duncan..."

Unless she was about to.

"You should probably know, I'm not much of a good bet," she said firmly. Like she'd really been thinking them over and had come to this very clear conclusion.

Except it made no sense.

He couldn't see her expression since he was standing behind her. He could only look down at the top of her head. There were a lot of complexities about Rosalie. No doubt. Hidden things under her brazen surface.

But she was not a woman who suffered from a lack of confidence. So he tried to unearth what she *really* meant by that, but couldn't. Because it just didn't add up. "You're not? Or I'm not?"

She didn't push away from him, and he'd expected her to. It kept his frustration with her in check, that she'd lean against him and have this conversation.

She didn't answer, and he wasn't in the mood to fight, so he figured they could set this aside for now. Get back to murder. Tonight, they could wade through all this.

So he kissed her cheek. "You seem like a pretty good bet from where I'm standing. I'm going to walk up to the main house. See if Dad can come up with a list of anyone who definitely couldn't have been at the bunkhouse between the detectives and us yesterday morning. Shouldn't take too long. You take your time waking up. I'll be back. It'll probably be another hour or two before we can get into the bunks undetected."

He felt her gaze as he released her and walked for the front door. He didn't look back, though he wanted to.

"Duncan?"

Slowly, he turned to face her. Standing in his kitchen, in his shirt, still looking half-asleep and gorgeous.

"Maybe it's not me. Maybe it's the whole…relationship thing. It's a lot of trust. I'm not sure I've got that in me."

He figured it was fair that trust had to be earned, and they had a ways to go on that front. But he was a patient man. A goal-oriented kind of guy. He could prove it, earn it. He would. Not with words. But with the same kind of stubborn tenacity that had led him to success in his career.

"So find it in you, Rosalie. I can wait," he replied, then went ahead and left rather than allow her to keep talking herself out of what they'd already started.

Because they were both people who saw through what they started. She'd come to that conclusion too.

He was *almost* sure of it.

He walked up to his parents' house and let himself in

after a brief tap on the door. They were both in the kitchen eating breakfast. They exchanged a look he didn't quite understand, then smiled at him.

"Morning," Mom offered. "What brings you up?"

"Some questions, unfortunately. Last night Rosalie and I had a bit of a break in the case, I guess you'd say. I need to know who on the ranch might have been unaccounted for between the time the ambulance took Owen away, and the time Rosalie and I looked through the bunkhouse yesterday."

Dad scratched a hand through his hair. "Well. Your mother and Terry were at the hospital. Everyone else would have been doing their assigned job."

"Is there a way to verify they were doing it? Especially if Terry wasn't here?"

Dad seemed to consider this. "Everyone had jobs to do since it's busy season," Dad said. "Terry and I sit down and discuss progress every other day during the busy season—and that's where he'd mention if someone was slacking off or something didn't get done. We didn't last night with the hospital hubbub. I can try to pin him down this morning. Get a rundown of yesterday."

"That'd be good." Would it give them answers? Before he could say anything else to Dad, his phone chimed. Duncan pulled it out of his pocket and read the text from Rosalie.

Owen's awake. Headed to the hospital to talk to him. Text after.

The phone on the wall rang, and Mom got up to answer. Duncan could tell by her reactions that she was getting the same information that Rosalie had just texted him.

She hung up then smiled over at him. "Owen's awake, and Sharon thinks she can get me in to see him today. So

I'm going to head up to the hospital. I know Terry is worried sick about that boy. I'm going to call down and see if he wants to ride together this time."

Duncan nodded but before his mother could lift the receiver again, the words caught up in his head. "This time? You two didn't ride together yesterday?" he demanded.

"No, Terry wanted to make sure everything was settled before he left. He couldn't have been more than twenty minutes behind me though. Waited all day with me too. But they wouldn't let us see Owen. Hopefully today."

"Yeah, hopefully." Duncan kept the smile in place and rejected the awful thought that wanted to take root. Sure, it gave Terry time to plant the map, but why would he? There was no reason. Not that anyone else had a reason. But the point was, anyone could have put that map there.

Anyone, including Terry.

Mom made the call, but Terry didn't answer. "Must already be out and about. I'll text his cell. You probably have things to handle this morning, Duncan," she said to him. She moved for the counter. "Here. Take some breakfast back with you." Mom handed him a big grocery bag full of food.

He frowned down at the amount. "Mom, this is enough for…"

"Two people?" Mom replied brightly. "I suppose it is. Would you like to discuss that?"

Since he absolutely would *not*, he took it without any other discussion, or mentioning that Rosalie was already leaving, and went back to his cabin.

Once Dad pinned down Terry, got the information on who else might have not done their chores yesterday morning, he'd have a list. A list of suspects. He'd present Rosalie or the detectives with it. It was progress. Steps, like Rosalie said.

And he'd include Terry on that list, even though he didn't want to.

They had to look at every angle, Rosalie had taught him that. So he'd follow every avenue, even when he didn't want to.

Rosalie pulled into the hospital parking lot. She'd made a quick stop at home for a clean change of clothes and was glad not to run into Audra and have to *explain* everything. Then she drove, faster than she should have, out to the hospital.

Maybe Owen really didn't know anything, but surely he'd remember if someone shoved those pills down his throat. And that was a clearer answer than whatever they *might* find on some cameras set up inside the bunkhouse.

Ideally, though, she'd have time for both. If she hurried.

She screeched into a parking spot and hopped out, plan already in her head. A little fast talking at the nurses' station, but she'd slip into Owen's room without permission if she needed to, a few questions, then…something.

Something.

It was a lot better than thinking about Duncan's parting shot this morning. When she got inside, there was a flurry of activity at the nurses' station. A few discreet questions and she got the gist.

Owen had crashed again. There was a lot of confusion because no one knew why. He'd been in good shape one minute, flatlining the next.

Rosalie wanted to stay and find out what happened, but the hospital hustle reminded her far too much of her father's unexpected death. She'd rather act than sit in *that*.

So she went back to her truck, refused to think about poor Owen crying over his dead friend, and considered her options. No answers from Owen, so she'd have to go back to the ranch and plant her cameras.

Her phone rang as she slid back into her driver's seat. It was Duncan. She thought about ignoring it. About finding some boundaries. When she was at work, she wasn't going to communicate with him.

But her work right now was *him* and his family, and she should probably tell him about Owen. So she answered on speakerphone, so she could drive back to the office while they talked.

"Hey," she answered. "Bad news."

"About Owen? Mom was halfway to the hospital when her friend who works at the hospital called and told her."

"They aren't sure what happened, so I'm headed back to put up those cameras. You got that list from your dad yet?"

"He's talking to everyone now." He paused for a moment. "Rosalie… I don't want to believe this is true. I know my dad doesn't, but… Mom mentioned that she and Terry didn't drive to the hospital together yesterday."

Something cold trickled into Rosalie's bloodstream. A few too many things clicking together with that simple fact. "So when did he?" she asked, careful to keep her tone neutral, even as her heart rate picked up.

"She said he was about twenty minutes behind her, making sure all the jobs were assigned for the day, and maybe he was. He could have been." But Duncan didn't sound convinced.

She found she couldn't argue with him, even though she knew better. There were too many coincidences adding up to Terry being a problem. Maybe not the whole problem, but part of this.

And if he was, everyone at that ranch was in danger, including Duncan. He wouldn't want to go to the cops yet.

He wasn't ready to fully believe Terry was the most likely suspect, but she was.

"Listen, Duncan, scratch the cameras. I'm going to head over to Bent County, talk all this through with Copeland," she said. "You stay put with your parents. Keep an eye on everything there. Call if anything seems even remotely fishy, especially with Terry. You have to be careful, even if you want to trust your gut. Okay?"

He sighed. She could just imagine the expression on his face. Frustrated resignation. "Yeah, okay. You be careful too, huh?"

"Sure, that's me."

He chuckled. "Uh-huh. Watch your back, Red. Give me a call when you're done with the detectives."

She should say no. She'd call him when she wanted. She didn't have to *check in* with him. Her job was dangerous, and if he was really so into this and waiting for her to trust him, he'd have to accept that.

But that would inevitably hurt his feelings in this moment, and if she hurt his feelings, she'd be thinking about *that* today, instead of what she needed to be thinking about. Which was how Terry Boothe might be connected to all this.

"I will. 'Bye."

"'Bye."

She ended the call on an irritated sigh. Not sure who or what she was irritated with, except maybe just this clutching, twisting feeling in her chest that was a tangle of feelings she most assuredly didn't want.

But had, for some damn reason.

She drove away from the hospital, which was more centrally located in the county, out north back toward the police station. She heard a faint shuffle of noise behind her.

Confused, she turned her head a little to peek in the back. And saw something wholly unexpected.

A gun. Pointed at her head.

Held by the man of the hour, who was sitting up from a crouched position behind her seat.

Terry, who was in the back seat of her truck, with a gun pulled on her. She'd been so distracted by everything happening, she hadn't paid *attention*. He'd been *hiding* back there? For how long?

"Keep driving," Terry ordered.

Rosalie said nothing as her mind whirled. She turned her gaze back to the road, to driving.

Terry had been at the hospital—that was the only time he could have gotten into her truck. *Maybe* at the ranch, but that just didn't add up. He'd been at the hospital.

He'd done something to Owen. *He* was the reason for his crash. He had to be.

"You tried to kill that poor boy. Twice?" She flicked a glance at him in the rearview mirror.

"Drive," he said again. His eyes were flat, his hand on the gun was steady. This was no panicked move. It was planned, and Terry was in charge of himself.

So Rosalie had to be in charge of herself. "Sure. Where are we driving to, boss?"

"You shouldn't have stuck your nose into this. Should have let trash like Hunter Villanova lay. It doesn't give me any joy to do this, but you ruined my plans."

A cold chill snuck up Rosalie's spine. She could handle a gun being pointed in her direction. Maybe it was misplaced confidence, but she figured she was in the driver's seat, so to speak, so she could get out of this.

But Terry having *plans* alarmed her. *Plans* spoke to time putting this all together, whatever this all was. Something she couldn't even begin to guess at. She swallowed her nerves. "What kind of plans, Ter?"

"You're going to turn around at the cut-through here. You're going to drive me back to the Kirk Ranch. And when we get where we're going, you're going to call that boyfriend of yours. I'll spare Norman and Natalie, because it makes sense to. But you two? You've overstayed your welcome."

Rosalie forced herself to laugh even though her throat was dry. "You think you're going to kill Duncan *and* me and get away with it?"

"I don't think I am. I know I am. I've got a plan, and since I know yours, mine'll win out. Go on then. Turn at the cut-through."

Like hell she would. As they came to the cut-through in the highway, Rosalie did everything at once—ducked her head away from the gun, jerked the wheel in the opposite direction toward the ditch instead of the cut-through, and hit the accelerator down to the floor.

When the truck crashed into the ditch, pain exploded in her head, but it wasn't a gunshot, so there was that.

Chapter Eighteen

Duncan hated the roiling feeling of betrayal in his gut. Hated worrying that a man who'd been his father's friend and right-hand man for…forever, really, might have… What? Murdered a kid? Shoved drugs down Owen's mouth?

It didn't make sense.

But nothing else did either. Until Dad came back with a list. Duncan looked at the clock on the oven. It was taking too long. And since Rosalie hadn't called Duncan back, he was going stir-crazy. There had to be something he could *do*.

He'd just walk out to the bunkhouse or stables or wherever Dad was. He'd just walk around until he found *someone* to give him *something* to do.

But when Duncan stepped out of his cabin, he saw Dad walking across the yard. He looked…gray. Not the exhausted pale he'd been dealing with for the past few days, but a kind of wounded gray. Like he was bleeding out from the inside.

"Dad…" Duncan met him at the bottom of the steps, then took him by the arm and led him inside. He pushed him onto the couch, a strange terror jittering through him. Because Dad was *fine*, so it shouldn't be *scary*, but Duncan had never seen his father look quite so weak and old, and it upended the way everything was supposed to be.

"Everyone was accounted for," Dad said, staring at his hands. "Granted, someone could be lying, but Dunc..." He lifted his gaze. Heartbreak in the dark brown eyes. "No one's seen Terry this morning. He was gone before sunup, before we got the call about Owen. Jeff stepped in and handled assignments this morning. Didn't tell me because he didn't want to worry me."

Something cold and foreboding settled in Duncan's gut.

"It can't be Terry, Duncan." Dad's head fell into his hands. "It has to be a mistake."

But Duncan knew Dad didn't actually believe that any more than Duncan himself did. "We'll figure it out," he muttered to his dad. He pulled out his phone and dialed Rosalie.

She didn't answer. If she was talking to the detectives, she might ignore the phone. So he didn't let himself worry. He just texted her. Call me. Emergency.

The text went unread.

She was just ignoring him. He wanted to believe that. Had to hold on to that possibility. It was the only thing that made sense. He knew that.

But he also had to act.

"I'm going to call the detective and give him this information," Duncan told his father. "And you're going to stay right here and rest for a minute, okay?"

Dad nodded without arguing, another terrifying turn of events. Duncan strode out onto his porch, not wanting him to hear this.

Heartbeat slamming into overdrive, he called the Bent County Sheriff's Department and jammed in the number for Detective Beckett's extension.

"Beckett," the man answered.

"Detective, it's Duncan Kirk."

"Great," he muttered. "What do you want?"

"Is Rosalie there?"

"I'm not an answering service, Kirk. You want to talk to your girlfriend, call her."

"She's not answering. And last I heard she was on her way to talk to you—"

"Me?" There was a slight hesitation. "You sure about that? Because I haven't seen or heard from Rosalie today."

That cold ball of ice in Duncan's gut turned into a full-on glacier. "What?"

"Do I need to repeat myself? Look, I'm busy, I—"

"I talked to her thirty minutes ago. She was leaving the hospital, and she was heading over to the sheriff's department to talk to you."

"Maybe she got sidetracked. Maybe she lied. Listen—"

"No, I need you to listen." Duncan took time for one careful breath, then laid everything out. Terry having the window of time to place that map. Terry not being on the ranch today. Everything pointing to Terry, Terry, Terry.

When he was done, the detective was silent so long Duncan was worried he'd lost the connection.

"Were you or your father aware that Mr. Boothe has been quietly buying up small sections of land in Idaho under an LLC?" Detective Beckett asked in that cop voice devoid of any emotion, even his usual irritation.

Duncan didn't fully understand the question, the information, but if they were looking into Terry... He just had to answer the questions and then this could all be over. "No. I wasn't, I can ask my dad but... No, I think he'd have mentioned it if he'd known."

"It also appears he's been stockpiling weapons—legally, in fairness—and storing them on this property. We haven't been able to get a search warrant yet since it's across state lines, but since the weapons confiscated from your parents' house don't match the murder weapon, we're trying."

Duncan felt like his foundation was crumbling. "You think he did it."

"It's a lead we're following, and your added information is helpful. It should put some weight behind the search warrant."

Which was essentially a "yes, we think he did it." But… "What about Rosalie?"

"She might be driving. She might be at her office or following a lead. What do you want me to do? She's a grown woman. I can't go searching for her when I've got a murder to solve."

"Fine. Don't do anything," Duncan muttered, and he hit End on his phone. "I'll do it."

He was in his truck before he'd shoved the phone into his pocket. And he was out on the highway in under a minute.

Rosalie ran.

She'd managed to unbuckle herself, kick open the door of her truck, and then crawl out of it. The pain didn't register at first. She was moving on adrenaline and the desperate need to get away from Terry and his gun.

She didn't look back at the wreck of her car. Didn't worry about seeing how long it would take him to crawl out of the wreck. She had to get out of gun range, then she could worry about all that.

She knew where she was, and the closest safe place to run would be toward Bent and the sheriff's department. The ranches were too far away and so was the hospital.

Oh, she was miles from Bent, and it'd be a miracle if she reached it considering there was a wet sticky substance dripping down her face. She didn't allow herself to think of it as blood. Acknowledging just how hurt she was would only slow her down.

She risked a look back toward the truck as she ran. She could see Terry crawling out of the back door. So she turned her attention forward and focused on running.

She had to get off the side of the road, even though someone might see her there and that might be help. It was too big of a risk considering how little traffic existed on this road. She needed to get out of Terry's line of sight. Or at least out of the range of his gun.

She pawed at her hip as she ran toward a cluster of trees. Her gun wasn't there. She'd lost it somewhere along the way. In the crash or the scramble out of the truck.

"Stupid," she muttered to herself. Careless. *Panic*. She knew better than to panic, but that's what she'd done. She cursed herself some more, but did it inwardly, so she could save all her breath for the run.

Once she was in the shade of the trees, she tried to get a better sense of her surroundings. She couldn't run much more. Her vision seemed to be getting…fuzzy, and not just from the sticky substance that kept leaking into her left eye. She was unsteady. Much more running and she'd fall and really hurt herself.

She leaned against a tree with both hands as she tried to catch her breath, tried to think through the whirling, nauseating chaos in her head. Pounding, pounding pain. By ducking the gun's aim when she'd crashed, the dashboard had given her a hell of a knock to the head.

But she wasn't shot, was she?

Luckily, her legs seemed to be holding her up. She just had to catch her breath and come up with a plan. She twisted so now it was her back leaning against the tree. She blinked her eyes a few times until she could see straight. Sort of.

She was in a copse of trees, probably planted by some long-dead pioneer. It gave her some cover, but no doubt if Terry thought she was hiding, this was what he'd go for.

She couldn't stay here. Not without a weapon. Not without her damn cell phone, which she'd left in the console of the truck.

But that wasn't too big of a mistake. If someone was smart enough to trace it, they'd find her truck crashed in that ditch. They could hopefully track her.

If Terry didn't first.

If worse came to worse and she was the next victim, surely some of Terry's prints or DNA would be in her truck. They'd find him. Justice would be served.

She tried to find some comfort in that, but was that all she wanted? *Justice?*

She thought about what this would do to Audra. Franny. Vi. The people who loved her.

Duncan. And maybe love wasn't in that equation. Too early, too soon for all that, but in this moment, Rosalie could be honest with herself, as little as she liked to be. It was somewhere in there, like a seed planted. Possibilities in all the things that brought them together, tied them together, made them *like* each other.

And sure, that was scary, but in *this* moment, the scarier thing was not getting a chance to see all that through.

So *hell no* she didn't just want justice. She wanted to live. She was going to have to fight. Creatively, sure, but fight nonetheless.

She hadn't paid close enough attention to how far she'd run off the highway route, but it couldn't have been more than a mile or two. Which meant she was smack-dab in the middle of nowhere on foot. The closest hint of civilization she could think of would be Hope Town—the former ghost town turned into a kind of community as a safe haven for people who needed it. But that still had to be miles off.

She could walk miles. She had concerns about the head injury, but she could walk miles. If she was slow and careful. If she kept to cover, like these trees. She could get there and then she could call the cops.

Something too close to panic bubbled in her chest.

But she couldn't panic. She had to think. Get out of the trees. Find new cover. Maybe if she could lure Terry deep enough away from the highway, she could double back and get back to the highway.

She pushed off the tree, had to close her eyes for a minute and breathe through the dizziness that threatened to take her out. She wouldn't let it.

She damn well wouldn't let anyone take her out.

Chapter Nineteen

Duncan sped his way toward Bent. His mind was racing in a million different directions. But he knew how to handle that, he reminded himself. He knew a million ways to focus. Back then, every game had felt like life or death.

Now that his situation *really* felt like life or death, he realized how ridiculous it had been to put so much pressure on himself for a *game*.

He gripped the steering wheel as hard as he could, especially with his bad arm, and focused on the throbbing pain in his shoulder. Sometimes pain could be a great focal point and motivator. He used it.

He drove with the idea he'd retrace Rosalie's steps. Drive to the hospital, then from there head to the sheriff's department. And if there was no sign of her, then to Wilde and Fool's Gold. And if she wasn't there, and hadn't gotten back to him, then what?

No. He couldn't deal in *then whats*. One step at a time. He made it to the hospital parking lot and finally had to force himself to loosen his grip on the wheel. He was sweating, a mix of worry and pain, and he needed to be more in control.

He did a quick circuit of the hospital parking lot. He saw his mother's car. Wondered how Owen was doing. He should stop in, make sure Mom was taking care of herself.

He would. He'd come back. Once he figured out what the hell was going on with Rosalie. It was probably something so ridiculous, and yet he couldn't get past this driving need to make *sure*.

Because maybe she was just ignoring him, but it didn't *feel* right. She'd said she would call him, and she'd said so reluctantly. Rosalie might want to push him away sometimes, but she wasn't a *liar*.

But she could have gotten caught up in something, and then wouldn't he feel stupid if he'd gone around tracing her steps?

"I'd rather feel stupid than guilty," he muttered to himself, driving back out of the parking lot of the hospital. He got back on the highway that would lead him to Bent and the sheriff's department.

He was so intent on getting there, he almost missed it. A glint of something on the side of the road. He didn't even fully mean to look into his rearview mirror to see what it was. But when he did, he slammed on the brakes. With his breath caught in his throat, he pulled an immediate and very illegal U-turn, going down the highway on the wrong side so he could pull up on the shoulder that allowed him the perfect view of a truck crashed into the ditch.

With a buzzing in his ears and his entire body feeling completely numb, he shoved the truck into Park, jumped out, and ran over to the crashed truck.

Rosalie's crashed truck.

The driver's-side door and back-seat door were open and when Duncan ran around the full length of it, he realized it was empty. Empty was good.

Right?

He let out a pained breath, then started a closer inspection of the car on the driver's side. He noted her phone was in the console, which wasn't...right. It couldn't be right. He didn't see anything else out of place or strange, except when he stepped away and realized the little smudge on the driver's-side door's window looked a lot like...blood.

He didn't let himself think about that, because there was no one *here*. Which meant if she'd had an accident, she'd gotten out. No one was dead here, and that was what mattered.

But why wouldn't she be here? Why wouldn't she have used her phone to call for help? It didn't add up and Duncan didn't know what to *do*. Where to even begin. She had to be around here somewhere. Bleeding. Maybe she'd tried to walk along the side of the road?

But why would she leave her phone?

Since he didn't have the first clue, and his gaze kept getting pulled back to the *blood* on the window, Duncan knew he needed help. He thought about what Rosalie had done when his place had been trashed—she'd called Detective Beckett directly on his cell.

A number Beckett had handed out to his parents that first night, and Duncan had the good sense to have added to his contacts. He dialed it now.

"Beckett," the man greeted tersely.

"It's Duncan—" Before he could even get his last name out, Beckett was cursing.

"If you call me again, I'm—"

There was no time for that. "I found Rosalie's truck crashed in a ditch on Route Two. She's nowhere to be found, but there's some blood."

For a moment, the detective said nothing. "Where on Route Two?"

Duncan looked around, tried to discern what mile marker he'd be at. Gave the detective an approximation.

"All right. You're going to stay put. Right by the truck. I'm going to send an ambulance, then I'll be out. Once I get there, you're going to get the hell out of our way."

Duncan knew Detective Beckett was right. The police knew what they were doing. Detectives knew what they were doing. But he couldn't bring himself to verbally agree.

"Listen. This is dangerous. Terry Boothe's truck was found parked in an abandoned garage not far from the hospital. There's a threat here. I'm on my way. You need to step back and let the police handle it."

Duncan considered it. For maybe two seconds. Terry had left his truck near the hospital? Where Rosalie had last been?

No.

"Sorry. Can't do that." He hung up. Surveyed the quiet world around him. What had happened here? An accident? A fight? She hadn't *just* crashed, or she'd still be here. She would have used that phone to call it in or at least taken it with her.

Something bad had happened. Maybe it wasn't Terry, but too much was adding up.

Duncan took a few steps away from the truck in the tall grass. He could kind of see where some of the blades had been depressed by someone stepping on them. He'd follow the trail as best he could.

But before he could take even two steps, his toe hit something hard. He looked down and saw the glint of metal. He crouched to examine it. He couldn't be sure it was Rosalie's, but it was definitely a gun. So he picked it up.

He had a bad feeling they were going to need it.

ROSALIE STUMBLED, her stomach roiling so much she thought for sure there was no way she'd breathe through the need to wretch.

But she managed. On her hands and knees, the muddy ground seeping into both, she managed to swallow down the need to be sick. She blinked at the gunk in her eyes, but she couldn't see. She wanted to believe it was just blood, but she knew better.

She was losing consciousness. The grip of black was edging around her brain, and she kept fighting it off, but only barely.

"Come on," she muttered to herself. "Get it together." She sucked in a deep, painful breath, then pushed off her arms so that she was upright on her knees.

But the sight that greeted her wasn't a good one. Terry was approaching. He'd caught up with her. Found her.

Now what?

She tried to get to her feet, but her legs wouldn't seem to move, so she tried to scoot back, away from him. She groped around on the ground for something, anything she could use as a weapon.

"You've made this much harder than it needed to be, Rosalie," Terry said, walking in slow, menacing steps toward her. "I could have buried you out here. It could have been easy, but you had to wreck that truck. Now, we've got to complicate things."

He moved toward her, and she tried to scramble away, but she couldn't seem to get to her feet. She just stumbled, and then she felt his hand on her arm and she was being dragged back. She *thought* she was kicking. She was trying to kick, but it didn't seem to change the steady slide of her body across the ground.

"You left a pretty nice blood trail. Now, do we think it'll be the cops or Duncan who comes to rescue you? My money's on our boy. If not, that'll be okay. It can still look like him. It'll look like him."

She tried to speak, tried to get her mouth to move, but it wouldn't.

"You shouldn't have crashed the truck, Rosalie. You shouldn't have done it. But you did, so we'll deal with it."

She tried to push him away, but she had such little strength left. He had one arm behind her, then the other, and shoved her back against the tree as something wrapped around her. A rope?

She tried to focus on breathing over panic. Understanding what Terry was saying over wanting to start sobbing.

"You can't really think you're going to get away with this," she rasped.

"Of course I am. I have a plan. You've been ten steps behind it this whole time. So I've got time. To perfect it. To make it right. You shouldn't have brought Duncan into it."

Duncan thought she was with the police, but how much time had passed? Would he be worried? Would he tell them to look for Terry? Would anyone find her wrecked truck?

They had to. If someone started looking for her, they'd have to find it. If she could just stay alive...

"Why?" she asked Terry, though she wasn't even sure what she was questioning. Just this whole damn horror.

"Why." He snorted. "Ten years of planning thwarted by some uppity kid who'd never seen a day of hard work in his whole sorry life? No. It wasn't happening. It's *not* happening. I never meant to kill him. If he hadn't gotten messed up in the cows, hadn't tried to blackmail me, they'd be mine and I'd be gone. But now? Now I'll kill whoever the hell gets in my way. Him. Owen. You. Duncan. It'll end there. I'll be out of here once you two are taken care of."

The cows. Somehow this had all been about the cows? She couldn't think it through clearly, but that was secondary right now. Because right now she had to save herself. Save Duncan.

There had to be some way out of this mess, but she was having a hard time keeping her eyes open. A hard time making sense of her scrambled thoughts and the gray mist over everything. Her head bobbed forward, the world black again. Then she felt a sharp, teeth-rattling sting against her cheek. Her eyes popped open, and she realized he'd slapped her.

"None of that," he growled.

Her cheek throbbed where he'd made impact.

"We need you awake. This isn't going to fall on me."

She used what little strength she had left to spit—a mix of blood and saliva—right at his face.

He reared back his arm, so she squeezed her eyes shut and braced herself for impact, for pain, for the awful, awful consequences.

But nothing happened. She opened her eyes to the foggy gray and saw him, still standing above her, but he'd dropped his arm and taken a step back.

"Not yet," he muttered to himself, whirling around and stalking away as he wiped his face on his sleeve. "Gotta make it right, so not yet."

Every "not yet" gave her a chance. That's what she told herself.

No matter how dire it all looked.

Chapter Twenty

Duncan was no expert tracker, but he managed to follow boot prints and drops of blood when there was no grass and only dirt. Away from the road, toward the trees.

Why would she do that? He made it into the grouping of trees. Pine needles littered the muddy ground below. Boot prints squelched into the mud. Was he ruining them? He tried to walk around them in case more help came.

He made it to one side, noted a tree that looked like it had been walked around quite a bit. He crouched, wondering if he studied the markings in the muddy ground, he'd be able to have an idea of what happened. But next to a tree, on an upturned curved leaf, was a tiny puddle of something dark, and a few more leaves around the area had the same.

Blood. It had to be blood. Way too much of it. His heart twisted into a pained pretzel. What was she doing? Heading away from help like this?

He shook his head. Answers didn't matter. He had to find her. So he searched the area for where the footprints came out on the other side. The terrain was pretty open here, and it was hard to note where any footprints were back in the tall grasses.

But in the distance, he saw another cluster of trees. If she had run away from the road and toward the cover of the first group of trees, then left this area, wouldn't she likely run for more cover?

He heard sirens in the distance. Maybe he should go back. The cops would know how to track. They'd have a better way of dealing with this, probably.

But he was already *out* here. She might be close, and if that was *her* blood, how could he possibly turn away? He surveyed the world around him again. The trees were the only place to go. Since there was no way of determining tracks, he decided to follow his intuition.

He began to walk straight for it, cutting through tall grass and focusing on not tripping over a random boulder, hole, or God forbid, a snake. He gripped the gun in his hand, ready to use it if he had to. He knew how to shoot it, probably, though it had been years since he'd even attempted to use a gun and his shooting hand was somewhat compromised.

He wouldn't need it. It was just a precaution. Everything would be fine once he found her. Everything his dad had taught him as a kid would come back to him, like muscle memory.

If he even needed it. Which he wouldn't, he told himself, over and over again.

Every once in a while, he paused. Looked around. Listened. It wouldn't be smart to get lost, but…

He heard it in one of those moments. A kind of *snick* sound, far away, but followed by something like a grunt. It all sounded very…human.

He rushed forward toward it. Then forced himself to think, to slow down. He couldn't rush into potential danger without thinking things through, even if he hoped with all he was this was just a strange misunderstanding, not danger.

He thought he maybe saw shadows moving around in the trees. But he couldn't be sure. So he tried to keep a low profile, crouching down as he walked so he was hopefully hidden by grass if anything...bad was out there.

Or should he just rush forward? Guns blazing? She'd been hurt. Bleeding. Why was he being patient?

But something inside of him seemed to insist upon it. A cautiousness. Because this was all wrong, so it required... tact.

He couldn't really see through the grasses, but once he was close to the trees where he thought he'd heard things, he straightened a little so he could see.

Across the way, Rosalie was sitting down. He nearly rushed forward, called out, did everything wrong in the moment. But her head was kind of bowed, and he realized she was *tied* to that tree. She lifted her head a little, and he could see even from a distance that her face was a bloody mess.

Duncan's whole body went ice-cold. Then, worse, another body moved into his vision. And even though the man's back was to him, Duncan knew who it was.

Terry. A man Duncan had *trusted*. The fury, the disgust, roiled through him along with the utter terror that he had Rosalie *tied up* and a gun in his hand.

But Duncan couldn't think about betrayal right now. He couldn't think about his worry for Rosalie. He had to think about how he was going to get her out of this.

He had a gun, but so did Terry. Duncan could see it there glinting in the man's hand. He thought Terry was speaking, the faint grumble of words on the breeze, but Duncan couldn't make them out.

Should he get closer? He had to get closer. He could hardly just crouch here hoping something magically worked out right. He had to get in there and somehow...

Hell, he was no cop, no white knight. The idea he should

be the one to *save* her seemed ludicrous, but there was no one else to do it.

He gave the cluster of trees a wide berth, trying to move closer *slowly*, with the grasses providing cover and the breeze distorting any noises he might be making. He found himself with a profile view of both Terry and Rosalie, and he could actually make out the words Terry was saying.

"We can wait him out. We can wait him out." It was the kind of repetitive thing someone said to themselves to convince themselves of something that was becoming less and less true.

"Seems to me there's sirens in the distance, Ter," Rosalie said. She sounded…tired, but she'd managed to infuse the sentence with some of her usual sarcasm. Even as awful as her face looked, bloody and bruised.

He swallowed down everything. This wasn't all that different than taking the mound in a World Series game. Sure, it was life or death, but if he shoved that away, it was the same process. Block out the noise. Settle into your body. Focus.

He carefully lifted the gun, using his right arm to support the dominant left one. His shoulder ached and throbbed and *burned*, which couldn't be good, but he knew how to play through pain.

He tried to remember all the advice his dad had given him, but that gun had been different. Hell, Duncan had been different—a kid, essentially, when his dad had taught him how to do this. Still, it had to be done, so…

He curled his finger around the trigger, aimed at Terry, and pulled. Swore at the jolt of sheer agony that went from shoulder to fingertip.

Duncan cursed his bad arm as the bullet hit a tree about two inches to Terry's right, and Terry whirled toward him, lifting his own gun.

He didn't shoot right away though. He aimed, Duncan aiming right back. He could hit his target this time. He would.

"You wouldn't shoot me, Duncan. You don't have it in you. And even if you did try again, you missed the first time."

"I won't this time," Duncan said, pulling the trigger after the word *won't*.

And he didn't miss—Terry jerked back, even as Terry's bullet whizzed past Duncan, far too close...but not close enough.

ROSALIE FIGURED SHE'D SCREAMED, and she didn't *think* she'd been hallucinating sirens, but who knew? Who knew?

Her teeth were chattering, and she could only barely make out what had happened with the second shot. Terry lay writhing on the ground. Duncan ran over to her.

He was saying things, but she couldn't quite make sense of them. She thought maybe he was trying to untie her.

"Well, I didn't have getting saved by a baseball player on my life bingo card." But he had. She really hadn't had a way out of this one. Tears threatened—not just emotion, but pain and relief and a million other things as her arms fell to her sides.

She couldn't really feel anything. A creeping numb feeling was overtaking her, but he'd untied her. And then she felt him lifting her to her feet. It took his grip on her arm and her leaning against the tree to manage to stay upright, but she was free and standing.

"I'm carrying you," he said.

She managed a huff of a laugh. "Hate to break it to you, but that bad arm's going to let you down there."

"Well, I'll just get another surgery. Come on."

She couldn't even seem to move her head to look at him, but she could see Terry. In front of her. Still moving. In fact...

She pawed at Duncan's arm. "Duncan, he's getting up."

Duncan shoved her behind him, and she wanted to shove him right back, but it was taking everything in her to stand on her own two feet.

Terry got to his knees. He was gripping his shoulder where blood was pouring out of the gunshot wound. He was white as a sheet, but he was getting up, and he still had a gun gripped in his hand. Luckily, the wound in his arm should keep him from getting a decent shot off, but still.

"Give me the gun," Rosalie ordered Duncan.

"Rosalie."

"I've got it, Ace. Give me the gun and hold me up. I'm a damn better shot."

"I should hope so. I haven't held a gun for over fifteen years," he muttered. "But you're covered in blood."

She didn't mention her vision wasn't all there, no more than her strength. "What are you going to do then?"

Duncan stood in front of her—a human shield she didn't want. Terry clearly was trying to raise the gun in his hand, but he couldn't because of the gunshot wound in his shoulder. Meanwhile, Duncan held his—*her*—gun pointed at Terry.

"Drop the gun, Terry. Just drop it."

"You couldn't shoot the broadside of a barn," Terry growled, but it was clear he couldn't aim his gun either.

"I don't know what happened, but you're not walking away from this. You're not hurting any more people. It's over."

"It's not over. It'll never be over." Terry's voice hitched. Despair and panic and something else Rosalie couldn't quite name. Maybe a mental break.

"I'm the victim here," he shouted, stumbling forward a little. He was sweating now, either from the pain, or the attempt to lift his arm.

"Victim? You're a murderer. You betrayed…everything my father did for you."

"Did *for* me? He *stole* everything from me." Terry stepped forward, eyes wild, shirt getting darker and darker as blood seeped out of his wound. "Norman Kirk always got everything. His parents bought my parents' ranch and I was left with nothing but a measly ranch-hand job. He married Natalie. Natalie was *mine*. I saw her first. She was always supposed to be mine."

"Holy hell," Rosalie muttered. This was deeper and more twisted than she could have imagined.

"I waited. I planned. I'll get mine now. I put in the work. I put in the damn work. It's all mine now. No matter what I have to do to get it."

"The police know Terry. About the land in Idaho. The stockpile. And I have a sneaking suspicion once they get the search warrant they're after, they'll find my father's missing cows."

Terry's entire face arrested in a kind of shocked horror that chilled Rosalie to the bone. She tried to reach out to take the gun from Duncan. If he wouldn't take Terry down, she would. Impaired vision and all.

"That'll be enough," a commanding voice interrupted. All eyes turned to Copeland stepping through the trees, gun drawn. There were a few other cops stepping into the shaded area as well, around Terry to make a circle. Detective Delaney-Carson. Sunrise's sheriff, Jack Hudson, and another Sunrise deputy.

"Drop it," Copeland instructed Terry. "Now."

Rosalie didn't know if she was the only one who saw

it—the wild desperation. The choice in Terry's eyes. Give up or go down swinging. She didn't wait to see if anyone else would recognize it. She just kicked out, so both she and Duncan fell in a heap on the ground.

Just as Terry swung his bad arm up, aimed and shot.

Aside from the pain in her head, she seemed to be okay, and Duncan had only grunted a little as he'd landed on his bad shoulder, she figured in an attempt to keep his full weight from falling on her.

Duncan looked up, so Rosalie did too. She saw the point where the wood had splintered from the bullet—where they likely both would have been hit dead-on if she hadn't pulled him down. Then he looked down at her.

"Well, I guess we're even, Red," he said, and he didn't shake, but his voice was raspy.

"I guess we are," she replied, though things were going a little grayer as Duncan detangled himself from her and helped her into a sitting position.

The cops were wrestling cuffs onto Terry, talking into their radios.

"She needs an ambulance," Duncan shouted at them.

She did. She knew she did. But still, she could hear the worry in his voice, feel it in the way he gripped her. "I'm okay." She squeezed his forearm until he looked away from the cops and at her.

"You don't look it," he grumbled.

"No. Probably need a few stitches. But I'm going to be okay. It's all going to be okay." She had never been any good at comforting people. Tended to shy away from it, but she pulled him into a hug anyway. Held on. "We're all going to be okay."

She felt him sigh against her. His grip on her was gentle, probably worried he was going to hurt her. But he held her all the same.

Because she wasn't lying. Everything was going to be *okay*. She'd make sure of it.

Chapter Twenty-One

Duncan hadn't wanted to let Rosalie go, but the paramedics had jogged onto the scene—stretchers and bags in tow. They'd loaded up Terry first, which had ticked him off, but one of the paramedics checked out Rosalie, right there with her sitting against the tree.

She'd argued with the woman, but the paramedic had been adamant. She'd have to ride in the ambulance to the hospital. Duncan had been somewhat relieved at how bitterly Rosalie had been against it. She had to be feeling at least a *little* like herself to mount that argument, no matter how terrible she looked.

He wasn't allowed to ride with her, which was infuriating, but he also didn't want Detective Beckett or even Detective Delaney-Carson explaining everything to his parents. It needed to be someone who would understand what a betrayal this would be to everything his parents held dear.

For thirty-plus years they had trusted Terry. That was an entire lifetime of believing someone was your friend. Someone you could trust and believe in. To have Terry be a murderer...

He sighed as he took the stairs to his parents' house. Rosalie had told him to go handle this. He hadn't even needed to explain—she'd understood. Since the paramedic had assured him that she'd need stitches, maybe go through a concussion protocol, but she would be okay, he'd let them wheel her away.

He'd given his statement to Detective Beckett. Gotten the clear to return to his truck and go break the news to his parents.

So here he was. Handling it. Audra would meet Rosalie at the hospital, and it wasn't like they'd let him in the room while they patched her up. He'd head out there later. Once he was sure his parents were okay.

He tapped on the door, then let himself in. Mom and Dad were in the kitchen, and as he approached, Mom stood from the table. She crossed to him, wrapped her arms around him and squeezed.

Dad stood next to the table looking pale and frail but determined to take it. They knew it was Terry now, but they didn't know the why of it.

"Just lay it all out," Mom said, pulling back, but gripping his hand.

He gave Mom's hand a squeeze then led her back to the table. He sat down and laid it all out to them. Terry hiding in Rosalie's truck at the hospital. Rosalie wrecking her truck to get away.

Terry having his own land, a stockpile of weapons. Duncan even shared his theory about the missing cattle. He didn't want to explain Terry's reasoning, but he had to.

"Saw me first?" Mom laughed bitterly. "I never gave Terry Boothe the time of day." She leaned into Dad, more troubled than Duncan wanted to accept.

"All these years..." Dad trailed off, and never finished that sentence.

"The police are still collecting all the information," Duncan said. "Terry made it sound like he's been resentful and planning this since his parents sold their ranch to Grandma and Grandpa, but the evidence doesn't support it. Maybe he always felt that bitterness, but he didn't start acting on it until a few years ago."

He'd hoped that might ease *some* of the hurt written all over his parents' faces, but it didn't. But they gripped each other's hands, leaned on each other.

They asked a few more questions, but mostly it would just take…time, Duncan supposed. And it would probably never fully heal that wound, but they'd survive. They had each other. They had him.

And despite Terry's attempt to take out Owen again in his hospital room, the kid was fighting. If he made it, he'd be able to testify against Terry over what Terry had done to him.

Nothing erased what Terry did, particularly to Hunter, but there would be justice. Duncan would use all of his resources to make sure of it.

Mom reached her free hand across the table to put it over his. "How's Rosalie?"

"They're patching her up. Audra was going to text me when they're done."

"You should be at the hospital. You don't need to worry about us."

Duncan looked from his mother to his father. He worried about them, and there was no stopping it. This was devastating. But there was nothing Duncan could do to fix that, and *that* sat on his chest like a heavy weight.

Dad stood, cleared his throat. "I'm going to need to go tell the ranch hands before the rumors go wild."

"I can—"

Dad shook his head. "This is my responsibility, Duncan. You stay with your mother." He strode out of the room.

Duncan looked at Mom, who was watching Dad with worry in her eyes. But she closed them, inhaled and exhaled carefully.

"He'll be all right. It'll be all right. It'll just take some time to…smooth out. You should go see Rosalie. And while you're gone, I'll make her a cake. Some cookies. A feast."

Duncan laughed in spite of himself. It felt almost normal. Bad things happened, and Mom swooped into action and comforted with food. It felt good and right.

He figured he could leave her and she and Dad would just be fine. After all, they had each other. Always had.

Still, he pulled her into a hug, and he squeezed her tight, wanting to transfer some kind of certainty that everything from here on out would be okay. For a moment, she even let him.

Then she pulled back, patted his cheek. "We'll all be all right. No one gets through life without some hard times. Love is what gets us through."

Because the sheen of tears in her eyes twisted painfully in his heart, he tried to lighten the mood. "Is that a not-so-subtle hint, Mother?"

She smiled at him. "I love you, Duncan. And I'm very proud of the man you are, who'd rush into help and save others, even though it's not your job."

"Everything good I am is because of you and Dad. Everything."

A tear slipped over onto her cheek, so he pulled her into another hug. Yeah, life was hard. But no matter the hard, he always had them, and they had each other all these years.

They'd all be just fine.

Rosalie felt nauseous. They'd stitched her up, done annoying tests on her cognitive situation, then yapped at her incessantly about concussions.

They were keeping her overnight, just to be sure she hadn't done more damage than they could see at the moment. Which was annoying as all get out.

Almost as annoying as Audra flittering around the room trying to make it *comfortable*. Rosalie was glad when someone else came into the room, even if that someone else *was* Copeland Beckett.

"She's resting," Audra said primly, scowling at the detective.

To Copeland's credit, he *almost* looked sheepishly at Audra. "No more questions. Just an apology."

"An apology?" Rosalie said. "Come on in."

Copeland's mouth quirked as he moved closer to Rosalie's bed, clearly ignoring Audra's scowl.

"I could have told you we'd narrowed in on Terry Boothe," he said, almost sounding contrite. "That might have avoided today's events."

"*Should* have told me. *Would* have avoided." Except she wasn't so sure about that. Everyone had been working for answers, and sometimes there was just no one right way to find them. They'd worked together, and just happened to coalesce on the same point without enough time to avoid Terry's violence.

"I don't owe you details on an ongoing investigation," Copeland said irritably. "It's not my fault we were coming to the same conclusions at the same time."

Rosalie grinned at him, immensely cheered at his bad attitude. "I thought this was an apology."

Copeland grumbled something under his breath. "I am sorry you got caught up in this. But you handled yourself."

He jerked his chin toward the bandage on her head. "You and your baseball player."

"Yeah, he saved the day. So did I. You...?"

"Arrived in the nick of time and arrested the guy? You're welcome."

She laughed, then winced a little when a dull pain sliced through her forehead. "All's well that ends well. Apology accepted. I plan to lord it over you every time we have to work together."

"I expect nothing else." He gave an uncharacteristic awkward wave, nodded at Audra, then strode for the door.

But the thing was, just as she'd told Duncan, she and Copeland were a little too much alike to get along. And too much alike not to understand each other.

"You're right. We all did what we could. No guilt, okay?"

He stopped at the door, looked back at her with an unreadable expression on his face. "I'm incapable of feeling guilt," he replied.

Of course that was a lie. He wouldn't have come here, apologized, without *guilt*. But she let him leave with that parting shot. Looked at her sister, who had a thoughtful expression on her face.

"You know, I'm fine. You don't have to be here."

"Don't be ridiculous, Rosalie," Audra said, her own brand of irritable. She pulled a chair next to the bed. "I think it's time to have a talk."

"Can it wait? I'm tired." And she was. Tired and feeling *gross*. She wanted tonight over with so she could go home tomorrow.

She refused to think about Duncan in this moment. Having to break the news to his parents, not just that Terry was a murderer, but that he had all that resentment for the Kirks all this time.

It made her heart clench, and she didn't want to deal with it.

"I'll let you sleep in just a minute. But for now, you're stuck in this bed and Duncan saved your life, so you're going to have to finally listen to what I've been trying to tell you for days now."

Rosalie shifted uncomfortably. "Come on, Audra. I'm in pain," she said, hoping to appeal to her sister's usually soft heart.

But Audra's expression was firm, and that was the thing about Audra. She had a lot of soft spots, but once she decided something, it was *decided*.

"Well, this is going to be painful, so it's the perfect time. I can't have you taking another step of your life thinking that because you loved Dad, you can't trust your feelings. There's nothing wrong with your instincts."

"Hell, Audra, can we—"

But Audra plowed right over her protests. "It was me. Every thoughtful present he ever gave you, every phone call he made on your birthday if he wasn't home. Mom too. The both of them were selfish and self-obsessed. And I hated that for *me*, so I set about to do something about it for *you*. I made them give you, or faked them giving you, everything I wanted."

Rosalie could only stare at her sister, stunned into complete silence. She knew her sister was just that kind of selfless. But it had never occurred to her...

"Audra. Why...?" She shook her head, trying to blink back the tears. She couldn't.

"I love you. I wanted better for you. If I'd known that meant you thought you had some sort of warped radar when it came to people, I wouldn't have. I thought I was doing the right thing."

Rosalie couldn't breathe for a minute. It was so awful. So...painful. Because if Audra had done all that, it meant... No one had ever done that for her. The thoughtfulness. The showing of care.

"You have always done the right thing," Rosalie rasped out.

Audra sniffled, blinking back tears. No doubt refusing to let them fall. "I hope that's true, but the only way you prove that to me is to realize Duncan is perfect for you. Natalie and I wouldn't have conspired to toss you two together at every opportunity if we didn't think so. And I shouldn't have to tell you that, because he saved your *life*."

"I saved his too," Rosalie said somewhat petulantly, because her heart felt big and bruised.

"Rosalie."

"You..." Rosalie couldn't decide if it was the head injury that felt like her brain was scrambled, or just these revelations.

The invitations. The Tupperware. She had been soundly and thoroughly *tricked* into being in Duncan's orbit.

She wanted to be offended, but a knock sounded on the hospital-room door and after a moment, Duncan stepped inside.

So tall and handsome and *good*. He *had* saved her life, even if she'd had the presence of mind to save his after. He'd done it first.

And all her life, Audra had been saving her heart. Stepping in to make her feel loved because their parents were incapable.

It felt...small and childish to keep thinking that all the ways Duncan was *perfect* for her, even if he wasn't perfect, wasn't good enough because of some internal, messed up thing on her end.

It would be betraying everything Audra had done for her.

"I guess I'll forgive you," she murmured to Audra.

"I should hope so. You owe me a hot, rich guy in return."

"I'll see what I can do." And she would. One way or another, she was going to find her sister exactly this. And better, she was going to be everything Audra had been to her growing up. She was going to step up in all the ways she hadn't for the people she loved.

She looked at Duncan as Audra got up, said a few words to him, then left them alone in the room.

He approached her bed. "Heya, Red."

"Heya, Ace." She wasn't going to blubber all over him. She *wasn't*. But it took some effort to blink back the tears. Especially when he bent over, tenderly brushed some hair out of her face, then gently pressed his mouth to hers. Just as easy as that.

And it was easy with him. It always had been. All the things that made him who he was just seemed to *fit*. Even though he'd saved her, he hadn't made her feel like…she'd somehow lost. He'd made it feel like a team effort.

Because it was and they were.

"Did you know your mother and my sister plotted to throw us together?" she asked, her voice tight.

His mouth curved. "I didn't know about Audra, but I had some suspicions about my mother. That a problem?"

She managed to shake her head, even though it hurt. "No. No problems here."

"Good," he replied, then kissed her again. Like this was just who they were now. Together. A team. A unit.

Because they were, and maybe that was a little scary, but it was mostly pretty amazing.

Epilogue

One month later

Duncan had never been so happy to be back home in his life. The trip to LA to deal with a charity obligation, check in with the shoulder specialist there, and tie up a few other loose ends had been an interminable four days.

He'd tried to convince Rosalie to come with him, but she'd been in the middle of a case. Someday—someday he'd get her out there. He'd take her anywhere she wanted to go.

It didn't bother him that he was head over heels in love with her. He sometimes worried that it would bother *her*, so he hadn't said that yet.

But she'd spent most nights at his cabin. She invited him to her family dinners with Audra, Franny, Hart, and his wife, and stepdaughter. She'd folded him into her life as much as he'd folded her into his.

And it felt right. Every day, it felt right to wake up with her in his bed. Giving him a hard time about something or another, worrying over his arm, which really was starting to heal. Specialist-approved and everything.

He still worried about his parents, but Mom had thrown herself into helping Owen. Dad had worked hard to find a replacement for Terry, and Duncan had helped. He took on more and more of the day-to-day ranching than he'd dreamed he would. But it was…enjoyable. Working side by side with Dad.

Especially knowing he didn't *have* to if they started to get on each other's nerves too much. There was an open job offer at the high school for coaching, and Duncan figured one of these days, he'd probably miss the game enough to take it.

But, with his baseball playing career done, the Kirk Ranch really was *home* now. And he was eager to be back. He pulled up to his cabin, and pushed the truck into Park, staring at Rosalie's own truck in the drive.

He didn't allow himself to picture it as it had been crashed into the ditch, though that still took some effort. Instead, he focused on the pleasant surprise. Though she often spent the night at his cabin, he hadn't expected to find her here before the end of her usual workday.

Pleased beyond telling, he hopped out of his truck and ignored his luggage in favor of going to find her.

She was in his kitchen.

"Are you…cooking?"

She looked up, a scowl on her face that smoothed out when she saw him. Which never failed to amaze him. He hadn't been looking for her, for this, but he had another stroke of amazing luck in his life to have found it.

"I tried. I failed. Appreciate the sentiment."

He crossed to her, just as she crossed to him. Meeting in the middle. She wrapped her arms around his neck as his came around her waist. She grinned up at him.

"How's the shoulder?"

"Doctor said exactly where it should be. So there, worrier."

"I never worry," she said, and she lifted to her toes and

pressed her mouth to his. A welcome-home kiss that was just what he'd needed. Four days in LA hadn't been terrible, but this was the only place he really wanted to be.

"I missed you," he murmured against her mouth.

"You were gone for four days," she replied, trying to wriggle away from him. He didn't let her.

"Yeah. Say it."

She tried to dim her smile, but she failed that too. "Does it count if you make me?"

"Say it, Red."

"I missed you too." She moved to kiss him again, but he held her off, studying her face. Maybe she wasn't ready.

But she damn well should be. And if she could admit she missed him over just four days, he figured she could take it.

"I love you, Rosalie."

She stilled in his arms. Her eyes immediately wary as she studied his face. But she didn't pull away. Didn't *look* away, so he didn't either. It took a few moments, but after a few careful breaths, she softened there against him.

"I love you too, Duncan."

Yeah, this was the best home he'd had yet.

* * * * *

COMING SOON!

We really hope you enjoyed reading this book.
If you're looking for more romance
be sure to head to the shops when
new books are available on

Thursday 25th September

To see which titles are coming soon, please visit
millsandboon.co.uk/nextmonth

MILLS & BOON

MILLS & BOON TRUE LOVE IS HAVING A MAKEOVER!

Introducing

Love Always

Marrying a Royal — Nina Milne, Suzanne Merchant

Summer with the Billionaire — Rachael Stewart, Justine Lewis

Swoon-worthy romances, where love takes center stage. Same heartwarming stories, stylish new look!

Look out for our brand new look

COMING SEPTEMBER 2025

MILLS & BOON

LET'S TALK
Romance

For exclusive extracts, competitions and special offers, find us online:

- **f** MillsandBoon
- **X** @MillsandBoon
- **◉** @MillsandBoonUK
- **♪** @MillsandBoonUK

Get in touch on 01413 063 232

For all the latest titles coming soon, visit
millsandboon.co.uk/nextmonth